The Shattered Kingdom
INVI WRIGHT

COMPLETED WORKS

STANDALONES
The Nanny | A Nanny/Single Father Romance
Lord of Dread | An Arranged Marriage Historical Romance
Aine | A Dark Shifter Romance

THE FEMALE SERIES
The Female is a why choose demon romance with a dark dystopian setting, declining fertility rates, captured women, and three irresistible men.
The Female
Her Males
Their War
Chev's Mate
Queens

THE CURSED KINGDOM SERIES
The Cursed Kingdom is a slow burning, why choose romance with a mystical faerie realm, two infuriatingly attractive princes, and high conflict between the faerie and shifter kingdoms.
The Cursed Kingdom
The Shattered Kingdom

TRIGGER WARNINGS CAN BE FOUND ON:
inviwright.com

UPCOMING WORKS

STANDALONES
His Assignment | A Bodyguard Mafia Romance (Coming 2026)
The Dragon's Agreement | A Dragon Fantasy Romance
(Release Date TBD)

LAND OF WOLVES DUOLOGY
Land of Wolves is a high intensity shifter romance with fated mates, government indoctrination that leads to painful betrayal, and impending war between the shifters and humans.
Land of Wolves | **Part One** (Coming 2026)
Land of Wolves | **Part Two** (Release Date TBD)

ONGOING SERIES

Fates | Book Six of *The Female* Series (Release Date TBD)
The Hidden Kingdom | Book Three of *The Cursed Kingdom* Series (Release date TBD)

STAY CONNECTED

SOCIAL MEDIA

Follow Invi Wright on social media to stay up to date on her newest releases, listen to her gab about romance & fantasy books, get regular book recs, and join a fun community of romance lovers!

TikTok & Instagram: @inviwright

EXCLUSIVE CONTENT & CHARACTER ART

Subscribe to **@inviwright** on Patreon for:

- Exclusive access to ongoing novellas
- Exclusive audio chapters
- SFW and NSFW character art
- Partake in polls (help decide what book she'll write next!)
- A free ebook copy of every book she publishes

THANK YOU

The largest thank you possible to my husband. You gave me the confidence and support to pursue writing, and none of this would be possible without you.

Also, to my Patreon subscribers: Joni S, Bhavini, Fnagirl, Krystin Baldwin, Nicole P., Cynthia T., Melissa Childs, Jack Lewis Landsmen, Tzahala Cofield, Danielle Bloome, Charline G., Lora Beth. Your support is the sole reason I'm able to do this, and I can't properly convey in words just how much you mean to me. I hope you enjoy this story.

COPYWRIGHT

Editing by: Amy McNulty
Map design by: Melissa Nash
Cover design by: Krafigs Design

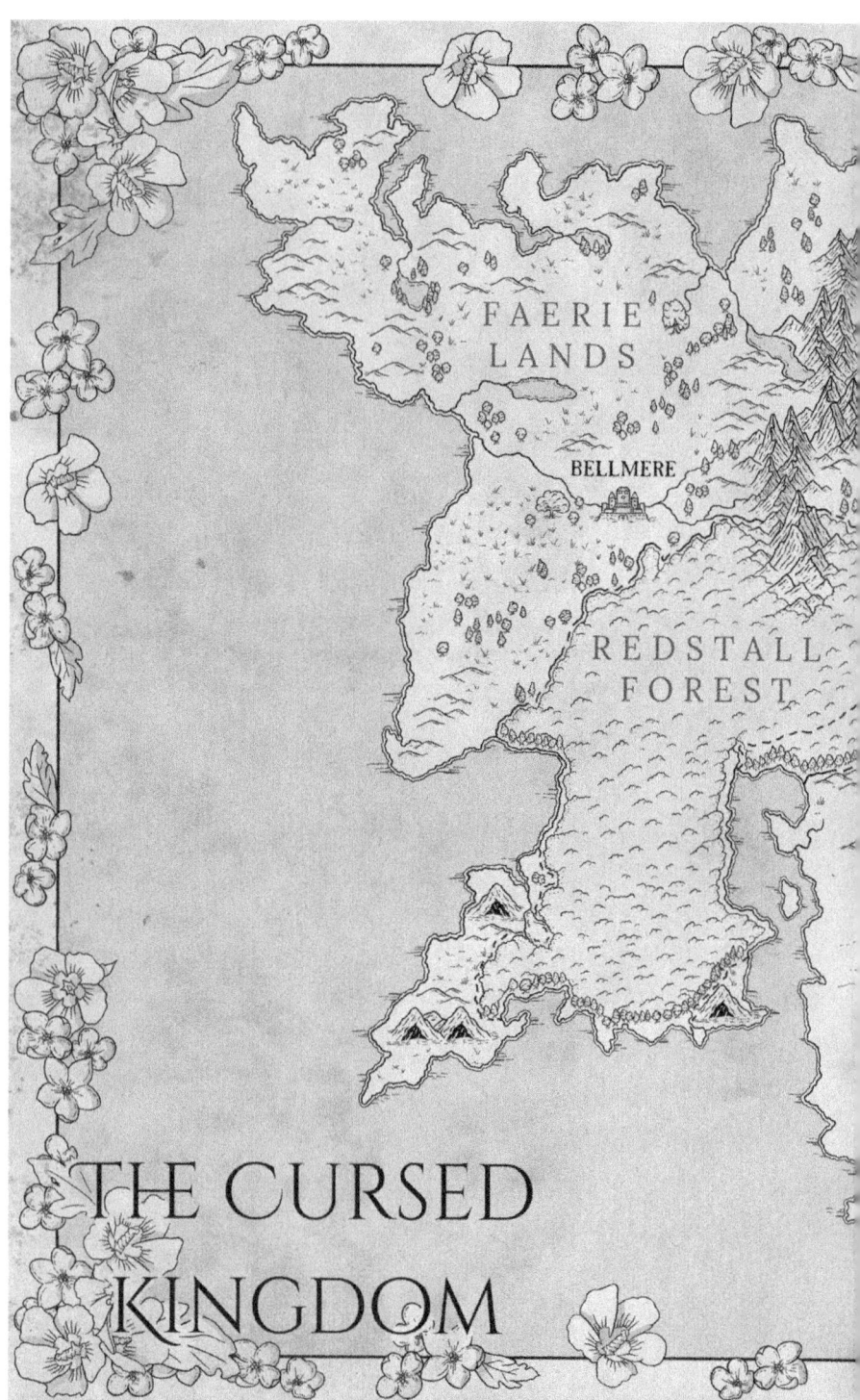

FAERIE LANDS

BELLMERE

REDSTALL FOREST

THE CURSED KINGDOM

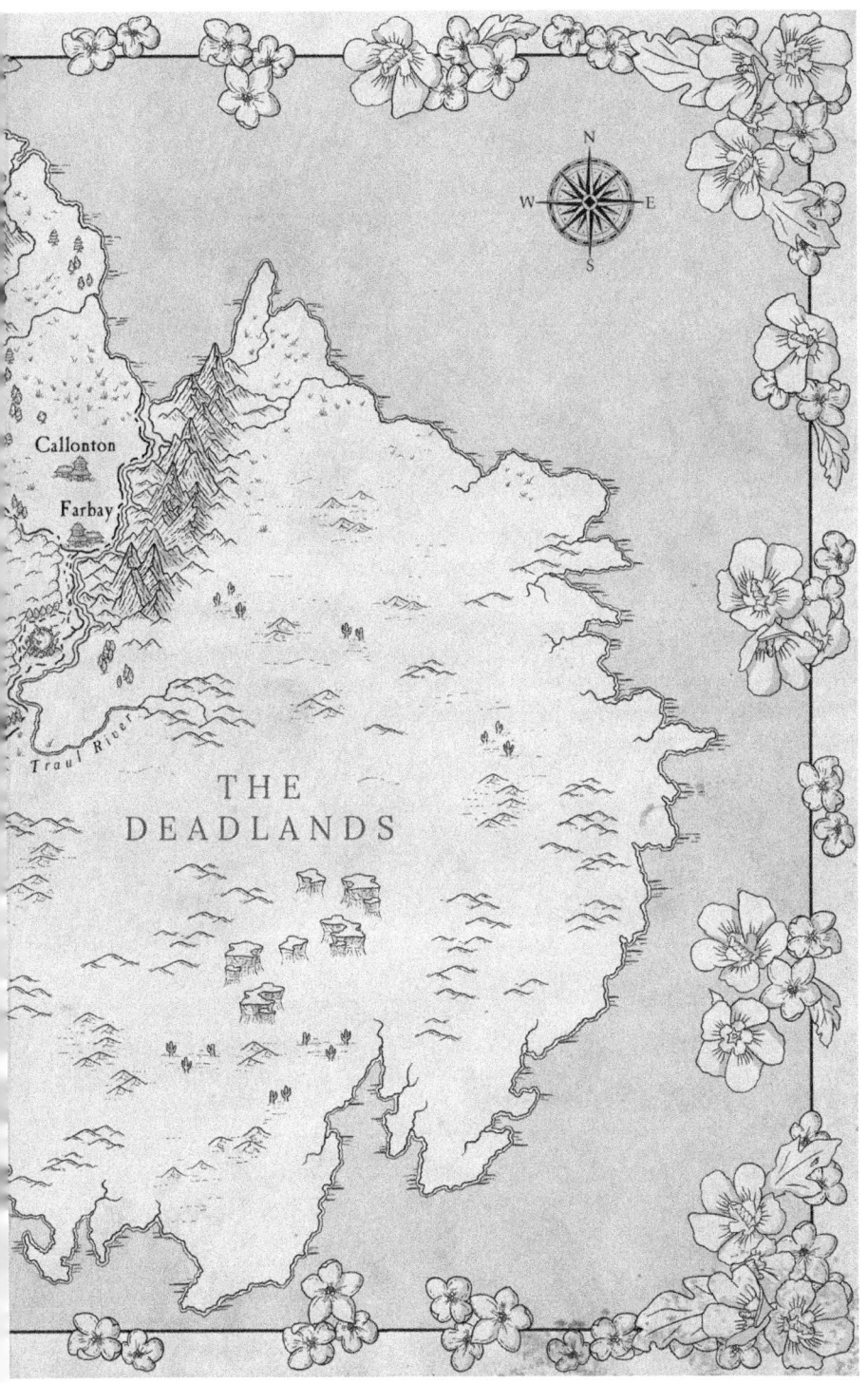

Callonton

Farbay

Traul River

THE
DEADLANDS

Chapter One

ABBY

ARE THEY GOING to kill us? I assume not, considering Lill is Kie and Mason's mate. It's a discovery I didn't expect, and I'm not sure how to feel about it. I'm avoiding thinking about it at all.

I walk beside Lill, my hand brushing hers. Her skin is cold, but the knowledge that she's alive brings me so much comfort. I spare her a glance, my attention captured by her gaunt cheeks and hollow violet eyes. She looks exhausted, and I can only imagine how hard my disappearance has been on her.

Kie and Mason walk ahead of us. They're both equally stiff, their movements just a little too purposeful to look natural. Both men are tall, but Kie's leaner form fits in amongst the faeries. Mason looks like a bulldozer. He stands out, clearly not one of them.

Their dark hair doesn't help. Kie's short black hair sticks out like a sore thumb against the sea of white blonde, as does Mason's dark brown strands. If it weren't for Kie's violet eyes and pointed features, I'd question whether he's actually a faerie.

Mason could never pass for one. I've not met another shifter, but I can tell he's one through and through.

Queen Gitta trails behind us with two of her guards. I can't

1

see her, but I can *feel* her presence.

Do they intend to lock Lill and me up inside that damned bedroom again?

We round a corner, one I vaguely recognize. The outdoor corridors separating the buildings are nearly identical, though, so maybe not. The walkways were beautiful in the light of day, but it's a different story when the sun is down.

The large, butterfly and vine covered trellises overhead are suffocating. It's too dark to see the details, and the sound of thousands of beating wings is unnerving.

We pass through a courtyard containing a large fountain, one with several women standing around it. They openly stare at us, their curious gazes darting rapidly between Kie and Mason before shifting toward me and Lill. Then they land on Queen Gitta and quickly dart away.

Her Majesty insists on following us back to Kie and Mason's home, probably to ensure Lill is locked away to her satisfaction. Mason accused Lill of murdering Kie's father, of murdering the faerie king. That's not to be taken lightly.

I still don't believe Mason's accusation, and I glare at the back of his head as we reach the small courtyard that separates the royal housing area from the remainder of the property. The walkways are open past the courtyard, no stifling trellis overhead, and there are no faeries lingering about.

Even Mason seems to relax as we find ourselves alone, his tense shoulders dropping and his gloved fists unclenching at his sides. I hate to admit that Mason looks different when freshly changed and showered. He seems less wild, less dangerous. I'm not quite so afraid he's going to shift into his animal form and tear out my throat at a moment's notice.

I grab the rolled waistband of my pants and pull them up, the fabric too loose to remain in place. While Mason dressed himself in a perfectly tailored, expensive-looking shirt and pants, he gave me lounge clothing. They're oversized and sloppy, and the well-dressed faeries with whom we've had the misfortune of crossing paths must think so little of me.

Hopefully Kie's shirtless and unshowered appearance distracted them. If not, then Lill definitely did. She's so visibly thin and sick, *and* she's wearing Kie's shirt. She wouldn't need to wear it had Kie done a better job watching over her. He may not have approved the whipping, but it happened on his watch.

The thought of one of those faerie guards tearing off Lill's shirt and hurting her has bile rising up the back of my throat, and I do my best to push the mental image of her bloodied skin and pained screams aside. I can *and will* fret over her later.

The royal houses are nestled inside a wooded area, and we weave through small paths lined with several trees before reaching Kie and Mason's home. The single-story brick building doesn't look very royal, which I assume is purposeful. They probably don't want their home to be easily identifiable. It would make it too easy for somebody to break in and murder them.

There's a smaller house beside theirs, and Kie guides us toward it. Four steps lead to a small porch and a dark, wooden front door. I thought he was bringing us to the house he shares with Mason, but I won't complain about having my own space. This house looks easy enough to escape from, assuming Lill wants to. I have no idea what to think or how to feel about the mate bond she supposedly feels with Kie and Mason, and she might decide it's best to remain here.

It's one of the many things we need to discuss.

"The guest house?" Queen Gitta asks the question, her voice loud as it travels from behind. She doesn't sound pleased.

Kie nods, then runs his fingers through his hair. The dark strands are knotted from our time in the forest, and he grimaces as he looks at Queen Gitta over his shoulder. His gaze briefly flashes toward Lill and me, but it doesn't linger.

I shift my focus toward Mason. The shifter hasn't spoken in several minutes, which isn't unusual. Still, I don't trust it. Zaha has decided that he's to be king, and I can only imagine the thoughts running through his mind right now.

He's going to side with the shifters and destroy the faeries. I just know it.

I hope to be present when Queen Gitta finds out. I don't appreciate how she had me brought to the meeting hall, throne-room area, nor do I appreciate how she looks at Lill and me with such open disgust. We didn't ask to be brought here, and despite the rumors that have spread regarding Lill's involvement in the king's murder, she was just a child. There's no way they're seriously going to accuse a seven-year-old child of murder. That's unbelievable.

Even if Lill *did* do it, there must be more to the story. Children don't just murder people.

Queen Gitta clears her throat. "Lillian and the human should be housed somewhere with—"

Kie interrupts. "Lillian is our mate. She will not be treated as a prisoner, and the guest suite is highly guarded."

"Then you should at least consider putting the human in—"

Mason spins, piercing Queen Gitta with his signature blank stare. "The human stays with us."

The human has a name. It's annoying that nobody seems keen to use it. I understand the faeries don't think highly of my kind, but to disregard me so openly is just plain disrespectful. For a species of beings who pride themselves on their grace, they're sure fucking rude.

Queen Gitta doesn't react to Mason's stare or tone, at least not outwardly. She appears utterly unaffected, which I'm sure infuriates the shifter.

"That's not your decision to make," she says. "Kieran is—"

This is my time to shine. "Kieran isn't anything. He agreed to give his title to Mason in exchange for Zaha stopping the growth of delysum." All attention shifts to me, and when neither Kie nor Mason dart forward to snap my neck, I continue. "Zaha's original plan was for Kieran to lead the faeries, Mason to lead the shifters, and for their mate to unite them, but that plan went to shit when Mason's parents abandoned him. Zaha doesn't believe the faeries need three rulers, and she's decided that Mason is the best option."

I'm fighting back a smile by the time I finish explaining this particular nugget of truth. Queen Gitta is red in the face, the elegant queen finally giving a reaction. I chose to keep this information to myself when Queen Gitta tried to humiliate me earlier. I wanted to keep my cards close to my chest, but there's no point.

Lill has been discovered, and it seems Kie and Mason don't intend to kill us. There's no reason for me not to overshare.

Queen Gitta takes a second to collect herself, smoothing down her black dress before tucking a strand of white-blonde hair behind her ear. Her gloves are black, and she clasps her hands politely in front of her waist. This appears to be her go-to stance.

"Is this true?" she asks Kie.

"Yes."

"And when were you planning on informing me?"

"Soon." Kie shrugs, the action oddly informal. He's comfortable around his mother, despite her title of queen and her haughty attitude. "After dealing with Lillian and Abby."

Queen Gitta's throat bobs. "Your coronation is to be held *three days* after your return, Kieran. That is what we promised our people. This is an immediate issue I should have been informed of directly upon your return."

I'm not a massive fan of Queen Gitta, but she makes a good point. Kie and Mason pretend to be in charge, but she's the acting ruler. They should've gone to her first and let her decide how to handle the issue, but I'm glad they didn't. Lill wouldn't have gotten the opportunity to touch Kie had he not decided to interrogate her first, and I don't even want to think about what her future would hold if she didn't have the security of the mate bond behind her.

I doubt Queen Gitta is above torture. The guard felt comfortable whipping Lill, so the action must not be foreign here. If things were left up to Queen Gitta, there's a fair possibility I'd currently be in the cells alongside Lill.

Queen Gitta sucks her cheeks into her mouth. "We should continue this discussion in private."

Her two guards are pretending not to be listening, but I'm sure they're tuned into every word. I'm willing to bet money they're going to be spreading the information I shared as soon as they can. The details I provided Queen Gitta are juicy, too juicy not to share.

Neither Kie nor Mason respond verbally to Queen Gitta, but they both turn around, facing forward, and resume walking toward the guest house.

The wooden steps are sturdy beneath my feet, and they creak slightly as Kie pushes open the front door and steps inside. Mason quickly follows, and I find myself holding my breath as Lill and I enter. I'm scared—I'm willing to admit that to myself—and I inch closer to Lill as we crowd together in the small foyer.

Queen Gitta enters behind us, then shuts the door. There are no guards present, but they're not needed. Lill and I would never stand a chance against two powerful faeries and a shifter, especially given Lill's current physical state.

The magic that floats through the air will heal her, I know it will, but it's going to take time. I hope not too much. I trust Lill with my life, but I'd feel better if she had her regular faerie strength and powers available.

The house's layout is nearly identical to Kie and Mason's, but on a smaller scale.

The foyer opens immediately into the living room, and there's an oversized couch filling most of the space. There's no fireplace, though, which is a shame. I love fireplaces.

Beyond the living room is a wall of windows, but it's too dark outside to see the view. I doubt it matters. The windows are likely reinforced, and if not, I'm sure Kie will use his magic to ensure they can't be opened. Escape won't come via the form of a window.

The kitchen is on the right, and on the left is a hallway that I assume leads to bedrooms and bathrooms. I eye the wide island separating me from the kitchen, debating whether or not searching for another knife is a good idea or a suicide mission. I highly doubt Mason will take kindly to me stabbing him twice.

"Don't even think about it." Mason's sharp command is startling. His green eyes are too bright, almost like he's recalling me stabbing him with fondness. He's fucking mad. "I allowed you your one strike, but it won't happen again. What you do to *me*, I'll do back to *you*."

Is he threatening to stab me? I take in his wild, brown hair, crazy eyes, and slight smirk. He most definitely is.

Kieran shifts, crossing his arms over his chest. If he's angry about me spilling the details of his conversation with Zaha, he isn't showing it. He looks generally annoyed, his lips pursed and posture tense, but that's how he looked even before I opened my mouth.

He's probably relieved I took it upon myself to speak up. I saved him the trouble.

Does he believe the accusation Mason spewed earlier? Does

he genuinely believe that Lill murdered his father? It's absurd.

Lill shifts her weight from foot to foot, her shoulder brushing mine. I have so many things I want to tell her, but I'd prefer to wait until we're alone to inform her of her mates' behaviors these past few days. They treated me like shit and tried to gift me to a god, and I'm going to make sure she knows it.

She should know who her mates are.

Then she's going to tell me every detail about her childhood. She's neglected to share some vital information, and I'm done being left in the dark. I deserve some damn answers.

"I won't lock you up," Kie says, finally breaking the silence. "But know that we *will* be alerted the moment you set foot outside."

His threats mean little to me.

Lill nods. "Okay."

Kie continues staring at her, not responding. I'm pleased he isn't paying me any mind. I've never liked his attention.

Besides, Mason is giving me enough to last a lifetime. The shifter is openly staring at me, and I can't recall the last time he blinked. He's probably upset I'm brushing shoulders with Lill, and I hope he doesn't become protective over her.

What does a protective shifter even look like? Will he try to pee on her? Maybe hump her leg like a rabid dog? Neither would surprise me, but she's my friend before she's his mate. If he wants her attention, he can get in line. The mate bond can eat dirt.

Silence continues to stretch between the five of us, and it's beyond awkward.

Mason is the one to break it with a low, gruff order. "Explain."

He's talking to Lill. I can't fathom whom else he'd be speaking to. Surely, not Kie or Queen Gitta. Or me. I'm just the lowly human here.

Chapter Two

ABBY

LILL LOOKS DOWN, staring at her bare feet. Kie didn't give her time to put on socks and shoes before shoving her through the portal and forcing her into the faerie realm, and I highly doubt either was offered between his questioning and her whipping.

I grind my teeth.

"Explain," Mason repeats. "How long were you and your mother plotting to murder King Malcolm? Why did you do it? How did you survive in the human realm for so long? Where is Callie?"

Lill shakes her head, but Queen Gitta interrupts before my friend has the opportunity to answer Mason's rapidly fired questions.

"This can wait," she says. "Malcolm is long dead, and Lill's answers won't change that. We need to meet with the council and inform them of your agreement with Zaha, preferably before they find out from another source. We must remain in control of this narrative."

"The council can wait five minutes," Kie says. "I'm particularly interested to hear what—"

Queen Gitta interrupts again. "It can wait." She brushes her hands down her dress once more, then pulls open the front door and disappears outside. "Come."

I raise a brow, secretly enjoying the way she commands Kie and Mason around like little children. I especially love the way Kie grows visibly frustrated. He glares at the open doorway Queen Gitta just disappeared through.

"We'll be back shortly," he finally says. "Don't do anything irrational while we're gone." The latter sentence is directed toward me.

Mason grunts. "I'll remain here."

The shifter is still staring at me. I'm doing my best to pretend not to notice it.

"This conversation involves you, Mace," Kie argues. "You should be present for it."

Mason shakes his head, his narrowed eyes darting rapidly between Lill and me. Where is his hostility coming from? I'm not a threat to Lill, and I highly doubt he cares whether or not she's a threat to me.

She's his mate, and I bet if he walked in on her trying to sever my head, he'd just be annoyed that she hadn't asked for his help. He'd be happy I was dead, and he'd probably try to fuck Lill over my corpse.

"I'll remain here," Mason repeats. "I don't want them slipping past the guards."

That's a lie if I've ever heard one.

Lill and I are in no position to attempt an escape. Lill can barely stand, and I'm human. We don't exactly make for the deadliest, or sneakiest, team. Especially against guards specifically ordered to keep an eye on us.

Kie puts a hand on Mason's shoulder. Mason almost immediately brushes him off.

"There's no need for you here," Kie says, gesturing toward

Lill and me. "They're not going anywhere, and we need to speak to the council before my mother does. She'll twist this in my favor, and you need to win Anox over before they concoct a workaround that strips you of power."

Why does Kie care about that? I understand that he and Mason are friends, but surely, he'd be eager to find a way to circumvent the agreement he made with Zaha. There's no way he's going to so willingly give his title, his birthright, over to Mason.

If Mason is surprised by Kie's support, he doesn't show it.

"I'm unconcerned with what the council members think of me," he says. "You speak with them. I'll remain here with Lilly and Abby."

Kie frowns. "It doesn't work like that, and you know it. Come with me, Mason."

Mason works his jaw side to side. He's still fucking staring at me. "No."

Kieran's composed façade falters. He recovers quickly, but I see the expression of sheer desperation that takes over his features. Why is he so desperate for Mason to join him? Maybe he's afraid to speak to the queen and the council members alone. I bet they're going to gang up on him. I hope they make him cry.

I hope the faeries revolt when they hear the news. I'm so excited.

"Mace..." Kie starts. He's going to beg. I can sense it.

Excited jitters travel down my spine.

Mason shakes his head. "No."

A tense silence passes between the two, and I watch with poorly concealed interest. I'm looking forward to being alone with Lill, but I love it when Kie and Mason fight. It's nothing new, but their arguments seemed to end in physical blows while inside the forest. What will they do here?

Kie turns, placing himself between us and Mason and

blocking our view of the shifter. My body feels infinitely lighter with Mason's piercing glare gone, and I reach out until the back of my hand finds Lill's. She wordlessly laces our fingers together. Kie and Mason speak to one another in hushed tones, keeping their voices too low for me to hear. I'm sure the exchanged words aren't pleasant, though, and I count seven seconds before Mason grunts and brushes past Kie.

He doesn't spare Lill or me another glance as he storms out of the front door, and Kieran quickly follows.

I squeeze Lill's hand as the door slams shut behind him. About damn time. I don't hesitate to pull Lill in for a hug, careful not to touch her back as I press my face against her neck and breathe the comforting scent of her perfume. Some of her hair gets into my mouth, which I usually hate, but I'm so happy hugging her that I don't care.

She wraps her arms around my waist and squeezes. "I'm so fucking mad at you."

"I figured." I choke out a laugh. "Your mates are assholes." I could go on and on for days about that particular topic, but there are more important things to discuss. I pull out of the hug and spin Lill by her shoulders. "Is your back okay? Let me see." I lift her shirt, needing to see her injuries for myself. "And why is Mason accusing you of murdering Kie's dad? Why did you and Callie escape to the human realm, and are—"

My voice dies out as I take in the mangled state of Lill's back. There are three long, deep lashes covering her mid-back and shoulders. One is actively bleeding, but the other two didn't split the skin too badly. Blood pebbled to the surface but didn't go beyond that.

"There might be bandages in the bathroom," I manage to say. "Let me check."

I trip over my feet in my mad search for the bathroom. It's in the hallway, the first door on the left, and I rip through the drawers until I find bandages. I wet two towels and return to the entryway, where Lill still stands.

She hasn't moved, and she shoots me a weak smile as I gesture for her to lean over the kitchen island.

"Well?" I urge as I lift the back of her shirt. My breath hitches as I take in the damage, and I shake my head before getting to work. "What's going on, Lill?"

Her ribcage expands with breath. She must be exhausted, but I don't know when we'll have another moment alone. If Lill and her mother *did* murder the king, now may be her only opportunity to tell me.

"My dad died when I was a baby," Lill starts. "He was a council member, and he had… strong opinions regarding how the royal family was handling shifter relations. He felt the faeries were too harsh. His death wasn't treated with much respect, which upset my mom."

I remain quiet, absorbing every word as I clean her back.

Lill continues. "Alpha Theon, Mason's father, got in her ear while he was here on business. He convinced my mom to begin sleeping with Kie's dad for information." Lill pauses to clear her throat, and when she speaks next, her voice is hushed. "Trolls run rampant inside the Redstall Forest, and several faerie troops were sent to help the shifters manage them. One of the troops was ordered to burn the shifter's supply of delysum on their way out. They failed, thanks to my mom. She told Alpha Theon of the plans, and hundreds of faeries died."

The bandages are sticky, meant to adhere to the skin, and I wince as I place one over Lill's deepest lash. I could kill the man who did this to her.

"And?" I ask. "What does this have to do with *you*?"

Lill sighs. "The failed mission created a lot of tension between faeries and shifters. We have a peace agreement, the Sylvan Harmony Treaty. It was created shortly after the shifters moved into the forest, and the failed mission almost broke it. I was too young to understand what was going on. A few days after the attack, I was asked to bring a pot of tea to the king. It's common for the young children of court to be given small tasks, so I didn't think anything of the request."

I fear I know where this is going.

"The tea was poisoned with delysum, and King Malcolm died," Lill says. "My mom and I left for the human realm that same day."

This is a lot to take in. "Who gave you the tea? Your mom?"

"No. My mom *was* working with Alpha Theon, but she would've never put me in that position." A momentary pause, then, "I don't remember who it was."

That's a lie. Lill's got the memory of a damn elephant, and there's no conceivable way she would forget who gave her that tea. She would never.

"Surely, you remember *something*," I say.

Lill spins around as I finish bandaging her back. Her eyes are begging. She doesn't want me to pry. Why? I'd dig for more, but we don't have time.

I change the subject. "You didn't kill the king, at least not intentionally. Why are they blaming you?"

Lill cracks a half smile. "Why wouldn't they? My mother and I ran away, and I'm sure it's been discovered by now that she was working with Alpha Theon."

"Well…" I scuff my foot against the ground, thinking. "You can tell them the truth now, can't you? You don't have to lie to protect your mom since, you know, she's already dead. I assume being Kie and Mason's mate will help."

"I hope so." Lill looks around, taking in the open space.

She seems to know a lot about mate bonds. I'm pissed she never mentioned them before. I've been in love with the concept of soulmates since I read my first werewolf romance book at thirteen.

I tap my fingers against my thighs. "I presume you were close with Kie and Mason. Mason calls you 'Lilly,' and Kie recognized your photo."

Lill moves into the living room and plops onto the couch, her shoulders slouched. She looks exhausted. I don't blame her.

"We were close," she admits, "but it was a long time ago." She clears her throat. "What happened in the forest? It seems you three went on quite an adventure."

That's one word for it.

Chapter Three

KIERAN

I SLIDE MY thumb down the side of my drinking glass, wiping away the condensation. Mason sits to my left, his plate of food untouched. Why isn't he eating? It's unlike him, and I shoot him a sideways glance before directing my attention toward Anox.

As the council leader, the faerie elder sits at the head of the table opposite my mother. He's wearing traditional faerie robes, the thick, brown fabric wrapped tightly around his torso and draped over his arms. It's an outdated style, which is likely why Anox prefers it. He wants to stand out.

"This is unacceptable," he says, looking between me and my mother. "This decision cannot be made without council permission."

Lady Cassandra makes a quiet noise of agreement, and Lord Bishop quickly does the same. They don't like Mason, and they make no attempts to pretend otherwise. I eye Lady Cassandra, noting she's chosen to wear her long white hair down this evening. The casual hairstyle is unlike her. I assume it's a result of how quickly this meeting was called.

Lord Bishop is also dressed down. He's traded his usual formal attire for a dark linen shirt and black pants. His short white hair is even mussed, not slicked back as he typically prefers.

I've never held him in high regard.

I hoped he'd come into usefulness with age, but he's yet to make a valuable contribution in the thirty-four years he's been alive. If it weren't for his family title and influence, he'd have been removed from the council years ago.

I might see to it myself when I—when Mason—takes control.

"There must be something we can do," Anox continues. He turns toward me. "Did Zaha seem open to compromise?"

I raise my glass to my mouth, letting my mother take charge of this conversation. I have no problems leading council meetings, and I've begun doing so with increasing frequency as my coronation approaches. Still, my mother insisted we meet with the council immediately. She can handle this.

She smacks her tongue against the roof of her mouth. "Zaha doesn't compromise, and we shouldn't risk angering her by trying. Delysum has been a growing problem for years, and if Zaha has agreed to halt its growth, we aren't in a position to risk anything more."

She's right. The shifters have been cultivating the plant for too long, and it's only a matter of time before they use it against us. We've prepared for it as best we can, but there's little we can do to defend ourselves. Delysum reacts violently with magic, and despite the thousands of hours of research we've poured into it, we've found no way to combat its devastating effects.

Lady Cassandra straightens up, preparing to speak. "I agree with Her Majesty. Prince Kieran made an agreement with Zaha, and we must honor it." She frowns, her violet gaze settling on Mason. "We'll have to be delicate in our announcement, and we should push back the coronation. Weeks, if we can manage it."

"No," Anox says. "Pushing back the coronation will be seen as hesitance. People will speculate that we're looking into alternatives, and the shifters will sink their claws into that weakness. The coronation should continue as scheduled."

Mother nods. "I agree. Kieran?"

"Yes. We shouldn't postpone the coronation." I drag my thumb through the condensation of my cup again, smearing the buildup. "What do you think, Mason?"

He's being largely ignored, and while that isn't unusual, it will only spell trouble. Mason is intelligent, and he holds grudges. He notices the subtle snubbing of the council members, and if they don't adjust their attitudes accordingly, it will only make the transition period harder.

Mason blinks, his expression perfectly composed. "I agree."

"Of course he does."

The snide remark comes from Lord Bishop, who quickly sinks into his seat when he notices the several sharp looks shot in his direction. The council members may not speak directly to Mason, but they remain respectful. They know better than to start a war with their future king.

Mother clears her throat. "We should sleep on the news and reconvene tomorrow morning." She turns toward Mason and me. "Would you care to share your *other* news?"

"There's more?" Anox sounds exhausted.

I feel the same.

Mason takes it upon himself to answer. "We've found our mate."

"The human you were spotted parading around the property?"

"No. The faerie."

"What faerie?"

"The human led us to her. Lillian Collins." There's a collective intake of breath as Mason shares her name. "Kie found her in the human realm, and the bond has been triggered."

Lady Cassandra shifts nervously in her chair, and Lord Bishop gapes with wide, shocked eyes. Mother and Anox are the only two who remain composed.

"She..." Anox visibly hesitates, then continues. "Lillian Collins, as in the young girl who was accused of murdering His Majesty?"

Mason nods. "That's the one. We haven't spoken with her yet, but we intend to do so as soon as this meeting is finished."

"We wish to be present while you speak to her," Mother says. "I'm most interested in hearing her side of the story. We know Callie was sharing information with Alpha Theon, and I suspect she manipulated her daughter into giving my husband the delysum-infused tea."

That's not going to happen. I have my suspicions regarding Lillian and her mother, but she's my mate. She's weak and so visibly frightened, and I won't allow her to be interrogated by the council. Mason and I will speak with her privately and decide which details to share.

"No," I say. "Mason and I wish to speak with her alone. We will relay any important information to you."

I pause, waiting for my mother or the council members to argue, but my decision is met with quiet reluctance. I've been taking charge of the council these past few years in preparation for my ascension, but I wasn't sure my authority would remain intact after they learned of the deal I made with Zaha.

"Kieran..." Mother starts.

I meet her gaze, unwavering in my position. She must sense it as she falls silent.

"We can't possibly announce that a shifter is taking the title of our king *and* that Lillian Collins is to be our queen," Anox says. "It's too much too quickly. We should keep your matehood quiet until the news of Prince Mason's ascension has settled."

That's not a bad idea.

"People have already seen her," Mason points out. "They're going to wonder who she is."

Anox dismissively waves a hand. "That's fine. Say she's a woman you encountered during your travels. Give her a fake name and say she's a trusted friend. You don't need to share the entire truth."

I grimace. "I publicly referred to her as Lillian."

"That's not a concern," Anox says. "I've met several Lillians throughout the years, and not once did I suspect they were Callie's girl. She was, what, seven when she and her mother vanished? It was twenty years ago. People stopped searching for her long ago, and most assume she's dead. I highly doubt anybody will recognize her, and if they do, we'll deal with it."

I release my glass and turn toward Mason, trying to read him. Shifters are notoriously territorial over their mates, and I'm treading carefully. He may not want to lie about Lillian. His lips flatten together as he stares at his untouched plate of food.

"Very well," he eventually says. "Are we done here? It's late, and I haven't slept in a real bed in days."

At least he had the opportunity to shower. That's more than I've been given. I smell like shit, and the fresh shirt I threw on before coming here isn't doing much to hide my stench. It's a painful mixture of sweat, river water, and the dirt I haven't been able to wash out of my hair.

Anox shakes his head, then rises. The other council members, and my mother, are quick to do the same. "We can continue this discussion tomorrow morning. As Her Majesty suggested, we should sleep on this information." He shifts his attention to Lady Cassandra and Lord Bishop. "I expect you to arrive tomorrow prepared with ideas. Enjoy your nights."

The room quickly empties. I remain where I am, hoping for a moment alone with Mason. We need to speak with Lillian tonight, and I want to ensure we're on the same page before facing her.

It appears I'm not getting that opportunity, though. Mason's out of his chair in a heartbeat, and he spares me one fleeting glance before storming out of the chamber room and down the wide corridor that leads outside.

Wonderful.

I debate calling him back, but I decide against it. Peace will make this transition easier. I'm the only person in this kingdom who can get through to Mason, and I'll need to act as a buffer until he's adjusted to his new role. It shouldn't be too hard. He may have originally been given the title of *prince* as a formality, but he's received the same education and training as me.

We attend the same meetings, and while we've historically filled separate roles and responsibilities, he should be familiar enough with mine to jump into action. He has no other choice. The coronation is in three days.

Chapter Four

ABBY

THUNDER RUMBLING BESIDE my ear drags me into consciousness, and I let out a quiet groan as I plant my palms beside my shoulders and push up off my stomach. I'm in a bed. It's comfortable and warm, but it's not mine.

Lill lets out another loud snore, her right cheek pressed into a pillow as she sleeps beside me. That explains the thunder.

I push myself up further, looking around. I'm in one of the spare bedrooms in the house Kie and Mason stuck us inside yesterday. How did I get here, though? I'm positive Lill and I fell asleep on the couch last night. We lay side by side as I told her about my time in the forest, not leaving out a single detail. I want her to know exactly who her mates are, but I'm known to drag out a story and we fell asleep as I neared the end. Lill must've woken me up and forced me to come in here.

It wouldn't be the first time that's happened.

Lill and I are underneath soft, beige sheets, and I carefully slide them off myself as I take in the room. There's a window to the right of the bed, but the curtains are drawn shut. Sunlight seeps in from the edges, though. It's morning.

Across from the bed is a short, wide dresser. There's a bright-blue vase, a shallow bowl, and a stack of decorative books placed on top. I don't waste my time admiring them. Above the dresser is a tall mirror, one I avoid looking at as I head toward the cracked-open door.

It leads into the hallway, and I peek to ensure the coast is clear before fully stepping out of the bedroom. I close the door behind me, wincing as it latches with a quiet click. I don't want to wake Lill.

I'm not foolish enough to attempt an escape, not when we're being so carefully watched. Besides, Kie knows where I live. Even if Lill and I did manage to escape, there's nowhere for us to go. It's a sobering thought.

I need weapons.

Mason's pants threaten to slide down my hips as I head toward the open living area at the end of the hallway, and I frown as I yank them up my waist. What are the odds Kie and Mason will supply me with fitting clothing? Hopefully, Lill's bond with them will afford me some liberties.

I make it two steps into the living room before freezing.

There's a man on the couch—an oversized, unwelcome man.

Mason sits up with a jolt as I step into the room. His hair is frazzled and his torso bare, and he blinks up at me with wide, green eyes before turning and grabbing his discarded shirt and gloves from the coffee table beside him.

Did he sleep here? Why? I wish he'd make himself scarce, but I suppose I should get used to seeing him around. I'm surprised he didn't wake Lill and me up and demand answers when he and Kie returned from the meeting with the council last night.

Mason tugs on his gloves before slipping his shirt over his head.

"Why are you here?" I ask.

"I like to keep an eye on things." His voice is rough with sleep.

Gravelly.

I snort. "You like to keep an eye on your *prisoners*."

The only response I receive is a blank stare. I'm half-expecting him to deny it and say something about Lill being his mate and it being his job to protect her, but he does nothing of the sort. I'm not surprised.

"Lill likes to sleep in," I say, jerking my thumb toward the hallway. "So don't wake her up."

Mason frowns but still doesn't respond. I don't take his silence as an agreement, and I subtly widen my stance. I've stabbed him once, and despite his threats, I'm not afraid to do so again.

"I'm serious, Mason. Leave her alone." I hope he hears the threat in my tone. "I know you have questions, but Lill's been sick for a long time and she needs rest." Mason cocks his head to the side. I continue speaking. "And I'm not telling you a damn thing about anything, so don't try me. You can talk to Lill when she wakes up."

It's Lill's story to tell, and given the severity of the accusations, I'm going to let her tell it as she sees fit. I'd hate to misspeak and get her into trouble, and I'm sure Mason will have a billion follow-up questions I don't have answers to.

"Is the council upset that Kie agreed to make you king?" I ask. I'm eager to know. What I wouldn't give to have been a fly on the wall for that particular conversation.

Mason takes a moment to respond. "I wouldn't say they are pleased."

"Good." I look around. "Where's Kie?"

"I anticipate he'll be here shortly." That's not an answer. "He disagreed with my decision to sleep here last night," Mason continues. "He thinks I should have left you and Lill alone. Something about privacy. I didn't listen."

Why is he telling me this? I shift my weight from foot to foot, my eyes darting toward the kitchen. I'm hungry, but I don't want to leave my spot. I'm protecting the hallway leading to Lill. Objectively, I know I don't stand a chance should Mason decide to push past me, but I at least hope the ruckus would wake Lill and warn her of the approaching shifter.

"I'll have food delivered later today," Mason says. "We weren't exactly expecting guests."

"What's the process of rejecting a mate?" I'm asking for Lill. I know her, and she would *never* be interested in men like Kie and Mason. She has standards, and she doesn't date losers. That's precisely what Kie and Mason are.

"There isn't one. Mate bonds are for life."

I hate the connection they have to Lill. I hate what that means for her. I doubt Kie and Mason will be willing to let her leave, not with the cursed bond between them. They're going to lock her up here. She'll never see the light of day again. Metaphorically.

My shoulders roll forward. "Are you sure?"

If there's a way to reject and destroy the bond, she'll want to know.

Mason nods. "Yes."

That's not the answer I was hoping for.

How many humans know about the faerie realm? Is it treated as some secret shared only amongst the wealthy and powerful? That wouldn't surprise me. Humans are notoriously stingy with their information.

Mason clears his throat. "I suppose I should apologize." He *supposes*? How kind of him to take that under consideration. "I'm sorry for how we treated you in the forest, and I hope you know it wasn't anything personal."

He must be joking.

"It sure was personal to me," I spit, unable to hold back my anger. "You treated me like an animal. You degraded me in more ways than I can count, and your half-assed apology means nothing to me."

Mason snaps his jaw shut with a quiet *click*. I'm glad to finally have his silence, but it only lasts a second. "How long have you and Lilly known one another?"

There he goes calling her 'Lilly' again. Something about it makes my blood boil, and I hold back a snarky remark. I'm not going to answer his questions. If he wants to know about Lill's and my relationship so badly, he can ask her himself.

I'm just about to tell him so when the quiet creak of a door fills the silence and Lill steps into the hallway. She looks better than she has in years. There's life behind her violet eyes, and she's not wearing the expression of complete exhaustion I've grown familiar with seeing these past few years.

I love to see her improvement, and I can't wait to watch it continue.

"Good morning," she murmurs as she brushes past me into the living room, her gaze darting between me and Mason. "Is everything all right?"

"Yes," Mason answers for us. I would have given a different answer.

I cross my arms over my chest, then drop them and yank my pants back up my hips. I'm curious to see how they act around one another. Mason is prone to violence and threats—at least, he was with me—but we're not in the forest anymore. We're in the heart of the faerie capital, and Lill's his mate.

Mason rises from the couch as Lill shuffles toward him. She pulls her bottom lip between her teeth, her violet eyes flickering over the length of his body. I remain rooted to my spot, watching their every interaction. I need to see it, even if it makes my stomach churn. I don't approve.

"I hope you're prepared to explain yourself," Mason starts.

"Do not think Kie and I will let the mate bond distract us from your actions."

I resist the urge to scoff. I'm not sure why I expected him to ask how she slept or how her back feels. I gave him more credit than he deserves. Mason's continually falling short of my expectations. Kie, too.

Lill's throat bobs. "I wouldn't expect you to." She looks around the room, falling silent. This is so fucking awkward. "I'm prepared to speak with the council whenever you are."

It's weird seeing her speak so comfortably and confidently about the faeries. I know she's one of them and spent the first several years of her life here, but I think of her as human. I keep expecting her to be as confused and overwhelmed as I am, but that's clearly not the case. She may not know everything, but she knows a hell of a lot more than I do.

"No," Mason says. "Kie and I wish to speak with you privately, and we'll decide what information to relay to the council."

Lill nods, and after a tense second, she reaches for Mason's hand. It's an innocent enough gesture, especially considering they share a mate bond, but Mason pulls away like she's poison. It's a dramatic response, and Lill recoils with a wince.

If I had to guess, I'd say it's because Mason's never experienced intimacy, even something as innocent as handholding. He was abandoned by his parents and made to grow up in a kingdom of faeries who hate him. I bet he's never even been kissed.

Fucking loser.

I bet he lies awake at night thinking about his first kiss, probably nervous he won't be any good at it.

"We're mates, Mace," Lill continues. "Does that upset you? You used to talk nonstop about how excited you were to find your mate. Has that changed?"

My stomach twists, tightening and tightening in a very uncomfortable fashion. How close were Lill and Mason before she came to the human realm? From the sounds of it, too close. She's remembering a little boy who no longer exists.

Mason doesn't respond to Lill, and her chest expands as she darts forward again and successfully takes his hand. I hold my breath as she pulls off his gloves, exposing his skin.

"It's me, Mace," she says. "I didn't kill King Malcolm. At least, not intentionally. I was nothing more than a pawn, and I don't have an explanation for my mother's decision to flee to the human realm. She had nothing to do with the king's murder, though. I know that."

Is she not going to mention her mother working for Alpha Theon?

Lill sets Mason's gloves on the couch and curls her hands around his now-bare ones. I crank my head to the side, trying to get a better view as she brushes her thumbs over the back of his fingers. Mason lets it happen, his lips pursed as he stares down at where they're touching.

Several seconds pass before he pulls his hand from hers and steps back, putting what feels like a mountain of space between them. Then he cocks his head toward the front door, and I look over just as Kie welcomes himself inside.

He's finally showered and cleaned himself up. The dirty, black clothing he wore in the forest has been replaced with light-beige pants and a white, linen shirt. It reminds me faintly of what Samuel wore, but Kie's clothing looks more expensive. The fabric seems thicker, and it fits him in a way that suggests it was tailored.

Mason's clothing is similar, but he wears all black.

"Good morning." Kie shuts the door behind him. "I'm pleased to see everybody is already awake." His gaze shifts toward Lill.

"Explain."

I frown. "You sure aren't wasting any time."

Kie shoots me a sharp look. "I chose not to wake you two up and demand answers last night, did I not? You're welcome."

I'm not thankful.

Lill drags her fingers through her hair. "I was asked to bring tea to King Malcolm. I thought nothing of it, and I had no idea it was poisoned. I ran to my mother once I realized what was happening. She was shocked and urged me to stay in our home while she dealt with things."

Lill pauses, giving Kie and Mason a chance to speak up before continuing. "She returned hours later with several canisters of delysum tea, and the next thing I knew, we were traveling through a portal to the human realm. She told me never to speak of my life here, which I haven't, and I was raised as a human. That's all I know."

"Lie." Mason is the one who throws out the accusation.

Kieran takes a different approach. "Who gave you the tea?"

"A servant," Lill says. "I didn't recognize her, and I don't know her name."

That's not the answer she gave me. She told me she didn't know in a way that signaled she was avoiding the question. The inconsistencies are slight, but they're enough. She's hiding something.

"Would you recognize her face?" Kie asks. "If I brought the servant before you, would you remember her?"

Lill shakes her head. "It was twenty years ago, and I was seven. I hardly remember anything from that day, let alone the face of a woman I briefly spoke to."

Mason paces the length of the room, his bare fingers tapping rhythmically against his thigh. He seems agitated, and he makes three trips around the room before abruptly bending and snatching his gloves off the couch cushion where Lill left them.

He tugs them on with movements significantly rougher than necessary.

"And your mother?" he asks. "Where is she?"

"Dead."

"Lie."

Mason has a favorite word this morning.

Kie steps further into the room, his violet eyes narrowing on Lill. "It was discovered in the weeks after your disappearance that Callie was working with Alpha Theon. She was sleeping with my father for information, and she's responsible for hundreds of faerie deaths."

"What?" Lill does an excellent job pretending this is new information to her. Her eyes grow wide, and she shakes her head in disbelief. "Why would she do that?"

"Your father was notoriously soft on shifters," Kie points out. "The death of a mate would be devastating for even the strongest of faeries, but coupled with the financial strain his death caused your family, it's not surprising your mother turned against us."

Mason halts his pacing. "Is she still in the human realm?"

"I already told you she died."

"Lie."

Mason resumes his pacing.

"You're more than welcome to go to the human realm and check for yourself," Lill snaps. "You'll find that she died nearly ten years ago, and I spent the remainder of my teenage years with Abby's family."

I don't particularly love the idea of Kie and Mason digging around the human realm, around my family, but I keep my mouth shut. I trust Lill knows what she's doing, but I'm tired of the lies. She hasn't been honest with me, and I don't appreciate it. Have I not proven to her already that I'm on her side? I would never betray her and share information she prefers to remain hidden, *even* if I disagreed with doing so.

"I already sent out a search party," Kie says, "and I expect them to return shortly with their findings."

Mason stops pacing. I'm getting the impression that he didn't know about Kie's decision. Poor Mason didn't get to sign off. What a shame.

"Don't touch my family," I say. I can't hold back any longer, not when I have confirmation that an undisclosed number of faeries are searching around my hometown.

"We won't." Kie's voice softens just slightly. It feels a lot like pity. "We have no interest in—"

Mason interrupts. "Don't tell her that. We *will* interrogate your family if we find the need, and should they be found guilty of any crime against the faeries, they will be punished."

Kie's silence is confirmation enough. I grind my teeth so hard my jaw hurts, but I don't further argue. My family is innocent, and I'm not trying to draw more attention to them than Lill seemingly already has.

"How did she die?" Mason asks.

Lill shrugs. "There's no magic in the human realm. We mixed crushed delysum leaves into tea to sustain us. It amplified the little magic we had, but there wasn't enough for us both. She decided to go without so I would have a better chance of survival."

Kie and Mason exchange glances, but neither voice their thoughts out loud.

Lill doesn't let that deter her. "Again, I was a child when all this occurred. If you want to punish me for unknowingly bringing our king a poisoned tea, very well, but I have no knowledge of the supposed relationship between my mother and the shifters."

There's a long beat of silence before Kie speaks. "I'm not in the interest of punishing children for the actions of adults."

Thank god. My entire body relaxes, relief sweeping through me. Lill isn't going to be punished.

"And the mate bond?" Lill asks.

Mason blinks. "What about it?"

"We intend to honor the bond, but we wish to remain quiet about it for the time being," Kie says, ignoring Mason. "We can discuss your position in court once we've had the opportunity to corroborate your story."

I was under the assumption that mate bonds were romantic, but the way Kie and Mason speak about theirs is anything but. I understand they're in a challenging position, considering Lill's role in the king's murder and Mason's new future title, but it wouldn't kill them to show the tiniest bit of compassion.

Lill nods, her gaze cast toward the floor. She's disappointed. "I understand."

"I'm pleased to hear it." Kie licks his lips. "I've requested that food and clothing be brought over. The delivery should be here shortly, and we'll give you a tour of the grounds once you're ready. It would look odd if we didn't treat you as we would any other guest." Kie's attention shifts toward Mason. "I need to speak with you. Now."

Lill takes that as her cue to leave, spinning away from the pair and storming toward me with her chin held high and lips pursed. She's upset, and she works her jaw side to side as she brushes past me and returns to the bedroom we shared last night.

I follow, my movements stiff. I'm trying to remain quiet and absorb as much information as possible, but it's hard. I want to go home, but I'm hesitant to ask on the odd chance that my request is approved. Lill hasn't asked me to stay, nor have we spoken about the possibility of me returning to the human realm, but I don't want to leave until I know she's safe.

I walk into the bedroom after her and shut the door behind us, then promptly sit on the ground. Lill does the same, sliding down the side of the bed and dropping her face between her knees.

"Did that go how you wanted?" I ask.

She shakes her head, then nods, then finally ends up shrugging. "I'm not sure. I didn't exactly plan for this to happen."

"I can tell by your changing story…" I mumble.

Lill lowers her head further between her knees, hiding her face entirely from my view. The way her shoulders roll forward practically screams *guilt*. I'm not going to pry, at least not when Kie and Mason are just down the hall, but I want Lill to know that I'm onto her.

Her lies haven't gone unnoticed.

Chapter Five

ABBY

I MAKE EYE contact with Lill through the dressing mirror, trying and failing to gauge her mood. I usually find her easy to read, but I'm having difficulty doing so today. She's closed off, and I'm not exactly in my best state of mind.

I'm behind on sleep, and the breakfast Kie requested to be delivered was hard to eat. The platter of vegetables was arguably healthy, but my body craves carbs and protein. I want eggs, sausage, and at least four pieces of toast.

We were given purple carrot-looking things and small, blue balls that could pass for blueberries if it weren't for the fact that they tasted eerily similar to celery instead. Still, I ate most of the platter while Lill picked at the pieces.

"Are you sure you're not hungry?" I ask.

She nods. "I still feel nauseous. I think it'll take a few days for the effects of magic to fix that."

"I can ask Kie and Mason to take you to a doctor."

I don't want to ask Kie and Mason for anything, but Lill won't do it. She hates asking for help.

"There's nothing a doctor can do," Lill says. "I'm sick because I've been starved of magic, and only exposure will fix it. I just need to be patient."

Patience isn't my strong suit.

Lill meets my eyes in the mirror, but I'm distracted by her exposed back. I've already cleaned her lashes and placed a new bandage over the deeper one, and I let my eyes travel to her sharp shoulder blades and visible ribcage.

"Are you done scanning me?" she snaps.

I shake my head. "No."

Lill huffs and pulls down her leggings, and I finally turn away as she grabs the dress Kie had delivered for her. He had two nearly identical dresses brought in, and I'm already wearing mine. It's not nearly as elegant or formal as the dress Her Majesty and the other women were wearing yesterday, but the fabric is thick and I like the blush color.

Lill slips hers over her head, letting the long fabric slide over her waist and settle at her calves. These dresses were made for tall faerie women, and the hem touches my ankles. It's not as flattering on short humans.

I take the laces at Lill's sides and tie them behind her back, pulling the fabric flush against her skin. I feared we'd be forced to wear corsets or something equally restricting, but the dresses are surprisingly comfortable.

I eye the square neckline and short butterfly sleeves.

"We look like bridesmaids," I say.

Lill cracks a smile. "You should've seen the faerie fashion twenty years ago. Some dresses were so heavy, I could barely stand in them." She clears her throat. "Mace used to help me tear off the inner layers so we could play."

I don't want to talk about Mason. "Is this place drastically different from when you were a kid?" I ask.

"It's hard to tell. I haven't had many opportunities to look around."

Right. I've spent ample time galivanting throughout the faerie lands while Lill has been slowly dying in the human realm.

"You look beautiful, Abbs," Lill says, changing the subject. "Our clothing looks good on you."

Our clothing. She's been here for less than twenty-four hours and already, she's acclimating. It's happening much too quickly for my liking.

"We should talk about—"

I fall silent as I take notice of the look Lill is giving me. She shakes her head, the movement subtle but precise. Now isn't the time to poke holes in her story. Very well.

"Does the magic feel good?" I ask instead.

"You have no idea."

"How long will it take you to be back to normal?"

Lill shrugs. "A couple of weeks, maybe. I've been deficient for most of my life, and I don't think my body will bounce back as quickly as it does for other faeries."

A couple of weeks? That's so long.

"So you intend to stay for a couple of weeks?" I'm fishing.

Lill's responding frown tells me she picks up on it. "I don't know. I need magic to survive, and the mate bond makes things tricky. I can't just up and leave, even if I wanted to. This is all as surprising to me as it is to you."

Hardly. Lill spent the first several years of her life here, and she knew of her ties to the faerie royals. She's not *nearly* as surprised as I am. I keep that particular thought to myself, though. Now isn't the time to start an argument, even if I can feel one beginning to brew.

It's in the early stages, but things are tense between us and I don't see a world where they improve without some serious communication. I'm not getting the impression that Lill is looking to talk through things, at least not the way I want. We're going to fight. Probably not today, but soon.

It's inevitable.

"What exactly is magic?" I wave my arm through the air, gesturing to the tiny flecks floating around us. "I know it's *this*, but what exactly do you do with it? How does it work?"

I'm desperate to know.

Lill teeters her head back and forth. "It's hard to explain. There's a lot of complexity, but you can think of it as a second pair of hands. Anything you can do with your hands, faeries can do with magic. It takes more energy to use magic than to just do something yourself, though, so it's not used that often."

"That's the most disappointing thing I've ever heard." I mean it, too. Magic is supposed to be, well, magical—not some useless tool that's rarely used.

"I can't open a portal with my hands," I point out. "But you and Kie did so with magic. I also met a man in Callonton who turned a stone into a giant, three-dimensional map."

Lill throws her hands out to the sides. "Magic is an impossible concept to explain to somebody who can't experience it. It's like describing color or taste. I'm trying my best here."

I pause, waiting for her to elaborate, but after a few seconds, I realize she's given up.

I brush my hands down my sides. "I suppose we can't hide in here forever."

I'd like to, but Kie and Mason are waiting to give us a tour, and we've taken our time dressing. Besides, I'm interested to learn the layout of this place. It will make our eventual escape easier.

I assumed Kie and Mason would be too busy to spend time with us. They should be preoccupied with planning for Mason's ascension, but it seems they're choosing to pretend everything is all right and continue their lives as usual. It's a transparent attempt to lull the faeries into a false sense of security.

Mason rises from the couch as Lill and I step into the living room, his eyes darting quickly between us. I'm expecting him to react to the sight of Lill dressed up in faerie attire, but he hardly bats an eye. He's a shitty mate.

"Where's Kie?" I ask.

The violet-eyed faerie isn't anywhere to be seen.

Mason sucks his cheeks into his mouth. "He's been called away. I'm taking you instead."

That's just wonderful. Mason looks about as pleased as I feel, which isn't at all. If I had to pick between him and Kie, I'd choose Kie. The faerie's an asshole, but he's considerably more stable than Mason. I don't trust the shifter not to get angry, transform into his ungodly horrifying beastly state, and start tearing apart faeries.

Lill shifts her weight, no doubt picking up on Mason's annoyance. He's not going out of his way to hide it, and I can only imagine how she feels having a mate who is so visibly displeased to be spending time with her.

I take back all the romantic notions I once held toward the idea of mates. It turns out even men who are destined to be with you are shitty.

"It wouldn't kill you to smile." I clear my throat. "You kidnapped, tortured, and offered me as a gift to Zaha. A tour is the least you can offer."

Mason scoffs. "I did *not* torture you."

That's a load of shit. He may not have tortured me physically, at least not in the traditional sense of the word, but he most definitely tortured me mentally. I was put under an inhumane amount of stress and fear, and he knows it.

A line forms between Mason's eyebrows, and he relaxes his shoulders in a way that looks forced and unnatural before extending an arm toward Lill. There's a tense moment where she stares at it, hopefully debating rejecting him, before she steps forward and takes it.

They're not touching skin. Mason's black gloves are firmly in place, signaling to the faeries that he hasn't and isn't interested in finding his mate. Does that upset Lill? She hasn't said anything about it, but I'm sure she's noticed.

Mason leads Lill outside, and I follow a few steps behind. I'm lingering so I can watch them, and I puff out my cheeks as the pair glide down the secluded wooded path separating the housing area from the larger property.

I don't understand this place. It's beautiful, but it's so different than how royals in the human realm live. There's no castle, no sprawling estate. Instead, there's a smattering of buildings nestled within one giant property. It's a compound.

Everything is so clean, but I suppose that's to be expected.

"Queen Gitta and a few council members reside here," Mason says. "So don't go sneaking around. Most guests stay in the housing on the other side of the property."

"Is this place open to the public?" I ask.

"Obviously not."

I bite my tongue at Mason's sharp reply. It was a good question, and unlike some people, I'm not afraid to acquire knowledge and grow as an individual. The faerie realm is new to me, and I'm eager to learn as much as possible in the short time I've got here. Once Kie and Mason verify Lill's story, I assume they'll shove me through the first available portal.

As I watch Lill speak quietly to Mason, her voice too low to make out the specific words, I realize she might not even want me here. This world isn't as foreign to her as I initially anticipated, and she's actually *trying* with Kie and Mason. I'm nothing more than a human-sized cockblock.

Mason leads us down several long, outdoor walkways.

They're beautiful, and I want to touch every flower and fancy decorative item we pass. If Mason weren't here, I probably would.

"Shouldn't there be guards with us?" I ask, interrupting their conversation.

It's not much of a conversation, anyway. Lill is doing about ninety-nine percent of the talking, and Mason is chiming in only occasionally with a grunt or one-word answer. I'm surprised Lill is still trying. I sure wouldn't be if I were in her position.

Mason slows as I speak, his long stride shortening just slightly. I'm relieved, and I take the opportunity to catch my breath. There aren't many people out and about this morning, probably because it's still early, but we're never entirely alone.

As a prince and the soon-to-be crowned king, shouldn't Mason have a bodyguard? Lill and I sure won't be of much assistance in an assassination attempt.

"Guards... with us? Why?" Mason spares me a glance over his shoulder. "The front gates are heavily monitored, and guards wander about. The property is safe, if that's what you're concerned about."

Is it, though? I'm not concerned about strangers attacking us. I'm worried about the faeries who are allowed inside doing so. They hate Mason, they don't know Lill, and I'm nothing more than a human pet to be kicked aside.

"If you head left, you'll find offices and assembly buildings," Mason says, moving away from the topic of guards. "They aren't of any interest to you."

Who's he to say that? They *could* be. I stare at the trellis above me, mesmerized by the thousands of butterflies fluttering around the vining flowers as I follow Lill and Mason around the corner. We're heading to the right, away from the offices and assembly buildings, and I let out a quiet yelp as I barely avoid barreling into a man.

He smoothly sidesteps me, his eyebrows disappearing into his hairline as he extends a hand. I think it's to help steady me, but I recover before he makes contact.

"My apologies," he starts. "I wasn't looking where I was walking. Are you—"

"Back away from the human."

Mason is between me and the faerie a heartbeat later, his back to me as he glares down at the faerie I almost steamrolled into. It's overly aggressive, and I scrunch my nose in disgust as I shift my gaze toward Lill. I want her to see this, want her to see how unnecessarily aggressive the shifter is. She's already looking. Good.

The faerie male steps away from Mason, his gaze darting between me and the shifter. "My apologies. It was an accident." He scurries away, not looking back.

I wait until he's out of sight before speaking. "That was uncalled for."

Mason spins, and it takes all my strength not to flinch as his anger directs itself toward me. "He wasn't wearing gloves, and he was fully intending to touch your arm. You humans may go around touching everything and everybody, but it's considered impolite here. He was taking advantage of your ignorance."

Mason retreats a second later, returning to Lill.

I glare at his back, grudgingly following behind. I'm not ignorant.

We make another sharp right, emerging in a giant field. It stretches as far as I can see, and it's carefully maintained. Walking paths are worn into the ground, and there are thankfully no trellises to be seen. I appreciate the unobstructed view of the clear sky.

There's a hill directly on the left and what looks to be tall hedges beyond it. Far off on the right are trees, and I spot a few buildings scattered about. Most of the land is clear, though.

The nearest building is dome-shaped. Shallow steps lead to a large, stone patio that appears to wrap around the side of the building, but it's the floor-to-ceiling windows that draw the most attention. It's stunning.

"This land makes up most of the property," Mason says. "You'll find the gardens, ballrooms, pretty much everything here."

I point to the building closest to us. "What's that?"

"The school."

I snort. "You have your own private school? How fitting."

Mason ignores me. "You'll find this area to be the busiest. Faeries love to stroll about. Socializing. I try to avoid it."

I move forward, brushing past Mason and Lill until I'm close enough to the school building to peer inside. It's empty, with only a few covered tables and chairs scattered about. The domed ceiling is a kaleidoscope of gold and red, and the crisp, white flooring is unnervingly clean.

"How many kids—"

"I'm leaving."

I turn, anger flushing my cheeks as Mason walks back underneath the trellis walkway, leaving me behind. He's not giving me enough time to take everything in. Lill frowns, also looking annoyed and left behind, before rushing after him.

I hesitate before doing the same. The faerie I ran into earlier seemed friendly, but most of the others haven't. I doubt they'll be much help if I get lost, and I'm admittedly petrified of running into *Her Majesty* without Kie or Mason present. They're the only thing standing between me and the frightening queen's wrath.

Mason weaves effortlessly through the covered walkways and open courtyards, and I almost immediately lose my sense of direction. I'm most definitely going to need a map.

"Kitchens and private dining halls are this way," Mason says, pointing down a walkway. "Stay out of the kitchens. The workers don't want your interruption, but you can usually find something to eat in one of the dining halls should you find yourself hungry."

I perk up at that. "We're allowed out of the house?"

"You can roam the grounds, although it's not encouraged."

"Not encouraged by whom?" By the faeries, or by Kie and Mason? Those are two very different things.

Mason turns, walking back the way we came. His refusal to answer my question is all the answer I need. It's not encouraged by him and Kie, but I don't care about their feelings.

He walks back into the open field. The hill that was on our left earlier is now on the right, and tall hedges block my view.

"The gardens," he says. He pauses, giving Lill and me just enough time to catch up before continuing. "This is the same park as before, just a different entrance." His green eyes meet mine. "In case you've lost your sense of direction."

Lill offers a laugh, but it's forced. "This place is different from the last time I was here."

"Of course it is," Mason says. "Queen Gitta ordered a restructure after King Malcolm was murdered. She didn't like our enemies knowing the ins and outs of the property."

To Lill's credit, she doesn't visibly react to the mention of the king's murder. I wonder if she blames herself. She shouldn't, but she was a child and they often can have a warped sense of reality and responsibility.

Mason resumes his infuriating tour, speed-walking us around the property and pointing out the important buildings. He doesn't give us enough time to look around and explore, and I'm getting the impression that he's intentionally making it as confusing as possible.

This is the worst tour I've ever been on, and my mood sours with every passing minute.

It takes almost an hour before we return to the royal housing area, and the second I spot the secluded wooded walkways, I storm forward. I have a headache, and I need space.

Chapter Six

MASON

LILLY BRINGS HER hands to my waist, and I bite my tongue so hard it bleeds. Her fingers are cold as she slips them underneath my shirt, touching my bare skin.

I fight the urge to flick her away.

It seems I'm not making enough attempts to hide my emotions, as she lets out a long, drawn-out sigh. Abby's always giving me the same noise, and I'm growing sick of it. I'm a prince and a shifter. People don't *sigh* at me.

It doesn't bother me so much when Abby does it because she's a human and, if I'm honest with myself, I deserve her irritation. Lilly should know better.

"Mace." Lilly's glancing between my eyes and my lips, but I'm not going to kiss her. "You're punishing me for something I didn't do. Not intentionally. I understand this isn't an ideal situation, but we're mates. I'm trying, and I'm only asking that you do the same."

My mate? She's a dirty fucking liar is what she is. I don't know what kind of magic she's using to make Kie feel the mate bond—it most definitely doesn't belong to the faeries—but it doesn't work on shifters. I feel nothing when I touch her. She isn't our mate.

I can't let her know I realize that, though. Lilly's playing a dangerous game, one I'm determined to understand. I figured it would be easy to pretend I feel the bond, but it's significantly more challenging than anticipated. I hate her touch, and she's going out of her way to be close to me.

Lilly slides her hands up my waist and to my front, resting her palms on my chest.

I've always known that I would eventually have to let a woman touch me, but I didn't realize just how dirty it would make me feel. It makes my skin crawl, and I fight the urge to shift into my animal form and put a protective layer of fur between us. The urge is becoming harder to control, and I'm nervous that I soon won't be able to contain my instincts.

The bathroom toilet flushes, and I tense as I wait for Abby's inevitable return. She refuses to leave Lilly and me alone, which is ideal. I don't trust the faerie's intentions, and I intend to keep a close eye on the human. Her loitering makes both tasks easy.

Lilly notices the way I shift, anticipating Abby's return. "You and Abby seem to have quite a…" She pauses, thinking through her following words. "Tumultuous relationship."

I suck my cheeks into my mouth, not wanting to discuss my relationship with the human. I feel guilty about how I treated Abby, but I already apologized and there isn't anything further to do. She's chosen not to forgive me, which I grudgingly accept, and that's all there is to it. I won't beg for her forgiveness. I've never done so before, and I will not start today.

I'll learn to live with the guilt. It occasionally steals my breath and makes my palms sweat, but I'm confident the intensity will lessen with time.

"It's tense," Lilly continues. "Would you like me to talk to her for you?"

Why is she offering this?

I shake my head. "No."

Abby finally enters the room, capturing my full attention. I'm becoming increasingly nervous regarding the safety of the human. I don't know what Lilly is capable of, and until I do, I refuse to leave them alone. Abby needs my protection.

She eyes Lilly and me, her gaze lingering on Lilly's hands on my chest, before she looks away and steps into the kitchen. The urge to brush Lilly away intensifies, and I let out a quiet breath when she retreats on her own. She was on me the second Abby left the room, and I'm relieved she's pulling back now that the human has returned.

The front door opens, and Kie comes sauntering inside a moment later. He glances around, taking in everybody's position, before shutting the door behind him. I can tell he's pissed by the tenseness of his shoulders and the furrow of his eyebrows. There's also the fact that he's openly glaring at me.

"Where have you been?" The question is directed toward me.

I was supposed to meet with him and the council almost an hour ago, but I chose not to go. I intended to, but the women took forever to get ready. I managed to make up the lost time on our tour, but then I couldn't bring myself to leave.

Kie turns toward Lilly. He's trying his best to act casual, but I notice the stiffness in his movements. He's fallen victim to the pseudo bond, but I can tell he feels a wrongness with it. He hasn't said as much to me, but I can read between the lines.

I want to tell him it's fake, but I worry he won't be able to maintain the charade.

We've long since accepted that we'd never meet our mate and trigger the bond. Our future marriage is to be a political move and nothing more. The kingdom needs a queen more than we need a mate.

That only works if the mate bond is never triggered, though. To deny an active bond and marry another would infuriate Zaha, and it's not a risk any faerie or shifter would ever take. Heavens, I can only imagine the punishment she'd dole out.

Kie and I never discussed the possibility of finding our mate, but I know he's always secretly hoped for it. I'd be lying if I said I never had, too. Giving up my mate isn't a sacrifice I've ever been happy to make, but a necessary evil.

He believes Lilly, and I don't enjoy lying to him. But if I tell him the bond is fake, his reaction will undoubtedly alert Lilly. I need her to think her magic is working, and to do that, I need Kie to believe the bond is real.

"Lillian." Kie's gaze falls to her dress. "You look beautiful."

Shit. I probably should've complimented her earlier. It didn't occur to me, and as I take in the way Lilly preens, I regret my oversight.

Kie closes the gap between him and Lilly, and I look away as he grabs her forearm and kisses her. It's chaste and awkward, and he clears his throat once it's over.

"Where have you been, Mason?" Kie repeats, pulling away from Lilly.

I wave my arm toward the women. "With them."

Kie hums. Abby's in the kitchen, and she refuses to look at us as she aggressively eats the few bites of her breakfast she didn't finish earlier. Kie mentioned having the kitchen stocked for them, but it's yet to be done. I'll look into it later.

"The council is waiting for us. Now," Kie says, drawing my attention. He gestures toward the front door, but I'm not leaving. "Mason." He sounds frustrated. "I'm not asking."

I raise a brow. As far as I'm concerned, he's no longer in a position to order me around.

"Yeah," Abby chimes in. "You should leave."

Someday soon, I'm going to tape her mouth shut. It's a miracle Kie hasn't used his magic to seal her lips together already. I shoot Abby a dirty look, hoping she gets the silent message to shut the fuck up, which only causes her to smile.

I miss the days when she was afraid of me. She was significantly less irritating.

"We'll behave," Lilly says. "You shouldn't leave the council waiting."

Her fingers curl loosely around my wrist, almost as if she's afraid of my reaction to her touch. I try not to appear too uncomfortable, but I can tell I'm not succeeding as Kie furrows his brows and cocks his head to the side.

Fuck.

I bring my hand to the back of Lilly's head. I've always preferred it when women wear their hair down, and I run my fingers through her soft strands before bringing my lips to her temple.

Her skin is warm as I quickly kiss the side of her head. It's all she's getting from me.

I resist the urge to wipe my mouth as I release her and step away. If she were truly my mate, I'd be all over her. I've heard that the mate bond is all-consuming, and soon my indifference toward the faerie will attract questions. I'll no longer have an excuse to hold back once we've confirmed Lilly's story.

I assume it's going to check out. Lilly's mother was cunning, and I doubt her daughter is much different. They had twenty years to cover their tracks, and it will take more than one surface-level investigation to uncover the truth.

I just need Kie not to impregnate Lilly in the time it takes me to do so. They aren't having sex, at least not yet, but I doubt Kie will be using protection when they do. It's our duty to create heirs, and it's not unheard of for mated pairs to begin trying almost immediately after triggering the bond. As far as the kingdom is concerned, we have no reason to wait.

The three of us are of a reasonable age, and we have the means to care for a child. The faeries won't care to hear any excuses.

"Go away, Mason," Abby repeats. "You're not welcome here."

Lilly makes a quiet noise of disagreement, but she doesn't argue on my behalf. She wants me gone, too, which is only more of a reason to stay. Is she planning something? Maybe she intends to run away with Abby. She won't get far, especially not while she's still so weak, but I wouldn't put an attempt past her.

"Tell the council I'm busy and will attend the next meeting," I say.

I shouldn't push them off. The council members hold power and influence, and they won't take kindly to my rejection. I don't have any other options. Somebody has to protect the infuriating human, and it sure isn't going to be the guards.

They don't know Lilly's true identity, and they'll choose her safety over a human's. Telling them to do otherwise would only draw attention, especially when they learn Lilly is our mate.

"Please don't make this any harder than it needs to be, Mace." Kie runs his hands through his hair, and I flinch as his composed façade momentarily drops. He's stressed, not to mention exhausted. He drained himself traveling through the forest and opening the portal, and now he's run thin with Lilly's discovery and my impending ascension.

Kie and I may not always see eye to eye, but he's important to me. I don't enjoy seeing this side of him, and I grind my teeth as I turn toward Abby.

"Behave," I order. My gaze shifts toward Lilly. "I will be back soon."

Kie follows me outside, silently judging as I order the guards stationed in the courtyard to keep a close eye on the house and alert us if either of the women attempts to leave. I'm fidgety as I head toward the chamber rooms, already anticipating the headache this meeting will be.

The faeries are scrambling, and the number of meetings they wish to have only proves it. We typically only have formal meetings once a week. Daily ones are practically unheard of outside of shifter conflict, and those I'm typically discouraged from attending.

Now, I'll be leading them. My father will be ecstatic when he hears the news.

Chapter Seven

ABBY

I SINK INTO the couch cushions, beyond bored, before pulling up the bottom of my dress and examining my scabbed knees.

"What happened?" Lill asks.

"Mason. He pushed me down while we were in the forest." I press my lips together, my anger renewed by the memory. "He was rough with me."

Lill's quiet for a long moment. "I'm so sorry."

I shrug. "Not your fault. How's your back feeling?"

"Better."

We fall silent. I should take this opportunity to ask her questions, but I don't. I doubt she'd give me genuine answers. The faerie realm is beautiful and I'm so glad she's feeling better, but it's clear I'm not welcome here.

I saw how Lill's face fell when I returned from the bathroom earlier. She was trying to cuddle up with Mason, and she backed away like a wounded puppy when I stepped into the room. She doesn't want me here.

I refuse to be somewhere I don't belong. I want to go home and forget this ever happened.

I trail my finger over the healing scab before fiddling with the hem of my dress. We've been alone for the better part of an hour, and Lill and I haven't exchanged more than a few words. I'm waiting for her to make the first move, which she doesn't seem inclined to do.

"Is there anything fun to do here?" I ask. I'm at my wit's end. "Maybe we could go to the big park."

Lill's responding grimace tells me she doesn't like that idea. "I don't think we'll be welcome there." I highly doubt we'll be welcome *anywhere*. Lill puffs air into her cheeks and glances at the ceiling, thinking. "We could go to the bathhouse, I suppose. There used to be one on the property."

A bathhouse? I'm imagining a giant tub full of naked faeries, but that can't be right. Lill would never suggest we do something like that. She's far from a nudist, and almost every faerie here hates us. I'm not interested in having their prying eyes on my naked body.

"A bathhouse?" I ask. "Explain."

Lill quirks a brow. "You know what a bathhouse is. It used to be popular among the faerie adults. I'm not sure if it still is, but it could be fun. I've always wanted to go."

"Fun for who?" I ask. "Surely not me."

I look into Lill's piercing, violet eyes. What do the faeries think about my brown ones? They must find them quite dull. Mason has green eyes, but they're unnaturally bright.

"Mason and Kie are acting…" Lill pauses, sucking on her teeth before continuing. "Mates are possessive, and I'd like to see how they react to me entering a public bathhouse."

I frown. She can't be serious. "We've been here for less than twenty-four hours, and they've spent the past twenty years convinced you murdered Kie's father. Give them some time." I can't believe I'm defending Mason and Kie, and I hate being put in a position where I feel the need to do so. It's outrageous, but it needs to be said. "I'm sure they'll soften once they've looked into your story and confirm you're telling the truth."

My stomach churns as the words leave my mouth, but I force myself to continue. I want nothing more than to bash Mason and Kie, but that's not what Lill needs. I've already told her my opinion of the two men, and she can do with that information what she pleases. I'm not going to push.

I'm putting our friendship before my personal feelings toward the princes, which I think is very mature of me. I'm a great friend.

"I know," Lill starts. "I just… I thought a mate bond would be, I don't know, *more*"—her voice cracks—"and I'm beginning to freak out."

Fuck me.

Lill chews on her bottom lip, rocking back on her heels. "What if something is wrong with it? What if Zaha altered our bond after I killed His Majesty? What if it's broken?" She's desperate, and my already fading resolve crumbles. "Mason refuses to look at me, let alone touch me," Lill continues, her voice low. "They're my mates, and I just want them to see me. I want to see that the bond affects them, even if they don't act on it."

"Okay." My heart pounds, and I yank my dress over my scabbed knees. "Fine. The bathhouse it is."

Lill practically beams, and I wave away her excitement with an exaggerated huff. I'll join her, but I won't be happy about it.

I follow her outside, mildly surprised we aren't immediately swarmed by guards with violet eyes and bayonets. The three lingering nearby turn toward us, though, and one heads in our direction.

"Can you take us to the bathhouse?" Lill asks as he approaches.

If he's surprised by her question, it doesn't show. His attention flickers between Lill and me before he nods and turns toward the two guards still in the courtyard. One takes off, probably to inform Mason and Kie of our plans. I wonder how long it will take the pair to hunt us down.

I'm going to guess under five minutes.

The guard brings us to a single-story brick building tucked away at the back of the property. It isn't much to look at, especially compared to the exteriors of the other buildings I've seen.

"Thank you," Lill says to the guard. "We won't be long." *I hope not.*

She grabs my arm and pulls me through the wooden front door. I expect a lobby, maybe a spot to check in, but the door opens immediately to a changing area. A long bench spans the room, and cubbies are built into the walls.

I'm relieved that only a few articles of clothing are folded and hung neatly inside. There must not be too many people here right now. *Good.* A woman in a simple black, linen dress stands beside an open doorway at the opposite end of the room. I assume it leads to the bathing pools.

The woman looks us over, her cheeks sucked into her mouth.

"Welcome," she eventually says. She sounds far from happy. "You can give me your clothing after undressing, and I'll ensure it's put away properly. The pool is through this doorway here." She looks pointedly at me as she gestures to the open doorway beside her. "This is a private space. Please act accordingly. No touching."

No shit. I'm not a child, and I understand what consensual touch is. Humans may not value touch as the faeries and shifters do, but we aren't heathens.

"So no underwater dick grabs?" I tut. "Shame."

Lill shoots me a sharp look.

I blink back at her, hoping she can see in my eyes that I'm not happy with this. I was hoping for gendered changing rooms at a minimum, and I awkwardly stand around before beginning to undress.

Lill is already two steps ahead of me. She hands her dress to the attendant and removes the bandage on her back. I'm pleased to see the one deep lash healing nicely, and at a faster rate than humanly possible. The magic here truly is good for her.

"Do you think they've been to a bathhouse before?" I ask Lill. She knows who the 'they' I'm speaking about are.

She shakes her head. "I doubt it. The risk of skin-to-skin contact is too high."

"And you think they'll come because you're here?"

"I hope."

I hand the attendant my clothing and cover my chest as we walk through the narrow hallway leading to the pool. The temperature rises with every step, and steam fills the air. By the time we enter the darkened room at the end of the hallway, I'm surprised I'm not choking on it. Several candles are lining the walls, illuminating the room with just enough light to see.

The room is made of stone, and vines grow up the walls. I'm not sure how they survive without sunlight, but I assume it's a faerie thing. The room isn't as big as I thought it would be, and the pool is surprisingly small. I'd estimate only ten or so faeries could comfortably fit inside.

Two faeries are at the far end of the pool, both men. Lill's the picture of confidence as she makes her way to the opposite end of the pool, and I scurry behind like an awkward mole rat. The men seem to be in the midst of a heated discussion, and I'm beyond relieved they don't look over as Lill and I sink into the water.

There's an underwater bench, and it's low enough that only my head and the tops of my shoulders stick out above the waterline.

Lill lets out a quiet groan. "My father used to go on and on about the bathhouses. They were his favorite place to unwind, and I've always wondered what they're like. This feels amazing."

I hate to admit that she's right. The water is warm, and my sore muscles immediately relax. The two men on the opposite end of the pool give us complete privacy, not once looking over. It's comforting, and I'm confident it would never happen in the human realm.

The relaxation doesn't last long. Two large figures storm into the room only minutes after we get situated.

Mason turns toward the faeries on the opposite end of the pool.

"Out."

The room is cleared within seconds. The men scramble out of the pool, water still dripping from their bodies as they disappear into the hallway leading to the changing room. That was rude. They weren't bothering anybody.

I pull my knees to my chest, hiding my body from view. Kie and Mason can see through the water, and I'm not offering a free show.

Kie lingers by the entrance. "What do you two think you're doing?"

Lill shrugs. "Relaxing."

Mason looks like he's about to burst a blood vessel. "Get out."

I don't appreciate being told what to do. Neither does Lill if the sudden stiffening of her spine is anything to read into. The four of us are at a standstill, nobody moving. I'm not leaving this pool until Kie and Mason are gone.

Kie is the first to break. He rolls his shoulders back, his jaw set firm.

"Very well," he says. "Let's make this quick."

He spins on his heel and storms away. I relax only slightly. Mason remains where he is, showing no signs of leaving. Lill must be quite pleased by his possessive, dramatic display.

I'm happy for her.

Those feelings vanish as Kie reemerges, now naked. *You've got to be kidding me.* I sink further into the water, averting my gaze as he slips into the pool beside Lill.

"What are you doing?" It's Mason who asks the question.

I'd also like to know what Kie thinks he's doing. I expected them to get angry with Lill and force us to leave, not *join* us. I would've never agreed if I had known this was how her half-cocked experiment would turn out.

"I'm joining our guests in the bathing pool," Kie says through clenched teeth. "Get. In."

Mason shakes his head. "No."

I love it when Kie and Mason argue, and I settle into the water as their explosive anger unfolds. I hope it's dramatic.

"Get in, Mace. They're already here and forcing them out will draw attention."

Mason shifts his weight from foot to foot. "I don't want to."

My lips twitch. He sounds like a pouting child.

"Very well," Kie finally says. "You can stand there and watch."

Kie's trying to poke at Mason's jealousy, but I can't tell if it's going to work. It doesn't seem likely. Mason is pissed, but his anger doesn't scream, *'I'm angry my naked mate is in a public bathing pool with Kieran.'*

My observation appears incorrect, though, as Mason glances between Lill and me one final time and stomps out of the room. He returns a minute later, and I avert my gaze as he slips into the water between me and Lill. He keeps a safe distance between the two of us.

I tilt my chin up, staring at the ceiling. This is awful, and I count the seconds until it's over. I'd dunk my head under the water if Kie and Mason's exposed balls weren't currently soaking in it.

Lill clears her throat. "Have either of you ever been inside the baths?"

"No." Kie and Mason speak at the same time, but Kie is the one who elaborates. "It's untraditional, and noblewomen can be opportunistic."

The water comes to the tops of my shoulders but ends at the center of Kie's and Mason's torsos. Both men are muscular, with broad shoulders and strong arms. Kie's frame is leaner, like maybe he was a runner at some point. Mason's bulky, which I suppose fits. He very literally turns into a wild animal.

Kie leans back and spreads his arms along the pool edge. His bicep is dangerously close to the back of Lill's head, his fingers ending near Mason's face. The shifter adjusts, moving farther away from the faerie. It brings him closer to me, so I stretch out my leg.

It has the intended effect. Mason jolts, darting away when my toe gets within a foot of where I assume his thigh to be. I want my space.

"Abby," Lill lightly scolds.

I won't apologize.

The action draws Kie's full attention, though. He meets my gaze before darting lower, the motion so quick, I wouldn't have noticed if I weren't watching. I know he and Mason can see through the water, and I hug my knees closer to my chest.

I'd say something about him keeping his eyes to himself if it wouldn't make things weird with Lill. Kie's her mate, and I'm not going to make snide comments about Kie trying to look at my bare body in front of her. That's wildly uncomfortable.

Kie finally looks away, his eyes squeezing shut. "And it begins."

And *what* begins?

Two women enter the bathhouse, their voices echoing off the stone walls. They're naked, which isn't surprising. Faerie women are tall and lithe, like they spend hours a day in a Pilates studio. It's bullshit.

They look around the room, and matching smiles spread over their lips as they spot Kie and Mason.

"Your Highnesses," the woman on the left says.

I faintly remember her from yesterday. She was reporting Kie's whereabouts to Queen Gitta, and she wore a red dress. I think her name is Jackie. Her hair is tied up at the nape of her neck, probably to keep it from getting wet, and she bows politely toward Kie and Mason before stepping into the pool.

She submerges herself to the neck before standing so her entire upper body is exposed. Water drips down her chest and waist, and I fight the urge to look away. The faeries are comfortable with nudity, and I don't want them knowing I'm uncomfortable.

Jackie faces Kie, and I exchange a look with Lill. Is she getting the same energy from the woman? Jackie hasn't done anything wrong, at least not outwardly, but I'm no fool. I know when a woman is attempting to stake a claim on a male, and Jackie is attempting to do so with Kie.

Jackie gestures toward Lill. "Who's this?"

She ignores me, which is to be expected. I'm a safe distance from the princes, but Kie's bicep is almost touching Lill. Kie makes no attempts to move it.

"This is Lillian," he says. "And that's Abby."

I guess I appreciate the introduction, but I'm happy fading into the background.

"Lillian," Jackie repeats. "How nice to meet you. I'm Jacqueline *Rowe*."

She overemphasizes her last name. I'm unimpressed. If Lill

notices, she doesn't let it show.

Lill offers a smile. "I'm aware. It's nice to meet you."

I sink low into the water, waiting for Jackie to ask about the relationship between Kie, Mason, and Lill. She turns toward me instead. She looks down, openly scanning my body beneath the water. It takes everything in me not to react. I may not look like the faerie women, but I won't be made to feel ashamed of myself.

I lift my chin as the corners of her lips twitch. She's laughing at me. I'm horrified.

There's a splash of water. Kie.

Four women step into the room, momentarily capturing my attention. They look around just as Jackie and her friend did, and they perk up the same way when they spot Kie and Mason. It almost makes me feel bad for the princes. They're treated like broodmares.

I'm sure they use that to their advantage, though. It's not an accident that there's a drawer full of condoms in their spare bedroom.

"That's enough, Jackie," Kie orders. "Take your seat."

Jackie's face turns red. The faerie prince is taking a human's side over hers. That must hurt.

"I'm only looking to meet the human who—"

The water shifts again.

"Sit." Mason's voice is lower than I've ever heard it. "Now."

Jackie's chest heaves, and she works her jaw side to side as she looks between me, Kie, and Mason. I'm surprised she's even debating continuing to argue. She must not know what Mason looks like in his animal form. If he ever used that voice on me, I'd be petrified.

Jackie's gaze travels back down my torso.

"Why does she—"

There's a flurry of movement as Lill storms past me at a speed

I've never seen from her before. Jackie looks just about as surprised as I feel, and within a second, she's being bent in half and her head held under the water.

"Laugh at her again," Lill spits. "Do it."

Water splashes as Jackie tries to rip Lill's hands off her, but Lill somehow manages to maintain her grip. Jackie's friend is of no help as she scampers back against the pool wall.

Mason laughs, because he's a maniac, and Kie runs his hands down his face.

"Enough!" Kie's voice bounces off the walls, and Lill takes that as her cue to release Jackie and step back. "We're leaving."

He exits the pool in one swift movement, and Mason doesn't hesitate to follow. You'd think the water were burning the shifter alive with how quickly he climbs out. I remain where I am.

Mason turns toward me. "Come."

His dick is out for the entire world to see, and I cringe at the sight of it. He's soft, thank fucking god, but it's at eye level and a little modesty would go a long way. I must admit I grudgingly respect his size, though, and I feel a tang of pity for Lill. That's going to be painful.

"In a second," I say.

My naked body was just publicly mocked, and I need a moment to collect myself and work up the courage to climb out of this pool. Everybody will see me, and I'm not prepared for that.

Mason hovers beside me, waiting for me to get out, and I avoid eye contact as I flick water at his feet. He's got surprisingly nice feet, and I wonder if he maintains his toenails himself or if there's a faerie who does it for him.

Mason crouches, bringing his soft penis even closer to my face.

I pointedly avoid looking at it.

"Do you mind?" I hiss.

Mason smiles. He knows exactly what I'm talking about.

"Why should I?" he asks. "Get out of the fucking pool before I drag you out myself."

He won't. If there's anything I'm certain of, it's that he's not going to touch me. He'll barely even touch Lill, and she's his mate. I'm prepared to call his bluff when Lill walks over with a towel.

Mason frowns. "Oh."

Lill can read my fucking mind, and I climb out of the pool and wrap myself in the towel with more speed and grace than I thought possible. Kie waits by the exit, and I brush past him and into the changing room.

"Stay here," Lill says from behind me. "Give us a minute to change first."

They listen, thank the fucking heavens, and I yank on my dress before waiting outside the building with Lill.

"I want to go home," I admit. "This place sucks."

Lill opens her mouth, then snaps it shut with a quiet click. "Of course. You should ask Kie to bring you home. I doubt he'll force you to remain here."

Kie and Mason emerge from the bathhouse, and I fall silent. If they heard our conversation, they don't address it. They also don't address our interaction with Jackie.

Mason shoots Lill and me a venomous glare instead. He's pissed.

"Never again," he hisses. "I have spent thirty years of my life avoiding public bathing houses, and you will never force me to enter one again."

I roll my eyes. "Nobody forced you to get in. Stop being such a drama queen. It's unattractive." I shove past the shifter, my shoulder slamming against his. "Move."

Kie snorts, and I only make it two steps before a hand is pressing into my spine and pushing me forward. I stumble, but the push isn't hard enough to completely topple me over. I know immediately that the shifter is to blame.

Lill gasps. "Mason!"

I knew it. I spin around, my budding anger growing as I lock eyes with the smirking shifter.

"Don't push me!"

Mason blinks, not looking the least bit apologetic. I may have technically pushed him first, but I'm half his size and he didn't even stumble. I almost ate shit.

"Don't be such a drama queen, Abby," he taunts. "It's unattractive."

I grind my teeth, mentally picturing his death as he saunters past me, taking the lead. I hate him. I hate him. I hate him.

Chapter Eight

KIERAN

EARLY MORNING SUNLIGHT shines through my office window. Several people are walking through the courtyard, heading toward the front entrance of the long building where most offices are located. Mine included.

I frown, shifting my attention to my oak desk. Lillian wasn't lying. Every bit of her story checks out, even the tiny details I was convinced were too ridiculous to be true. We went as far as to test the blood from one of her discarded bandages, and sure enough, hints of delysum were found mixed within her blood.

I flip through page after page of the toxicology report, reading every sentence in excruciating detail. I was pleased to see it waiting for me on my desk this morning, but my stomach has since dropped.

I can't fathom why. I should be relieved to discover my mate is being truthful with me, that she had no intentional part in my father's death. Who did, then? Probably Callie, but I have no leads to her whereabouts.

Lillian claims she's dead, and Abby's parents confirmed that. The missing person reports they've recently filed for Abby and Lillian contained all the information we needed, and the faerie who impersonated an investigator and spoke with them found nothing suspicious.

Callie died, or vanished, almost ten years ago. Abby's parents raised Lillian, and she's grown progressively sicker with each passing year.

The deadly side effects of delysum have been well established, and I'm surprised Callie took the risk of drinking it. Even when the leaves are steeped and their potency diminished, the plant still reacts too violently with existing magic. Lillian only survived because there was none in the human realm.

Why remain with the humans, though? If what Lillian says is true, she had no reason not to return once her mother died. She's hiding something from us, and I can't fathom what it could be. I've been flirting with the possibility that Callie is still alive, but I'm trying to trust Lillian. She insists her mother is dead, and I want to believe her.

We're mates, and that has to mean something. I have to make it mean something, even if instinct tells me not to trust it.

A knock on the door pulls me from my thoughts.

I reorganize the toxicology report, then tuck it into the folder where I keep all my files on Lillian. "Come in."

Mason comes sauntering inside. He wasn't in his bedroom this morning, and I suspect he chose to sleep on the couch in the guest house where Lillian and Abby are staying.

"Somebody wishes to see you," he says, stepping aside to reveal Abby.

Oh? And he chose to escort her himself? When did Mason become the human's personal bodyguard?

Abby purses her lips, her eyes flickering around my office. The space is bland, and I can tell she's judging it. My desk faces the door, and behind me are shelves filled with decorative books I've never read. There's a long table along the right side of the room for when I hold private meetings, but the surface is empty.

Mason welcomes himself to my things, and he fingers through the paperwork on my desk before snatching up Lillian's report. Abby awkwardly lingers in the doorway.

I have to meet with my mother and Anox in fifteen minutes, and I glance at the clock on the corner of my desk to confirm the time.

"What can I help you with?" I ask.

"I'd like to go home," Abby says. "When can I leave?"

I lace my fingers together and rest my hands on my desk. "We'd like you to remain here until we confirm Lillian's story."

Mason pauses, his movements stilling. He's already put two and two together that Lillian's story has checked out and I'm lying to Abby. I wait for him to contradict me, but he doesn't.

"If this is because of Jackie's behavior in the bathing house..." I start.

Abby's eyes narrow, the human silently daring me to continue. I clear my throat instead, letting the rest of my sentence die out. I shouldn't acknowledge it. Jackie was out of line, and I've already had her removed from the estate. Her open access has been revoked, and she can only enter on business.

"I'm asking to return home because my family loves and misses me. Lill and I already discussed this, and she agreed it would be best if I returned home. I don't belong here."

Abby chews at the dead skin on her bottom lip. She needs to drink more water.

"Am I a prisoner, then?" Abby blurts out.

I blink. Does she think she's a prisoner? I haven't offered to send her home, but I've been under the impression that she wants to be here. She's protective of Lillian, and she hasn't mentioned anything about returning to the human realm before today.

"Of course not," I say. "I'll have a portal readied for you as soon as we confirm Lillian's claims."

"And when will that be?" Mason asks. He's taunting me.

I clench my jaw. "Soon."

I won't force Abby to stay, not when she has a life in the human realm she wishes to return to. It's probably dull and monotonous, but it's hers. I just wish to re-read the report and discuss the findings with my mother and Anox before making any decisions. I'm thorough, a trait Mason could stand to pick up.

I eye the bodice of Abby's dress as Mason resumes flicking through Lillian's file. I've asked for a small handful of garments to be delivered to her and Lillian, and today, Abby chose a summery, white dress. The sleeves are thin, and the fabric hugs her chest and torso before flaring at the waist.

It complements her shape.

Abby's brown eyes narrow, and I look away before she says something snarky. I've never known somebody with brown eyes, and it's quite exciting. The men of court have also noticed, if Lord Bishop's reports are anything to go by. He was discussing her during the council meeting yesterday, happily sharing the details being spread about her.

People suspect we found her in the forest and brought her here out of pity. Some believe her to be secretly working for the shifters, but most don't agree. They don't think a human is capable of that.

"Do you intend to join the meeting this morning?" I ask Mason. "We're looking to discuss your coronation."

The coronation that's taking place tomorrow afternoon. We're announcing it later this morning, and I anticipate our statement will be met with a healthy amount of panic and outrage. We can't put it off any longer, though.

"I'm leaving now," Abby decides. "Let me know when you're ready to send me home."

She brushes her hands down her dress before spinning toward the door. Faeries wait until I excuse them, and I can't help but smile at Abby's rudeness. She'd make a terrible faerie.

Mason worries his bottom lip between his teeth, his gaze darting between me and Abby. The human takes notice.

"I remember how to get back," she says. "I'll make a right at the courtyard, and when I can't go straight any longer, I'll turn right again."

Mason frowns, and Abby looks pleased with herself as she throws her hair back and storms out of the room. She slams the door shut behind her, which I think is an attempt to anger Mason. It doesn't work.

"Why did you lie to her?" he asks.

I shrug. "I had my men look into Lillian's claims, and they found that—"

Mason lifts his arm, showcasing the file he's been flipping through. "I can read. Lilly's been drinking delysum to stay alive, and Abby's parents have confirmed that Callie died several years ago. Lilly is telling the truth."

He sets the file down, his fingers brushing against the top drawer of my desk as he pulls away. I twitch. It's a slight movement, one I shouldn't have made. Mason's too perceptive, and I know I've been caught when he cocks his head to the side. His eyes roam over my face, but I keep my expression neutral.

"What's in there?" His voice is heavy with accusation.

I blink. "Nothing."

Mason lunges. I dart forward, trying to stop him, but he's already ripping open my top drawer. The wood splinters, and everything falls to the floor.

The tiara I stole from Abby's bedroom snaps as it lands on the ground, and the peanut container she used in the woods falls alongside it. I ignore both as I reach for the red fabric hidden in the back of the drawer. Mason reaches it first. I doubt he even realizes what it is, but it's red and I was going for it. That's enough for him.

Shame warms my cheeks as I snatch the fabric out of his hand. "Don't touch my things," I snap.

Mason stares at my hands for a long moment before meeting my gaze. His pupils are fully expanded and his shoulders are quivering, both telltale signs that he's holding back a shift. He knows what the red fabric is, and it's not hard to guess to whom it belongs.

It was hidden with Abby's tiara and peanut container.

I adjust, placing myself between him and the door. Hoarding Abby's things is a betrayal to our mate, and I'm fully prepared to physically stop Mason from running to Lillian with the truth. I intend to dispose of these objects. I just haven't gotten around to it.

Mason holds out his hand. "Give them to me."

I shake my head. That's not going to happen.

"It's not right," Mason continues. "It's a gross invasion of Abby's privacy, especially after what we did to her in that forest. Give. Them. To. Me."

I tense, beyond annoyed. I didn't expect Mason to take this side of the argument, and I don't have a good response. I thought he'd be angry on Lillian's behalf, not Abby's. I shift my weight, debating the consequences of keeping Abby's underwear.

Mason's judging me, but I don't care what he thinks of me. I'm too busy trying to keep the entire faerie kingdom from crumbling. I *do* care what Abby thinks of me, though. I never wanted to give her to Zaha, nor did I want to do all the other things I felt I had no choice but to do in the forest. I took her free will, and I haven't even apologized for it. I'm not sure where to start.

I slide the underwear between my fingers, then drop it into

Mason's outstretched hand.

Mason shoves them into his back pocket. "I'll dispose of them."

I shouldn't have stolen them in the first place. It's below my station to do something so depraved, especially to a human. I was having fun looking through her bedroom, and I stole them thinking I'd leave her in the human realm and never see her again. I wanted a memento.

I clear my throat. "Our meeting is in five minutes. Your coronation is tomorrow morning, and we should—"

Mason shakes his head. "I'm already up to speed, and I have things to do. You can handle this without me."

He leaves the room in a flurry, and I want to pull my fucking hair out.

Chapter Nine

MASON

KIE'S AN IDIOT. Getting him to hand over Abby's underwear was almost too easy. I've never been jealous of the faeries, but I'm admittedly upset I can't manipulate portals. I'd love to go to Abby's home and look through her things.

It's not fair that Kie got to do so and I haven't.

"It's a gross invasion of Abby's privacy." I can't believe he fell for that. I don't care about Abby's privacy. Just a few days ago, she stabbed me in the stomach. I could've *died*.

My pace is fast as I shove open the door to my bedroom, letting it slam behind me. I can count on one hand the number of personal items I own. It's never been something I've cared much about, but Abby's underwear is most definitely being added to the list. I just need to store them somewhere Kie won't find them.

I'd like to believe he doesn't look through my things, but you can never be too certain. I'm sure he thinks I give him privacy, but I have no issues searching his room and office whenever I suspect he's hiding something.

I run my fingers over the red lace, then pull off my gloves so I can touch them with my bare hands. They're clean, which isn't surprising. Kie may be hoarding Abby's possessions, but he'd never steal her dirty underwear. It would be too far, too invasive. Even I wouldn't do that.

Clean underwear is different, though. At least, that's what I'm telling myself. The lace is rough, nothing like what women here wear. I should hate it, but I find myself entranced by the cheap material. Is Abby poor? I've never considered the possibility. The quality of her underwear suggests that she just might be.

We can't send her back to the human realm if that's the case. Has she ever gone hungry? Does she struggle to meet her basic necessities? Sending her back into that situation is not an option I'm willing to consider.

I'll discuss the matter with Kie later, once things have settled. It's hard to wrap my head around the fact that I'll be crowned king tomorrow, not that I've had much time to think about it. Abby and Lilly have been keeping me busy.

I should return to them soon.

I don't like leaving the human alone with Lilly, and if it weren't for the faerie's aggressive actions toward Jackie yesterday, I'd never consider doing so. I want to kill Jackie for laughing at Abby. I was so pleased to finally glimpse Abby's bare skin, but the memory has been tainted.

The human's shoulders rolled forward as Jackie mocked her, and I just knew she felt humiliated.

I was moments away from stepping in during the exchange, but it's best that Lilly took the initiative to defend Abby. There wasn't time for me to cover myself, and word would've spread that I touched Jackie's bare skin while drowning her.

Although I suppose it doesn't matter as much anymore. The faeries heavily suspect that Lilly is our mate, so touching another woman isn't quite as scandalous. There's no risk of igniting a bond, everyone would think. Only I know there actually is, if our real mate is out there somewhere.

I liked how Lilly held Jackie's head under the water. Lilly's a dirty fucking liar, but I don't think she's going to hurt Abby. She seemed genuine in her anger.

I'll give her and Abby a few minutes of privacy.

I have business to attend to. My gaze flickers around my bedroom, from my freshly made bedsheets to the wardrobe pushed up against the left wall. I pace the length of my room, my feet pounding against the ground. I could hide the underwear in my desk, but that's the first place Kie would look.

I drag my thumb over the lace, searching for an adequate hiding spot.

Has Abby worn these for another man? I'll kill him.

I groan. "Fuck!" *What am I doing?*

Something clatters, and I freeze as I snap my head toward my ensuite bathroom. Somebody's in there, and I'm willing to bet the culprit has buggy brown eyes, clenched fists, and an infuriating knack of getting on my every damn nerve.

Chapter Ten

ABBY

I'VE FUCKED UP. I've fucked up big time.

Does Mason know I'm here? He has to know I'm here. He can probably smell me, or maybe he can hear my panicked, uneven breathing.

I press my back against the bathroom door, my heart pounding as I listen to him through the wall. He's been watching me like a hawk these past few days, and I never imagined he'd return to his home after meeting with Kie. He's going as far as to sleep on the couch outside Lill's and my bedroom, for fuck's sake.

The guards who linger around the royal housing area weren't paying attention to me, and Mason and Kie's house was just a few doors down.

How could I not snoop?

If I'm going to be stuck in the faerie realm for the indefinite future, I might as well use it to my advantage. I planned to search through Mason's things and find leverage to use against him. It was a foolproof idea.

My pulse skyrockets as Mason's footfalls near the door I'm hiding behind, and I hold my breath until he retreats. He's pacing, probably upset about something. He's going to murder me. He's going to rip out my spine and leave me to bleed out on his bathroom floor.

What are the odds he comes in here? Too high to leave to chance.

The only way out is through Mason's bedroom, and the window above the walk-in shower is too narrow to fit through. It's also high on the wall, and I'm not sure I can do the pull-up required to escape.

There's a cabinet underneath the sink. It'll be tight, but I think I can fit inside. It's my only option.

I'm careful to keep quiet as I open the cabinet door and peek inside. There's a ton of stuff in here, and I grimace as I slide Mason's products aside. How many grooming items can one person possibly need?

"Fuck!"

Mason's sudden shout has me flinching, and my heart stops as one of the bottles tips over. I dart forward to catch it, but I'm not fast enough. Mason's pacing comes to an abrupt halt the second the bottle clatters against the bottom of the cabinet, and I hang my head. He heard.

The bathroom door slams against the wall with a loud bang, but I'm expecting it.

I remain where I am, not having the courage to face Mason.

Instead, I shut the cabinet door and press my forehead against it, waiting for death. I can only hope it comes quickly. When several seconds pass and my head is still connected to the rest of my body, I accept defeat and face Mason.

He's not pleased. He's glaring daggers at me, his gloved hands clenching and unclenching as I rise to my feet. I imagine he doesn't enjoy people sneaking into his room and going through his things, but it's not my fault I wasn't stopped. You'd think that as the crowned prince and soon-to-be king, his home would be better protected.

Mason blinks. "Why?"

He steps farther into the room, and I curl my fingers around the sink as I try to think of an excuse. Anything will do, but nothing comes to mind.

"I wanted to go through your things," I admit. I've never been a good liar, and I don't see the point in trying. "I don't trust you, and I wanted to see what I could learn."

"Oh?" Mason quirks a brow. "And what have you learned?"

"Nothing useful."

I only had a few minutes to explore before Mason came storming into his bedroom, and other than the copious amount of hair products hidden beneath his sink, his room is void of personality. I suppose that's what I learned about Mason. He's bland.

Bland and boring, like unseasoned chicken.

I did find one item of interest, but I won't mention it until I need to.

"Sorry to hear that." Mason doesn't sound the least bit sorry. The corner of his lip curls. "I've learned something quite interesting about you this morning."

He sounds proud of himself, and I don't like it.

"And what's that?" I ask.

Mason reaches into his back pocket and pulls out a piece of red lace. It takes approximately half a second to realize it's a pair of underwear dangling off his finger, and I scrunch my nose while I wait for him to explain.

Are they his? Maybe Mason has a thing for wearing women's underwear.

"Are you poor?" he asks instead.

"What?"

Mason tosses the underwear toward me, and I clamp my arms

to my sides. I'm not catching them. That's disgusting.

The lace hits my stomach before landing on the floor by my feet. I peer down at the fabric, still confused, before sucking in a shaky breath when I spot the branded tag on the back. I highly doubt the small boutique I purchase my lingerie from exists in this realm.

My heart pounds as I snatch the underwear up off the floor, anger mounting as I come to the horrible realization that they're mine. Fucking Kie. He went through my dresser drawers when Zaha brought us to the human realm, but I didn't realize he'd stolen anything. I should've known better.

I don't understand why they're in Mason's possession, though, or why he's carrying them around in his back pocket.

Mason points toward them. "The fabric quality is poor, and I'm concerned you're impoverished. Are you?"

It takes several seconds for me to work up the strength to speak. "Why do you have these?"

Mason shrugs. "I was flirting with the idea of keeping them as a memento of our time together. Maybe wearing them for the council members who insist on probing up my ass. I haven't decided."

"That's not funny."

"I'm not trying to be."

"Lill's my best friend," I say, "and *your* mate. You shouldn't be walking around with my underwear in your pocket."

It's beyond inappropriate, and I won't stand for it. Mason shifts his weight from foot to foot, visibly contemplating, before speaking.

"She's not our mate," he says. What the hell is that supposed to mean? "Lilly's using some sort of magic to trick Kie. I don't know how it works or why she's doing it, but I'm certain she isn't our mate."

That's simply not true. Lill wouldn't lie about that, especially to me. I've seen how she talks about Kie and Mason and how desperate she is to make their bond work. She may be lying about a few things, but not that. I don't believe it.

"I'm telling the truth, Abby." Mason steps toward me. "Lilly is not our mate. I feel nothing when I touch her."

Nothing? That's just not possible. Lill and Kie clearly feel something when they touch one another.

"Have you considered the possibility that it's *you* who's broken?" I snap. "That maybe Zaha decided to punish you and take away your mate?"

Mason nods. "Yes, I did, but I still feel a connection with Kie. Lilly is lying to us, you included."

"Why would she do that?"

"Your guess is as good as mine."

I cross my arms over my chest. "And why are you telling me this?"

"Because I feel inclined to be honest with you, even when that includes telling you things I shouldn't." Mason scowls, running his fingers through his hair.

"Why?"

"I don't know. I don't particularly enjoy it."

"Yes, you do. Touch me." The words are out of my mouth before I truly register what I'm saying. "With your skin. Touch me."

I have suspicions.

Mason gulps, shaking his head. "No. Don't ask that of me."

I don't see why I shouldn't. He's obsessed with me, and if Lill isn't his mate, then I want him to touch me. I want to confirm that *I'm* not his mate. If Lill *is* lying, which I'm still doubtful of, she and Callie must have ulterior motives. Maybe those motives included me. Perhaps they came to my town and Lill befriended me because I'm Kie and Mason's mate.

I reach for Mason, fully intent on taking matters into my own hands, but he snatches my wrist with his gloved hand before I make contact.

"I'll break your wrist," he threatens.

"No, you won't."

Mason tightens his grip, trying to scare me. It doesn't work, and he awkwardly releases me after a second. I attempt to touch him again, but he snatches my wrist once more. He doesn't break it, even when I try for the third time.

"Enough!" Mason hisses. "You're being inappropriate."

I bark out a laugh. "*I'm* being inappropriate?" I can't believe he'd even say that. "You're carrying my lingerie around in your pocket."

Mason's left shoulder rises in a halfhearted, lazy shrug.

"Why won't you touch me?" I ask.

Mason retreats into the bathroom doorway, putting space between us. "Because Kie's hoarding purple, plastic tiaras, and I'm searching for places to hide your cheap, scratchy underwear."

His admission is unspoken, but I hear it loud and clear. He thinks I could be his mate. I'm not the only one with suspicions.

I cross my arms over my chest. "If you think I'm your mate, you should touch me and prove it."

A part of me is terrified that he might be.

"And what if you are?" Mason asks.

I don't know.

"Are you prepared to live permanently in the faerie realm? Are you prepared to be a queen?" Mason hammers me with questions I don't have the answer to. "Are you prepared to love us? Because that's what would happen. Once a mate bond is triggered, it's all-consuming. You'll beg for me, you'll beg for Kie, and you won't be able to stop it."

Kie and Mason kidnapped me, threatened to murder me, and then tried to gift me to Zaha. Begging them will never happen, mate bond or not.

Mason licks his lips and peers down at me, and I look away when his stare grows too intense.

"Why do you think Lill is lying?" I ask. "*If* the bond *were* fake, that doesn't mean she's responsible. Have you considered the possibility that she's being tricked, too?"

"She didn't return when Callie died," Mason says. "If what she says is true, why remain hidden in the human realm? You may not like Kie and me, but we aren't unreasonable men, nor are we malevolent leaders. We don't punish children for the actions of adults, and she knew that." He throws his hands in the air. "We were best friends! Lilly was my best fucking friend, and she chose death over me. Why?"

I gulp, not having a good answer. I haven't thought of that.

"She couldn't have known she wouldn't be punished," I say. "Callie probably told her she'd be killed or imprisoned for treason."

Mason shakes his head. "That's not it." He sounds confident, and a tiny, minuscule piece of me believes him. "I think she knows something, and she's scared of us finding out what it is. Maybe Callie told her something before she died, or maybe Callie is still alive. I don't know."

Why are they so convinced Callie is alive? She's dead. I know she's dead.

"And why shouldn't I tell Lill everything you've told me?" I ask.

Mason darts forward, snatching my underwear out of my hand. My jaw drops as he shoves them into his back pocket, not the least bit embarrassed of himself.

"You're not going to tell her," Mason taunts. What makes him think that? "Deep down inside, I know you believe me. It's written all over your face. You're guilty, probably because you already suspect she's keeping secrets."

Mason steps aside, moving out of the bathroom doorway. I ignore the hint to leave.

"If you gave us some time alone, I could speak to her," I say. "She'll tell me the truth."

"No."

"Ple—"

"No."

I sigh. "Mason, I—"

"I said *no*."

"Fuck you."

I push off the sink and storm toward the doorway, done with this conversation. Mason doesn't try to stop me, and in a fit of anger, I throw my bare hand toward his face as I pass by. It's a sad attempt to touch him, and Mason doesn't even flinch as he grabs my forearm and pulls my fingers out of his space.

"I hope you're my mate," I spit. "I'll never forgive you and Kie for what you two did to me, and I'd enjoy making your life miserable."

Mason releases my arm, his expression a cool mask of indifference. "If you were my mate, you wouldn't have a choice. The bond would drive us together, and you'd be helpless to stop it."

Mason has no idea how petty I can be. My ability to hold a grudge is unparalleled.

Chapter Eleven

ABBY

I KEEP MY pace fast in an attempt to put space between Mason and me, but he easily matches my speed.

He probably suspects what I'm trying to do, but he doesn't acknowledge it. Neither do I, and when we reach the front door of the house Lill and I have been staying in, I rush inside and try to slam the door in his face.

I'm hoping to lock him out. Mason's huge, but I doubt he can break down a door.

It seems I'm not going to find out today.

Mason sticks his arm through the open doorway at the last second, preventing me from shutting it. I still try, because I'm not one to give up easily, but I quickly realize it's useless. Mason doesn't even seem to be struggling.

I release the door, and Mason steps inside with a shit-eating grin.

He's amused, and I turn away before my anger gets the best of me. I can't let it. I'm still reeling over his earlier accusations, and there are more important things to focus on than wiping that grin off his face.

What if his suspicions are true? He has no reason to lie about not feeling a mate bond with Lill. It makes no sense. If she were lying, why wouldn't she tell me? Does she think I would run to Kie and Mason with the truth? I'd never betray her, and I think she knows that.

Lill emerges from the hallway, her hands behind her head as she works on braiding her hair out of her face. She's already looking healthier. It's only been two days, but I can see the effects of finally having magic coursing through her system.

The dark bags under her eyes are vanishing, and her shoulders no longer slouch forward as if holding up the weight of the world. She's still exceptionally thin, but that's not something that'll be improved overnight. She's eating, and the weight will come with time.

Her violet eyes widen as they land on me.

"You're still here," she blurts out. "Are they not letting you leave?"

Her gaze flickers between Mason and me, her eyebrows furrowed in genuine confusion.

"Nope." I shake my head. "Kie wants me to stay until everything with you is cleared up. He claims that should be soon, but I'm not holding my breath."

Lill drops her arms to her sides. "I'm sorry, Abbs. I didn't think he'd force you to stay here with me."

I'm sure not surprised by it. Kie and Mason like to say we're not prisoners, but I know better. It just frustrates me that I understand where they're coming from. Somebody was murdered, and I'd also want answers if I were in their position.

Mason brushes past me and takes his usual spot on the couch. He's not much fun to be around, and I glare at the side of his head as he flops onto the cushions. I've known Lill for most of my life, and she's never given me any reason to believe she's untrustworthy. She's a good friend—a good person.

Mason's conspiracy theories won't change my mind on that matter.

Lill purses her lips, then turns toward Mason. I slip out of the entryway, fading into the background as I watch them from behind the kitchen island. What's Mason thinking? What's Lill thinking?

Mason's already told me his secrets, so I focus on Lill. She appears earnest as she peers across the room at the shifter, her hands twisting around themselves. Unless she's magically turned into an award-winning actress, there's no way she's faking the desperately longing looks she gives the shifter.

She truly believes him to be her mate. She very well might be.

I still haven't ruled out the possibility that it's Mason who is broken. I much prefer that option because if Lill *is* lying, then who is Kie and Mason's mate? Mason hinted that he believes it to be me, which is a terrifying thought. If I can get my hands on one of them and prove there's nothing there, I'll feel a thousand times better. Mason's on high alert, though. Kie will be my best bet.

"Are you all right?" Lill asks Mason. "You look tense."

Mason crosses his ankle over his knee, the picture of confidence. "I'm just fine."

I wish he would leave. I've been avoiding poking the small holes in Lill's story, but it's time to pry. She should know that Mason suspects her.

"Are you nervous for your coronation tomorrow?" Lill tries. "It's a big day."

"Nervous? No."

Lill nods, her head slowly bobbing as her tentative smile falls. Mason's doing a shit job pretending to be her mate, and I chew at my bottom lip as Lill closes the distance between them. Mason doesn't pull away, but he doesn't appear particularly welcoming as Lill bends and kisses his forehead. It's forced and so painfully awkward, and I fight back a wince as Lill immediately retreats.

"Are either of you hungry?" Lill clears her throat. "I've been looking for a reason to cook. I can pick some ingredients up from the kitchens and make lunch."

Despite the thousands of conflicting emotions roiling through me, my lips curl. Lill has always loved cooking—really anything related to homemaking—and it warms my heart to see her returning to her old habits. I give it only another day or two before she begins redecorating.

"I could eat," I say.

My appetite is practically nonexistent, but I'm willing to force something down if it breaks the ungodly tension between Lill and Mason. He's cold, refusing to speak more than a handful of words at a time. It's a drastic change from the way he was behaving with me just a few minutes ago. He was spilling all his secrets, and I didn't even have to work that hard for them.

Is that because I'm his mate? If that were the case, shouldn't I feel something more for him? He infuriates and annoys me, and I find myself wishing for his death more than anything else. I don't enjoy the thought of him and Kie with Lill, but that's because I see their true colors. Lill deserves better than them.

I deserve better than them.

I brush my fingertips over my lips, my thoughts wandering. What would it be like to kiss Kie and Mason? I haven't seen much of the faerie recently, but I can't get rid of Mason.

He's probably a poor kisser. He has full lips, so maybe it wouldn't be too horrible. I'm willing to bet he's never done it before, and I'm not interested in teaching. I don't have the patience, and I highly doubt Mason's a quick learner.

Kie would be the better lover. Kie seems like the type of person to enjoy the act of sex. Mason rushes to the end, impatient and eager to get his fill and retreat into solitude. Kie would have fun with it.

Has Mason ever made a woman orgasm? Has he ever tried? I very highly doubt it.

Does he have a big dick? Is it pretty? Is he circumcised? I caught a glimpse in the bathhouse, but I didn't take a close look. I don't have a strong preference as long as he keeps it clean. What does he look like when he cums? Does he moan? I'd guess not. He's probably broody and silent. Or he grunts. Like a caveman.

Lill brushes past me, and I flinch.

"What are you hungry for?" she asks. "Something sweet? Savory? Do you want a whole meal or just a snack?"

Mason's head snaps in my direction when I don't immediately answer. We make brief eye contact, but it's enough to send a cold chill down my spine. I don't want him looking at me. I don't want any more of his wild accusations getting into my head.

I shrug, trying to focus on Lill. "Anything. I'll come with you."

Lill hums and slips on her shoes. "No need. I'll just be a minute."

I linger, my heart hammering as she pulls open the front door. Is she lying to me? Is Mason lying to me? Is everybody fucking lying to me? I may be a human, but I'm not less than them.

Lill shoots Mason a smile. It's sweet, filled with so much fucking emotion. I'm going to be sick. "I'll be right back."

The door shuts. Mason rises from the couch.

I lift a hand. "Stay away from me!"

My legs shake as I rush to the bathroom, slamming the door shut behind me. My mind is swimming, and I hang my head between my shoulders and lean over the sink, taking deep breaths. I'm in a full panic. It's not ideal.

The door opens, and I groan as a shadow larger than Lill appears beside me.

"Get out." I point to the door. "Go."

All I want is one fucking minute of privacy.

"This is your fault," I continue. "And you should leave."

Mason steps farther into the room, thoroughly ignoring me, and he takes his sweet time looking me over before shutting the bathroom door, trapping me inside. I push away from the sink, refusing to take my eyes off him as he wets a washcloth.

"Abby…" Mason pauses. "Is this truly my fault?"

He gestures for me to look down. I obey, still frowning as he brings the wet cloth to the back of my neck. The cold feels good, and I take a moment to focus on my breathing. I'll kick him out in a second.

"Kie's better at these things," Mason admits. "I don't have much experience with women. I've only ever been with prostitutes, and the interactions are simple. Kie has spent much time with the noblewomen, and they have a lot of feelings. He's quite skilled at navigating these situations."

"I don't care to hear about your and Kie's romantic history."

Mason falls silent, then nods. "Look up."

Despite his usual brutish behavior, he's surprisingly gentle as he slides the washcloth along my forehead. I don't know why I'm letting him do this.

"She believes the bond is real," I say.

Mason doesn't respond, but I know his silence is a denial. He doesn't believe me. I push his hand away from my face.

"Let me speak with her," I order. "Give me a chance to clear things up."

Mason shakes his head. "I said *no*, and I'm not changing my mind."

I'm not going to accept that answer.

"You are." I mean it, too. "Or I'll walk out of this bathroom and tell Lill everything you told me earlier." I'm about to make him really upset, but I don't care. "I found the map of the Redstall

Forest in your bedroom. It was hidden in a pocket at the bottom of your wardrobe. You're looking for something. Your family, maybe? I'll tell everybody. I'll tell Kie."

Mason's jaw drops. I caught him by surprise.

"How do you think the faeries will feel to learn their future king is looking for his shifter family? That he misses his mommy and daddy and wants to know where they're hiding out?"

Mason is furious, his nostrils flaring and chest heaving. The washcloth falls to the ground with a *splat*, and Mason's gloved hands are around my head a heartbeat later.

"I should crush your skull." He squeezes my head. Not enough to hurt, but enough that I know he's fantasizing about following through on his words. I bet he gets off on the thought of hurting me. "I should've killed you when I had the chance. Should've snapped your neck the second I met you and been done with it."

He doesn't mean that.

I ignore my pounding heart as I meet Mason's eye, daring him to hurt me.

"You won't," I taunt. "Pussy."

Mason squeezes his eyes shut and sucks in a slow, even breath, giving me the perfect opportunity to do what I've been trying to accomplish. I dart forward before he realizes what I'm intending, and I shove my bare finger straight down his throat.

Chapter Twelve

ABBY

MASON GAGS, A noise that brings me immense satisfaction.

It's almost enough to distract me from the colossal mistake I've just made. Almost.

Mason curls his fingers around my wrist and yanks my now-limp finger out of his mouth. He doesn't release my arm, holding it between us instead. I'm not sure if he's aware of what he's doing. I'm not sure *I'm* aware of what I'm doing.

I shudder, a full-body shiver working its way up my spine. "It was an accident." I blurt out the first thing that comes to mind. "That didn't count."

It's too late. I've already touched him—placed my bare skin on his.

Mason's so close that I can make out the dark-green ring at the outer rim of his eye and the few freckles lining the bridge of his nose and cheekbones. When he exhales, his breath warms my skin.

He licks his lips, his tongue running over his bottom lip before he sinks his teeth into the soft flesh. "I told you not to do that."

"I didn't," I lie. "I didn't touch you."

Mason finally releases my wrist, and my arm drops limp. My

body is shivering, the sensation entirely out of my control. I might as well have been struck by lightning with how hard I'm shaking.

I imagined that triggering a bond would be romantic, maybe even overwhelming. When I kissed Samuel, I fantasized about fireworks, sparks, and a minor heart attack. I feel none of those things right now.

My emotions toward Mason haven't magically changed. I don't want to confess my undying love or write romantic sonnets or draw his naked portrait. I'm not even sure why or how I know he's my mate. I just do. I know it to my very bones, and there's nothing anybody could ever tell me that would convince me otherwise. It's like I've spent my entire life only breathing with half a lung, and now I have two fully functioning ones.

It's right. I feel right, which I objectively know is very, *very* wrong.

"You shouldn't have done that," Mason says. "I told you the bond with Lilly was—"

I interrupt without thinking. "Stop calling her that."

There's more poison in my voice than intended. Mason's nickname for Lill has always annoyed me, but just slightly. It's one of those things I frown at and move on from.

Mason closes in on me. He moves like the predator he is, quiet and agile.

"I told you the bond with *Lillian* was fake," he corrects himself. "She's found a way to imitate it, and she's lying to us all." I begin to shake my head, but Mason's following words stop me. "She went out of her way to touch Kie. She forced contact. She knew he'd feel something. She knows what she's doing, Abby."

The thought is too painful to consider. Has she been lying to me this entire time? Have I just been some pawn to her and Callie? The coincidence is too great.

Mason is mine. I don't even want him.

Something falls to the ground. Mason's gloves.

His throat bobs, and his bare fingers skirt over my face. He continues forward until he's cradling my skull in his palms, his thumbs brushing over my cheekbones. His earnest expression is too much to bear.

My fingernails bite into my palms, the pain the only thing keeping me grounded.

"I don't want it," I admit. "I don't want to be your mate."

"I know."

"I take it back."

"You can't."

"Mason." My voice cracks. "Please. I don't want it."

The calloused pad of Mason's thumbs swipes under my eyes, wiping away the tears beginning to fall. "I told you not to touch me."

"This isn't my world," I say. "I have family to go home to."

I have to return to them. It's not an option.

"We can bring them here."

"I'm human," I say. "Happily human. I have a whole life to return to, a life I'm *excited* to return to."

Mason's silence isn't encouraging.

I continue. "We can go to Zaha. She can fix this."

Mason shakes his head. "She won't, and she'll punish us for asking."

I believe that. Zaha knew we were mates when we came to her, which explains her surprise when Mason and Kie offered me up on a silver platter. Was that why she rejected me? Why she sent Kie and me to my childhood home? Did she plan for this to happen?

"You tried to kill me," I say.

"I'm aware."

"You forcibly bathed me. You humiliated me."

"Yes."

The memories flash through my mind, each more painful than the last. I thought they were going to rape me. I had no reason to believe otherwise, not when they practically held me down and stripped off my clothes.

"You offered me to Zaha as a human slave."

A beat of silence, then, "Yes."

"Is that all you have to say?"

Mason's fingers tighten against the back of my head. He's holding my skull like it's a bowling ball he's terrified of dropping, and he looks awkward doing it. His shoulders are hunched and his back bent, and he's worrying his bottom lip between his teeth so hard, I'm surprised there's any lip left.

It's because he's never held a woman. He doesn't know how to do any of this.

I don't let that realization soften me.

"Well?" I urge. "Is that all you have to say?"

"What do you want me to say?" Mason asks. "I did those things, and I very well can't take them back. The fact of the matter is that hundreds of thousands, if not millions, of faeries will die if the shifters continue cultivating delysum. Shifters will die, too. You are innocent, but so are they. We shouldn't have been so rough with you, and we shouldn't have taken things to the extent we did, but we did. I live with that, and I'll continue to live with that for the remainder of my life, and there's nothing I can do about it."

Everything Mason says is true, but I don't feel satisfied. I grab his arms and pull his hands away from my head, not wanting his touch. His retreat leaves me feeling cold, but I ignore the unpleasant sensation.

Mason's touch is like a warm, gooey cookie on a chilled, snowy day. I know it's unhealthy, but fuck if I don't want to shove the entire cookie in my mouth in one bite. I want to choke on it.

It's the damn bond.

Mason's gaze travels to my mouth. "I'm sorry about this."

Before I so much as have the opportunity to consider what he's apologizing for, his mouth is on mine. I'm expecting a rough kiss, but he barely touches me. He's uncharacteristically hesitant. Fearful, even.

My lips curl, the humor of this situation too great to ignore.

Mason's hands find my waist and his mouth trails to my jaw. My smile falls. I should most definitely stop this, but my arms are glued to my sides. It feels too good, and my skin is on fire.

"I wanted to touch you so badly," he admits. "I knew you were my mate. I knew it."

Mason's the only thing keeping the burning from spreading. He grabs the short sleeves of my dress and eases them down my shoulders. I'm not wearing a bra.

"Just for a second," Mason says. "I promise."

His green eyes are vibrant as he stares at my exposed chest, his pupils darting from one nipple to the other before returning to my face. He looks devastated, like he's confident this is the only chance he'll ever get to see and touch me. It is.

It's just that his attention feels so good, and I can't remember the last time I've been touched. I've spent the past several years caring for Lill, and there hasn't been time for a relationship, casual or otherwise. I've been lonely, and Mason's desperate, and who am I to say *no*?

"I want more," he admits.

Me, too. Fuck. I hate that.

I place my hand on Mason's head. His hair is soft, and I allow myself only half a second to enjoy it before pushing him downward.

"This will never happen again," I say. "Make it count."

His warm tongue lashes over my nipple, and a hand slips up

the bottom of my dress. He's not letting this opportunity go to waste. My underwear is pushed to the side, and I jolt as Mason's finger trails along my slit.

He's panting against my chest.

I gasp, leaning against the wall. "Mason!"

"I know. I'll be quick."

Mason drops to his knees, yanking my dress up my legs with one hand and my underwear down with the other. There's a rip of fabric, and then my thigh is pulled over his shoulder and his face is between them.

"Mace! We shouldn't—"

I slam my head against the wall as he licks up my slit. Then he moans—fucking moans—and licks me again. Zaha's a bitch to make the bond feel this good. The mere thought of stopping Mason is agonizing.

My hips twitch. "*More.*"

Mason finds my clit, and each lash of his tongue is accompanied by a low, throaty moan. If I didn't know any better, I'd say he's enjoying this even more than I am. He's exploring, too. Soft, tentative licks are quickly followed up with rough, confident ones.

Mason's a fast learner and surprisingly observant.

"Show me what you like," he orders, pulling back just slightly. "I want to make this good for you."

Happy to. I grab a handful of Mason's hair and rock against his tongue, my thighs shaking. I don't think I could stop if I wanted, my every thought consumed by Mason and his tongue and my rapidly approaching orgasm. I'm pulling his hair in every direction, probably ripping out the strands, but he doesn't seem to mind.

I use it to guide his mouth, fearful he will change the position and I'll have to start over. He doesn't, though. For once in his life, he's obedient.

"Don't stop," I order. "I'm so close."

Mason's fingers dig into my ass, helping to hold me steady as I rub myself against his tongue. Just a few more seconds and I'll be there. The orgasm is coiling, building between my thighs with an intensity I'm not expecting.

I dig my heel into Mason's back and slam a hand over my mouth, muffling my cry as it hits me. Mason licks me through it, continuing until I shiver and push him away.

"I…" I'm at a loss for words.

Mason peers up at me, smirking as he wipes his lips and jaw with the back of his hand. "Never thought I'd find so much enjoyment in being on my knees."

"That's not—"

Mason jumps to his feet, all traces of amusement vanishing as he rips open the bathroom door and disappears into the hallway. Where is he going? It's not unusual for Mason to storm off in a flurry—it's one of his least attractive traits—but I wasn't expecting him to do so only seconds after having his mouth on me.

I fix my dress, pulling the sleeves back up and smoothing down the hem. My underwear is nowhere to be seen, I suspect having been stolen by the shifter. I fear what he's going to do with it.

The mirror above the sink taunts me, tempting me to look. I avoid it. I'm not proud of myself, and I'm not interested in seeing my reflection at this very moment. I won't like the person looking back at me.

Lill is Mason's mate. Or, at least, she believes she is.

I spend another several seconds adjusting my already-fixed dress. What am I going to say to her? This isn't me. I don't fuck men in bathrooms, especially men who are tied to my best friend.

I wasn't thinking.

I stare at the ground as I step out of the bathroom, mentally preparing for what awaits me. I made a mistake, and I'm adult enough to own up to it. I won't make excuses for myself.

I'm going to tell Lill what happened. I'm going to tell her everything I know.

My movements halt as I step into the living room. Mason's at the door, facing two visibly panicked guards. Lill is nowhere to be seen, probably still getting food, and Mason's entire body is quivering as he turns toward me.

"Lillian's gone." He shakes his head, like he doesn't believe what he's about to say next. "And she murdered Her Majesty on her way out."

Chapter Thirteen

ABBY

OF ALL THE times for Mason to abandon me, I didn't expect it to be in the face of actual danger. I stare at the five guards I've been left with, then shift my gaze toward the front door Mason practically broke on his way out of here.

"The queen is dead?" I ask. I already know the answer.

The guard closest to me nods.

My heart lurches. "Is Kie okay?" I clear my throat. "His Highness, I mean. The prince. Kieran. Whatever the fuck you call him."

The guards exchange glances. What does that mean? Is that a no? Did Lill hurt Kie? Was that part of her plan? And she killed the queen? Are they sure? Did anybody actually see it happen?

"Well?" My voice cracks. "Is Kie okay?"

The door bursts open, and Mason comes barreling inside. "Fuck!" He storms through the guards, grabs my arm, and pulls me into his side. "Lillian can open fucking portals, so you need to stay with me. Can't have her hurting you."

It seems he's changed his mind on abandoning me with the stone-faced guards, but I don't think Lill would ever hurt me. She's been lying about some things, I'm willing to admit that, but

I believe our friendship is genuine. We've been through too much together for it not to be.

"Is Kie okay?" I ask Mason.

He nods. "Yes. Come on."

Mason drags me out of the house, his pace nearly impossible to keep up with. Long gone is the man who was on his knees begging me to take control. He's been replaced by the angry Mason I'm most familiar with—the one who was raised as a prince and is prepared to be king.

The coronation is tomorrow. *The coronation is tomorrow.* Mason's going to be a king. I'm his mate. What the fuck does that mean for me? Where the fuck is Kie? Where the fuck is Lill?

We pass by several faeries, but none appear alert. They look at Mason and me with their usual level of caution and general disapproval, but nothing more. They don't yet know about the attack. The news hasn't spread, but I doubt that will be the case for much longer. Things like this are hard to hide.

"Stay close," Mason orders. "Now isn't the time to be rebellious."

I wasn't planning on it. The faeries and shifters may think little about humans, but we aren't idiots. The queen was just murdered, and it's in my best interest to remain close to Mason. He's the scariest motherfucker here, and he has an vested interest in keeping me alive. I'm going to be this man's shadow until told otherwise.

Do I need to be a shadow if the threat is Lill? I don't know, and that isn't a position I ever thought I'd be in. Just a few weeks ago, I was fully prepared to die in the faerie realm in the name of securing her delysum and saving her life, and now people are afraid of her hurting me.

Does she know what Mason and I did? That I touched him? That I exposed the bond between her, Mason, and Kie as false? I should've been careful. I should've been patient. I should've been a lot of things I wasn't.

"Are you sure she killed the queen?" I ask Mason.

"Yes. She asked a guard to bring her to the queen, slit her throat, and vanished through a portal."

Why would she do that? Lill's always had a violent side to her, and it's been used to my benefit several times, but it's never gotten out of hand. I didn't think she had that in her. This is the woman who cooks me elaborate dinners and yells at me for placing a glass on the coffee table without a coaster. She listens to Billy Joel, cries during movies, and has an unhealthy obsession with mint ice cream. She doesn't murder.

Mason leads us to the building where Kie works. The faerie stands outside with two guards and an older man wearing elegant robes. I'm not prepared for the relief I feel at seeing Kie. He appears uninjured and significantly more composed than I would be if my mother had just been murdered.

"Lock down the grounds." Kie's rough order has even me standing up straight. "I don't want anybody coming in or out."

The two guards beside Kie take off, but the man in robes remains.

Kie looks over as we approach, his gaze lingering on where Mason's holding my arm. The shifter isn't wearing gloves. He must have forgotten to put them back on, or perhaps it was a deliberate decision. Either way, he's openly touching me. He just dragged me across the property with his bare hand on my arm.

"Yes," is all Mason says.

Kie blinks.

Mason continues. "If you tell her not to touch you, she'll make it a personal mission to do the opposite. Abby doesn't listen."

"Does Lillian know?" Kie asks.

"I don't know."

"How don't you know?" Kie turns toward me. "Did you tell her?"

"This only just happened." Mason jumps in to answer for me. "It was a surprise to us both, and we got carried away in the bathroom. Lill was out of the house, but she may have overheard. I don't know. The guards were at the door when we finished."

The robed man beside Kie groans and walks away, beginning to pace. I've seen him before, but we've never interacted. I assume he's important if he's allowed to eavesdrop on this private conversation.

"What do you know?" Mason asks, changing the subject.

He's yet to remove his hand from my arm, and I'm getting the impression he has no intention to do so. I highly doubt Lill will appear and snatch me out of thin air. At least, I like to believe so. She's probably too weak to open two portals back-to-back. She was on the verge of death just a few days ago, and I'm certain she wasn't faking it.

Kie frowns. "Nothing of use. We're sweeping the property, but I highly doubt she's here. She's long gone, probably with the shifters."

Mason scoffs. "She's with Callie."

Callie's dead. Instinct tells me to say it, but logic keeps me quiet. I was told that Callie was dead, but I never saw the body. I can't confirm it.

The man in the robes returns, his crooked finger pointed in my direction. "Take the human somewhere safe," he tells Kie. "We don't need to top this day off with your mate's death." His gaze shifts toward Mason. "Come with me."

Mason tightens his grip on my arm. "Abby stays with me."

"No." The man shakes his head. "Abby stays with Kie. She has two mates, and you are busy. Hand her over. We don't have time to waste."

The man doesn't wait for an answer before spinning on his heel and vanishing into the building. He flings open the door with more force than necessary, and he doesn't look back. *Who is he?*

There's a moment of awkward silence before Kie gestures to Mason's unmoving grip on my arm. "He's right. With the queen's death, you're now our acting king. You need to be the face of this. I'll bring Abby to our home. Lillian's never been inside, so it won't be easy for her to open a portal there. Abby will be safe with me."

Mason's thumb brushes over the inside of my bicep, and he worries his lips together before finally releasing me. I'd prefer to stay with him, but I won't make a fuss.

"I won't be long," Mason promises me.

I nod, and he follows after the robed man. Kie places a hand on the small of my back and begins guiding me away, back in the direction Mason and I came from. Unlike Mason, he keeps a casual pace. I'm willing to bet it's to send the impression of control. It wouldn't look good for the faeries to see him running around in a panic.

"Why does Mason have to handle this himself?" I ask. "Shouldn't you two do it together?"

"In theory, yes," Kie says. "But you complicate things. The mate bond is fresh, and Mason won't be able to think clearly with you around. It's best you two are separated, and I'm the only person he'll trust you to be left with."

Should I mention the five guards he briefly left me with immediately upon hearing the news? His first instinct was to leave me with them, even if it only lasted approximately forty-five seconds.

"Do the faeries know about your agreement with Zaha?"

"Yes. They aren't pleased."

The private paths leading to the royal houses are swarming

with guards. They part to let Kie through, several bowing their heads as they do so.

The house Lill and I have been staying in taunts me, and I can't help but stare at it as Kie leads me to the one he shares with Mason. I was just here, and I immediately walk through the open entryway and sit on the oversized black couch.

Kie silently shuts the door behind him, then lights the fireplace. It provides some background noise, but not enough to drown out the awkwardness. I haven't seen much of Kie these past few days. He's been busy preparing for Mason's coronation, and my few interactions with him have been brief.

"I'm not going to touch you," I say. "If that's what you're concerned about. I've learned my lesson."

Kie paces the length of the room, his long legs carrying him from wall to wall in fourteen easy strides. I've always found Mason to be the more frightening of the two, but as I take in the dead, empty look in Kie's eye, I can't help but wonder if my assumption was off.

Five minutes pass. My anxiety grows.

I clear my throat. "Are you okay?"

Kie doesn't answer.

Of course he's not all right. He's been forced to give away the title many would argue was his birthright, and the woman he believed to be his mate just murdered his mother. He's been cast aside, forced to hide away in his home as humans do with women and children.

Kie continues to pace, his strides quickening and quickening. I'm not sure what to do other than stare, my hands tucked under my thighs and my feet tapping against the ground. Should I continue trying to speak with him?

Another ten minutes pass, and every one is spent in complete silence.

Kie turns his back to me, retreating into the open dining area. My toes curl in my shoes as he abruptly stops at the table. He leans forward and plants his palms onto the dark wood, his head dropping between his shoulders. The rapid expansion and contraction of his ribcage suggests he's panting, maybe even hyperventilating.

I can't hear his breathing from the couch, nor can I see his face to confirm. Still, I know what I'm looking at. Is he having a panic attack? Do faeries get them?

"Did you know?" Kie's question is full of accusation. "Did you know she was planning on murdering my mother?"

I physically recoil. "Of course not."

Kie turns, his violet eyes narrowed in on me. "Lillian was your best friend, was she not? You claim she told you everything. Did you know? Is that why you wanted to leave this morning? Were you hoping to escape before she followed through?"

He's hurting, and I'd wonder the same thing if I were in his position. I remind myself of this fact to keep my anger in check. It works, and I manage to keep a level head as I answer his question.

"I did *not* know," I repeat. "And had I suspected, I would have told you. I'm willing to overlook and excuse several things in the name of friendship, but murder is crossing the line. I had no idea what Lill was planning. I'm just as shocked as you are."

Kie cocks his head to the side. "But you suspected she wasn't my true mate? Is that why you touched Mason? To confirm your hypothesis?"

"Mason was the one who suspected, and he put the idea in my mind approximately twenty minutes before I touched him." I have no problem placing blame on the shifter. "He was the one keeping secrets from you, not me."

Kie stares at me for a long minute, then resumes his pacing.

Another five minutes pass. Where is Mason? How long is he going to be gone? I want to know what's happening. Have they found Lill? Does Mason have it under control? It's hard to imagine him in a leadership position. He seems too brutish, too ruled by emotion.

"Do you know where she would go?" Kie asks.

"No," I admit. "I could suggest a few locations in the human realm, but I'm not sure they'll help much."

The front door flies open, smacking against the wall with a loud bang. Mason comes storming inside a moment later. Two guards stand in the doorway behind him but make no moves to enter.

Mason immediately finds me, and his shoulders relax as we make eye contact.

"Can you make a list?" he asks. He must've heard me through the door.

I hesitate, then nod. Lill's killed somebody, and I can't continue playing the middle. She had more than enough opportunity to tell me what was going on, and she chose to keep her secrets. She looked me in the eye and lied to me, purposefully keeping details of her story hidden. Maybe she had a good reason, but from where I stand, I struggle to understand what it might be.

Mason turns, gesturing for one of the guards to enter. Well, I thought he was gesturing for the guards. They part instead, revealing three poised faeries. The one wearing robes is in front, and trailing behind him is a woman with white, shoulder-length curly hair and a man staring at me with an uneasy amount of interest.

They file inside the house and into the dining room. Kieran takes a seat, and the others follow. They leave the spot at the head of the table empty, I assume for Mason. The shifter doesn't take it.

He chooses to stand beside me in the living room.

"These are the council members," he says, his voice low. "The council leader is Anox." He's the one in the robes. "Beside him is Lady Cassandra, and the other is Lord Bishop. Would you like to sit with us?"

Anox looks over, his violet eyes unblinking. It's like he's looking through me, and it's painfully unnerving. Everything about him is unnerving.

"Am I allowed?" I ask.

Mason hesitates. "You're technically not welcome to sit in on council meetings, but this is a special circumstance. The other alternative is for you to sit in the living room pretending not to eavesdrop, which will be uncomfortable for everybody present."

As tempting as lurking in the living room sounds, I choose the less unpleasant option. Mason walks beside me as I approach the table, and he waits until I settle into an open seat before taking his own.

"Lillian isn't on the property," Mason begins, filling Kie and me in. "Two scouts have been sent to the outpost in the Redstall Forest with a message for my father—" Anox clears his throat, and Mason shoots him a glare before continuing. "With a message for *Alpha Theon*. We're informing him of our suspicions that Lillian Collins is hiding within his lands and an order for him to return her to us should she be found."

Kie taps his finger against the table. "Are you sure it's wise for your first decision as acting king to involve communication with the shifters?"

"We've considered this," Anox chimes in. "And we've decided it's in our best interests to do so. Given the severity of the situation, it's imperative for Mason to exhaust every possible avenue to getting Lillian in our custody."

"What will you do to her?" I ask.

Kie is the one who answers. "We provide fair trials, Abby. No snap decisions will be made."

I let out a sigh, beyond happy to hear that.

"We've put out a notice of Her Majesty's death," Mason continues. "And we're moving my coronation up to tomorrow morning."

Lady Cassandra leans forward, and a strand of hair falls over her eye. She smoothly tucks it behind her ear before speaking. "What about..." She pauses, grimaces, and turns toward Kie. "What's your mate's full name?"

Why doesn't she ask *me* that? Have I suddenly turned invisible? I think not.

"Abby," Kie answers.

"Abby *what*?"

Kie falls silent.

"You don't know your mate's family name?" Lady Cassandra raises a brow. The subtle movement contains a significant amount of judgment.

"My full name is Abigail Williams," I say, answering her.

She leans back in her chair. "I am not ignoring you to be rude. I am ignoring you because you're not allowed to participate in this meeting. Despite Mason's unconventional demand for us to convene outside the chamber rooms, I wish to honor tradition. Especially in a time of unrest."

Annoying, but I suppose honorable.

Lady Cassandra shifts her attention to Mason. "What do you intend to do about Abigail Williams?" she asks. "Do you wish to have her crowned as your queen consort? As your mate, she's entitled to the title, and it'll give her protection should something happen to you and Prince Kieran."

Mason chews on his bottom lip. "What do you think?" he finally asks Kie.

I'm interested to see if either of them will bother to ask me how I feel about the matter. I have little interest in becoming Mason's queen consort, mate bond or not.

"I think we should hold off on that," Kie says. "We can deal with Abby after today's events have settled."

Deal with Abby.

"I agree," Anox chimes in.

Both Lady Cassandra and Lord Bishop let out murmurs of agreement.

I rest my chin on my knees as the topic changes, returning to Her Majesty's death and Mason's coronation. There's a lot to discuss, but the council manages to fit everything into one thirty-minute meeting.

The council members leave immediately after, returning to work. Kie resumes pacing the minute we're alone, hardly speaking and staring ahead with a detached, cold expression.

Dinner is spent with me curled up in a ball on the couch while Kie and Mason pore over the short list of places I think Lill could have gone. They ultimately decide to send a small unit of soldiers to each location, which I think is overkill.

It's dark by the time the men are sent out. Four per location. Lill may have murdered the queen, but she's still physically quite frail. If found, it won't be hard to overpower her.

"Are you tired, Abby?" Kie eventually asks.

The sun fell hours ago, and I'm beyond exhausted. I can barely keep my eyes open, and I blink heavily before shrugging.

"I guess," I mumble.

Kie frowns, pushing away from the table. It looks like he's about to approach me, but he changes course and returns to his position at the table after a visible hesitation.

Mason looks over, his green eyes piercing. "You'll sleep with me tonight."

"No."

Mason opens his mouth, probably to argue, but Kie quickly intervenes. "You can sleep in the guest room. Do you wish to shower? I'll bring you a change of clothing."

I shake my head. "I'm fine out here."

I want to know if there are any updates on Lill's whereabouts.

Kie frowns again. He's always frowning. "Go to sleep, Abby. Tomorrow will be busy, and you'll want to be rested for it. Mason's coronation is early."

I shake my head again.

Kie sighs. "We'll wake you if we hear anything about Lill."

My eyes narrow.

"We promise," Mason chimes in.

My next blink is exceptionally heavy. "If you're lying, I'll kill you."

"We're aware." Kie gestures down the hallway. "Do you remember where the guest room is?"

"Wouldn't forget it." I'll never forget the room he locked me inside while Lill was being tortured in the cells.

I climb off the couch and head down the hallway. The door is ajar, and I eye the scuff marks from my failed attempts to kick it down. It's only been a few days since I was locked in here, but it feels like a lifetime.

My limbs are heavy as I strip off my dress and slip between the covers, but sleep doesn't immediately find me. I roll around for what feels like hours, unable to get my mind to stop racing long enough to fall asleep. I'm not happy with today.

Chapter Fourteen

ABBY

THE BED DIPS, and I instinctively clutch the bedsheets to my chest as I jolt upright. Mason is sitting on the edge of my bed.

Kie is lingering in the doorway, already showered and dressed. His hair is still wet.

"What?" I snap. "What time is it?"

"Early," Mason says. "The coronation is at sunrise, and it's time to get ready."

He places his hand on the sheets, directly over my hip. I brush him away, then kick at his leg until he takes the hint to get off the bed. He doesn't, choosing to remain firmly planted in his spot.

"Your clothing is in the bathroom," Kie says from the doorway. "We're leaving in thirty minutes."

With that, he spins on his heel and leaves. I stare at his retreating form, my eyebrows furrowed. He's not usually like that. In the forest, he was the friendlier of the two. I mean, he was still an asshole, but not like this.

"Is he okay?" I ask Mason.

"He's stressed, and he feels foolish for believing the bond with Lillian was genuine. He's skeptical you're truly our mate, which is absurd, considering I've confirmed it myself."

I shoot the shifter a sideways look. "He told you that?"

"He didn't need to."

I hum. "Is there an update on Lill?"

"No. She wasn't at any of the locations you provided, so we're inclined to believe she's still in this realm. I suspect she's hiding with Alpha Theon and Callie in the shifter lands."

I'm done insisting that Callie is dead. Nobody seems inclined to believe me, and I've already been wrong several times when it comes to Lill.

Mason continues. "We should have a clearer idea once we hear back from my father."

If we hear back from his father. From what I've gathered, it doesn't seem that Mason and his dad have the best relationship. The shifter alpha abandoned his son in the faerie kingdom after Mason's shared mate bond with Kie was discovered, and there hasn't been any contact since.

The thought no longer fills me with as much joy as it once did, which I blame on the bond.

I eye last night's dress lying on the floor beside the bed. Mason follows my line of sight but makes no attempts to leave. He knows I'm naked under these sheets, and he's hoping to catch a glimpse.

"Get out," I order.

"Why?"

"Because I want privacy."

"Why do you need privacy?" The corner of Mason's lips twitch upward. "I've already seen and tasted you. Have you forgotten about that? You shoved my face into your cunt, and—"

"Get out, Mason!" I kick at his leg again.

This time, he listens, his smile remaining as he lifts his hands in surrender and backs out of the room. "We leave in thirty minutes."

Thirty minutes isn't enough time, but the rush keeps me busy enough not to dwell on our current situation. I'm stressed about Lill, and I'm stressed about what the mate bond means for me.

I still want to go home. I miss my family, and I'm sure they miss me. I didn't tell them I was leaving, and they're undoubtedly worried sick. Have they already contacted the police? Is there an investigation?

There's a navy-blue dress hanging in the bathroom. It's significantly more formal than the day dresses I've been given these past few days, and it has a corset-style lacing up the back.

I shower before squeezing myself into it, pleased I can do the laces myself. The dress is a bit long, the hem dragging along the ground. It doesn't help that the faeries exclusively wear slipper-style shoes. They're comfortable, but they offer no additional height.

Mason and Kie are standing around the dining room table when I emerge, both leaning over a large map that must have been brought in after I went to bed. It's of the Redstall Forest, and there are several locations marked.

Are they searching for Alpha Theon? Did these two get any sleep last night? It doesn't appear so.

I look toward Mason, but he refuses to make eye contact. Is he afraid I'll bring up the secret map I found in his bedroom? I won't, not until I need to. Not until it benefits me.

"The crowning ceremony is private, and it will be quick." Mason glances toward Kie before continuing. "We'll be attending an observance for Queen Gitta afterward."

Kie winces, the movement so subtle, I wouldn't have noticed if I hadn't been looking. I've never seen Kie lose control, and I'm nervous he's at his breaking point. It's a miracle he hasn't lost control already.

Mason lets himself feel every emotion that comes his way,

good or bad, but Kie's reserved. What if the observance is what breaks him? What if he throws himself over Queen Gitta's casket or tries to climb inside with her?

"I expect to hear back from my father within the next day or two," Mason continues. "If I don't, we have a unit of soldiers prepared to scout his lands for her."

That explains the maps.

"They aren't *his* lands." Kie's quick to correct Mason. "The Redstall Forest belongs to the faeries, and it always has. We gave the shifters a place to live after they destroyed their kingdom, but that doesn't make the land any less ours."

I suck my cheeks into my mouth. That's an argument I have no interest in getting involved in.

It's odd being around the pair now that I know they're my mates, especially Mason. The bond is subtle, but it's there. I want to be near the shifter, preferably pressed against him in whatever way possible.

Mason walks behind me, disappearing from my line of sight. "Are you ready to go?" His bare fingers slide up my covered shoulders, dangerously close to my exposed neck. Half of me wants to push him away, but the other half wants to let him touch me. I want to feel the warmth and comfort. I'm craving it, and it's hard to ignore when he's so close.

"I knew you were my mate," he whispers. His fingers finally touch my bare skin, and I unsuccessfully suppress a shiver. "And I'm pleased my assumption was correct. I'm pleased you're mine."

I don't know how to respond to that. I love compliments, but I want to be angry with Mason. I'm not ready to give up my grudge, and if I start acting like a giddy fool whenever he gives me attention, that's precisely what will happen. I have to remain strong.

"I'm not yours." I step forward and brush his fingers away. "Back off, rat."

"'Rat'?"

I nod, and Kie lets out a low chuckle. It's the first bit of emotion he's shown in days.

He clears his throat. "Let's go."

It's a short walk to the ceremony location, which I quickly recognize is the meeting hall the queen brought me to on my first day here. The three-story dome-topped building is exactly how I remember it. A wide, shallow staircase leads to the front glass doors and immediately upon entering is a large hall. The marble flooring, stone pillars, arched ceilings, and giant chandeliers are just as breathtaking as the first time I saw them.

The early morning sunlight is just beginning to stream through the windows, casting the entire room in a golden haze. It's stunning.

Mason walks inside first, with Kie and me immediately behind.

The throne at the back of the room is the first thing I notice. A set of wide, shallow steps leads to the oversized, elegant chair. Queen Gitta sat on it the last time I was here, but I try not to think of that as I eye the dark-red cushion and detailed wooden armrests.

I gulp, shifting my attention to Anox. He stands several feet from the door, and beside him are the other two council members I met last night. Lady Cassandra has dressed up for the occasion. She's in a floor-length silver gown, and her hair is pulled away from her face in four neat braids. Lord Bishop is wearing a blue suit with gold detailing, and he thankfully keeps his eyes away from me.

I don't particularly like the way he stares.

All three faeries bend at the waist as Mason approaches.

"Are you ready?" Anox asks.

Mason nods. "Yes."

There's a pair of double doors to the left of the room. They blend in with the wall, seamless and nondescript, and Anox bows to them before grabbing the golden knobs and pulling.

"The anointing room is sacred," Kie says, his voice low as the doors are pulled open. "Only royals and council members are allowed inside, but we're making an exception for you. There's a pool of water in the center of the room. You'll want to avoid that. You and I will stand along the back wall while Mason and Anox perform the ceremony."

I nod, happy to know what to expect. I don't like surprises.

Anox and Mason walk inside, Kie and I head in after, and Lady Cassandra and Lord Bishop take up the rear.

There's indeed a shallow, black pool taking up a majority of the room. In the center of it is a large, shiny black stone. What's it for? The edges are jagged, and the shine resembles obsidian.

Kie guides me to the back of the room. Lady Cassandra and Lord Bishop join us. Mason said the crowning ceremony would be private, but I still anticipated more flair. He tugs off his shoes and socks before stepping inside the pool. The water laps at his ankles as he walks toward the black stone. It juts out of the water, just reaching the tops of his knees.

Anox waits for Mason to get situated before approaching, his robes trailing along the ground behind him. He pauses once he's standing at the edge of the pool, and he bows at the waist before beginning to speak in a language I don't understand.

Several minutes pass before Mason nods and responds, also in the foreign language. It sounds like he's repeating what Anox is saying, probably taking an oath or something similar.

I'll have to ask Kie and Mason later.

Anox and Mason go back and forth for several minutes, and I shift my weight from foot to foot. This is tedious, but I'm in no hurry for it to end. Mason said there's an observance for the queen afterward, and I'm truthfully dreading it.

I'm holding out hope that Lill didn't kill the queen and this is all some elaborate trick, but I won't be able to hold on to that when facing the aftermath of the queen's murder. I wasn't a fan of Kie's mother, I'd be the first to admit that, but she didn't deserve to die. If I killed everybody who made me mad, I fear there wouldn't be many humans left on Earth.

Anox reaches into his robes and pulls out a green, jeweled knife. It's objectively beautiful, but I just know Mason's going to cut himself with it. It's too exquisite and ceremonial to be used for anything other than a good old blood rite.

Mason tugs off a glove and extends his arm, and Anox cuts into his hand. It almost immediately begins to bleed, the red blood flowing out onto his palm before dripping down his fingers. I hate blood.

Mason waits until it's covered the entirety of his palm before bending and pressing it against a flat part of the stone. I wait for the ground to shake or the gods to come bestow their blessing, but nothing of the sort happens. I count to fifteen before Mason removes his hand.

He leaves a thick smear of blood behind, but the cut on his palm already seems to be healing. I continually forget just how fast faeries and shifters heal. It's a lot to get used to.

What would it take to kill Mason? Stabbing him in the chest didn't work, and he healed quickly after having his guts practically spilled in the forest. My knee has yet to recover. A small scab remains, and I'm tempted to peel it off so it scars.

I want a physical reminder of what Mason did to me, and I want Mason to remember every time he sees it. Kie, too.

Mason rises, saying some final words in the foreign language. Anox and the other council members bow again, but Kie doesn't.

I'm not sure what I'm supposed to do, so I default to copying the council members.

"No," Kie murmurs. "We don't bow to Mason."

"Why?"

"As his mate, you're his equal. As for me, I just have personal feelings against it."

Good to know.

Mason climbs out of the pool, his gaze meeting mine as he slips his socks and shoes back on. The council members bow again. It's getting repetitive. If they're upset about his position as king, they don't show it.

Is this how the faeries are going to treat him now? They were more than comfortable showing their contempt when they believed he was a prince with no real power.

"Is that all?" I ask.

Kie nods. "What else did you expect?"

"I'm not sure. More flair, maybe."

Mason clears his throat, I suspect holding back an amused chuckle.

"I will have this recorded immediately into our texts," Anox says. "I will see you at Her Majesty Queen Gitta's observance shortly."

Right. His reminder has me falling silent, and I stare at my feet as Kie and Mason guide me out of the room. Kie waits until we're outside before speaking.

"Do you have a speech prepared?" he asks Mason.

Mason curls his fingers against my lower back. "I do not."

I'm not surprised to hear that.

Chapter Fifteen

ABBY

THE GARDENS ARE beautiful. The particular one I've been brought to is hidden within a circular wall of tall bushes, and it's filled with shrubby trees, stone paths, and fountains. It makes the gardens of Versailles look like a playground.

It's shaping up to be a beautiful day, too. The sky is clear, and there's a slight breeze.

The barrier of giant hedges provides surprising privacy, and lining them are tall, stone vases, all filled with blooming flowers. I've never seen such vibrant colors. There are only fifty or so faeries within the small area, but what appear to be hundreds are waiting on the hill beyond the gardens.

It feels like every pair of eyes is on me, but I hope that's just my paranoia talking. They're most likely looking at Mason. He's their new king. Their new *shifter* king.

The quiet murmuring within the garden falls silent as we enter. Then the faeries bow, bending lowly at the waist and parting to reveal a stone slab. *Fuck no.* The queen has been wrapped in thin brown cloth, her body covered from shoulder to toe, and she's been laid on the large stone slab in the garden's center. I've never seen anything like this, and I avoid looking too closely at her form.

The faeries continue to part, and Mason and Kie shift to stand on either side of me. I would love nothing more than to linger behind, but I'm not granted that opportunity. I'm guided forward, toward the stone slab and the body on top of it.

Her Majesty is gray and waxy, clearly dead. I've been fortunate enough never to see a dead body before today. My grandparents had closed caskets, and all my childhood pets were put down at the vet's office and cremated. I wasn't involved.

Kie steps ahead of me, and I linger behind with Mason as he bends over the slab and whispers a few words too quiet to hear. Does he not have the opportunity to see his mother privately? That's awful.

I stare at my feet, giving him privacy, even if the faeries surrounding me don't offer the same courtesy. Only a minute or two passes before Kie returns to my side, and Mason takes his turn. He says a few quiet words before turning and facing the crowd.

They're probably waiting for the speech Kie mentioned.

Mason begins, again in the language I don't understand. I listen, trying to see if I recognize anything. Nothing stands out. This isn't a language that exists in the human realm.

"I understand many of you are hesitant to see me rule," Mason says, shifting into a language I understand. Somebody behind me scoffs, and Mason clears his throat before continuing. "I'm not interested in giving useless promises to mollify you, and I won't stand here pretending I'm not the firstborn son of Alpha Theon."

Mason wasn't lying when he said he didn't have a speech planned. He's only two sentences in, and already, he's fucking up. He's supposed to comfort the faeries, not remind them that he's not one of them.

Kie lets out a quiet sigh and drops his chin to his chest.

"But I've made a commitment to the faeries, and to Zaha, and

I intend to honor it." Mason licks his lips, his green eyes darting from faerie to faerie. "I am a good leader, and Prince Kieran will remain by my side as a valued council member."

Several seconds pass in tense silence. I listen to trees, focusing on the quiet flapping of bird wings. The garden is peaceful, and I wonder if this area is reserved exclusively for funerals. I hope not.

Mason continues. "Please do not hesitate to come to the council and myself with any concerns. We understand Her Majesty's death frightens many, and we assure you we have everything under control."

I wait for further elaboration, but Mason offers none. He steps away from the queen's body, letting Anox take a turn. I didn't notice the robed faerie's entrance.

He places a hand on Queen Gitta's wrappings, then faces the crowd with just as much confidence as Mason. "In light of recent events, we will be holding court tomorrow evening. We invite you all to join."

Pressure on my arm pulls my focus from Anox. It's coming from Mason. He nudges his head to the side, gesturing toward the exit. Are we leaving already? We've only just gotten here. I wait until we're safely away from the crowd before speaking.

"Why aren't we staying?"

"The royal family does not mourn," Kie says. "We move forward. Always."

That's a shitty tradition. Kie lost his mother. He deserves to mourn.

We pass dozens of faeries on our way out of the gardens. Each one bows deeply to Mason. It's unsettling, and I quickly find myself eager to be away from prying eyes. The grounds are significantly busier today, I assume because of Queen Gitta's remembrance.

I'm surprised they don't hold it outside the property, but I'm not looking to question faerie tradition. Not today.

"What now?" I ask.

It's Kie who answers. "We continue with our day as normal. I have some work to wrap up, so you'll stay with Mason for the remainder of the morning. I'll be back shortly."

Mason halts. "What do you mean? What work?"

"I'll be back shortly."

Kie's avoiding the question, and he breaks away from us a moment later. Mason visibly hesitates, looking like he wants to chase after Kie and demand that he remain with us. I hope he doesn't. Kie needs space.

I do, too, if I'm being honest with myself. I still haven't wrapped my mind around the fact that he's my mate, and it's significantly easier to avoid thinking about it when he isn't nearby. Mason isn't giving me the same opportunity, and the mate bond is annoying.

It's not changing my overall perception of the shifter, but I'm continually finding myself drawn to him. I'm impressed with how he's handled himself today, and I'm excited to have the morning with him. Neither of those emotions are welcome, and I doubt I'd be feeling them if it weren't for the bond.

"When will I be allowed to go home?" I ask. "I need to contact my family. They must be worried sick about me."

We walk along the wooded path leading to the royal houses. I scuff my feet along the worn path.

"You're our mate," Mason says. "You'll remain with us. I haven't had the opportunity to speak with Kie about it, but we'll arrange for your family to be brought here. They can live on the property if they wish, or within Bellmere."

"They have jobs, friends, commitments. Their entire lives are within the human realm. So is mine. I can't stay here. I need to go home."

"That's not an option."

Of course not. Heaven forbid Kie and Mason do something that doesn't directly benefit them. We reach the house, and I storm ahead and push open the door before the shifter gets it into his head to do it for me. I don't need him to do anything nice for me.

"You can't bring my family here," I argue. "They don't know about faeries."

Mason walks into the kitchen. "Then they'll learn. Are you hungry?"

He pulls something wrapped in cloth out of a cabinet, and I inch forward as I realize it's a loaf of fresh bread. I haven't had breakfast, and the bread looks good. Mason grabs two plates, and I come to the painful realization that he has no idea how to cook as he places two slices of bread and a handful of fruit on each plate.

"I won't cook for you," I say. "Don't think that because I'm your mate, I will become your personal chef."

Mason stares me down. "Okay."

He shoves a piece of bread into his mouth, and I do the same. Mason's jaw shifts with each bite, the muscle clenching and unclenching. He has a nice, square jawline. I know several human men who would kill to have it.

Everything about Mason's physical appearance is objectively nice, though. He's big and strong and sometimes I just want to sink my teeth into him. Would he let me? He let me stab him, so I'm inclined to believe he would.

I should've never touched him. It was a mistake.

"What should I do with my bedroom?"

It takes me approximately ten business days to try to make sense of Mason's question, and I still come up empty-handed.

"What?" I give in and ask.

Mason sighs, the noise dramatic and unnecessary, before

walking down the hallway that leads to the bedrooms. I absentmindedly follow him, still not understanding what he's getting at.

"You refused to sleep in my room last night," he says, opening his bedroom door. "Tell me what I need to change so you'll sleep with me."

I blink.

Mason is useless, and I don't know what I've done to deserve being paired with him. Maybe I offended Zaha in another life, and this is her way of getting revenge. It wouldn't surprise me.

"I'm not going to sleep with you," I say. "I don't trust you. I frankly don't even like you."

And I mean it, too.

Mason rolls his eyes. "You don't need to trust me to share a room with me. My bed is comfortable, my sheets are soft, and I am warm."

"Don't you have work to do?" I ask, changing the subject. "Maybe a meeting to attend or a letter to write?"

"I'll work better after a night of good sleep with my mate." Mason pulls open his wardrobe doors and gestures to the clothing inside. "I'll make room for you to put your dresses, and I won't use them to masturbate."

Oh, wow. I'm so fucking charmed. How kind of him to offer not to desecrate my clothing. I've never felt so lucky.

"I'll sleep with you if you get on your knees and beg for my forgiveness," I say. "I want you to tell me how meaningless your life is without me and how ashamed you are of the way you treated me. Then I want you to suckle on my big toe while you call me 'Daddy.'"

Mason slams his wardrobe drawers shut. He's pissed.

"I'm being serious," he says.

I'm sure he is. I don't doubt that for a second, but that doesn't mean I want to sleep with him. I understand and accept that it's safest to stay here instead of the house I shared with Lill, but I'm happy with the condom-filled spare bedroom.

I take a seat on the edge of Mason's bed. The shifter seems excited as I settle on the mattress, and I hold eye contact with him as I lift the hem of my dress up my thighs. I'm tired of him acting like I'm some object he can bark orders at and boss around.

If he wants to treat me like an object, I'll treat him like one, too.

"If you're so desperate to waste my time"—I sneer—"you might as well be useful."

I'm surprised steam isn't billowing out from Mason's ears. That's a sight I'd enjoy. He clenches his fists, his eyes narrowing. I've made him angry.

"Come on, now," I taunt. "I don't have all day."

Mason steps away from the bed. "I don't want to."

I fake a pout. "Why not?"

"Because putting my mouth on you meant something to me, and now you're mocking it."

I snap my legs shut and pull down my dress. *Fuck.* Leave it to Mason to make me feel guilty for giving him a taste of his own medicine.

"I—"

I barely have time to react as Mason darts forward and rips my dress back up my legs. I fall back onto his bed, my heart pounding.

"Don't be so gullible, Abby. I like your spitefulness, and if I need to lick my way to your heart, so be it." Mason pauses, hesitating, before continuing. "I want you to know this does mean something to me, though. *You* mean something to me, even if you hate me."

I don't know what to say. Mason's admission makes me feel

unnervingly pleased, but I don't want to feel pleased with him. I don't want any soft emotions toward Mason.

Without responding, I place a hand on top of his head and push it between my thighs. It's easy not to think when he's down there.

Chapter Sixteen

KIERAN

I HEAR THEM the second I walk through the front door.

Abby's moans are muffled but loud, and I follow them to Mason's bedroom. The door is cracked, and I can't resist the urge to peer inside. I haven't explicitly told Mason I don't want him having sex with her, but I shouldn't need to.

Forked mate bonds are rare, but there are established rules. Mason and I share Abby, which means our first time with her will be together.

I'm pleased to see Mason isn't fucking her. He's on his knees at the foot of his bed, his face buried between her thighs. Abby's on her back, her legs wrapped around his shoulders and her hands lost in his hair.

I lean against the doorframe. I'm exhausted, my body begging for rest, but sleep is the last thing on my mind.

I never imagined Mason would so eagerly drop to his knees for a woman—even his mate. It's an advancement I didn't expect, but I'm not surprised Abby's drawn it out of him. She's mean and bossy, and Mason seems to enjoy it when she believes she controls him.

How long will it take her to realize she doesn't?

Abby moans, rocking her hips. My throat is suddenly dry.

Mason seems to think I'm in denial of the bond I share with Abby, which couldn't be further from the truth. I've been drawn to the human since I first laid eyes on her, but she doesn't want my bond. She doesn't want me, and I won't touch her and force it.

The distraction of my mother and Lillian is making it easier to avoid her. I was a fool for believing the bond with Lillian was real, despite all the signs warning me that something was wrong. I wasn't drawn to Lillian the way mates should be—the way I am with Abby. Mason's reluctance should've been another warning sign.

It was, but I ignored it.

Now my mother is dead, and my true mate wants nothing to do with me. I have nobody to blame but myself.

I'm trying to remain impartial and give Abby space. It's working. She doesn't look at me the same way she looks at Mason, which is another form of torture. I'm willing to endure it, though. I have too much on my plate, and adding the complexity of a mate bond with a human who wants nothing to do with me isn't feasible.

Mason slips a hand between Abby's thighs, and her entire body jolts a second later. I wonder if this is the first time he's put his fingers inside her, and I'm pleased he waited until I was present to do so.

I'm avoiding her, but I don't want to miss too many firsts. They're still important to me.

Abby slams a hand over her mouth, trying to quiet her moans. She's largely unsuccessful, and I can't help but wish I were in Mason's position. Is she soft inside? I shake my head. Of course she is. She's soft and warm, and I bet she feels incredible around his fingers.

I'm surprised she's letting him touch her.

Abby continues rocking against Mason's tongue, her moans growing louder until she buries her heels into his back and arches off the bed. She's cumming. Mason's arm flexes as he works her through it, and he continues until she relaxes and drops her legs from around his shoulders.

The movement fully exposes her, and I force my expression to remain neutral as I finally see her slick cunt. She's soaked, but that's not what captures my attention. Mason's fingers are still inside her, his middle and ring, and she's stretched tightly around them.

I have to look away.

I've fucked plenty of women, but none have made me as desperate as the human.

Abby hasn't noticed me leaning against the doorway, her focus entirely on the shifter. It doesn't bother me nearly as much as I feared it would. I've never felt jealousy toward Mason, but a small part of me always worried that would change if we ever found our mate.

If anything, I'm pleased they're together, even if it only appears to be in a sexual manner. We haven't been kind to Abby, and she's entitled to keep Mason on his knees.

I want her underwear back, though.

Mason pulls Abby's dress down her thighs before throwing himself on top of her, pinning her to his mattress. She lets out a muffled grunt and almost immediately begins punching him in the arms and back.

"Get off me!"

Mason laughs. It's genuine, and my heart lurches. I haven't heard Mason laugh so freely in years, and the irrational bolt of jealousy I've been fearing travels up my spine. He's getting everything. I used to be the carefree one, and all my loss has been his gain.

He has our mate. He has the title that's been promised to me since birth. He is working to reconnect with his parents after I just put my remaining one in the ground. He can pretend his decision to reach out to Alpha Theon is within the kingdom's best interests, and maybe it is, but I know Mason. He's always held out hope of reconnecting with his parents.

They abandoned him, and he's looking for any excuse to forgive them. He's also desperate enough to take whatever shitty excuse they give him, which will undoubtedly cause issues.

He believes everything will be solved after one conversation with his father, that Alpha Theon will choose Mason over the woman and daughter who successfully brought down the ruling faerie family.

"Mason." Abby releases another loud shriek. "Get off me!"

Mason laughs again. "I got on my knees and begged my forgiveness into your pussy, and now I'll tell you my life is meaningless without you—which it is—and how ashamed I am of the way I treated you—which I am." Mason slides a hand down her leg, then curls his fingers around her ankle. "And now, Daddy, I'll suckle your big toe."

I'm not following.

Abby screams absurdly loud as she kicks her legs, trying to keep Mason away from her feet.

I suck in a shaky breath, trying and failing to rein in my anger. I should be happy that Mason is finally finding companionship. He's been dealt a challenging life, abandoned as a child and forced to live with strangers who openly hated him. I shouldn't let Mason's newfound happiness make me bitter. He deserves this.

"Stop it, Mason." Abby continues to scream. "Stop it right now!"

Mason releases her ankle. "Does this mean you'll sleep in my bed? I've done everything you asked, and I get so, so, so cold at night." He lowers his voice, and I roll my eyes. He's so fucking dramatic. "I need my mate to keep me warm."

"I hate to interrupt," I lie. Abby's about to answer him, but spitefulness prevents me from letting her do so. "But I thought you'd want to know I've returned."

Mason ignores me, fully intent on pretending he hasn't been aware of my presence since the second I opened our front door. Abby isn't keen to do the same. She pushes at Mason's shoulder until he gives in and rolls off her.

He shoots me daggers. I don't acknowledge them.

Abby's face is red. Is she embarrassed to have been caught with Mason? She's doing her best to keep up the appearance of hating the shifter. She must be upset to have been caught being soft with him.

She slides off the bed and fixes her dress, a blush spreading down her neck. It's hard to keep my expression neutral as she collects herself. I'm desperate to know how it feels to touch her. I felt something with Lillian, but it wasn't what I always imagined a bond to be. Will it feel different with Abby?

She's already touched Mason and tied herself to us, so there's no reason for me to postpone. If it weren't for her hatred of us, I would've done so already. I'd like comfort. I would've liked to hold my mate as I spoke my final words to my mother earlier today.

"The faeries will be testing you tomorrow," I say to Mason. "They want to prove you aren't fit to lead, and they'll be eager to embarrass you during court."

We don't hold court often, mainly because it's time-consuming and nobody ever comes. I suspect the throne room will be filled tomorrow. The faeries will have plenty to say and ask, and Mason needs to make a good impression.

Things are unstable, and it's only a matter of time before the shifters, and other noble families, try to exploit it. We need to maintain a united front.

"The faeries are never going to accept me," Mason says.

"That doesn't mean they won't respect you."

"I beg to differ."

Mason has spent years ruining relationships with the faeries. They never gave him a chance, and he acted accordingly. Mason left a trail of bodies everywhere he went, and he never bothered hiding his hatred toward my people.

It wasn't ideal, but considering there were no plans for him to ever step into real power, my mother and the council didn't spend much energy trying to repair the relationship. They focused on me instead.

Abby clears her throat. "Kie—"

I shake my head, stopping her. I already know where she's going with this, and I don't care to discuss my mother's death right now. There are more important matters to focus on, and the royal family doesn't mourn. The kingdom doesn't stop moving, so neither can we.

It's what my mother said to me after my father's death, and it's what she'd advise me to do now.

"I should brush up on foreign policy," Mason says. "Given my ties with the shifters, that's where the faeries will be aiming their jabs."

I nod, in complete agreement.

Abby chews at her bottom lip. "Do I need to come to court?"

"Yes." Mason and I speak in union, but it's Mason who continues. "You'll remain with us until we find Lillian and Callie."

Abby's presence will raise questions, specifically about Lillian and our lack of a wife or mate. We aren't formally announcing Abby's position, but we aren't going out of our way to hide it like we were with Lillian. I hesitate to make any formal announcements until things have settled.

Abby is weak, and if we confirm our tie to her, she'll become a target. Mason and I were set to have a political marriage, and many will feel jilted when they discover we've chosen a human female. Abby doesn't know how to lead a kingdom, and she doesn't show much interest in learning.

She doesn't even want to be here, for fuck's sake. Just yesterday, she was asking me to take her home.

Mason gestures to the door. "Shall we?"

"Yes." I shoot Abby a fleeting glance before exiting Mason's room. "I've had study materials brought to my office."

Mason takes a long moment to respond. "We shouldn't be out." He glances at Abby, concern written plainly across his features. "We can better protect Abby from our home."

"We need to convey the impression of confidence. Abby is safe with us."

I say the last bit for her benefit. The kingdom is on high alert, and there's no way for Lillian or Callie to enter without us noticing. My mother wasn't prepared, but we aren't going to put ourselves, or Abby, in a similar position.

It's a short walk to my office, and Abby is suspiciously quiet the entire way. What's she thinking? Does she worry we can't protect her? She walks between Mason and me, pointedly avoiding touching either of us, and storms ahead once we enter my office.

Abby helps herself to my desk chair while Mason and I stand at the long table in the corner of the room. It's piled high with books, most of which are on foreign policy. We have a human mate and a shifter king. The faeries will be most concerned about how we intend to handle that.

A map of the shifter lands is laid out, and I brush it aside before reaching for the policy book our tutors forced us to memorize when we were teenagers. Mason groans the same way he did back then, and he swipes the book from my hand before sinking into a chair.

Abby rips open my desk drawers, and I avoid looking over. She's going to find the plastic tiara and peanut container, and I don't care to see her angry expression when she does. I keep my focus on Mason instead.

"I don't remember this book being quite so thick," he says.

I hum. "That's because you were given a modified version."

His discussed the most critical topics, but my copy dove deep. As a prince, Mason was expected to learn more than most, and he probably has more knowledge than even our most involved nobles, but I was held to an even higher standard.

"The benefits of being king," I say, cracking a smile. It's almost genuine.

Chapter Seventeen

ABBY

THE BEDROOM DOOR creaks open, the noise just loud enough to pull me from the deepest edges of sleep. I'm still heavy, though, my body weighed down with exhaustion. Kie and Mason spent all day studying policies, traditions, and polite responses for court. I was excited to listen in at first, but the conversation quickly grew tedious.

Mason would say something ninety-five percent correct, and Kie would quickly intervene with alternatives. Then they'd bicker like an old married couple.

My sheets are pulled back, the movement further waking me. I already know who it is, and I bury my face into my pillow as I work up the strength to speak. I just want to be left alone.

"Go away."

My mattress dips at my waist. "But—"

Mason sounds like a wounded puppy. I don't care.

"When and *if* I'm ever ready to sleep with you, I'll let you know," I say. "Stop pushing the issue and go back to your room."

Mason sighs, and a second later, he retreats.

Despite my rejection, my body tingles with excitement at the thought of sharing a bed with him. It's the infuriating bond. I want

Mason wrapped around me, his chest pressing against my back and our legs tangled together. I want to wake up suffocated by him, and I want to push my hips back until he's hard and ready to slide inside me.

I want it so badly I can feel it, but I've already given in to him twice. If he offered again, I'm not sure I'd have the strength to turn him away.

I squeeze my eyes shut, hating myself for my desperate thoughts. Mason warned me that the bond would do this, would cause these unwanted feelings, but I never imagined it would be this intense. I thought I'd have more control over it.

"What does it feel like?" I ask before Mason leaves. "The bond. What does it feel like for you?"

Mason pauses by the door. "I imagine it's what you feel, but amplified. Shifters traditionally feel mate bonds the strongest. We're ruled by emotion and instinct, which pairs well with a mate bond. Humans feel them the least. They're not naturally occurring for your species, so you won't be quite as affected. Faeries are somewhere in the middle, but closer to shifters."

I can't imagine the bond feeling any stronger than it does right now.

"How are you…" I trail off, not sure how to word my next question. I don't want to give too much away. I don't want to admit how much I want him. "How are you controlling yourself?"

Mason laughs, sounding mildly deranged. "Do you think I'm controlling myself? I'm attempting to sneak into your bed while you're sleeping."

"Yeah, but not to…" I trail off. I thought he was sneaking into my bed because he wanted to be near me. Was this sexually charged? I don't like that. "Were you—"

Mason is quick to interrupt. "No, Abby. No. That was a bad example. I wasn't going to touch you, not in any sexual manner. I just…" He pauses, thinking, before continuing. "I'm desperate for you, but in *any* manner. I obviously want to have sex with you, but I just as equally want to be beside you. I can't breathe when we aren't in the same room."

I fear what I would do if I felt the bond any more than I do now. Mason may claim it's not entirely sexual on his end, but that's the emotion that's standing out most to me.

"Will the feelings subside if I give in to them?" I ask.

I'll fuck Mason if it means I can spend the next several days ignoring him. I need him out of my head, and I'm exceptionally skilled at sex without feelings. I went to a state school for accounting, which was mind-numbingly dull. Sex and alcohol were the only forms of entertainment I had.

"Do you think Zaha would make things that easy?" Mason asks. He steps toward me, and a part of me dies as I realize he's wearing only a pair of tight, black underwear.

He was going to sneak into my bed like that? My immediate reaction is to be angry, but the emotion doesn't come. He's never cuddled—never felt skin against his—and I'm sure he's excited to experience it. I don't believe he was trying to be a pervert.

Mason kneels beside my bed, bringing us to the same level.

"Everybody says bonds are overwhelming at first," he explains. "It'll settle over the next few days, maybe weeks if we continue to ignore it."

Weeks? I have to go weeks like this? The mere thought fills me with dread. I don't have that level of patience. I predict I have only days before I'm begging Mason to fuck me. I know who I am, and I'm fairly confident my willpower won't last that long.

Frustrated, overwhelmed tears fill my eyes, and Mason frowns as one spills down my cheek.

"I'm so angry with you," I choke out. "You were cruel, and I'm not ready to forgive you."

Mason warned me this would happen when I first tried to touch him. He said the bond would make me forgive him, would make me want him, but I didn't believe him. I thought I would be stronger than it.

I hate Zaha.

Mason brushes the wetness off my cheek. "You knew the risks involved in touching me, and I'm not going to make us both miserable by denying it. I'm not a good man, Abby. You're going to forgive me, and I'll let you."

A second tear soaks into my pillow.

Mason continues. "But there'll always be a piece of me that knows it isn't real. Even in thirty years when we have a dozen happy children running around, I'll remember that you're only with me because of our bond. I'll always know your love isn't genuine, that it's been forced and artificially created, and I promise you that knowledge will haunt me."

Mason offers a weak smile. I can't breathe.

I don't know what I want, but it surely isn't that.

"You're deranged if you think I'm going to push twelve children out of my body," I say. I'm unsure how to respond to the other bits of his confession, so I'm choosing to ignore them. I'm good at that.

Mason smirks, accepting the topic change. "But your womb is so fertile…"

I groan. "Get out!" I kick my leg, fighting with the blankets before breaking free and kicking Mason in the ribcage. He howls in laughter, finding himself quite the comedian as he retreats to the door. "Don't ever say that to me again!"

Mason's laughter only grows. I hear it even after he shuts the door and returns to his bedroom. I hate him more than I've ever hated anybody, and I hope he knows it.

It takes me a long time to fall asleep, my thoughts bouncing rapidly between Lill, my family, Mason's confession, and Kie's stony silence. I never thought I'd miss my days working at the marketing firm or my infuriating meetings with Mark. I'd give anything to sit across his cluttered desk reviewing expense reports.

A lightweight, red linen dress hangs over my bedroom door the next morning. I stare at it for half a second before ripping it off the hanger. It's a fucking milkmaid dress, and I just know Mason is the culprit.

It's thankfully not as revealing as I feared, and I mentally curse the shifter as I slip it over my head and tug it over my torso. At least it fits. For once, the hem doesn't drag against the floor or my ankles. The dress ends squarely at my calves, where it's meant to.

Mason and Kie stare when I finally leave the bedroom, and Kie wordlessly slides me a plate of food before returning to the giant book he and Mason are leaning over.

"When is court?" I ask.

"This evening."

Great. They spend the day studying, and I sit on the couch staring at the ceiling. Hours pass at a snail's pace, and by the time the sun begins to drop, I just might die of boredom.

Kie shuts the book he's spent the past two hours reading. "It's time to go." *Finally.*

I look over as he and Mason pull on their signature black gloves. They're pretending they haven't found their mate, which bothers me more than I'd care to admit. They wore their gloves yesterday, too.

Mason forces me to walk between him and Kie, and he drops his hand from my back as we reach the meeting hall. The building was empty yesterday for Mason's ceremony, but not today. The throne room is packed, and I estimate there must be well over a hundred faeries present.

They look rich.

The room falls silent as we enter, all eyes on us. I can't tell which of us is getting the most attention, and I don't look hard enough to find out. The knowledge will only make me nervous.

Mason guides me up the steps leading to the throne. There are now two, one for Mason and a figurative one for Kie. I'm forced to stand behind Mason. I don't think it would've killed them to have a chair brought in for me, even if it's plastic and folded up. It's not too much to ask for.

They're hoping to avoid drawing too much attention to me, but making me join them on the small stage defeats the whole purpose. Mason wasn't willing to entertain the idea of me standing down below with Anox, and he snapped at Kie the one time it was mentioned last night.

Anox and the other council members stand at the bottom of the stairs, and Anox makes a short announcement about prosperity and strength. Does he actually believe that?

Faeries begin loosely lining up at the bottom of the steps. They chat amongst themselves, and servers walk around the room with platters of refreshments. I always imagined court was a solemn and serious affair, but this is more of a cocktail hour.

Anox calls out the name and title of the first person in line. It's a young man, maybe only fourteen or so, and he bows deeply before approaching Mason. I'd expect somebody of his age to be nervous, but he's the picture of confidence.

"Your Majesties," he says.

Kie isn't technically a 'majesty,' I don't think. He's still a prince, which I've gathered is 'highness' here. Is calling Kie a majesty considered a slight against Mason? I can't see the shifter's face, so I look toward Anox instead.

He's giving away nothing. Not helpful.

The boy faces Mason directly and bows again. "My King."

I'd bet money Mason's a little bit hard right now. These faeries have spent their entire life openly hating them, and now they're lining up to earn his favor. I peek at his lap, wanting to confirm, but I don't see anything unusual.

"As you may know, my family's land borders Redstall Forest," the boy starts. "We're worried about shifters trying to claim them now that one of their own is in power."

Damn. They aren't starting with softball questions.

Kie and Mason prepared for about fifty variations of this exact question, and I rock back on my heels as Mason gives a perfectly rehearsed answer about honoring property lines and the strict penalties for unlawfully infringing upon them.

The answer is painfully diplomatic and filled with political correctness, but the boy looks pleased at the end of it.

He steps down, and the next person is announced.

This pattern continues. Some of the faeries have genuine concerns, but most are looking to test Mason. They find sly ways to question his loyalty to the faeries, but Mason takes it in stride. I've never seen him so composed, and I'm impressed.

I didn't think he'd be able to do it.

Does it make a difference? The faeries hate shifters, and I'm not sure Mason's composure will change their perception of him. He needs to start gargling faerie dicks if he wants acceptance. Kie, too. They can gargle together. One takes the shaft and the other takes the balls.

I'll stand in the doorway collecting payment.

Kie remains silent, his chin held high as he stares into the room. He's the picture of grace, and even without a fancy crown sitting on his head, I can tell he's royal. It emanates from him, and it's kind of hot. I'm not sure I've ever seen him disheveled.

Our time in the forest doesn't count.

He's different here, less carefree and open.

"Miss Jacqueline Rowe," Anox announces the next person in line, "and Sir Arthur Rowe."

Jackie stands at the bottom of the steps, patiently waiting her turn to speak with Mason. She's wearing a red dress, not dissimilar to my own, and her white-blonde hair is pulled out of her face in an elegant bun. I can't help but compare myself to her. It's impossible not to.

I didn't bother doing my hair today. It hangs loosely around my shoulders.

How long were Jackie and Kie together? It's obvious they were, but I have no idea how serious it was. I'm not entirely sure I want to know.

Beside Jackie is an older man, I assume her father, given that they share a last name. He looks just like her, and she places her hand on his arm as they walk up the steps. Neither he nor Jackie glance in my direction.

It offends me more than I'd care to admit.

Chapter Eighteen

ABBY

JACKIE CURTSEYS, AND her father gives a deep bow.

"Your Majesties," he says.

I grind my teeth as Jackie copies him, practically purring the words.

Arthur turns toward Kie. "I'm so sorry to hear about the late queen. She was truly a marvelous woman, stolen from us much too soon. You have my sincerest condolences."

This is the first time today someone has acknowledged Kie's mother.

"Thank you," he says. "Your condolences are appreciated."

Arthur continues. "I'd like to revisit the tentative agreement we were sorting through prior to your meeting with Zaha." He shifts his attention to Mason. "I'm sure you're under great pressure to take a wife, and my daughter is still available."

She's available because she's a bitch. I bite my tongue.

Jackie's dad pauses, clearly waiting for Kie or Mason to speak, but he's met with silence. It's awkward, and he clears his throat before continuing. "Jacqueline is greatly respected, and she exhibits the grace and poise befitting a queen. A marriage between our families would be highly advantageous."

142

Jackie smiles, showcasing a mouth full of beautiful, white teeth. I want to punch them out of her head. I want to curb-stomp her face into the fucking ground until her brains are leaking out of her ears and her skull is fragmented into a million tiny pieces.

I blame the bond.

Mason straightens up in his seat, but it's Kie who responds. They didn't plan for this question, and Mason has no rehearsed answer.

"We aren't looking for a wife at the moment," Kie says. He sounds calm. "But we'll take your offer under consideration and be in contact should circumstances change."

Neither Jackie nor her dad looks particularly pleased, and I curl my hand around the back of Mason's throne as they take their leave. That's not the answer I was expecting Kie to give.

I didn't think they'd declare me their mate or anything, but a firm 'no' wouldn't have hurt.

Mason lifts his hand, and Anox calls for a brief recess.

Once chatter has resumed, Kie spins around. "Arthur won't speak against us if he thinks there's a possibility we'll marry his daughter," he explains, his voice low so he isn't overheard. "We need his support, so we can't outright dismiss Jackie."

I hum. "I understand."

Mason turns, and I feel only slightly comforted by the fire in his eyes. He stares at me for a long moment, his gaze shifting from my downturned lips to my heaving chest. I flush when angry, and I can only imagine how red I am right now.

He spins back around without speaking, which Kie also hurries to explain. "It's against tradition for the king to have private conversations while court is being held. This is a public affair, and it's seen as a slight."

Mason groans, shifting in his seat. "I can practically taste her jealousy."

He speaks into the room, to nobody in particular. I look out, but the faeries are busy getting refreshments and chatting. Even the ones in line aren't paying attention.

"Whose?" I ask. "Jackie's?"

Mason shakes his head. "Yours." His voice is so low, I can barely hear what he's saying.

He places a hand over his lap, adjusting himself. Is he hard? Is my jealousy turning him on? I hate men.

"Do you like it?" Mason asks, still speaking to the room. "You can play with it later."

I refuse to let myself so much as consider the offer.

Kie sighs. "Mason…"

It's a quiet warning, but Mason ignores him. "I never had a mouth on it. I want to know what it feels like."

Even if the faeries can't hear Mason's words, they can still see him. He's practically humping the air, his hips twitching every few seconds. The movements are muted, but Mason seems unable to remain entirely still.

"Stop teasing Abby," Kie says.

"*Teasing?*" I can't help but snort, mildly amused. "Mason's poor impulse control isn't having the effect he's hoping for."

Kie raises a brow. "I'm sure."

I wish I could curb-stomp his face into the ground, too.

"I'm not sure what you—" My voice dies out as an intense pain erupts in my chest.

I release a choked gasp, and one hand flies over my heart while the other clutches Mason's throne. I lean over it, unable to make a noise or breathe or even fucking think. The pain lessens as Kie jolts up, and I dig my nails into his arms as he grabs me around the waist and shoves me entirely behind Mason.

His grip is so tight, it hurts, and I wince as he pushes me down, hiding me behind Mason's throne.

Mason's voice echoes through the room. "Shut and lock the doors. Bring anybody lingering in the hallways inside."

There are several undignified shouts. I don't understand what's happening, not in the slightest, and it's impossible to think through the burning pain. Kie's hovering above me, fretting over my chest.

He rips open the front of my dress, and I screech as he exposes my breasts.

"They're still doing it," he says to Mason. He sounds like he's in pain. "They're trying to stop her heart, and they're strong. There's more than one. They're working together."

They're trying to do *what*? Stop my heart? What does that even mean? The pain intensifies, and I instinctively thrash out my arms. My head hits the wooden leg of Mason's chair, but I don't really notice.

Kie winces. "Fuck."

He rips off his gloves and presses his palm flat against my chest. There's an immediate jolt as he ignites the bond, but the intensity is overshadowed by the warmth that erupts where he touches. The pain dissipates, and I grab his wrist as I slump against the ground.

Tears begin pooling and pouring down my cheeks, my physical reaction to the shock and pain impossible to control. I'm faintly aware I'm shaking as Kie presses his forehead against mine. The touch doesn't last long as Mason shoves Kie aside and rips me off the ground.

The shifter is trembling, and he groans as he buries his face into the top of my head.

"I need you to keep me from shifting and killing every faerie inside this room." He sounds desperate. "I need you to do it *now*, Abby."

I don't know how the hell I'm supposed to do that.

I act on instinct as I slide my hand up his torso and around the back of his neck, and I hope he doesn't mind that I'm actively crying as I guide his head down and smash my lips against his.

There's a brief moment of pause, maybe even panic, before Mason relaxes. I'm all too aware this is his second kiss, but his hesitance doesn't last for long. He learns quickly, picking up the movements with ease.

It's a good kiss. I wasn't expecting that.

Mason groans, but it's not a noise of desire. He's fighting with himself, and I hope I'm helping because I have no idea what else to do. I'm pretty sure I read this in a fated mates book once, and it worked.

"You two need to leave," Kie orders. "Preferably now."

Mason disconnects his mouth from mine, and he makes brief eye contact with Kie before carrying me from the room. The faeries part for us, their movements panicked and frantic as they scramble to get out of Mason's way.

Over his shoulder, I see Kie. He still stands near the throne, and he's giving orders I can't hear over the erupting chaos. His eyes briefly meet mine just before the doors are slammed shut behind Mason. They block out all the noise, leaving Mason and me in heavy silence.

His deep breathing is the only sound I hear as he carries me away. His brisk walking pace is faster than my running.

"Keep touching me."

I do, sliding my hands through his hair and pressing my cheek against his.

Mason quickens, and the few faeries we pass dart out of the way when they see us coming. They look scared, and I don't blame them. If Mason weren't begging me to touch him, I'd be afraid he was going to kill me, too.

"What just happened?" I ask.

"Somebody in that room tried to kill you." Mason tightens his grip on my waist as he shoves open the front door to his home. "Kie will take care of it. I will keep you safe. And you will prevent me from losing control and murdering every faerie on the property."

Mason storms toward his bedroom.

"It's easiest for faeries to open portals to locations they've been before," Mason explains. "No faerie has ever been inside my bedroom. You're safest here."

I'm shaking. I didn't realize it until now, but as Mason sets me on his bed, I realize I can't keep myself from shivering. Somebody just tried to kill me—to stop my heart. I don't understand why. Nobody's ever wanted to kill me before, Mason excluded.

Mason tears at the fabric of my dress and places his hand over my bare chest. Feeling my beating heart seems to calm him briefly, but it doesn't last long. He pulls away and rips off his shirt, the buttons scattering. I stare at his chest, not the least bit intrigued by the muscles and skin that typically send me into a flurry.

Mason isn't spending much time admiring me, either.

He pulls me in for a hug, pressing our bare skin together.

He's still shaking. Every muscle in his body is tensing and releasing irregularly, and I hesitate before nudging him to lie down. He does, and I straddle his waist. He can't leave and kill people when I'm sitting on him.

"Please!" Mason gasps. "I can't—"

His back arches in a way I've only seen in horror movies, and a low, pained groan seeps from his throat. I'm not the least bit sure how I'm supposed to keep him calm, and I'm doing a shit job at it.

Mason looks seconds away from losing control.

His shoulder pops forward, dislocating from the joint. It's arguably the most disgusting thing I've ever seen, and I grimace as I grab the muscle and shove it back into place.

"Stop that," I hiss.

Mason thrashes, and his other shoulder shifts forward. I shove that one back into place, too.

"Stop this right now," I say. "Put your shoulders back."

He ignores me, and if one more part of him pops out of place, I will lose the little bit of sanity I have left. I didn't sign up for this when I touched him. I signed up to be a pretty queen consort who frolics through fields of daisies, not an emotional support human.

"I'm a sister," I blurt out. "I have an older brother. His name is Aaron, and he's turning thirty this year. People used to tell me I looked just like him, which I always hated growing up. I thought they were telling me I looked like a boy."

Mason's shoulders return to their sockets.

"Growing up, he was best friends with this boy named Tommy Knocker, who I thought was so cute—" A shoulder pops back out. "I was six!"

Mason glares up at me. "I. Don't. Care!"

"Anyway," I continue. "He and Aaron used to call me a 'troll.' I hated it, and I'm looking forward to rubbing it in Aaron's face that I'm mated to a faerie prince and a shifter king. He's going to be jealous."

Mason chuckles, but it sounds more like a whine than anything else. I'd tell him just how unattractive he's being if I weren't afraid of those damn shoulders popping back out.

"Tell me about your siblings," I order.

"I don't know where to start." Mason gulps. "Kalix is my brother. He's set to become the next Alpha after my father, but I don't have many memories of him. He's two years younger than me…"

Chapter Nineteen

KIERAN

THE ROOM IS angry. Our guests quickly shift between shouting at me, shouting at one another, and shouting at the guards who have trapped them inside the room. They've figured out what just happened to Abby, and they accuse one another with baseless accusations.

I look around, planning my next move. Almost every faerie in this room is from an influential family, and they all know how to manipulate magic.

My bloodline is in power for a reason, though. My ability to manipulate magic is better than any others in the room. I struggled to keep Abby's heart beating and had to go as far as to touch her to do so, so there must have been more than one attacker.

My hands are shaking, a side effect of having used so much magic in such a short period of time. I clasp my hands behind my back to hide it.

Faeries continue shouting, and it takes every bit of concentration I have not to think about Abby. The desperate need to find her is consuming me, but I must deal with this first. I'm going to find out who tried to kill her, and I'm going to serve them to Mason on a silver platter.

It's the worst punishment I can think of.

I keep my hands clasped behind my back as I find and approach Jackie. She's lingering in the center of the room, sipping a glass of water with practiced indifference. She's watching, scanning, and clocking every movement around her. That's her specialty.

Her eyes narrow as I approach, and I just know she's thinking about Abby. Jackie's never been a jealous woman, but she doesn't like my human. The fact that Abby is still alive is how I know Jackie didn't have a part in this.

She's painfully cunning, and if she truly wanted Abby dead, Abby would be dead.

"Is she your mate?" Jackie's voice is loud, drawing attention. It's not an accident. Everybody wants to know, and Jackie's always been good at pleasing the masses. "Well?" she prompts when I don't immediately answer. "Is the human your mate?"

I shake my head. "No."

"You're lying."

"If she were my mate, do you truly think I'd be here dealing with this mess right now?"

I'm fighting with myself not to drop everything and run to Abby. I don't know if she and Mason returned home safely, and the unknown is killing me. What if they were ambushed on their way back? Mason is quick to kill, a trait I've never appreciated more than I do now, but it doesn't take long to stop a heart.

If she were attacked again, Mason would have only seconds to find and eliminate the threat.

I'm taking the fact that he hasn't burst through these doors and begun ripping through the faeries as a good sign. I have to. It's the only way I'm keeping my sanity.

Jackie rocks back on her heels. "You touched her. Mason kissed her."

I shrug. "She has ties to Lillian. She's valuable. Abby can't die, and I did what I needed to keep her alive." My hands have stopped shaking, and I let my arms fall to my sides. "And we all know Mason will fuck anything. Abby's... available."

The lies are sharp on my tongue, disgusting and bitter. I hate saying it, hate insinuating that Abby is a whore Mason's found himself fascinated by. He'd kill me if he heard me talking about Abby like this. Abby probably would, too.

She tends to grow violent when she feels she's been slighted.

I lower my voice. "Do you know anything?"

Jackie takes another sip of water, finishing the glass before gesturing for one of the servers to come forward. She sets her empty glass on the platter, her eyes still flickering around.

"I might," she says.

I roll my shoulders, already knowing this will cause me problems later, before leading her out of the room. Rumors will spread. Mason and Abby will be upset.

"Nobody leaves," I order.

The walkways are dead silent as I bring her to my office. The walls are soundproofed, so we won't be overheard. Indulging a past lover with a private discussion is unheard of for a mated man. I'm putting myself in a position to have my loyalty called into question, which I'm not proud of.

If Jackie realizes Abby is my mate and there's no possibility of marriage, she won't be particularly inclined to help me, though. I need to keep rumors of Abby and me at bay, which means I must do things a mated man would never consider.

I sit behind my desk, eager to put some physical distance between Jackie and me. Guilt is hitting me like a sledgehammer, leaving me burning from the inside out. I need to touch Abby. I need to strip us both bare and feel every inch of her skin pressed against mine, and I fear I might die if I don't get it soon.

Mason has been acting odd lately, desperate and antsy. I knew it was because of the bond, but I didn't truly understand until now. I would give anything to be near Abby, and I don't care who I hurt in the process.

It's a terrible predicament to be in. Mason and I are meant to put the kingdom first, but I know with absolute certainty that I would let it, and everybody inside it, burn if it meant keeping Abby alive.

"Why did you revoke my access to the estate?" Jackie asks, breaking the silence.

I tap my fingers against my desk. She won't give me any useful information until I answer her questions.

"You made Lillian angry," I say, "and I was under the impression she was my mate."

It's not a complete lie. She *did* make Lillian angry, and I *was* under the impression she was my mate. That's not why I had her access revoked, though. She made Abby feel insecure and small, and I couldn't tolerate it.

"You thought Lillian was your mate?" she asks.

I nod.

"But she isn't?"

"She's the daughter of Callie Collins," I admit. "She used magic to forge a mate bond between us. It didn't work on Mason, which is how we discovered the truth."

Jackie hums. I can't tell whether or not she believes me. I'm mostly telling the truth, so I hope she does. I need her help, but I'm not looking to spill every secret with her. My true relationships with Abby and Lillian don't involve her.

Jackie paces the length of my office. "Are you genuinely considering my father's proposal?" She looks around the room as if she hasn't been here a thousand times. "I thought we were in a good place when you left to meet with Zaha."

I don't respond. I'm unsure what to say, and I won't trip over myself making excuses. We both know what Jackie says is true, so there's no point denying it. I'm not going to apologize for it, either.

"I would make a good queen. You admitted so yourself," Jackie continues. "If your concern is my relationship with the shifter, you don't need to worry. I have visited the brothels he favors and learned what he likes. It's nothing unusual, and I'm happy to do it."

I regret ever telling Jackie I believed she would make a good queen. I meant it when I said it, and I still believe that to be true, but it only amplifies my guilt. I gave Jackie a compliment I can't give my own mate.

As much as I enjoy being around Abby, I don't think she'll be a good leader. She's combative and petty, and she seems disinterested in anything that has to do with ruling a kingdom.

I tried encouraging her to participate in my foreign policy discussions with Mason, but she made it abundantly clear that she had no interest in doing so. She was too busy playing with the glued-together crown she found in my desk drawer. I'm excited to see her reaction when she realizes that, as our mate, she has access to over a dozen real ones.

Jackie sits on my couch, her dress fanning around her. I've never seen her wear something so revealing, the fabric sheer and the top practically nonexistent. I know why she did it, but I feel zero interest in the breasts that once enticed me to pull her into dark corners and small nooks.

We have shared almost every first, and it was assumed we'd marry after my coronation. That was until I turned seventeen and realized there were more women out there—women who were excited and eager for my attention. Jackie and I still pulled one another into corners, but I pretended not to notice when I found a dark hickey sucked into her skin and she pretended not to notice when my bed smelled like perfume.

"My father's proposal?" Jackie repeats.

I clear my throat. "My mother died two days ago, and Mason's yet to settle into his position. We're not ready to decide."

Jackie nods. She doesn't look pleased, but she doesn't seem angry.

"I haven't heard anything about an attack against Abby," she says. "The faeries who planned this are tight-lipped, which means we can eliminate about half of the people in that room. Do you have a list of attendees?"

"Yes." I sift through the paperwork on my desk. I was given a list last night, and I frown as I slide it toward Jackie.

She grabs a pen off my desk and immediately begins crossing off names. She's quick, and I chew at my bottom lip as she jumps into action. Her help is going to come with a steep price. She's going to demand something once this is over. It may not be a marriage, but it won't be innocuous. It'll be something I can't provide. I'll need Mason's permission, and knowing him, he won't be eager to give it.

Chapter Twenty

ABBY

MASON'S TAKING ADVANTAGE of my kindness.

He lies below me, his arms sprawled to the sides as he discusses his extensive family history. I'm still straddling him, but only because he claims he'll lose control if I get up. I stopped believing him a long time ago, around the same time his erection began pressing between my thighs.

His pants and my underwear are the only things separating us, and it's all I can think about.

Mason shifts, and I curl my fingers into my thighs. It feels good, but Mason doesn't seem to notice as he continues discussing what he remembers of his childhood home.

"I used to love swimming in the Traul River," he says. "The swimming hole I preferred isn't too far from where we stopped for water." It's also where he and Kie forcibly bathed me, but he avoids mentioning that. "I was the best swimmer."

Mason thinks he's the best at everything he does. Humility isn't a concept he's familiar with.

I shift my weight from side to side, subtly seeking friction between my thighs. The slight movements aren't nearly as satisfying as I'd like, but they're better than nothing. The bond has me so needy, I could probably cum from this alone, which is sad.

"I loved fighting, too," Mason continues.

I hum, staring at his chest. He's muscular, and I so badly want to touch him. My fingers twitch with the urge, the digits threatening to betray me and slide up his torso. He'd let me, and he's probably hoping I'll do precisely that, if not more. He wouldn't be so hard if he weren't.

Mason clears his throat and moves again, fully rolling his hips. It provides me with proper friction, and my eyelids flutter shut as a bolt of pleasure shoots up my spine. I might actually cum from this.

"Mason," I say in warning.

He smiles as his hands curl around my waist, holding me in place. I peer down at him, my stomach in knots. His pupils are blown out, and he licks his lips before pointedly rocking his hips again. It's a confident action, one he's doing because I haven't been as subtle as I'd hoped.

Fuck. "How long have you known?"

Mason snorts. "How long have I known my mate is using my cock to masturbate? I'm clocked into your every movement, Abby, even the ones you think are too small to notice."

So, he's known the entire time. *Wonderful.*

He taps my hip, silently encouraging me to lift. I'm not sure I want to, mainly because Mason can't be trusted. Still, because I love to do things I know I'll later regret, I rise.

"Shifters aren't allowed to train until they're ten, not in any serious manner," Mason says, resuming his earlier conversation. "I was nine when I was given to the faeries."

It takes me several seconds to remember what he was talking about. It's hard to think when he's fiddling between my thighs. I expect him to touch me, but he pulls down his zipper instead.

Does he think we're going to have sex? Not a chance.

"I dreamed of the day I'd be old enough to fight," Mason continues. "I thought myself a little killer, and I even attacked Kie the first time I met him." My underwear is pulled to the side, and something warm smacks against my sex. "I was obviously unsuccessful in my attempt to kill him."

I don't know how he can carry on a conversation at a time like this. One movement, and he'd be inside me. It's all I can think about.

Mason lays his cock flat against his stomach, then pulls me on top. I sit, letting the length of him press between my slit. "This is more comfortable for us both," he says. "You may continue rocking. I'll pretend not to notice. I know you like that."

Mason doesn't know anything about what I like. I have half a mind to get up, rejecting his invitation and hurting his feelings, but I don't. The head of his cock is pressing directly against my clit, and it feels good.

"Kie's back," Mason warns. He props himself up on his elbows and adjusts my dress, covering me. Kie bursts through the bedroom door a second later.

My back is to the door, and I avoid looking at Kie for fear of giving myself and Mason away.

I'm frozen in place. *Kie's back.* Kie was gone because somebody tried to stop my heart. I've been so distracted by Mason that it almost completely slipped my mind. It's only been an hour. How can I have forgotten somebody tried to murder me only an hour ago?

I blame the mate bond. It's messing with my head, warping my sense of importance.

"Jackie and I have narrowed the list to fourteen people," Kie says. "They're being monitored. I want to know what they're up to."

Mason sits up further, and I flinch as his cock drags against my slit. He doesn't spare me a glance as he places a hand against my lower back, keeping me in place.

"Are you kidding me?" he asks. He shakes his head. "You let them go, and you're working with Jackie? What the fuck, Kie? You said you'd take care of this."

Mason's asking the right questions.

Kie sighs, stepping farther into the room. "I can't order the execution of nobility over a hunch. I need proof, and I wasn't going to get it today. Jackie knows everything. You know that as well as I do, and you also know she wasn't involved in the attack."

I hate hearing Jackie's name.

Mason shifts, and I shoot him a warning look. Every movement rubs him against me. It's too much, and I don't want Kie to know what we were up to. It's humiliating. I hate Mason, yet here I am grinding against his bare cock.

I'm ashamed of my attraction toward the shifter, and I don't want anybody, not even Kie, to know about it.

"Who's on the list?" Mason asks.

He presses against my lower back, urging me to grind against him as I was earlier. I shut my eyes, hoping the lack of visual stimulation will help me focus on Kie. My arms are shaking with the effort of holding myself back.

Kie rattles off several names I don't bother listening to, his voice growing louder as he nears. I'm acutely aware of his presence as he walks up behind me.

"Your heart is strong," he says.

He pulls off his gloves, and I twitch against Mason as Kie brings his bare fingers toward me. I feel like a dog begging for pets as I lean into him, desperate for his touch.

Kie skims my shoulder, and I draw in a shaky breath as he pushes my dress sleeve down my arm. He ripped the fabric earlier, making it easy to remove. Mason rolls his hips beneath me, and I pretend to need more stability as I slide my hands up his torso. I doubt I'm fooling anybody.

"Two of them are known shifter supporters," Kie says. He brushes my other sleeve off my shoulder, and his throat bobs as he pulls the front of my dress down. "Jackie thinks—"

Mason grunts. "Stop talking about her."

It's like he's read my mind, and I'm grateful he said it instead of me. I'd rather die than let my jealousy show. It gives Kie and Mason too much power.

Kie's violet eyes flash toward Mason. I take the chance to admire Kie. I've seen Mason's body several times, but I've never really seen Kie. Even when we were in the forest, he was discreet with his nudity.

Mason pushes against my lower back again. The movement rocks me forward, and I hiss as my clit rubs directly against Mason's length. The stimulation is almost constant now. It's too much.

"We should remain open to the possibility that the shifters were behind this," Kie says.

Mason grunts, the vein in his neck bulging as he reaches behind himself and grabs the bed's headboard. He's fully thrusting against me now, meeting each of my slight movements with desperate ones of his own.

"The shifters had no part in this," he says. His knuckles are turning white from how hard he's gripping the headboard.

Kie brushes my hair out of my face, his bare fingers barely grazing my skin. I want more, but I won't ask.

"Harder," Mason orders.

I plant my hands against his chest, growing desperate. This is too much. My hips begin to rock on their own accord.

"Yes." Mason gasps. "Use me."

His moans grow louder, continuing until something sticky

covers my sex and thighs. Did he just cum? I lift my dress to see, and I immediately wish I hadn't. It was one thing to know I'm riding the length of his cock, but it's another to *see* it.

Cum pools from him and spreads against me with every movement. I whine, wanting nothing more than to grab his messy length and slide it inside me. He's beyond thick, and I just know it would feel so good.

Mason continues gripping the headboard. I want to know why he's restraining himself, but I'm afraid asking will encourage him. I'm worried that if he tries to fuck me, I'll let him. It's a miracle I haven't put him inside me yet. It would be so easy.

Kie trails his fingers up and down my neck, but it's all he gives.

"Kie," I plead. I'm not sure what I want from him, but it's more than this.

He *tsks*. "Not yet."

I snap my jaw shut with a quiet click. *Not yet?* What's that supposed to mean?

I brush him away, flicking his fingers off my neck. I won't beg him to touch me, not after the way he's treated me. Mason, despite his faults, is at least trying. He's apologized, and I can tell it's sincere.

Kie can't even muster up one measly apology.

He can suck my balls.

I continue grinding against Mason, moving in the way that feels best for me. I'm so close, and the way Mason's staring at me as if this is the best thing he's ever witnessed isn't helping.

"You prefer me." He moans. "My mate prefers me. My cock, my affection, and my touch."

Oh, for fuck's sake. Give an inch, and he takes a mile.

Mason wraps an arm around my waist and pulls me against his chest, quickly replacing Kie's removed fingers with his mouth.

The feeling of his tongue on my neck is enough to push me over the edge, and my movements grow jerky as I finally find my orgasm.

It's everything I hoped it would be, and I drop my head against Mason's chest as I struggle to catch my breath. I needed this, and I take a moment to compose myself before smoothly sliding off the shifter's lap.

I made a mess of him, but I refuse to look as I straighten out my dress and attempt to pull the sleeves back up my shoulders. I need to change, and then I need to take a long shower and contemplate my life. This has been fun and all, but attempted murder is where I draw the line.

Kie lingers in the corner of the room. He looks upset, but I refuse to allow myself to care.

I clear my throat. "What happened after we left?"

The sudden guilty expression that crosses Kie's face is unexpected. He grimaces and glances away, his lips pursing. I immediately know it has something to do with Jackie. I cross my arms over my chest and tap my foot against the ground.

Mason remains where he is, lying on the bed with his arms sprawled to the sides. He looks content, and he doesn't even attempt to cover himself up.

I focus on Kie. "Well?"

Chapter Twenty-One

ABBY

KIE BLOWS A strand of hair out of his eye. "Jackie is well-connected," he starts. "I brought her to my office so we could talk privately, and we reviewed the list of faeries in attendance today. We were alone, but nothing happened between us. I promise."

Mason props himself up on his elbows, a smile toying at the corners of his lips as he glances between me and Kie. He's enjoying this, probably because it further pushes his agenda of being my favorite.

I resist the urge to grab one of the study books off his desk and throw it at him.

"Did Jackie ask about our relationship with Abby?" Mason asks. He's fanning the flames. Kie recognizes it, too, if his frosty glare is anything to go by.

"She did." Kie offers no further explanation.

He's stupid if he thinks I'll let him leave it at that. This is my assassination attempt we're talking about. I don't like Jackie, but I don't care that he spoke to her alone. I deserve to know every little detail.

"…And?" I ask.

Kie hesitates. "And I said you weren't our mate. I told her

your connection to Lillian makes you valuable and that Mason kissed you because he's a whore and you're available."

Mason's smile falls, but I have a feeling it has little to do with Kie calling him a whore.

Kie ignores the angry shifter. "I'm sorry, Abby. I didn't—" He stops to collect his thoughts before continuing. "I'm sorry."

I wait for him to elaborate further, but he doesn't. He's not trying to make excuses or defend his actions, which I surprisingly admire. If I'm honest with myself, I don't mind what Kie said. If people are going to try to kill me off nothing more than assumptions, I don't want to know what they'll do when they have confirmations.

Mason rises, finally putting his cock away, and approaches Kie. I'm not interested in their dick-measuring contest, and I shove my hair out of my face before spinning around and leaving the room. I need to shower.

Two pairs of footfalls follow me into the hallway bathroom.

"Go away."

Two pairs of footfalls retreat from the hallway bathroom, and the door shuts quietly behind me.

Mason's cum covers my inner thighs, and I want it gone. Intimacy was a good distraction from today's attempted murder, but the moment is over and I've been pulled back into reality. There's a small pile of clothing sitting on the counter by the time I finish showering. Men's clothing I deduce belongs to Kie. I'm ready to own some things of my own.

They supply me with women's clothing every morning, but I want a wardrobe to choose from. I'd like to pick my daily outfits, not rely on whatever they've decided I should wear.

Kie's waiting for me outside the bathroom door. "Mason and I will bring our mattresses into your bedroom and sleep on the floor tonight."

I frown. "That seems unnecessary."

"It's far from unnecessary," Mason says, stepping out of his bedroom. His hair is wet, and he's in fresh clothing. "We don't know who tried to harm you, and we intend to stay close until we do."

"Why me?" I ask. "It's *you* they don't like, so why kill me?"

Kie swallows. "We can't survive without you. At least not in any meaningful way. We wouldn't be fit to lead, and we'd be stripped of our titles. Killing you is the easiest way to remove Mason and me from power."

"But nobody knows I'm your mate," I point out.

"We've not confirmed anything, but I'm sure some people assume," Kie says. "Mason publicly touched you after my mother's murder, but it's been largely overlooked. There's a possibility somebody is reading into that, or maybe Lill said something before leaving."

Was Lill involved? Mason and Kie probably think she was. I'm trying hard not to think about it. For years, it's been her and me against the world. When we were fourteen, she pushed my boyfriend to the ground and kicked out his knee because he tried flirting with her. I struggle to believe she would knowingly steal my mates. Or send an assassin after me.

She's not a bad person.

I walk into my bedroom, and Kie and Mason take turns dragging in their mattresses. I partially thought they were joking, and I sit in the center of my bed while they get situated. My bed is large enough to fit the three of us, but I don't invite them to share.

The bond is urging me to. It's forcing me to fantasize about sleeping with both of them wrapped around me, but I fight it.

Their mattresses barely fit in my room, and I purse my lips as Mason and Kie struggle to lay them flat beside one another.

"Why don't you two share?" I eventually ask. Their

mattresses are comically large, and there's more than enough room for them to squeeze together on one.

Mason shoots me a sideways look. "Because I don't want to share a bed with Kie."

"Have you two truly never slept together?" They've denied it several times, but I've always suspected. I gesture between them. "It's entirely platonic?"

Mason rolls his eyes. He looks mildly annoyed, which I'm choosing to believe isn't because of me. "Yes, Abby." He huffs. "It's entirely platonic. I've never had sex with Kie, nor do I want to."

I hum, dropping the subject. I'm curious if they've ever shared a woman, but I'm not mentally prepared for that answer.

There are several annoyed grunts and muffled curses until they get their mattresses situated, conveniently in a position that has Mason pressed up against the side of my bed. I'm sure it isn't accidental, and I debate threatening him to stay away before ultimately deciding against it. I don't think he'll try to sneak into my bed after the rejection he faced last time. Plus, a small, minuscule part of me wants him close.

I'm terrified of the faeries trying to kill me again, and I trust Mason to keep me safe. He's big and scary, and he likes to kill people.

The bedroom light is shut off, and I settle as best I can. I already know I won't find sleep, but shutting my eyes and trying is better than nothing. Kie and Mason toss and turn, their sheets rustling as they move around.

What does my family think happened to me? I haven't spent nearly as much time thinking about them as I should, maybe because none of this seems real. There's been a lingering feeling that all of this is fake, that I'm going to wake up in bed to discover I've been dreaming. That's what I hoped would happen while traveling through the forest. I must've pinched myself a million times trying to wake up.

"Abby?"

My mattress dips as Kie sits on the edge of my bed, his vibrant violet eyes practically shining in the dark. What's with these men welcoming themselves to my bed? Kie scoots closer, his movements silent and cautious.

I peer around him, eyeing the shifter on the floor. Mason lies on his stomach, his face buried into his pillow. I doubt he's sleeping, but he pretends.

Kie's significantly more reserved than the shifter, and we haven't spent any meaningful time together since returning from the Redstall Forest. He's practically a stranger now. I don't recognize the man I traveled through the forest with. That Kie was easygoing and loud, almost to the point of being annoying. This one is pensive and quiet, constantly focused on completing the next task.

If I'm honest with myself, I'm not even sure he's interested in me. Not the way Mason is. Mason's obsessed with everything I do, but Kie doesn't show much emotion. It's the only reason I'm not pushing him away right now. This is the most he's given me, and I'm curious.

Kie pulls my comforter to my waist. I'm still wearing his shirt, and his lips twitch as he eyes the material. It's almost a smile, and I swallow past the lump in my throat as he begins lifting the fabric up my torso, exposing my stomach. He pauses below my breasts.

"May I?" he asks.

I hesitate, then nod. Kie raises my shirt over my chest, then places his palm over my heart. His bare fingers curl into my skin, and I suppress a shiver. Several heartbeats pass before he drops his hand into his lap, and I pull my shirt back down.

"I didn't want to trigger our bond," he admits.

I've gathered as much.

"You don't trust me," he continues. "I see how you're fighting the bond with Mason, and I didn't want to add to that. I wanted to build trust between us first, maybe even become friends, before touching."

Kie pulls the bedsheets back up my torso, covering me.

"I'm sorry I spoke to Jackie privately," he says. "You don't seem too upset, but it was inappropriate. The faeries would view it as a form of infidelity."

I shrug. "I don't like Jackie, but I dislike being murdered even more."

I'm pleased they were able to narrow down the list of suspects, and I hope he has answers soon.

Kie cracks a half smile. "You're supposed to be angry with me."

"I am," I admit. "Just not about that."

I lick my lips, working up the courage to ask a question I really want an answer to. There's a good chance Kie's response will hurt my feelings, but I need to know.

"Are you disappointed to have a human as your mate?"

Kie's answer is immediate. "I'm not disappointed—not even close. You being human doesn't bother me in the slightest, just like I'm not bothered that Mason is a shifter. It makes you who you are." He taps his fingers against my mattress. "I just wish we'd met under better circumstances."

He climbs off my bed and returns to his mattress. I stare at where he sat, ruminating over his words, before lying back down. I wish that, too.

Chapter Twenty-Two

MASON

ABBY SITS ON the couch, her knees tucked into her chest as she stares into the fireplace. She's been catatonic for the better part of the morning, pretty much from the moment she woke up. She gasped as she jolted upright in bed, her sudden movements putting Kie and me on high alert.

She refuses to tell me what she dreams about, but it's weighing heavily on her.

I fear it was about me or Kie, about the bonds she's made more than apparent she doesn't want. Or maybe it was about Lillian. Or possibly Jackie. It could also be about the attempted murder. Or maybe about her family. There are too many options.

Kie stands in the kitchen. He's staring at the counter, which he's been doing for the past forty-five minutes. Things never used to be this awkward between us. I want to crawl out of my skin and disappear.

"You should relocate to my mother's office today," Kie says, breaking the silence.

Abby looks over. I shrug, my gaze flickering between the two before returning to the map on the dining table. Why hasn't Abby told Kie about the map she found in my bedroom? What's she waiting for?

"I don't want your mother's office," I admit.

Each council member and several high-ranking nobles have offices on the property, but I was never given one. I attend meetings when requested, but I never held my own. The queen never found it necessary to provide me with an office despite my title of prince. Kie and I shared more often than not, much to her annoyance.

The queen was never unkind to me, and I'd go as far as to say she treated me well when I was a young, frightened child, but we grew apart as I ventured into adulthood. She found me too troublesome to bother with, and I decided that every faerie besides Kie wasn't worth my time.

"You should still take it," Kie urges. "It sends the impression that you're settling into your position."

"Hm." I'm not going to do that. "I'll consider it."

There's shuffling outside, boots scraping against dirt before somebody knocks on our front door. I've never been more relieved to have a distraction. Kie is closer to the door, but he doesn't answer. He moves toward Abby instead. I wait until he's in position before responding.

Anox stands on the doorstep, frowning.

"What?" I ask.

"Do you two intend to hide in your home all day?" He sounds just like the queen, and I press my lips together as he continues. "We received word from Alpha Theon this morning." He extends an arm, gesturing inside my home. "May I come in?"

My gaze shifts to the guards behind Anox. They're pretending not to be eavesdropping, but I know better.

I move aside, allowing Anox to enter. I hate this little robed man, and I glare at the top of his head as he saunters inside with more confidence than he deserves. I'd strip him of his position if it wouldn't cause such intense backlash.

Kie remains where he is, continuing to block Anox's view of Abby. The council leader is wise to avoid looking even remotely in her direction.

Anox is an intelligent man. He knows better than to push the limits of a shifter whose mate was just attacked. Inviting himself inside my home is already teetering on the edge, but we didn't leave him many options. Kie and I couldn't agree on who should remain with Abby today, so we both decided to stay.

The mere thought of leaving her fills me with all-consuming dread. There's no conceivable way I'll be able to get anything productive done without her in my direct line of sight, not until we've dealt with the faeries who attacked her.

Anox clears his throat. "The scouts you sent to the Redstall Forest outpost met with one of Alpha Theon's representatives late last night. It wasn't the friendliest of exchanges, but we received this letter from Alpha Theon."

Anox pulls a sealed letter from his robes. I'm surprised he didn't take it upon himself to read the contents.

"Was there any mention of Callie or Lillian?" I ask, taking the letter.

"No." Anox shakes his head. "Alpha Theon's representative refused to speak with our scouts about anything of value. The letter was passed off, poorly concealed threats were shared, and our scouts were dismissed."

Not surprising. Relations between the shifters and faeries have been steadily declining for years.

Anox gestures to the letter. "What does it say?"

Wouldn't he like to know? I blink, pointedly tucking the letter into my pocket. Anox would never have been so daring with Queen Gitta. He's testing my boundaries, seeing how much he can get away with.

"We'll come to the council should we have any concerns," I say.

Anox purses his lips. "Very well."

He lowers his gaze and excuses himself, slamming the front door with more force than necessary. He's upset with my dismissal. I don't give a fuck. I wait until he's gone before ripping open the letter.

There's not much here—a date, time, and location.

"Alpha Theon has requested a meeting at the mouth of Traul River tomorrow morning," I say.

Kie snorts. "He wants to meet on shifter lands? That's not going to happen. We can meet on neutral ground, and—"

Traul River is deep within the forest. It's easily a two-day trip for a faerie. If there were magic, they could teleport, but it's rare for a faerie to possess enough power to open back-to-back portals, especially in a location without magic to draw from. Kie and maybe a few nobles can do it, but the list is small.

In theory, we could have a unit of faeries travel into the forest through a portal made by Kie. It would weaken him to hold it open for so long, which wouldn't leave him with enough strength to adequately protect Abby. The soldiers can then open themselves a portal and retreat should things go south, but it's risky. There's not enough margin for error, and it puts Abby at risk.

I don't know any other faeries who can hold open a portal long enough for a unit of soldiers to travel through. I can make it if I shift into my animal form and run through the night.

I doubt my father would invite me onto his lands if he didn't have something to share. He has either Callie or Lillian, probably both. He's willing to negotiate.

"It's not possible," Kie says. "I'm not sure what game Alpha Theon is playing at, but—"

"I can do it," I interrupt. I have no other choice. "If I take off from the entrance at Farbay and run throughout the night, I'll make it to Traul River just before sunrise."

Abby's chewing her fingernails, gnawing at the skin like a little cannibal. She's nervous for my safety. I can see it in her eyes. I can't remember the last time somebody was worried about me, and my chest fills with warmth as her gaze flickers rapidly between me and Kie.

Kie shakes his head. "I can open a portal there and back. I'll go."

"Why?" His offer makes no sense. "Alpha Theon will be expecting me. He won't be willing to negotiate with you, especially considering your recent title change. He wants to meet with the king. Me."

My words are harsh, but they're true. For the first time in our lives, my word holds more value than Kie's.

"You can't go, Mace," Kie says. His voice is deceptively soft. He uses it when he's trying not to upset me. "Your father isn't the honorable man you think he is. He'll take advantage of you, and it's best if you remain here with Abby."

I work my jaw side to side, my eyes darting toward Abby. I don't appreciate what Kie's implying, but I don't want to lose my composure in front of her. I'm trying really fucking hard not to frighten her, and I've been doing an excellent job these past few days.

"I am perfectly capable of handling this meeting myself," I insist.

Faeries hate shifters, especially my father. They want to see us eradicated, they always have, and Kie is no different. He may not voice his feelings out loud, especially not to me, but they're there. He hates my kind, and he'll disrespect my father. He can't be the one to go.

Kie drags his fingers through his hair. "There are things you don't know about Alpha Theon."

"Like what?"

I'm under no illusions that my father is a wonderful, loving man. He abandoned me to the faeries. He's a shit father, I know that, but that doesn't mean he isn't a fair leader. Besides, I'm still his son. Family means something to shifters.

Kie looks like he wants to scream, but he won't. He won't lose composure. It's not the way faeries operate.

Kie sucks in a deep breath before continuing. "My mother offered your family to visit you on neutral grounds every summer for fifteen years, and she even offered to give you leave, allowing you to enter the shifter lands for a week for your eighteenth birthday. Every attempt, and there were hundreds, she made to reconnect you with your family was rejected."

My heart thumps, and I swallow down the painful disappointment.

Kie continues. "My mother only ever received one letter from Alpha Theon that addressed you, and—"

"Where is it?"

Kie blinks. "What?"

"Where is the letter?"

I don't care to hear his inaccurate interpretation of what my father said, and the queen was notorious for saving her correspondence. She was painfully organized, and nobody knows her office better than Kie. It was meant to be his one day, after all.

"I don't think you—"

"Where. Is. It."

Kie sighs. "Top left drawer of her desk."

I turn toward Abby. "Stay here."

Leaving her makes my skin itch, but I push the discomfort aside. Kie is more than capable of watching her for a few minutes. I repeat that to myself as I storm through the property.

The late queen's office is beside Kie's, and it's locked. I break the handle and force my way inside, my ears ringing as I rip open the top drawer of her desk. There are several letters inside, and I flick through them before finding the one from my father. I faintly recognize his handwriting.

There are only two sentences inside.

Mason's health is not my concern. Do not contact me regarding this issue again.

I check the date, sinking to the floor. I was a child when I was sent here, and my immune system wasn't yet developed. I fell sick about four months after arriving, and the faeries didn't have the means to treat me.

Queen Gitta promised to write to my father and ask him to send the pack doctor, but nothing ever came of it. I got better on my own after a few weeks.

I chew at my bottom lip, rereading those two sentences. This doesn't change anything. We've secured a meeting with Alpha Theon, and I intend to go. If not for myself, then for Kie. Callie and Lillian betrayed the faeries and murdered his parents. He deserves answers.

Footfalls near, both with gaits I'm familiar with. I turn toward the broken door just as Abby and Kie walk inside. I don't appreciate them following me.

Abby glances at the letter resting on my thighs, and she lingers by the door before slowly approaching. I remain seated, hating the pitying look in her eye as she reads my father's calloused words.

I don't want her pity.

Still, I don't reject her comfort as she sets the letter aside and lowers herself onto my lap, straddling me. She never openly touches me, and I'm just desperate enough to let it happen.

She brushes her fingers down the side of my jaw. "I'm sorry, Mace."

Abby rarely uses my nickname, but I like it when she does. I especially like it when she follows it up by kissing my jaw. Her lips are soft, and my eyelids slip shut as her warm breath fans over my neck.

"Let Kie go." My eyes fly open. Abby continues. "Stay here with me."

"No." I pull my face away from her lips, not appreciating her using kisses to mollify me. "There's no magic. Kie will be weak and vulnerable."

Abby trails her fingers down the side of my neck, her touch distracting. "What if both of you go? Kie opens the portals, and you keep him safe."

"And what about you?" I ask. "We can't leave you here. It's not an option."

Abby shrugs. "I can come, too."

That's never going to happen. Not in a million years.

Chapter Twenty-Three

ABBY

KIE AND MASON are upset. It's evident in the way Mason stomps around the room and Kie barks orders. Kie's usually polite, but not today. He's taking a page out of Mason's book.

Kie grunts. "Let me know when it's done."

He slams the front door shut and turns back to the room. We're leaving for the forest early tomorrow morning, and Kie is losing it. Mason isn't far behind. I'm nervous, but I'm also secretly pleased to be getting my way.

We're going to the meeting together.

Kie and Mason hate this plan. It's obvious they hate it with every fiber of their beings, but there are no other options. Mason can't meet Alpha Theon alone, and Mason insists his father won't speak to Kie. Both men insist I can't be left alone here.

The only solution is for all three of us to go.

It's dangerous, but I suspect there's just as much danger here. Somebody already tried to kill me, a fact I'm doing my best to forget. I look down, fiddling with the plastic tiara I stole from Kie's office.

Mason paces the living room, then disappears down the hallway. His bedroom door slams shut a second later. He's been unnervingly quiet since finding that letter. He must be devastated.

Kie shifts, placing himself in front of me. The bond has my fingers twitching with the urge to touch him, to feel his bare skin against mine. I run my thumbs over the fake stones on the tiara instead, distracting myself with it.

"I don't know what to say to you." Kie lets out a dry laugh. "I don't know how to have a relationship with you after everything. I thought I was doing right by my people, but at what cost?" He stares at the tiara, refusing to make eye contact with me. "And now we're bonded. I can see how you're fighting the pull to Mason. You're going to fall in love with us. You have no choice, and I'd do anything to stop it." Kie's voice cracks. "I wish I could kill our bond."

I step back. What am I supposed to say to that?

Kie continues. "I'd rather spend the rest of my life alone than with a woman who's forced to love me."

"But you can't." I set the tiara on the edge of the couch. "You can regret what you did to me, but you can't take it back. You regret touching me and igniting the bond, but you can't take it back. What's done is done, and I'm sick and tired of you and Mason acting like I'm so entranced by the bond that I don't have a functioning brain behind it."

Kie gulps.

I continue. "I'm attracted to you two, but I'm not some damsel hopelessly in love with you. I haven't been robbed of coherent thought, and it's time you two stop bitching about things you can't change and do something productive. Buy me flowers or cook me a romantic meal. Be vulnerable. I honestly don't fucking care, just—"

"Vulnerable?" Kie cuts my sentence short. "I'm terrified. I'm terrified Alpha Theon is plotting something. I'm terrified Mason is going to be hurt. I'm terrified of letting my people down. Is that vulnerable enough for you? Do you need more? I can't stop listening to your heart, and I've been funneling magic into it since you were attacked. I haven't slept because I can't use magic when sleeping, and I can't leave you unprotected."

His words take a moment to register. That's a lot to take in, but one part stands out.

"When was the last time you slept?" I ask.

I know he didn't the day his mother died. He was up all night trying to make sense of Lill's attack and preparing for Mason's coronation. The following night, he and Mason were up until the early morning reviewing those foreign policy books.

We went to bed early last night, and I was under the impression that Kie, Mason, and I all got a whole night of sleep. I was certainly exhausted after the execution attempt, and Mason slept so deeply that his heavy breathing woke me several times.

"Kie?" I urge.

He looks away, refusing to answer.

"Mason!" My voice is shrill, and the ground vibrates as Mason storms out of his bedroom. He's on us within seconds.

"What?" He glances between Kie and me. "Is Kie bothering you?"

His face is suspiciously red and splotchy, and the green of his eyes looks extra vibrant. Was he crying? The thought has my heart thumping. I want to ask if he's okay, but I don't think he'd appreciate me acknowledging it.

"How long can faeries go without sleep?" I ask instead.

Kie shoots me a look of betrayal, but I don't care. I don't trust Alpha Theon, and Kie needs to not be on the verge of a mental breakdown when we meet him.

Mason shrugs. "A day, maybe two. Why?"

I meet Kie's glare. I won't feel guilty for caring about his health. "Kie hasn't slept in three days, and he's been funneling magic into me since the attack."

Mason cocks his head to the side. "Kie? Is that true?"

"I'm fine." Kie snatches my tiara off the couch. "I need to pack."

"You need sleep." Mason and I speak at the same time. It's unnerving, and I shoot the shifter a dirty look before continuing. "I'm safe with Mason, and you're nearby if anything happens."

Kie rocks back on his heels.

"Abby will sleep with you," Mason offers. Excuse me? "She needs rest, too."

Abby can decide for herself if she needs rest, which she doesn't. I'm managing perfectly fine, and I don't want to sleep with Kie. I don't want to sleep with either of them. Besides, it's too early for bed. I've never been one for naps.

"I said I'm fine," Kie urges. "We need to brush up on the terrain surrounding Traul River. I'm thinking—"

I want to rip out my hair. "For fuck's sake!"

I grab Kie's wrist, and I do my best to ignore the way the contact makes my heart swell as I drag him toward Mason's bedroom. Kie's had women in his bed, and given the sheer number of condoms in the bedside drawer of the guest room, I'm willing to bet he's entertained women there, too. I don't want my first time sleeping with my mate to be in a bed he's shared with others.

Mason admitted that he has never had a woman in his room, so I'm taking ownership of his bed for the evening.

I'm half-expecting Mason to make a fuss as I drag Kie into his room. He doesn't say anything, though. Neither does Kie.

"Strip," I order the faerie.

Kie hesitates, his violet eyes looking everywhere but at me, before he blows out a long breath and tugs his shirt over his head. I do my best not to stare at his toned abdomen as I begin undressing.

"I don't want to wear a dress in the forest," I say. "I want pants and a shirt, preferably stretchy and form-fitting."

Kie nods, stripping to his underwear. The tight black fabric does little to hide the skin underneath. I want to see him, mainly out of pure curiosity, but I won't ask. He doesn't deserve my eyes on his penis. Mason doesn't, either, but that ship has already sailed.

I point to the bed. "Lie down."

Mason's dresser is full of lounge clothing, and I find the lounge pants he gave me to wear on my first day here and a comfortable shirt.

Kie slides under the sheets, his movements robotic and tense. He acts like a midday nap is going to kill him.

I draw in a slow breath before joining him in bed. It's awkward, and we shift until he wraps himself around me, my back to his front. I'm allowing the man who tried gifting me to a god to spoon me. I've lost all control of my life.

I clear my throat. "Go to sleep."

Kie slips a hand up my shirt and presses his palm over my heart, and I involuntarily shiver. Our bond is working overtime to make me comfortable with him, and it's succeeding.

"You're okay," he whispers.

I don't think he's talking to me. Still, I respond.

"I'm okay. Go to sleep, Kie."

Chapter Twenty-Four

ABBY

ONCE KIE FALLS asleep, he's out cold. The hand he insisted on resting over my heart falls limp, and his arm on my waist grows heavy. I feel a strange sense of accomplishment at having successfully gotten him to sleep.

Mason sneaks into the room, his eyes darting rapidly between Kie and me as he packs a bag for tomorrow. I assume he's going to pack one for me, too. I hope so, at least. We don't plan on being gone for long, but Kie and Mason want to be prepared.

"Are you hungry?" Mason whispers.

I shrug, and Mason returns several minutes later with a platter of food. Kie groans, rolling over, and I take that as my opportunity to sit up and eat. I'd leave the bed altogether if I didn't fear it would wake Kie up.

Mason finds excuses to linger in the room while I eat, but we don't speak out of fear of waking the testy faerie. Should I ask Mason about his father? Does he even *want* to talk about it? I can't tell.

"You should rest, too," Mason eventually says.

"I'm not tired."

Mason raises a brow. "You sound like Kie."

He shuts his curtains, plunging the room into darkness. I glare in his general direction, or at least what I assume to be his general direction.

"What are you doing?" I ask.

"Go to sleep, Abby."

The empty platter is eased out of my hands, and the bedroom door shuts a second later. I'm not tired, and I cross my arms over my chest as I sink back down. Kie rolls over again, pulling me into his arms.

He hooks a thigh over my waist for good measure, trapping me in place. I let myself enjoy it, but only because he's sleeping and won't know. I can't remember the last time I was cuddled, and it's nice. I feel warm, and safe.

I fall asleep.

I don't wake up until the next morning.

I'm in only my underwear, and my skin is slick with sweat. The faerie beside me is a furnace, and our sticky bodies are practically fused together.

Something is quietly vibrating on the bedside table on my left, and I fight back a yawn as I turn to see what it is. On the table is a dark shard of glass that wasn't there yesterday, and I raise my brows as I realize it's one of those magic enhancers Samuel used.

He used his to create a map of the realm. I haven't seen one since. Mason must have placed it here last night.

Kie groans, drawing my attention. We shifted while sleeping, and he's practically sprawled over me. His violet eyes blink open, and he plants his palms beside my shoulders before pushing his upper body off me. His shoulders and biceps flex, the muscles bulging as he leans forward and touches the dark glass.

"I didn't know you had one of those," I say.

Kie shrugs. "Most faeries in the capital don't use them. We're strong, and the magic boost they provide is negligible. It is helpful for small things, though, like this. Mine has been infused to vibrate every morning."

The buzzing stops, and I relax back into the mattress. Then I remember we need to leave for the shifter lands and jolt out of bed. I left my dress on the floor last night, but it's gone. I bet Mason stole it, and I chew at the inside of my cheek until I spot two piles of folded clothing on his desk.

They weren't here last night.

Both outfits are black, and I fight back a smile as I realize one is meant for me. Mason found me a pair of tight pants and a stretchy long-sleeved shirt. The ensemble is identical to the outfits they wore in the forest. We're going to match.

"Do you feel better?" I ask Kie.

He sits up, watching me dress.

"I do," he admits. "I always thought sharing a bed would be uncomfortable, but I enjoyed it."

My movements falter, but I quickly regain my composure. It never occurred to me that this would be the first time Kie shared a bed. I suppose the risk of accidentally touching skin during sleep was too high.

Kie clears his throat. "Did you enjoy sleeping with me?"

Yes. I'm not going to tell him that, though.

I grab the second pile of clothing and toss it toward Kie. He smoothly catches the fabric, his piercing gaze never once leaving mine. It feels like he's staring into my soul, and I don't like it.

"I should find Mason," I say.

I'm surprised the shifter didn't crawl into bed last night or, at the very least, drag in a mattress and sleep on the floor. Mason's been vocal about his desire to be near me, and I doubt he'd allow me to have alone time with Kie out of the goodness of his heart.

He'll weasel his way between us, and he'll do it with a smile.

I push open the bedroom door and walk down the hallway,

peering into every room I pass. They're all empty, and when I round the corner that leads to the open living space, I finally spot Mason.

He's sprawled across the couch, still in yesterday's clothing, with his feet dangling off one side and an arm hanging off the other. Sitting on his chest is a folded piece of paper, and upon closer inspection, I realize it's the letter his father wrote.

Mason fell asleep rereading this.

My heart lurches.

Three backpacks are resting against the edge of the couch, and I step over them before snatching the letter off Mason's chest. His nose crinkles, and I just know he's awake and smelling to see who's near him.

He relaxes once he realizes it's just me. I'm not sure what I'm doing, and I drag my fingers through my hair before setting the letter on the coffee table and throwing myself on top of Mason. I feel bad for him, and instinct tells me this is what I should do.

The shifter immediately wraps his arms around my waist, trapping me against him. My knee falls between his thighs, and my arms are squished between our torsos.

"Mason," I grunt.

"I'm jealous you slept with Kie first," he says. "And in *my* bed, no less."

He's not really upset. He walked into his bedroom several times while Kie was sleeping, and not once did he look the least bit jealous. He's only making a big deal about it because he's hoping to guilt me into agreeing to sleep with him, too. It's not going to work.

I huff, pushing myself off Mason as Kie walks into the room.

The faerie's gaze flickers between us and the letter on the table. Mason clocks the action, and he snatches up the letter and shoves it into his pocket.

"Give me five minutes to change," Mason says, rising from the couch. "We should leave soon."

Kie nods, his lips flattened into a straight line. What's he thinking? I wonder what Mason's thinking, too. My mom used to make my brother and me hold hands and share compliments whenever we got on her nerves with our fights, and I'm contemplating making Kie and Mason do the same. I would if we weren't in a time crunch.

Mason disappears, taking his letter with him, and Kie retreats into the kitchen. He fills a platter with food, then slides it in my direction. It's a healthy breakfast, full of protein.

"Eat up," he orders. "We have a long morning ahead of us."

We plan to be back before anybody notices we're gone. Kie and Mason don't want the council, Anox specifically, to know we've left. Anox will throw a fit, and Kie and Mason don't want to risk anybody finding out. It would be too easy for an opportunistic faerie to take advantage of the kingdom being temporarily left without leadership.

I'm shoving the last bite of food in my mouth when Mason returns, now dressed in matching black attire. I want to joke about it, but now doesn't seem like the right time. Things are too tense, too awkward. I wish I had been paired with mates who don't have such complicated relationships with their families. It's not something I'm familiar with, and I don't know how to address it.

"Let's go," Mason says.

He throws his and my bags over his shoulder. I extend my arm, not needing him to carry my things, but Mason doesn't hand it over. If anything, he looks amused by the mere thought of him *not* carrying my bag.

"I wish I had that treatment," Kie mumbles, brushing past me.

Mason shoots him a sharp look. "Sleep tonight and I'll consider it."

Kie secures his bag over his shoulders before ordering Mason and me to stand aside so he can open a portal. He's opened them a few times in front of me. The one after finding Lill was violent, and he practically poured magic into the ground to open the portal to the gods' realm.

This time, it's closer to what Lill did. There's no abrupt or aggressive tearing of the world. The air begins to ripple, then splits open like a zipper unlatching. Instead of the black couch I've been familiar with, I'm now staring into thick woodlands.

Mason takes my hand, his gloved fingers curling around my palm, before pulling me through the portal. I squeeze my eyes shut as dizzying weightlessness hits me, and I only open them once the smell of earthy dirt hits my nose.

Kie has joined us, and the portal is gone.

I look around, an uncomfortable feeling of déjà vu hitting me. The last time I was in these woods, I was angry, hungry, and so fucking scared. Kie and Mason were still planning on giving me to Zaha, and I was half-convinced they were going to rape me. I thought Lill was totally innocent.

Now we stand here as mates. Mates who don't get along, but mates nonetheless. Queen Gitta is dead, my best friend is a wanted murderer, the shifter who tried to kill me begs me to share a bed with him, and Kie's refusing to sleep out of fear my heart will stop beating.

I turn toward Mason. "Are there any shifters nearby?"

He shakes his head, the column of his throat bobbing as he gulps. He's nervous. I don't blame him. This will be his first time seeing his father since he was sent to live with the faeries, and emotions are high after finding that letter.

"My senses are better in my animal form," Mason admits.

"I see." I reach for my bag, intending to pull it off his shoulder so he can shift.

Mason shakes his head and pulls the bag out of my reach.

"What're you doing?" I ask.

Mason meets Kie's eye over my head, the pair having a silent conversation. I hate it when they do that. I don't appreciate feeling left out, and I glare at the underside of Mason's chin until he shifts his attention back to me.

Mason clears his throat. "You're afraid of my animal form."

What? Is this man stupid?

"I'm afraid of dying even more," I say. I had to explain this to Kie after he confessed to meeting with Jackie, and I hope this is the last time I have to say it. "I don't understand why I need to keep explaining this."

Mason hesitates before setting the bags on the ground and removing his clothes. I used to avoid looking at him when he stripped, but now I let myself stare. Mason hands his clothes to me, and I shove them into his bag before stepping back and gesturing for him to get to it.

His shoulders pop out. I turn away. I'm not interested in seeing, after all.

Several seconds pass before Kie taps my hip. "It's safe to look."

I appreciate the warning, and I steel myself as I lock eyes with the giant shifter. Mason's terrifying, his animal form large, intimidating, and incredibly fucking deadly. I can't be scared of him, though. We already have enough working against us.

"Hit him."

"What?" I must not have heard Kie correctly.

The faerie chuckles. "Hit him, preferably as hard as you can. See for yourself that it's still Mason. He's not going to hurt you."

The mere thought has my hands shaking. Still, I widen my stance, shove away my fear, and swing. Mason doesn't move so much as an inch as I connect my palm with the side of his head.

My hand stings like a bitch, though, and I let out a pained gasp as I clutch my fingers to my chest.

Mason plops down on his butt. He's still as tall as I am.

"I'm overcoming my fear," I whisper to myself. I'm shaking, adrenaline rushing as I eye Mason's muzzle and the teeth I know live behind his lips. "Open your mouth."

Mason's jaw drops, and I stare into his throat before sticking my hand inside it. I wiggle my fist inside his mouth like a fish before pulling it back out. He didn't bite me. Good.

"His ears are sensitive," Kie says.

I grab the fuzzy, pointed ear and yank. This time, Mason reacts. A pained whine pours from his throat as he throws his body toward his ear, following my tugging. Still, he doesn't attack me.

I release his ear, guilty as he rubs it against the ground.

"I'm sorry," I say.

Kie chuckles. "He deserves it."

Kie's in a better mood already. He's laughing and encouraging me to hurt Mason, two things he hasn't done since finding Lill. I wonder if the sleep has anything to do with it.

I zip up Mason's backpack, and Kie smoothly throws it over his shoulder. He also tries to take my bag, but I pull it out of his reach before he gets his grubby hands on it. It isn't that heavy, and I can manage just fine.

I turn toward Mason.

"Lead the way, Scooby."

Chapter Twenty-Five

KIERAN

ABBY MARCHES AHEAD of us, leading the way. She doesn't know where she's going, but she's following the sound of the river, heading toward the shoreline. It's accurate enough.

Mason walks alongside her, his body so close that his fur brushes against her fingers. I suspect asking him to give her space will be about as successful as splitting hairs. He's protective of her, and anybody who sees us will recognize it.

"Mace…" I start.

He turns his head, peering at me over my shoulder.

I open my mouth, but then I realize I have nothing to say and clamp it shut. Mason doesn't accept that. He smacks his jaw against Abby's hip to stop her, and we both pretend not to notice her quiet, nervous shriek. She's still wary of Mason, but it won't last forever.

Mason stares, waiting for me to speak.

"Do you sense anything?" I ask.

It's a stupid question. Mason would make it abundantly clear if somebody were nearby. This area isn't highly trafficked by the shifters, which is precisely why I brought us here. Shifters aren't kind to faeries, and if they see us outside the meeting grounds, they'll attack first and ask questions later.

I'm willing to bet the entire forest from the entrance at Farbay to Traul River is crawling with shifters. Alpha Theon requested a meeting that only Mason would be able to make for a reason. He wants his son to come alone, and I'm sure the shifters are waiting for him to come running through.

Mason stares at me. I imagine he'd be saying something snarky if he were in his skin form. After a moment, he turns back around, not bothering to engage further with me.

I release a quiet breath, and we continue walking.

"It helps to think of you as a pet," Abby says to Mason.

Her voice is low, cautious even. She's scared to be loud. I hate her fear, but I'm appreciative of it. It's better to be safe than sorry.

"Do you have dogs here?" Abby continues.

Mason can't answer in this form, so I answer for him.

"No."

Abby makes a quiet noise of surprise. "Humans have domesticated wolves, and we call them dogs. They come in all shapes and sizes, and some larger breeds resemble a smaller version of Mason."

I think I understand what she's talking about. We don't have pets, but we occasionally purchase mammals to keep rodents out of barns. They look nothing like Mason, though.

"Anyway," Abby continues, "it helps when I think of Mason as a pet. I like them, and I'm pretending Mason's a large dog. If you were, I'd put a bow in your fur and feed you treats."

Mason ignores every word that comes out of her mouth. I try to listen, I really do, but she loses me at bows and treats. Our mate is odd.

I'm trying to think of something to say, something to humor her, but my mind is blank. I'm usually good at speaking, quick on my feet and comfortable owning conversations, but Abby's exceptionally skilled at turning me into a wordless fool.

Mason doesn't seem to have that problem. If he weren't in his animal form, I'm sure he'd respond with something rude or sexual.

He'd tell her he'd wear a thousand bows for her treats. Then he'd slide his hand down her backside to show her precisely what treat he has in mind. Abby would huff and push him away, but then her face would turn red and her arousal would saturate the air.

If I tried that, I'd get elbowed in the throat. Abby doesn't lust for me like she does for Mason. It's my fault. I pulled away, throwing myself into work and Lillian.

Burning-hot shame rushes through me whenever I think about the faerie woman. Mason knew something was wrong with the bond—he made that clear from the very start—but I ignored his visible discomfort and reluctance. I was convinced Lillian was ours, and I ignored every sign that suggested otherwise.

I touched Lillian in front of Abby. I *kissed* Lillian in front of Abby.

Does Abby think about it? When she looks at me, does she think of my lips and hands on Lillian? I want to scrub the memories from her brain. It's no wonder she prefers Mason. He never indulged Lillian, and the few times he allowed the faerie to touch him, he looked like he'd been swallowing nails. He visibly hated it.

Mason takes off into the forest. He says and indicates nothing before darting away, his muscular frame pushing him out of sight. I close the distance between me and Abby, keeping her close.

"Give me your bag," I order.

I let her carry it for fun, but the time for her spiteful independence is over.

Abby wordlessly slips the bag off her shoulders. I throw it

over mine, then place a hand on the back of her neck. My fingers curl around her throat, and I slowly guide us to stand so my back is to the river and I can see into the surrounding woods.

Abby buries her face into my chest, her body shaking. She's terrified.

Mason's not within my sight or hearing range, and I brush my thumb over the back of Abby's neck to keep her calm and her heart steady. I've developed an obsession with listening to it, and it's hard to focus when it's pounding so aggressively in her chest.

"You're okay," I whisper.

She grabs my waist, and I continue surveilling the woods as she slips her fingers under my shirt and touches my bare skin. She isn't wearing gloves, and I can't help but shiver at the contact. It's surprisingly steadying.

Does she remember when Lillian touched me like this? I can't lie and say Lillian's touch was unpleasant. It was the first skin-to-skin contact I'd ever had with a woman who wasn't a blood relative. It was nothing compared to this, though.

I want to wrap myself around Abby and cling to her until I'm dead. I crave it. I *need* it.

There's commotion to my left, and I shift Abby to the right. Mason is out there alone, but I won't leave Abby unprotected. I have to trust Mason to take care of it. He's a better fighter than I am, anyway.

I rely on my magic, but Mason is pure brute strength. I can hold my own against a shifter or two, but Mason moves through them with an easy I can't match. He's not threatened until surrounded by a minimum of five or six full-grown adult males.

There's more rustling, and I tighten my grip on Abby's neck as fur weaves through the trees. It's not Mason.

I slide our bags off my shoulders. "Get on the ground, put the bags on top of you, and don't move."

For once, Abby listens. She drops to the dirt and drags our bags over the top of her. They're thick, and they'll act as a barrier between her skin and a pair of sharp teeth.

Two shifters come darting in our direction a second later. I step in front of Abby, fighting the instinct to use magic as the shifters approach. These two must've slipped past Mason.

The one on the left favors his right side, overcompensating for an injury. He's Priority Number Two. Priority Number One is fast and covered in thick muscle. He's going to rip off my fucking arm, and I shake out my limbs as I crouch down and meet him head-on.

He lunges for my neck, a move I expect and just barely dodge. Shifters always go for the necks. It's where Mason went the first time we met.

Abby's pounding heart is all I can hear. It's all I *want* to hear, and I listen to every pump as I turn to the side and kick the shifter in the hip.

Priority Number Two doesn't come for me. He goes straight for Abby, bumping him to Priority Number One. I reach him before he reaches her, and when he opens his mouth to bite me, I grab the upper and lower parts of his jaw and rip them apart.

A tooth impales my palm, but adrenaline makes the pain easy to ignore.

The whine the shifter lets out is sickening, and I try not to think about the fact that he's a person with a family as I rip his head in two. He crumples to the floor, but I don't have time to ensure he's dead before turning back to the remaining shifter.

He's taken advantage of my distraction, and I watch in slow motion as he lunges for Abby.

She screams and throws a bag at his head, slowing him enough for me to reach them. Blood pumps through my veins, panic rendering me unable to think as I throw myself against his side and knock him off-balance.

Four claws gouge my arm as he falls, the sharp nails easily tearing through my skin. It burns, and I grunt as I throw my fist into his eye socket. His position on his back puts him at a disadvantage, and I avoid his kicking feet as his skull shatters beneath my fist.

The area around his eye caves in, and at least one of my fingers breaks. Still, I don't stop until the shifter falls limp. Are there more? I don't hear anything, but that's not reliable.

This is their land, and they know it better than I do.

Abby digs through our bags, and cold fingers wrap around my wrist a second later. I hold still while Abby pushes the torn skin on my arm together and staples it in place. Mason and I have been taught how to use stitches, but we packed the stapler for Abby.

She takes advantage of it, and I wince as she works her way up my arm.

Then she rises, her breath hitting the back of my neck. "Thank you."

I nod, only relaxing when Mason finally emerges from the woods. He's covered in blood, and his eyes dart between me and the two shifters who snuck past him. He doesn't speak, but I know what he wants.

"Help me clean my arm?" I ask Abby.

Mason needs to dump his kills in the river, and he doesn't want Abby to see them. My kills were brutal, but they were quick and relatively clean. Shifters fight differently, and the ones Mason fought will be shredded into pieces. He doesn't want Abby to fear him more than she already does.

I place myself between her and the bodies, blocking her view as I crouch beside the water. Abby quickly joins me.

"Is Mason okay?" she asks, peering at him over my shoulder.

He's sniffing around my kills, probably ensuring they're dead.

The one whose face I tore apart must be hanging on because Mason darts forward and sinks his jaws into his neck. Abby flinches, and I grab her chin and guide her head away.

"He's fine," I say. "Don't look at him."

"Why?"

"Because he's embarrassed." *Embarrassed* isn't the right word, but it's close enough. "He's going to drag the bodies into the water and rub mud over the blood trail, and he doesn't want you to see."

"Why?"

"Because he doesn't want you to be afraid of him."

Abby makes a quiet noise, then falls silent. She looks deep in thought, which I won't interrupt. I busy myself instead, searching through our bags until I find soap.

I'm covered in blood, and the scent will carry. I need to wash it off before any other shifters wander into the area. It's one thing if Mason kills a few, but it's another if I do.

I can't meet with Alpha Theon covered in shifter blood—not if I want anything productive to come from our meeting.

Chapter Twenty-Six

ABBY

I'VE SPENT ALL this time thinking Mason is the dangerous one. It makes sense. He's mean and turns into a giant, terrifying animal. I realize now that I was wrong. Kie ripped a shifter's head in half. Then he smashed in the head of another—all with his bare hands. He didn't need sharp teeth or long claws.

I continue replaying the scene in my head, over and over and over again.

Whine. Rip. Crunch.

Whine. Rip. Crunch.

My hands shake as Kie cleans his arms and face, washing off the blood. I must have a few specks on my face, and I wince as he runs his thumbs over my forehead and eyebrow. Then he cleans my upper lip.

Mason drags bodies into the river. I see him out of the corner of my eye.

There's so much blood.

This isn't the first time Mason's fought shifters, but this is the first time I've seen the aftermath. I prefer *not* seeing it.

"Where is the mouth of the river?" I ask. That's where Alpha Theon said he wanted to meet.

"We're about an hour away," Kie says. "We should get there early enough to stake out the area."

I'm ready to return home. Well, to Kie and Mason's home. I'm slowly giving up hope of ever returning to the human realm.

"Anox is going to be upset." I'm talking to myself, mainly to fill the silence. "He's going to do that thing where he gets red and slams doors."

"He absolutely will." Kie chuckles. "He practically raised Mason and me, but his disrespect shouldn't be tolerated. I'm sure not going to say anything about it, and I highly doubt Mason will, either. I suspect we're both secretly afraid of the old man."

I bite back a smile.

"I've been meaning to thank you for last night. I know you're not interested in sleeping with us, but having you close was… It was comfortable. I enjoyed it." Kie snorts, then continues. "Mason went through four mattresses before settling on one he liked, and he's incredibly possessive over it. It was fun stealing it for a night."

My gaze drifts behind Kie. Mason's finally finished dumping the bodies into the river and wiggling around on the blood trails, and now he's in the water shaking out his fur.

"You should warn Mason if you ever plan to share a bed with him," Kie says. "So he can ready himself for you."

I pause. "Ready himself?"

Kie tosses the soap into the river and rises. I do the same.

"What does he have to ready?" I repeat.

Kie shoots me a sideways glance. "His asshole, obviously."

He throws our bags over his shoulder and walks away, heading toward Mason. I stare at his retreating form, pretty sure he's joking but not one hundred percent sure. Mason doesn't have to ready his asshole.

I have no interest in Mason's asshole.

Why would Kie joke about that, though? Kie doesn't make jokes.

I hurry behind the faerie, eager to keep close. Mason steps out of the river and shakes out his fur one last time. Water splatters everywhere, thankfully not on me. The bodies he dumped just a few minutes ago have already been swept away, conveniently in the direction opposite of where we're heading.

We continue walking, but there's no more conversation. Not that there was much before.

Kie and Mason slow as we near the meeting point, and we adjust to walk in the woods instead of along the riverbank. I'm placed between the two men, a familiar position. I used to hate when they'd trap me between them, but I don't mind it as much now. It's actually comforting, and I don't pull away when my arm brushes against Kie's.

"So, what's the plan?" I ask.

Kie and Mason never agreed on how they wanted to handle this meeting. Mason wants Kie and me to remain quiet and let him lead the discussion. Kie wants Mason and me to remain quiet while he leads. Both men want to hide me in a cave with an open portal for the duration of the meeting.

It'd be a good idea if holding open a portal for an extended length of time wouldn't drain Kie, leaving him and Mason vulnerable.

I think we should've told Alpha Theon to fuck off and suggest a meeting that doesn't put us at such a disadvantage, but Mason is convinced this is our only option. Kie seems to agree with him.

"We go together," Kie grumbles. "And I let Mason lead the conversation, at least to start."

Mason huffs in agreement, then pauses and transforms out of his animal form.

I dig through his bag for his clothes, freezing when I notice the giant gash on his torso. It trails from the center of his chest to his hip, and it's still bleeding. He's hurt. He's been hurt this entire fucking time. Why didn't he say anything?

"You can't—" I huff, too angry to finish my lecture. "You're stupid, Mace."

Mason heals quickly, and I can't imagine how deep this gash must've been if it's not already healed. I'm brimming with anger. It's uncontrollable, and I fight back several snarky comments as I trail my fingers alongside the wound, careful not to touch it.

"I'm okay," Mason says. He pulls his clothes from my hand. "You can fret over me later."

I'm *not* fretting.

We abandon our bags to travel light the remainder of the way. Mason takes the lead. "We're almost there," he eventually says. "About ten minutes away. Watch what you say."

Because there are shifters nearby. It goes unsaid, and I manage a jerky nod as the three of us resume walking. The sound of running water grows louder as we head toward the river, and Mason places a hand on the small of my back as we finally reach the meeting spot.

I expected more fanfare.

There's a man up ahead. He's standing on the water's edge, his back to us. He's alone, but he's not vulnerable. He's fucking massive, and he has the same build as Mason. This must be Alpha Theon. I take this moment to study him. He and Mason look similar from behind, but Alpha Theon's hair is shorter. Mason's wavy dark strands touch his ears, but his father's ends close to the skull.

I thought we'd be surrounded by shifters. Maybe we are.

We come to a halt a few feet behind Alpha Theon.

"And here I thought this would be a private meeting with my son."

Alpha Theon turns around, his gaze landing immediately on Mason. The two may share a physical build, but Mason must get his looks from his mother. Alpha Theon is one ugly motherfucker, and he looks like he's sucking on something sour.

"You brought your human," he says. His gaze shifts to me. My heart stops. "Are you looking for a trade? I heard Zaha didn't want her, but I might be interested."

Disgust roils through me. We're off to a great start.

Alpha Theon smiles. *Are you looking for a trade?* What a loaded question to begin this meeting with. He's trying to rile us up, and he's not even bothering to present himself as a nice guy.

It's not what I was expecting—not that I had high expectations to start. It's so much worse.

Alpha Theon isn't going to offer Mason any sort of kindness. Not for a second. He's going to be callous and cruel, and it's going to kill my mate. I want to grab Mason's hand, but I don't want to initiate physical contact in front of the shifter alpha.

Nobody knows we're mates, and Kie and Mason intend to keep it that way.

I chew on my bottom lip instead, scanning Alpha Theon from head to toe. Had Mason never been sent to live with the faeries, he'd probably be alpha by now. He'd have taken a shifter wife, and he'd likely already have a child or two.

I would've never met him.

Queen Gitta would still be alive. Kie would be the faerie king.

Alpha Theon exudes confidence. Not one part of him looks nervous or worried about meeting his son for the first time in over twenty years. Is he planning to kill us today?

Mason and Kie would win in a fight against Alpha Theon. The alpha is built like a truck, but so are my mates. Kie's at a disadvantage because he can't use magic here, but after seeing what he did to the two shifters who attacked us, I won't underestimate him. He can hold his own.

"I'd be willing to give you delysum in exchange for the human."

"No." Mason's answer is curt. I appreciate it.

Alpha Theon finally shifts his gaze to his son. "I wished to meet with you alone."

He hasn't acknowledged Kie's presence. It's almost as if the faerie is invisible to him. I don't need to look at Kie to know it's pissing him off, which I'm sure is Alpha Theon's intention. I highly doubt anything he says or does is unintentional.

Mason clears his throat. "We didn't feel that was appropriate, given the circumstances."

I scan the woods surrounding us, searching for shifters. Nothing stands out, but I don't believe it. I don't know Alpha Theon, and I don't trust him.

"We?" Alpha Theon laughs. "I heard the faeries softened you, but I didn't realize they also stripped you of your manhood."

Mason stiffens beside me, and his arms begin to tremble. He's going to lose control.

Alpha Theon continues. "The moment you failed to kill Kieran, I knew you'd never grow to be a man I'd be proud of. I must admit I always held on to some hope. I'm disappointed."

I slide my hand up the back of Mason's shirt, pressing my bare palm against his warm skin. Alpha Theon's eyes follow my movement, silently clocking the action. I don't care. I drag my nails down Mason's back, hoping the touch is distracting.

Alpha Theon smirks. "The rumors about her being your mate are true, then?"

"You already know that," Mason says. "Why else would Callie have brought Abby and Lillian together? I assume she used gods' magic to find our mate."

Alpha Theon shrugs, not denying Mason's accusation. I

suppose we can consider that one question answered. It's already more than I thought we'd get out of this.

I ignore the pang of hurt that travels down my spine. Did Lill know? Did she suspect?

Kie interrupts. "We also assume Callie is still alive, and you've been hiding her on your lands for several years." Kie clears his throat. "You don't have Lillian, though."

A look of shock crosses Alpha Theon's expression, but it vanishes almost immediately. What makes Kie think Lill isn't with Alpha Theon? I have many questions, and I expect a full debriefing when we get home.

"What do you intend to do with our lands?" Alpha Theon asks, changing the subject. "Now that you're king, I'm interested to hear how you plan to handle the Redstall Forest."

"I intend to make no changes to our land agreements."

Alpha Theon scoffs. "Our numbers were decimated by Zaha, and we haven't had the opportunity to repopulate because your beloved faeries have trapped us within this forest. We aren't thriving."

I don't see how the forest is preventing the shifters from repopulating. The trees aren't stopping them from humping, and the forest is huge. I suppose they have to share the area with the trolls, but I'm under the impression the trolls aren't much of a threat.

"Repopulate?" Mason cocks his head to the side. "That's an interesting concern coming from the man who left his child for dead."

Ah. Here it comes.

Alpha Theon blinks, his eyebrows furrowing together. He doesn't know what Mason's referring to.

Mason reaches into his pocket and pulls out the crumpled letter he found in Queen Gitta's desk. I didn't realize he brought it, and I press my lips together as he tosses it toward his dad. Alpha Theon takes two seconds to read the letter before shrugging and dropping it to the ground.

I can practically *feel* the last remaining bit of Mason's patience vanishing.

Alpha Theon was in a great position to manipulate Mason. Had he come to this meeting with a better attitude, perhaps the promise of reconciliation, even if not earnest, he could have very likely gotten Mason to do just about anything for him. I'm sure he'll realize later it was a huge mistake.

Alpha Theon didn't think Mason held any loyalty toward the shifters. He didn't realize the lengths to which Mason went to defend his family.

Mason shifts his weight from foot to foot. His back muscles tighten and loosen with each movement, and I continue stroking my fingers over them. I'm not sure if it's helping, but it doesn't hurt to try. It's better than nothing.

Kie speaks, killing the quiet that's fallen over us.

"Callie must be desperate to find her daughter," he says. "That's why you agreed to meet with us, isn't it? You don't know where Lillian is, and you're hoping Abby can give you information."

Alpha Theon grows stiff. I now understand why Kie was adamant about coming to the meeting. I'm not sure Mason is in a state of mind to read all the hidden things Alpha Theon is saying with his silence and snarky responses. Kie's perceptive, though. He's making accusations, and judging by Alpha Theon's physical response to them, he's on the right track.

"Lillian was given a black stone necklace as a child," Alpha Theon says. "She was told to use it if she ever needed access to magic. Callie failed to mention that it was gods' magic she'd be using."

What? I blink, faintly recalling Lill using a necklace to help her open the portal. I knew every article of clothing and jewelry Lill owned, but I'd never seen the necklace before then. The way the gold chain shimmered in the sunlight caught my attention, and there was a small black stone in the center of it.

I was so preoccupied with Lill opening the portal that I didn't think twice about it, and she wasn't wearing it when Kie brought her to the faerie realm.

Alpha Theon continues. He's smiling, his lips curling into a cruel smirk. He's pleased with whatever he's about to say. "You're correct that Callie knew who Abby was, but Lillian didn't. When that magic made her feel a mate bond with Kie and Mason, she would've had no reason not to believe it."

It feels like I've been punched in the gut. I've been punched, kicked, scratched, burned, and fucking frayed. Lill thought the bond was real.

Alpha Theon doesn't give me time to recover before continuing. "You're also correct that she's not with us. We don't know where she is."

We. He said *we*. So Callie is still alive? Did Lill know that? It doesn't matter. I betrayed her. She thought Kie and Mason were hers. She was telling the truth.

A hand lands on my back. It's Kie's. He's removed his glove, and he's touching me the same way I'm touching Mason. He's afraid I'm going to do something. I bite my tongue until it bleeds.

"I agreed to this meeting because I need your help," Alpha Theon says. He's talking to me now. "We must work together to find Lillian."

That's not right. Lill's a strong and capable faerie. If she wanted to be with her mother and Alpha Theon, she would be. She could've easily opened a portal to the shifter lands and found her way here.

Kie trails his fingers up and down my spine. I do the same to Mason.

Mason hasn't spoken in a suspiciously long time, but I can't bring myself to look at him. I'm frantic, and I don't want his emotions to rub off on me.

"I believe we're past the point of helping one another," Kie says.

"I'm speaking to your mate," Alpha Theon snaps. "She's the one who knows Lillian, and—"

Mason interrupts. "Kie."

His tone is sharp, and within half a second, a portal is violently ripped open and I'm shoved through. I land on my hands and knees, and two heavy bodies follow immediately behind, crushing me.

Chapter Twenty-Seven

ABBY

MY KNEES SCRAPE against the ground, the skin most definitely shredding. They just fucking healed, but I suppose it's better than landing on my face.

Kie lands on my back, but he plants his hands beside my head and pivots at the last second so he doesn't completely flatten me. The pained grunt he lets out tells me Mason didn't offer him the same courtesy.

Dead silence fills the air, the absence of sound a stark contrast to the river's running water. I didn't realize how loud it was until it disappeared, and it takes me several moments to regain my bearings.

"Are you okay?" It's Kie who asks. He grabs my waist, pulling me to my feet. We're back at the royal grounds, surrounded by three panicked guards. "I don't know why Mason pushed us through like that."

Mason's quick to respond. "There were shifters behind us. The rushing water covered their footfalls, and they found a way to mask their scent. One of them was too nervous, and I overheard his pounding heart. There wasn't time to waste, and Abby's slow."

"I'm not slow." My hands sting, and several tiny pebbles are lodged in my palms. At least they're not bleeding. "And you didn't need to be so rough."

The guards surrounding us awkwardly back away, their movements clunky as they glance between one another. We didn't tell anybody we were leaving. It must have been a shock for us to suddenly appear through a portal. Did they see the shifter lands on the other side of it?

Anox will be pissed.

"How many were there?" Kie asks.

Mason shrugs. "No idea. I didn't have time to count."

I look between Mason, Kie, and my palms, still trying to dissect Alpha Theon's final words. Was he being honest? Why would he lie? Callie is alive, but Theon doesn't know where Lill is. What does he want her for, and if she didn't run to the shifters, then where did she go?

Anxiety twists my stomach into painful knots. Is she okay?

The thought of Callie faking her death and escaping to live with the shifters, leaving Lill behind in the human realm to rot and die, makes my blood boil. Does Lill know what her mother did to her? Does she still believe Kie and Mason are her mates? I went out of my way to touch Mason, and I chose to believe the worst after discovering the bond.

"She wasn't lying," I say.

Mason extends his arm, reaching for me, and I flinch away. I do it without thinking, and Mason wordlessly drops his arm back to his side.

"She murdered Queen Gitta," he points out. "She's not as innocent as you want to believe."

Kie grabs my shoulder, physically turning me toward him. There's panic in his violet eyes, and they flicker up and down my frame in rapid, flighty movements. Is he listening to my heart? It wouldn't surprise me.

His lips twist as his gaze lands on my palms.

"You're hurt."

I hide my hands behind my back. "Hardly."

Kie sucks his cheeks into his mouth, visibly contemplating, before nodding to himself and turning toward Mason. "Call a council meeting."

"Yeah." Mason waves a hand through the air. "I'm not looking forward to this."

It's a short walk to the chambers where the council meetings are held. It's in the same building as Kie's office, and the room is just as elaborate as the others I've seen. I've yet to leave the estate and visit the faerie capital, and I wonder if it's just as beautiful.

Probably.

Anox and the other council members are already waiting inside. None stand as we enter, nor do they look pleased to see us. I suspect they know we left.

Mason takes a seat at the head of the table. Kie and I take the spots beside him. I'm not supposed to be in these meetings, but it seems another exception is being made.

Anox is the first to break the silence. "We came by your house first thing this morning," he says. "We wanted to give you space after Abby's attack, but we needed to discuss Alpha Theon's response." He taps his fingers against the table. "Where were you?"

"Kie and I decided it was best to meet with Alpha Theon alone." Mason doesn't sound the least bit apologetic. "Alpha Theon has confirmed our suspicions that Callie's alive and hiding on his lands, but it doesn't appear he has Lillian within his possession. He's anxious about my rule, and he wanted to hear how I intend to move forward with our land agreements."

Anox puckers his lips. "What else?"

"We ran into some complications. Our meeting was cut short."

"What complications?"

Kie shrugs. "Nothing of importance."

Is he not going to share how the shifters attempted to sneak up on us from behind? Is that for Mason's benefit? I spare a glance at Mason, but he avoids acknowledging my look. I suspect it's intentional.

Lady Cassandra clears her throat. "If Alpha Theon's unwilling to give Callie up, we should send troops into Redstall to retrieve her. We've never had enough proof to outright accuse the shifters of orchestrating the attack against King Malcolm and breaking the Sylvan Harmony Treaty, but their harboring Callie is an act against it."

Kie groans. "We can't break the treaty over a hunch and a fugitive. They need to take definitive action against us."

Lady Cassandra points toward me. "They tried to kill your human, did they not? She's not a faerie, but she's here as an esteemed guest of the crown."

It's a good point, but not one I wish to use. There's so much bad blood between the faeries and shifters, and I have no interest in being used as the catalyst for a war that will undoubtedly result in thousands of deaths. That would weigh too heavily on my conscience.

"Technically," Anox says, "*faeries* tried to kill Abigail. We can't prove the shifters had any involvement."

I'm still waiting for answers to that. Kie claims that Jackie is digging into it and several faeries are being put under close surveillance, but the unknown makes me anxious. It's scary to think that somebody out there tried to kill me. Somebody who may still have access to me.

"We should consider announcing your bonds with Abigail," Anox continues. "It will offer her an extra layer of protection. Due to the circumstances, we can rush her coronation. The sooner she holds the title of queen consort, the better."

My heart pounds, and I force myself to breathe evenly despite the raw panic coursing through my veins. I haven't even decided whether or not I want to stay here, let alone become a queen. I don't care about the faeries, not really.

They don't care for me, either.

"We'll consider it," Kie says, dismissing the question. "We'll discuss the matter privately and get back to you soon with an answer."

Anox nods, but he looks to be sucking on something sour while he does so. I don't get the impression his recommendations are often rejected.

"Alpha Theon harboring Callie isn't enough to break the treaty," Mason says, "but his refusal to hand over a faerie fugitive *is* enough to publicly call his leadership into question."

What? A stunned silence falls over the room. They're shocked. I'm feeling the same way. This is an observation I'd expect one of the council members, maybe even Kie, to make, but never Mason.

Anox cocks his head to the side, his mouth opening and shutting. It takes him several seconds to find words. "Are you suggesting we—"

"I'm suggesting that my first official act as king is to denounce Alpha Theon's leadership. The shifters live on faerie lands, and Alpha Theon no longer serves us as he should." Mason's throat bobs. "We were kind to give them land after they angered Zaha and destroyed their kingdom, but Alpha Theon is taking advantage of that kindness. If he insists on keeping Callie, he won't be doing it as Alpha. It's time for Kalix to step up."

Anox leans back in his chair. He doesn't speak, but I can tell his mind is moving a million miles a minute.

Mason continues. "I'm a shifter, and if the faeries want any semblance of control over my kind, it'll have to be done through me. I'm the only person the shifters would ever consider listening to."

The rest of the meeting goes in one ear and out the other. There's talk of the logistics of making such a statement and a little bit more on whether or not Alpha Theon's claims of not knowing where Lillian is are genuine.

What feels like several hours pass before the meeting ends and I'm ushered back to Kie and Mason's house. They're silent on the walk, which is fine with me. I don't have anything to say. I don't know what to say.

I can't imagine what Mason must be feeling right now. He just found out yesterday that on top of his parents abandoning him to the faeries, Alpha Theon also refused him the medical care he desperately needed. His father left him to die.

What did Alpha Theon intend to do to us had Mason not heard the shifters sneaking up on us? Would he have killed us? Tortured us? I doubt, whatever it was, that it would've been friendly.

I begin stripping to my underwear the second we're inside the house. My clothes are covered in dirt, and most likely some blood from when the shifters attacked Kie and me. I want them off, and I grimace as I drop them to the floor and kick them away.

Mason stalks out of the room, his bedroom door slamming shut a second later. Kie remains in the foyer with me.

"If what Alpha Theon said about Lillian is true..." He shifts his weight from foot to foot. "I hope you know that we belong to you. We've always belonged to you. Lillian was wronged, but it isn't your fault." He drags his hand through his hair. "You felt a pull to us. A pull that, even before triggering the bond, was strong and hard to ignore. A pull you shouldn't feel guilty about."

I can't even begin to imagine the pain and anger I'd feel if I caught Kie or Mason touching another woman. It would ruin me, and I'm not sure I'd ever recover. I'm not sure I'd want to.

I did that to Lill. I didn't believe her.

I should've never touched Mason.

I'm going to be sick. I haven't eaten in hours, but bile finds its way up my throat as I tumble headfirst into a vortex of self-hatred and disgust.

Kie reaches for me, but I step out of his grasp. The little voice in my head tells me to run away, to deny the bond and everything related to it.

"No," he hisses. "Mason has worked too fucking hard to earn the sad, minuscule affection you give him. You can't take that from him, not now. You touched him because you knew something was there, even if you didn't want to admit it. It's a shitty situation, but Mason doesn't deserve your regret."

Tears blur my vision.

Kie continues. "His father just tried to kill him, and that outweighs your guilt toward feeling like a shitty friend." He rubs his face. "If you can't do that…" He points down the hallway that leads to our bedrooms. "Then I think it's best you remain in your room. At least until Mason's settled."

Kie heads for the shifter, shutting Mason's bedroom door behind him.

I just want things to be easy. Mate bonds are supposed to be romantic and effortless. I fell in love with the idea the moment the words slipped out of Samuel's mouth. He was so desperate to find a mate, and he bought me food and gloves just for the opportunity to touch me.

I wanted him to be my mate. It would've been a love story for the ages.

My bonds with Kie and Mason are far from a love story. It's complicated and hard and not at all what I wanted. Kie's right, though. Mason doesn't deserve my regret, not now. He's dealing with enough as it is.

I grab the item nearest me, one of the barstools tucked underneath the kitchen island, and slam it against the ground. I've never intentionally broken something, and I don't feel the least bit better as the wood splinters into a million pieces.

Footfalls thunder in my direction.

Kie's face is void of emotion as he steps into the room, and his back stiffens as he surveys the shattered barstool. Mason does the same.

I storm toward the shifter, not sure what I plan to do until I throw my arms around his neck and pull him in for a kiss. I'm done thinking, and I'm done talking. This stupid oaf is my mate, and he needs me. I fear I might need him, too, but I'm not quite ready to admit that. Not yet.

Mason groans, peppering kisses down my neck. It feels good, and I tilt my chin so he has more skin to play with. It's exactly what I need, and I lean into him as I shift my attention to Kie.

"Touch me," I order the faerie.

I need to know I betrayed Lill for something real.

Chapter Twenty-Eight

MASON

ABBY'S MOUTH IS so soft. Her thighs are so soft.

Everything about her is so soft.

My hand tangles in her hair, and I hold her close as I lift her onto the kitchen island. I'm careful to avoid her wreckage, navigating around the shattered wood. If I weren't so distracted by Abby's softness, I'd be impressed by her ability to so thoroughly ruin our furniture.

I wish I had seen her do it. Maybe I can get her to do it again for me later. I need there to be a later.

My father sent shifters after us. They were approaching from behind, and I'm sure they weren't planning on exchanging pleasantries once they reached us.

They were going to kill me. Kill Kie. *Kill Abby.*

I remove my hand from her head, scared I'm going to hurt her. I grab her thighs instead. They're thicker and can handle a bit of squeezing. They're meant for my hands, and she seems to enjoy it when I touch them.

Her breath hitches, and a full-body shiver works down her spine before she snatches up the hem of my shirt and tugs upward. She wants my shirt off? Easy. I break our kiss just long enough to rip my shirt over my head. If my mate wants my clothes off, my clothes will be off.

Kie is still lingering across the room. He hasn't moved.

I don't know what his problem is, and I'll kill him if he ruins this for me. Abby told him to touch her. It's an easy ask, and it doesn't leave much room for confusion. Kie wants her—I know he does—and it's about time he stops holding himself back. It's not earning him any favors.

I love letting Abby know when I'm happy, or angry, or horny, or really fucking needy. She likes it. I needed her to keep me calm after the attack, and she was more than happy to oblige. She kissed me, touched me, and told me so much about herself.

I learned all about her family and life before meeting us, and I know more about her than Kie does. I'm closer to her than he is.

It's something I never thought would happen. I feared our mate would be a faerie who loved Kie but tolerated me, and for once, Zaha's done right by me. I like my human. I want her, and I'm happy she's stuck with us for the rest of our lives.

"Mace," Abby starts. "I need to feel you."

Her eyes flicker to the side, toward Kie, and I'm on her before she thinks too deeply about his odd lingering. She doesn't need him. I can be enough for her.

I trail my hands up her thighs, letting myself bask in the knowledge that I'm touching my mate with my bare hands. I never thought I'd have this. Arousal seeps from Abby, the heady scent pouring from her pores in intoxicating waves. I would die without this woman.

"Our mate's cunt has already been covered in my cum," I taunt Kie. "And she hasn't even kissed you."

Kie frowns, finally stepping closer. "Fuck you."

"I have everything you've ever wanted, and I didn't even have to try," I say. Kie's face contorts, shifting into anger. This is good.

I continue. "I have your title, and I'm about to have our mate's cunt. She won't be thinking about you when I'm inside her, and you have nobody but yourself to blame."

Abby gasps, her fingers curling into my shoulder. She likes this, and I shoot her a wide smile as Kie storms toward us. The faerie is upset, and he roughly shoves his way between Abby and me, taking my place.

I let him, happy to stand back as he wraps one arm around her waist and buries another into her hair. The start of a gasp erupts from her before his mouth is on hers, cutting the noise short.

Abby jolts, but then her body practically melts in Kie's arms. He's showing passion. Need. They both need this.

"Mine." He groans. "You're mine."

Kie's kiss is rough, and I can't help but wonder where he gained the confidence. He kissed Lillian a few times, but never with real passion. I was terrified the first time Abby put her lips on mine, but Kie shows none of the hesitation I felt. It pisses me off.

Abby fucking loves it. She moans and rubs against him, my mate a whore for her men. I've never seen Kie fuck, but I've heard rumors. She's going to love him. I hope she loves me more.

Kie's the first to break the kiss, and he pulls back just enough to rip her soft black bra over her head. Abby has pretty pink nipples, and she sinks her fingers into Kie's arms as he sucks one into his mouth.

He moans. "I've been fantasizing about touching you since I saw you in the bathhouse. I love your body. It's so fucking…" Kie groans, at a loss for words. "It's everything. I want to sink my teeth into you, cover you in my marks."

I lick my lips, enjoying the idea of covering her in love bites. We spent a long time outdoors today, and I bet Abby's skin is salty. I'm also willing to bet the skin would be easy to bruise. Humans have weak blood vessels.

Abby's panting. She doesn't seem put off by Kie's admission, and I can't help but take a taste. I pull her thigh outward, making room for myself. Abby's hips rock forward, my mate looking for friction, but I have other matters to attend to. I crouch, sucking the skin of her inner thigh into my mouth, fully intending to leave a dark mark behind.

Kie shifts, doing the same to her other thigh. I'm pleased we're on the same page, and we take our time covering our mate's inner thighs as she fruitlessly rolls and thrusts her hips, silently begging for friction we aren't giving her.

She needs to learn patience.

Only when I'm satisfied with my work do I pull away. Abby is indeed covered in marks, ones I hope remain for several days. She will think of Kie and me every time she sees them.

"So pretty," I murmur, lightly tracing the largest one. "This one's my favorite."

Abby cries, still twitching. Kie chuckles, then moves inward. He wants a taste of her cunt. I've tried to be polite and contain my comments about how good it is, and I'm excited he's finally going to experience it himself.

"Is this okay?" I ask. "Is this too much?"

Has Abby been with two men at the same time? Is this new to her? It's not a question I want an answer to, but one I'm grudgingly willing to admit would be helpful to know.

Abby nods, then shakes her head, then nods again. "This is good," she eventually blurts out. "I want more. I want... I need to know. You two are my mates, and I need to know that—"

I quiet her with a kiss, cutting off her rambling. I know what she needs, and I don't want her thinking of Lillian right now. We're *her* mates, and I fully intend to prove that. Kie better not disappoint.

I pull off her mouth so I can look into her eyes, wanting to see her expression the moment the faerie puts his tongue on her. Abby shifts, trying to peer down at Kie, but I cup her chin and force her to look at me. I'm being rough with her, but she likes it. She'd sure let me know if she didn't.

Abby's pupils dilate as he runs the tip of his nose along her covered slit.

"You smell like Mason," he says.

I smirk, pleased with the observation. I've worked hard to cover our mate with my scent, and I'm proud of what I've accomplished these past few days.

There's a tear of fabric, most definitely her underwear, and Abby's eyes grow comically wide as Kie finally licks her. She's so fucking beautiful.

Kie moans, and Abby's nails dig into my forearms. My birth family may not want me, but my mate does. Even when Kie is pleasuring her, licking and sucking her sensitive skin, she holds on to *me*. She loves me. I know it.

"How much do you want?" I ask.

I love pleasuring my mate, but I'm eager for more. I want inside her. I want to take.

Abby's back arches, and the column of her throat bobs as she struggles to focus on my words. I sneak a look, my lips curling as Kie sucks her clit into his mouth. I've never tried that and haven't thought to, but Abby seems to enjoy it. I'll try it next time.

"How much?" I repeat. "Do you want us to take you to my bedroom?"

She likes my room, likes that I've never had another woman in there. It drives Kie mad, but I don't feel sorry for him. He's facing the consequences of his actions, and I'm reaping the benefits. Our mate prefers my bed, and I'm not above using that to my advantage.

Abby rolls her hips, but Kie pins them to the counter. I always let her take control and ride my mouth, but Kie keeps her in place.

"My room?" I repeat.

Abby blinks, still processing my question, before giving a jerky nod.

Thank the fucking gods. I don't know what I'd do if she turned us away. My cock is aching, and I'm desperate for release. Men are discouraged from masturbating between the time they trigger the bond and have sex with their mate, and these past several days have been the toughest of my life.

Had Abby made me wait much longer, I might have broken that unspoken rule. It's a faerie rule, anyway. Shifter mates have no issues with self-pleasure.

Abby releases my forearms, her eyes lighting with fire as she trails a hand down my torso. I let her, excited to see where she's going with this. It's about time she touches my cock, and I bite back a hiss as she grabs me over the fabric of my pants.

"This is mine."

She's looking for confirmation. I'm more than happy to give it. I've been waiting for the day she claims me. I've never belonged to somebody, and I've always wanted it.

"Yes," I say. "It's all yours."

Kie nudges me aside, always so impatient, and carries Abby to my bedroom. She wraps her legs around his waist, happily letting him carry her over the destroyed furniture. I've had several intimate moments with Abby, but this is Kie's first.

I have half a mind to leave them alone, to let them have this moment to connect without me, but then I decide I don't want to and follow behind them. Abby's my mate, and Kie can't hoard her.

Kie already has her fully naked in my bed when I step into the room, and she lies on the center of the mattress watching him undress. I begin removing my clothing, too, and poor Abby grows panicked. She doesn't know who to look at, and her gaze whips back and forth between us.

She looks close to fainting when we're both finally naked. She's nervous. She's never taken two men before. The realization has me shaking, struggling to hold back the urge to crawl over her and take what the gods have promised is mine.

Abby is mine. My woman. *My mate.*

"Who do you want inside you?" I ask.

I'd love to fuck her at the same time as Kie, both of us filling her, but I don't want to overwhelm her. I've done some research on human men, and they're smaller than we are. Abby's no virgin—it's a fact she's made a pointed effort to inform me of— but I refuse to hurt her.

"I have to decide?" Abby drags her fingers through her hair. My poor human is stressed, unsure which one of us to choose.

I fist my cock, drawing attention to it, before kneeling on the edge of the bed. I want her to pick me. I want it so fucking badly, and when her attention shifts momentarily to Kie, I realize I need to decide for her.

Abby needs my cock inside her. It's evident by her heavy breathing and needy little pants. It would be cruel to continue denying her.

I spread her thighs, making room for myself. It's about time I fuck my mate.

Chapter Twenty-Nine

ABBY

MASON'S FRANTIC. I share the emotion.

I need them to fuck me, and I need it to be so good that it leaves no doubt that we're meant to be together. I need to know that Zaha didn't make a mistake or this isn't another one of Callie's tricks.

I still can't wrap my head around her being alive.

Mason creeps his way between my thighs, the shifter surprisingly agile. I can't help but gawk, my mind running a million miles a minute as my gaze darts toward the giant man crawling over me and the quiet one standing at the edge of the bed.

I expect Kie to be upset with Mason's intrusion, but he doesn't look the least bit bothered. If anything, he seems to find the entire situation humorous. His lips are curled into a sly smile, and his violet eyes are looking me over in a way that feels more predatory than it has any business being.

Mason's cock presses against my inner thigh, so close to where I want it. I'm relieved he didn't make me pick between them. I wouldn't have been able to choose. I want them both.

Kie walks around the side of the bed, his fingers trailing along the bedsheets. His muscular arms are taunting me, begging me to reach out and touch, but I have a feeling Mason will lose his mind if I make any moves for the faerie.

The shifter is possessive, and he's made it obvious he wants me first. Kie must've suspected this would happen. Kie's the well-trained dog who waits patiently for his bone. Mason is the puppy who gets too excited and snaps it out of the owner's hand.

The thought has me giggling, which captures the attention of both men. They look equally offended, glancing between one another with matching frowns.

"What's so funny?" Mason asks.

He sits back on his knees, staring down at me. It's hard not to look between his thighs. I've seen his cock a few times now, and I'm nervous to take it inside me. I have half a mind to tell him and Kie to use one of the many condoms in the guest room nightstand, but I don't. I'm on birth control, and I'm selfishly excited to be the first woman either man is bare inside of.

"What's so funny, Abby?" Kie repeats Mason's question.

I smile. "I just wasn't expecting Mason to be so excited."

I expect the shifter to return with a snarky response, but he gives a halfhearted shrug instead. "You're my mate. Of course I'm excited."

He's lining himself up and pushing inside me a second later, filling me with a low, drawn-out moan. I have no words, and I grab helplessly at his arms and neck as my body stretches around him.

"Fuck." Mason gasps, grabbing my thighs. "I knew you'd feel too good."

He pulls out halfway and pushes back in.

I slam my head against the sheets, faintly aware of Kie brushing my hair out of my face. The bed dips as he kneels beside my head. I know where this is going, but when I turn to take him in my mouth, he moves behind me.

"Kie?" I whine, my voice shaky as Mason rocks his hips

against me. He presses against all the right spots, making it impossible to think. "What're you doing?"

Hands hook underneath my elbows, and I release a shocked gasp as I'm hauled backward up the bed. Kie's pulling me onto his lap. My back is flush against his chest, and his hardness presses against my lower spine.

Mason smoothly adjusts, his hands traveling to my hips as he settles into an easy rhythm.

"Look at her," he tells Kie. "She was made for us."

The faerie's breath warms my neck as he peers over my shoulder, watching Mason fuck me. I don't need to look to know it's a vulgar sight. My wetness is dripping down my inner thighs, and I suspect Mason's covered in it.

"How does she feel?" Kie asks.

"Fucking amazing." Mason grunts. "You'll find out soon enough."

He's deep inside me, and each thrust has my lower back rubbing against Kie's length. I want more of the faerie, but I'm not able to touch him. He's underneath me, and I can't reach him at this angle.

I settle for grabbing his thighs, but it's not enough.

Mason seems to sense my inner turmoil as he pulls out and flips me onto my hands and knees. Then he grabs my hips and guides me back onto his cock, not missing a beat.

Kie's lounging against the headboard. He looks much too relaxed, but I know it's an act. He's already leaking precum, and his hips are twitching of their own accord. He wishes he was the one fucking me right now, and I make eye contact with him as I lean forward.

Mason admitted to me once that he's never had a mouth on him, and I'm willing to bet the same is true for Kie.

Kie hisses. "*Abby!*"

He squeezes his eyes shut as I close my lips around the head of his cock, and his hands immediately fly to my shoulders. It's like he can't decide whether to push me away or pull me in. It's a confidence booster, and I fight back a smile as I take him further into my mouth.

He's too big to take all the way, or even most of the way, and he's too thick to stretch around comfortably. Still, I try my best.

Mason leans over me, bringing his lips to my ear. "You look so fucking good with Kie's cock in your mouth." He's palming my ass, squeezing and massaging the flesh. I can tell he's not entering me all the way, and I huff before pushing back against his next thrust.

Mason curses, and I pull off Kie.

"I can take more than you think," I say. "You won't break me."

Mason takes my words to heart. His grip on me tightens, and I almost fall forward from the force of his next thrust. He shoves the entirety of himself inside, stretching me more than I thought possible.

Kie takes action, too. He grabs my head and guides me back to his cock. Long gone is his relaxed façade. He's panting, his chest heaving as I take him into my mouth. I barely get halfway.

"Gods," Kie moans. "It's so good."

I like it when he takes control, when Mason does, too, and I let myself drown in the feel and taste of my mates. It's overpowering all my other senses, and I love it. I love this.

Tears fill my eyes and stream down my cheeks. I needed this to be good, and it is.

Mason begins rubbing my clit, his movements perfectly timed with his thrusts. He's learned what I like, and I thrash against him and Kie as the pleasure builds. I assumed Mason would be the one to cum first, but at this rate, it's going to be me. My orgasm is close, and Mason rubs my clit until every muscle in my body is shaking.

"Let it go," Mason orders. He's grinding against me now, the head of his cock repeatedly rubbing against a spot that's making me see stars. "I want to feel my mate cum."

Kie pulls out of my mouth, letting me breathe. I bury my forehead into his hip, my eyes clenched shut as Mason drives me to release. I'm so fucking close.

"Mason—" I cry.

My voice dies out as Mason pulls me up onto my knees. My back presses against his chest, and I make eye contact with Kie. I'm not sure if it's rude to make eye contact with a man while orgasming on another man's cock, but Kie doesn't seem to mind.

He squeezes the base of his shaft, his jaw slack as I come undone.

Mason continues fucking me, his moans growing louder as his movements become erratic. He's close, and immense satisfaction washes over me when he finally pushes in deep and stills.

He buries his face against my neck, peppering my skin with kisses as he finishes inside me. He's panting, and I'm left feeling painfully empty when he finally pulls out several moments later.

Cum is pouring down my inner thighs. It's a feeling I typically hate, but I can't bring myself to care as I move for Kie. I want him too. He sits back on the bed, his lazy smile returning as I straddle his lap. He's mine, and I want him finishing inside me just like Mason.

"You don't need to—" Mason starts.

Kie shushes him, his voice low. "She can take it." He tucks my hair behind my ears, his movements gentle. "You can take it, can't you?"

I nod. I can take it.

I use his shoulder for leverage as I line him up, beyond desperate to have him inside. Mason already stretched me out, leaving me mildly sore, and Kie is no better. He's just as thick as the shifter, and this angle allows him to sink in deeper.

I ride him gently, rocking my hips back in soft movements. Kie's grip on my hips helps guide me, and when I attempt to speed up, they slow me down.

"Don't hurt yourself," Kie mutters. "I'm already so close. Just a few more thrusts and I'll fill you. Can you cum from penetration alone?"

I hesitate, then nod. I've only been able to cum that way when I'm by myself, and it's not easy.

Kie releases his grip on my hips. "Show me."

"I don't know that I can..." My voice trails off as I take in Kie's unbothered expression. "It might take a while."

Kie cocks his head to the side. "Cum on my cock, Abby."

Fine. I grab his shoulders, adjusting our positioning until I find the one that feels best. Kie's the picture of patience as I begin rocking my hips, moving them in small, jerky motions that have gotten me there before.

Kie watches my every movement with rapt attention, and I suspect he's memorizing them so he can do it himself later. I enjoy the thought more than I should, and I let my head fall back as I focus on the sensations.

Mason is behind me, his presence comforting, but he doesn't interfere. I suspect he, too, is memorizing my every movement.

My second orgasm hits me like a freight train. It's fast and intense, and my back curls as I drop against Kie's chest. He holds me steady, and I'm almost too distracted to notice that he's cumming, too.

I didn't realize he was so close to the edge, but there's no mistaking the deep moan that pours from his throat as his hips jerk up against me. He finishes inside, his cum mixing with Mason's. I take it, greedy for it all.

"You're my family." Mason's declaration pulls me from my post-orgasmic haze. "I've been desperate to hold together the idea of family I shared with my father, but I realize now I didn't need to. You're mine, Abby. You and Kie are my family."

Fuck. I need a moment to process that.

I need to make a decision.

I can't continue torturing Mason. He's fighting for me, and it's cruel to keep throwing him small crumbs while actively denying our bond. I can't expect him to give himself to me while simultaneously pulling away.

Despite everything that's happened between us, he doesn't deserve that. I need to decide. Either I'm in, or I'm out. My heart pounds, and I'm faintly aware I'm taking too long to respond.

Mason slips off the bed and disappears into his ensuite bathroom. He's disappointed in me. Kie is, too. The faerie doesn't say anything, but his lack of reaction is enough.

I climb off Kie, and he clears his throat before sliding off the bed.

"I'll get you something to clean yourself with," he says.

His voice is monotone—the fevered way he spoke to me just minutes ago now long gone. I clasp my hands in front of me, hating myself for not speaking up.

The shower turns on, the water loud as it erupts from the showerhead and smacks against the tile. It's probably Mason. He wants to clean me off of him. He doesn't want the remnants of our sex to stick to his skin any longer than necessary.

The realization hurts more than I'd care to admit, and it urges me to join him and Kie in the bathroom. Mason's indeed in the shower, his back facing me as he angrily scrubs at his skin.

Kie's in front of the sink, his hands pressed against the marble and his head hanging between his shoulders. He straightens up as I step into the room, and he runs a hand towel under the faucet before spinning toward me.

"Here," he says, handing it over. "You can shower after Mason, but this should hold you over while he finishes. I'm going to bring in my mattress."

He moves to walk past me, but I grab his bicep, stopping his retreat.

Chapter Thirty

ABBY

KIE STARES DOWN at me. His gaze is intense and heavy—a weighted vest. I resist the urge to shrink into myself as I tighten my grip on his bicep.

Say something, Abby. Anything.

"I—" I start.

I don't know what to say. I'm not so mad anymore. They regret how they treated me, and while I have every right to hold it over their heads for the rest of our lives, I don't want to. Being angry is hard work, and it's exhausting. I'm denying myself mates, something I really do want, and it's making us all miserable. At this point, I'm punishing myself just as much as I'm punishing them.

They've earned a second chance.

I'm not in love with either of them, but they deserve the opportunity to earn my love.

Kie sucks his lips into his mouth, his patience waning. I suspect he knows what I want to say, but he isn't going to help me get the words out. I almost wish he would. It would make this easier.

My attention shifts to Mason. He's still showering, his head bowed as he scrubs the remnants of sex off himself. I'm sure he's listening to me and Kie, though. He's always listening.

"I—" I start again.

I fall short, and Kie pulls his arm out of my hand. He's not rough, but I feel like I've been slapped as he walks out of the room, continuing as if I hadn't stopped him.

Mason finishes showering, and he avoids eye contact as he dries off and wraps a towel around himself. Then he walks out of the room, leaving me alone. I drag my fingers through my hair, tugging on the strands as I swallow a frustrated scream.

I'm making this more complicated than it needs to be.

I hurry to shower, hoping it will clear my mind. It doesn't work, not that I honestly expected it to. I'm just as tongue-tied when I return to Mason's bedroom, if not more.

Two mattresses have been dragged into the room. They're squished next to one another, and Kie and Mason are lounging on them. They take turns flipping through a stack of papers, the pair looking more like two best friends preparing for a sleepover than two royals.

The sight warms my heart.

"You can have Mason's bed," Kie says.

Mason looks up as I pull open his wardrobe and dig out some clothing, his narrowed, green eyes following my every move. It's not helping my nerves, and I do my best to ignore it as I organize my thoughts.

I need to address what was said. No more avoiding it.

"I would like you two to meet my family," I start. "You offered once to bring them here, and I think that would be best. They must be worried sick about me, and they'll want to meet the men I'm in a relationship with."

They might not want to stay, but they'll at least want to visit. They'll want to see that I'm healthy and safe. Most importantly, they'll want to see that I'm not dead.

Kie finally looks up.

I continue. "Mates don't exist in the human realm, and it's not considered appropriate for a woman to be in a relationship with multiple men, or vice versa. You should probably know that going into this."

Mason quirks a brow. "*Are* we in a relationship, Abby?"

"Yes." I bob my head. "Yes. I believe we are."

Mason taps his fingers against the papers he's flipping through, and he exchanges a silent look with Kie before handing the faerie the stack and rising. I hold my breath, afraid the slightest movement will ruin things.

Mason continues forward, not stopping until I'm pinned between him and his wardrobe. My heart is pounding with hard, rhythmic thumps that block out my loudest thoughts.

I'm sweating. "I want this," I blurt out. My eyes dart toward Kie. "I want you both."

"You already have us," Kie says.

Mason tucks a strand of hair behind my ear. "We want to have you, too. Do you want that?"

I'm going to vomit. "Yes."

Mason blinks down at me. It feels like he's reading into my soul, and I don't like it. I'm scared to give either of them access to my emotions, to my heart. I'm terrified of the power it gives them.

But I've made my decision.

I want to let them in—even if the thought is petrifying.

Kie finally rises from the floor, and my gaze darts between his approaching form and Mason's. The shifter glides to the side as Kie nears, making room for both men to trap me against the wardrobe.

This would've terrified me once, but now my heart is pounding for an entirely different reason.

"Are you certain?" Kie asks. "Mason and I aren't perfect, and we've made plenty of mistakes with you. Don't tell us we have you if you aren't certain. We'll wait as long as it takes until you are."

Fingers graze the back of my hand. I'm not sure which man they belong to, and I highly doubt I'll ever get used to the energy that vibrates between us.

"I don't want to be afraid of disagreeing with you," Kie continues. "I don't want to live life afraid of your anger, terrified if I say the wrong thing, you'll pull away with the excuse that you never truly forgave us in the first place. I don't want to feel like a monster for the rest of my life. I can't erase our history, I know I can't, but I—"

"I don't think you're a monster," I interrupt. I mean it, too. They made terrible decisions, but I don't think either of them is anything close to monstrous. "And I know what I'm agreeing to."

Mason isn't saying anything, and he sucks in a long, shaky breath before stepping away and stacking the spare mattresses on top of one another. Then he kicks them aside, and he makes sure I'm looking at him as he slides into his bed.

The message is loud and clear. I'll share the bed with him and Kie tonight, and probably every night thereafter.

It's intimate. Sex is one thing, especially when I know how much of it they've had in their lifetimes, but cuddling is different. Cuddling is meaningful to the faeries, and to the shifters. It means touching. It means hope.

Kie nudges me forward. "Go."

I take only one step before pausing. Kie's words from earlier today need to be addressed.

I make eye contact with Mason. "Do you expect me to touch your asshole?" Mason blinks. I gesture toward Kie. "Kie said you need to ready your asshole for me."

Silence. Nothing but awkward, painful silence. It's broken by a sharp intake of breath, then a cackling laugh from Kie. It comes from deep in his belly, and my face immediately turns a thousand shades of red.

Mason doesn't justify my question with a response. His stare is full of judgment, though, as he pulls back the sheet covers and gestures for me to join him in bed.

Kie continues snickering, clearly proud of himself. I want to be annoyed, but the emotion is impossible to find. This is my first time hearing Kie's genuine, unrestrained laughter, and something sweet pours through my veins as I climb into bed with Mason.

The sheets are already warm. I enjoy it, and I preemptively tug off my clothes and toss them onto the floor. I'm going to be hot, especially if Kie joins us. I assume he will.

Once he's done laughing at his bad joke.

Mason wraps an arm around my waist and pulls my back flush against his chest. He's wearing only his underwear, and so much of our skin is touching. I refuse to let myself overthink it as I relax against him.

"I would die for you," Mason whispers, "but you're not welcome to touch my asshole. I will push you to the ground if you try."

Kie's shoulders are shaking with the force of his snickers. They're practically giggles. My big, royal faerie mate is giggling because I fell for a joke about Mason liking ass-play.

"That's enough," Mason eventually says.

I sink my teeth into my bottom lip, chewing at the skin as Kie finally joins us in bed. He traps me between him and Mason, and I take this time to admire him. I've always found Kie beautiful.

Faeries have dainty features—pointed noses, high cheekbones, and big eyes. Kie is no different, but nothing about him screams delicate. I touch his jaw, sliding my fingers across his stubble. Despite everything, I don't regret our bond.

Mason buries his face in my hair at the back of my neck. "You smell like me. At this rate, we won't be able to hide your connection to us. We're with you every minute of every day, you're living in our home, and you smell of us." He adjusts, his lips brushing against my shoulder. "We smell like you, too. It's going to draw attention."

Anox suggested earlier that Kie and Mason announce that I'm their mate. He said they can rush my coronation. They can make me a queen consort.

I don't know how to feel about that. It's so much, so soon.

I clear my throat, wanting to change the topic. "Once people know who we are to one another, will you stop wearing your gloves?"

"Why?" It's Kie who asks. "We don't have to, but I assumed you'd want us to. It's symbolic to wear them after—"

"They're ugly," I blurt out. Honesty, they are. "They're ugly, and they make you look like corny supervillains. It's not just you two, but everybody who wears them. I've tried hard to get past it, but I can't."

I've refused to allow myself to make the connection until now. It felt rude, but I can't live the rest of my life like this. Kie and Mason already go out of their way to avoid touching others. Besides, what's the worst that will happen?

A woman trips over her feet, and when Kie darts forward to catch her, he accidentally grabs her bare arms. It truly wouldn't devastate me. Humans touch all the time. We don't value it the way faeries and shifters do.

"I understand if you two feel more comfortable with them," I continue. I'm backtracking, already regretting insulting something so important to them. "Actually, you should just continue wearing them. I shouldn't have brought it up. It was rude."

Mason chuckles, his warm breath hitting my shoulder. "You're rambling, Abby. We wear the gloves out of respect for you, not for ourselves. Truth be told, I find them uncomfortable. I'll be glad not to wear them anymore."

Kie nods, a smile toying at the corners of his lips. He's laughing at me. He's not stopping, either. His smile grows, continuing until he's burying his face into his pillow to hide it. He's so giddy tonight, and I hesitate before grabbing his hip and gesturing for him to flip around.

He does so without complaint. I'm surprised he isn't fighting this, and I wrap my arm around his waist before pulling him against my front.

"We call this spooning," I whisper in his ear. "I'm spooning you."

Kie stiffens, and a long beat of silence stretches before he finally responds. "Never say that to me again."

I smirk. I knew he wouldn't like it, but that's what he deserves for making me ask Mason about his asshole. I've caught glimpses, and it's not a forest I'm looking to explore. I never want to think about Mason's asshole again.

Chapter Thirty-One

ABBY

A SHIFT IN the mattress wakes me, and I peek open my eyes just as Kie slinks out of bed. He's trying to be sneaky, and he's unsuccessful.

We changed positions during the night. I'm still between Kie and Mason, but we've flipped. Kie's now behind me, hugging me to his chest while I hug Mason to mine. It must be a comical sight. I'm smaller than the two, and our bodies don't align properly.

Both men easily wrap around me, but I can't do the same. My knees dig into the tops of Mason's thighs, and my face is buried against his shoulder blades.

"Come back," I order Kie, my words muffled as they vibrate against Mason's back.

"In a minute," Kie says. "I have to use the restroom."

Quiet footfalls patter away, and I dig my face into Mason's shoulder with an exaggerated yawn. Last night was arguably the best sleep of my life, and I hate to admit it might have something to do with the two men who shared my bed.

Mason flips over, half-rolling on top of me in the process. He's warm, and I frown as I'm pushed onto my back and a sleepy, mussed-hair shifter flops over me. His morning erection is pressing against my hip, incessant and needy.

Mason seems satiated, though. He's not looking at me with the crazed, horny eyes I've grown familiar with seeing these past few days. I'm sure he'd have sex with me in a heartbeat if I asked for it, but he won't be disappointed when I push him away.

Which I intend to do.

I buck my hips and shove at his shoulder, lifting him just enough that I can wiggle out from underneath him. He drops more weight onto my chest, playfully fighting. His refusal to release me typically flares my anger, but I play along.

I fight Mason, twisting and shimmying until I'm on my stomach. Then I attempt to army crawl off the bed, practically fighting for my life as I slide onto the floor. I'm panting by the time I land on the hard ground, and Mason beams at me from over the side of the bed.

"You're weak," he says. "Weak and small and frail." He raises both his eyebrows. "It's good that you have a strong mate to protect you."

"You're right," I admit. Pride practically emanates from him in waves, and I shoot him a sickly-sweet smile as Kie returns to the room. "I'm so grateful to have you, *Kie*."

The faerie shoots me a look, then flicks his fingers in a gesture I'm pretty sure means *fuck off* in faerie.

Mason huffs. "I'm stronger than Kie."

"I'm not getting involved," Kie says, sauntering past me.

Mason slinks off the bed, all long limbs and smooth movements. He's a predator, and I can't take my eyes off him. I had sex with him last night. It's all I can think about as he changes into a fresh pair of underwear.

I needed the sex to be good. I needed to know I betrayed Lill for something.

I know now.

I owe Lill a giant apology for doubting her, but I'm not the one who betrayed her. Callie gave her that necklace. Callie tricked Lill into igniting the gods' magic, making her feel a mate bond with Kie and Mason. Callie betrayed Lill, not me.

Mason tugs on a shirt. "I have a meeting with Anox this morning. I suspect he'll demand again that you be formally crowned as my queen consort…" He shoots me a sideways glance. "How would you like me to respond?"

My heart lurches. This is the first time either of them has taken my feelings into consideration.

I clear my throat. "I would be… agreeable to that. I'm not interested in dying, and if the formal title offers me some protection, I'd be a fool not to take it."

After last night, I'm fairly certain I will be staying here. I don't think I'll ever find peace in the human realm, not when I know what and who awaits me here. I agreed to give Kie and Mason a chance, and I meant it.

"And should he demand more?" Mason urges. "Anox will scent you on me, and it's only a matter of time before they begin asking about heirs."

Heirs? Children? I haven't even *begun* to think about that.

"I want a child someday," I admit. "But not now. Not anytime soon."

Mason sits on the edge of the bed. He's staring at me, but I can tell he's lost in thought. What's he thinking? Has what I said shocked him? I've gathered that faeries and shifters don't wait long to have children, shifters especially. It seems it's the cultural norm for them to begin popping them out with a frequency my vagina will *never* know.

"*A* child," Mason eventually says. "Just one?"

Understanding washes over me. "I'm willing to tentatively commit to one *each*," I say, "but I won't agree to anything more.

Not until I better understand what I'm signing myself up for."

Mason visibly perks up, his head bobbing.

Kie returns to the room, a white dress thrown over his arm, and Mason wordlessly takes that as his cue to leave. He pats Kie's shoulder as he passes but says nothing. Did Kie overhear our conversation? I assume he did, but he doesn't address it.

"Can I dress you?" he asks.

Dress me? "Why?"

Kie's lips twitch, the shadow of a smile appearing. "It's symbolic to the faeries. If we're to be mates, I want to do it right. I want to dress you."

"Okay." I eye the white fabric in his arms. "Sure."

Kie beams, offering me a rare full smile as he straightens out the dress and tugs it over my head. I lift my arms, helping Kie slip the lightweight cotton fabric over me, and obediently spin so he can tie the laces in the back.

I'm not nearly as comfortable around Kie as I am with Mason. The shifter forced his affection on me, and he was persistent enough to break through my defenses. I'm still adjusting to Kie, but it seems he's making a genuine effort.

"All done," Kie says, patting my back.

I clear my throat. "Thank you."

"Jackie and I have a scheduled meeting this morning. An update on your attack." Kie's words come tumbling out, almost like he's scared to say them. "I'd like you to come with me. I'm going to tell her the truth about us, which I should've done from the beginning. She'll be angry, and I fear she might say things meant to hurt you. I don't know what they'll be, but we have a long history and there are a lot of truths for her to pick from."

Truths.

Kie takes a deep breath before continuing, not giving me time to think. "She probably won't want to help us after she learns the truth, but—"

"Does she love you?" I ask. I speak without thinking, but I don't regret the question.

Kie pauses. My question has caught him off guard, and he takes a long moment to think before answering. Every second feels like a battering ram to my chest.

"I don't think so," he eventually says. "She likes power, and I've always been an easy way to access it. I believe she likes who I am as a person, but she doesn't love me. I fear she won't help once she realizes marriage is off the table."

I don't understand why we even need her help. Is there nobody else who can investigate the issue? Is Jackie truly the most connected person here?

I suppose it shouldn't surprise me. A tentative marriage agreement was in place between Jackie, Kie, and Mason. They were going to marry her. Jackie was raised to fill the role of queen consort, and she's positioned herself accordingly.

She's well-connected, and she's smart.

She's so well prepared for the role that we have no choice but to come to her with our tails tucked between our legs, begging for help. If she were in my position, I doubt Kie and Mason would be dealing with this. She'd have it handled herself.

She'd made a good leader.

"You should offer her a position on the council." The words are bitter on my tongue. "Do you think that would make her happy?"

Kie shakes his head, immediately dismissing the idea. "Council members are active members of court. If Jackie were given a position, she'd become a permanent fixture in our lives. I've already made so many mistakes, Abby, and I won't do that to you. We'll figure something out."

Jackie's been rude the few times we've met, and I can

confidently say I'm not a fan of her, but I'm capable of remaining objective. She's an important asset. Our desperation for her to look into my attack proves it. Kie and Mason should be working to secure her loyalty.

The faeries are already so upset with the recent turn of events. They're displeased with Mason's new title, and I doubt they'll be happy to learn I'm Kie and Mason's mate. We need all the support we can get. We aren't in a position to be picky.

"You need her," I push.

Kie purses his lips. I can't help but smile, my cheeks growing warm. I secretly like Kie's hesitance. Jackie throws herself at him, and I don't want him taking her up on her advances. Humans don't have mating bonds, and cheating runs rampant within relationships.

"Abby," Kie starts. He closes the distance between us, his movements filled with a nervous energy. "I'm scared she'll say something to hurt you when she discovers you're my mate." He's returning to his earlier conversation. It must be weighing heavily on his mind.

I grab Kie's hands and pull them to my waist, silently telling him it's okay to touch me. He curls his fingers around my hips, his grip tight.

"I've dated other men, Kie," I say. "I've had good sex. I've been in love." Kie looks like he's about to combust. I continue. "I don't like Jackie, but I won't be devastated to hear you fingered her at a dinner party or fucked her underneath a waterfall. Annoyed? Yes. Jealous? Probably a little. But I'll be okay. We're both adults with pasts, Kie."

"I've never had sex underneath a waterfall."

"That's not the point of what I was saying."

Kie sighs, pressing his forehead against mine. "I know."

I don't get the feeling that he believes me, but I don't know what else to say to assure him. Mason told me before that humans don't feel the mate bond as strongly as faeries and shifters, and maybe this is a part of it.

I have no interest in sharing Kie and Mason, but I won't lose my head over being around Jackie. I can handle a few rude remarks. I'm the one who shares a bed with the men she wants. Kie held *me* last night while Mason fucked me, not her. He'll never hold her, and she'll never feel Mason. I've already won.

Kie and I leave the room, only to find Mason lingering in the kitchen. He's standing in the center of the room, a piece of pink fruit in one hand and a broken wooden spoon in the other. He points the snapped end at me.

"Don't *ever* talk to me about other men."

I snort. "Don't eavesdrop on my private conversations."

I would never acknowledge other men with Mason. I'm not stupid. Kie and Mason are wildly different people. Kie can handle adult conversations, and Mason is a toddler who breaks spoons.

"I was a virgin before you," I tell Mason. "I've never so much as laid eyes on another man."

Mason stomps out of the kitchen. "Obviously." He grabs my chin and tilts my face toward his, urging me to look him in the eye. "I was a virgin, too. You're my only."

He's such a liar. He's been with plenty of women, but I like pretending they don't exist. I'll never meet any of his lovers, and he'll never meet mine. The lie is harmless, and we both know it.

There's a sharp knock on the front door. I'd bet money it's Anox, or a guard sent by Anox, to remind Mason of his council meeting this morning. It's enough to ruin the mood, and I let out a quiet sigh as Kie and Mason snap into work mode. Their teasing smiles disappear, now replaced with stern expressions and purposeful movements.

Here we go.

Chapter Thirty-Two

ABBY

KIE SLIPS HIS hand into mine, his bare palm pressing against me. He's not wearing his gloves, and he's openly touching me. He's making a statement.

Mason should be well into his council meeting by now, and he will approve Anox's request to have me formally titled. It's a terrifying thought, one I'm not ready for. I'm not what the faeries want in a queen, and I'm okay with that. Zaha must have picked me for a reason, though.

Kie brings me to his office, and I sit on his oversized couch. I'm nervous and antsy to meet with Jackie, and I instinctively rub a hand over my chest. I still feel phantom pain from when the faeries tried to kill me, and it's giving me anxiety. I'm scared they're going to try again.

I don't want to die.

I'm sure Kie and Mason are also eager to resolve this issue. It's been days of hovering, the pair not letting so much as five feet of distance come between us. I have to practically beg to shower alone.

There's a knock on the door.

"Come in," Kie says.

The door cracks open, and a guard I don't recognize pops his head inside. His gaze lands on me, then shifts immediately to Kie. Has he already heard about me being Kie and Mason's mate? I doubt it will take long for word to spread once Mason gives permission.

"Jackie just entered the grounds," the guard says. "Shall we permit her entry?"

"Yes," Kie says. "Ensure she's escorted directly here. I don't want her wandering around."

The guard nods, his gaze briefly flashing toward me before he leaves, shutting the door behind him.

"Do you think he knows?" I ask the second we're alone.

"Most definitely."

"Do you think he's upset?"

Kie frowns, lacing his hands together on his desk. "Most faeries will be disappointed, but I anticipate the guards are quite fond of you. You've calmed Mason considerably, making working here less…well… less dangerous."

I still remember how Mason attacked that guard on my first day here. It was violent and abrupt, and I can only imagine the terror the guards felt whenever the shifter was near. Mason's an asshole through and through. Maybe that's why he's so protective of his. He identifies with it.

Kie leans back in his chair. "You're going to be a queen. Queen Abigail Williams. It has a nice ring to it, don't you think?"

I agree. I want a gold scepter, one with a ruby on top. I bet Kie and Mason could procure one for me. I'll carry it around everywhere I go. I'm not going to be a good ruler, I'm fully aware of that, but I still want to be remembered for something. Being known as the human queen who carried around a scepter would be kind of fun.

"It's a good thing you're here," I admit. "The faeries would revolt if it were just Mason and me. They like you. They respect you."

Kie gives me a forced smile. They respect him, but it still might not be enough. They don't believe he has any control over Mason. There's a good chance they'll revolt after learning their queen consort is a human.

"I—" I start. "I'm sorry Zaha took your title from you. You'd make a wonderful king."

Kie shrugs, glancing away. "I don't need to be a wonderful king." There's a nervous energy to his words, like he's afraid of my response. "I just need to be yours."

He whispers the last part, and his violet eyes flicker anxiously in my direction. It makes me wonder. Everything he's ever cared about has been taken from him—quite publicly, too. That's enough to make even the most confident person insecure.

"Kie." I swallow past the lump in my throat. "You—"

Kie shakes his head, turning away from me just as Jackie pushes open the door. She welcomes herself inside, confidently stepping into Kie's office as if she'd been here a million times. She probably has.

She looks beautiful. She's in a long silver dress, and her blonde-white hair has been pinned behind her ears. I resist the urge to smooth down my frizzy strands as Jackie's gaze flickers toward me.

"Why?" is all she asks.

The question is directed toward Kie.

"Sit," he says, gesturing toward the chair opposite his desk.

All signs of vulnerability are gone, and now there stands a man who has spent his life preparing to be king. There's not one hint of emotion in his expression, not one hint of Kie behind his cold, dead eyes and stiff posture.

Jackie glances at me again before taking the seat Kie offered her. She walks with natural grace, and I can see why she was chosen to be queen.

"What have you learned?" Kie asks.

He wants to extract as much information as possible before telling her I'm his mate. Jackie doesn't take the bait. She crosses her arms over her chest and leans back in her chair. Then her head swivels toward me.

I maintain eye contact, refusing to cower.

"I'd like to know who tried killing me," I say, hoping it explains why I'm here.

Jackie rolls her eyes. "I'm sure."

She knows. She knows who I am to Kie, and she won't tell us anything. She purses her lips together and wrinkles her nose, subtle disgust shining through her otherwise-neutral expression.

"What do you know, Jackie?" Kie says, drawing attention back toward him.

He's calm and even-tempered. It's impressive. Attractive, even. I've never seen Kie in a professional setting, and he's good at it. He would've made a wonderful king, and while Mason is great, he's less... *diplomatic*. I don't understand why Zaha forced them to switch positions.

"Why should I tell you anything?" Jackie asks. "My prospects only stand to diminish with Abby as our queen, and I don't want to be on the wrong side of the divide."

"Mason is your king, and I'm acting on his behalf. Do you truly wish to deny your—"

I interrupt. "There's an open spot on the council."

Kie shut down my idea when I suggested it earlier, but I stand by it. Jackie wants power, and this gives it to her. He won't win her over with poorly concealed threats, but bribery always works. It's how humans get things done.

Kie shoots me a sharp look, one that screams *shut the fuck up and let me handle this.* I'm going to be getting an earful from him later.

"That isn't—" Kie starts.

Jackie lifts her hand, silencing Kie. Then she turns toward me, her violet eyes piercing. "Continue."

Happy to. "You can't be queen, at least not in title, but the work still needs to be done. Kie and Mason need somebody with influence, and you were raised for the position. There's an open spot on the council for the duties I can't fulfill, which is just about everything."

There's no arguing a mate bond. Jackie can't be queen while I'm in the picture. This is the best offer she will get, and I hope she can see it.

"Lady Cassandra and Lord Bishop have shown interest in the position," Kie says, continuing my lie. I fight back a victorious smirk. "They're always looking for higher council positions, but we wanted to speak with you first."

Jackie sucks her lips into her mouth, almost appearing as if she doesn't know whether or not to believe us. Vanity seems to win out, though, as she straightens her shoulders and bobs her head.

"Lady Cassandra doesn't understand strategy, and everybody knows Lord Bishop only got the position through his family name," she says. "Giving either of them meaningful responsibility would be a mistake." She hums, tapping her fingers against her thigh. "New members must be voted in by the council and approved by Mason. I wish for them to be present for this conversation."

Why?

My leg begins to bounce, and I press my palm against the top of my knee to keep it still. I don't want Jackie to see how nervous I am. Anox and the other council members will probably cream their pants when they hear we've made this offer, but Mason will be livid.

I didn't discuss my plan with him, mainly because I didn't realize we'd need his approval. He'll never go for it.

"In front of Mason?" Kie asks.

Jackie nods, confirming. "Yes." She rises from her chair. "I heard there's a council meeting currently in session. Shall we go?"

She exits the room before Kie responds.

I avoid looking at Kie. Instead, I clear my throat and rise from the couch. Kie meets me there, and he places a hand on the small of my back as he guides me outside, where Jackie's impatiently waiting.

"We *will* be discussing this later," he whispers, his tone sharp.

Jackie turns and smiles at us over her shoulder, her eyes twinkling. She heard Kie's threat, and she's pleased he's angry with me. I hope I don't come to regret my decision.

Chapter Thirty-Three

MASON

THE COUNCIL MEMBERS are already waiting in the chamber room. They used to smile and rise for Queen Gitta and Kie, but I receive nothing more than silent stares. It doesn't bother me, not when I know I'll be returning to Abby and Kie this evening.

I have the respect of the people who are important to me.

The council members are nothing more than nuisances I'm forced to work with.

In the center of the room is a long table, and I sit in the head seat that Queen Gitta once occupied. The spot on my left is reserved for Kie and remains empty. Lord Bishop is on my right, and Lady Cassandra is beside him. Directly across from me is Anox.

I tap my fingers against the table, eyeing the platter of food in the center. I'm hungry, but it's not customary to eat during council meetings. Queen Gitta hated the distraction.

I maintain eye contact with Anox as I lean forward and snatch a piece of fruit. Lord Bishop makes a quiet noise in the back of his throat, his violet eyes growing wide, before he follows my lead. Lady Cassandra and Anox remain where they are, refusing the food.

I'm not surprised. Anox is a stickler for what he believes to be the proper way, and Lady Cassandra has hated me since I rejected her sexual advances on my fifteenth birthday. She would deny it if asked, but I suspect she still feels spurned.

Kie believes I'm reading into things that don't exist.

"I presume you slept well," Anox starts, breaking the tense silence. "You seem in good spirits this morning, Your Majesty."

I bite into my fruit to hide my smile. I slept exceptionally well last night, all thanks to Abby. Having Kie in my bed was new, and I don't appreciate how we occasionally brushed legs or arms, but it was tolerable. I imagine I'll get used to his presence with time.

Abby likes it, so I won't complain. I'm also not going to suggest alternating nights with her. That's simply not an option.

I frown. "You can call me Mason."

"I will not," is Anox's smooth reply. He turns toward Lady Cassandra and Lord Bishop. "And neither will you."

I shove my hand into my pocket, playing with the red lace I stole from Kie. I enjoy having something of Abby's to carry around. It helps calm me, but she'd be angry if she learned what I was doing. I don't see why. The underwear is clean, and it's not like I'm walking around the property swinging them around my finger.

I also saved one of the legs from the barstool she broke last night. I enjoy my trinkets, and I want one from the night she gave herself to us. I wonder if she'd let me fuck her with it.

"We've decided to move forward with Abby's coronation," I begin. "We've considered the points you laid out yesterday, and we agree that the protection the title provides outweighs the negatives."

Anox falls silent. I lean back in my chair. There. It's been decided. My mate is not a secret to be ashamed of, and we can only realistically hide her for so long. The sooner we break the news, the sooner we can move past it. People already suspect, especially after our display during court.

Kie touched her, and she was the only thing that kept me stable.

I almost murdered every faerie in my vicinity when she was attacked, and she alone prevented me from doing so. And when my father was baiting me, Abby's touch kept me in place. I'd thank her for it if I didn't fear she'd hold it above my head.

Lord Bishop presses his palms against the table, his lips pursed as he searches for the right words. He's afraid of angering me, which he should be. I won't tolerate his disrespect, especially not toward my mate.

"She is…" he starts. "You mentioned she handled human finances, yes? Is she experienced? Educated? If we push that information out alongside her crowning, perhaps we can assuage some fears regarding having a human queen consort."

I straighten up. That's not a bad idea.

"Or they'll be worried we're going to allow a human to manage the kingdom's finances," Lady Cassandra chimes in. "We shouldn't—"

Anox raises a hand. "No. I like this idea. Our financial affairs are covered by a team of six and overseen by me. Abigail's expected to take a position on the council, but given her lack of royal experience, we can start her off underneath me. She will shadow me, and when I feel she is ready, she will be fully enveloped within the council."

I'm not sure about this. I don't know if Abby wishes to work, let alone in something as dull as finances. Even if she does, I don't know how *I* feel about her working underneath Anox. Title will place her above him, but title technically put Kie and me above him when we were children. It wasn't respected.

Anox is admittedly an excellent mentor. He ensured Kie and I received the best education, but he was stern. He worked us to our breaking point, and he did so without mercy. I'm not sure if I can sign Abby up for that, especially without her permission.

"Let me discuss with Abby," I say.

"Why?" Lord Bishop cocks his head to the side. "You are her king, are you not?"

"Do you have a mate, Lord Bishop?"

He shakes his head.

I snort. "Then you simply do not understand."

I am terrified of Abby.

Anox sucks his cheeks into his mouth. "Have you been intimate? I don't ask because I care to know the details of your private lives, but with Queen Gitta gone…" I work my jaw side to side. "You and Prince Kieran are the last of the royal bloodline, and after the attack on Abigail's life, I don't think it will benefit anybody to postpone heirs."

I knew he'd bring this up. I clasp my hands in my lap, my anger mounting. They are prying.

"People will be quite pleased to hear she is trying with Prince Kieran," Lady Cassandra says. "If you allow her firstborn to be faerie, and you claim him as your heir, it would solve several of our issues. This generation may be lost to a shifter and human, but our future remains faerie."

Lord Bishop opens his mouth, but Anox lifts a hand to stop him. Even he doesn't care to hear Lord Bishop's asinine comments. They're rarely helpful.

"I can see you're getting upset." Anox gestures to my quivering arms. "I trust that you and Prince Kieran understand your responsibilities, and I will let you come to me when you're ready to share."

That might be the kindest thing Anox has ever said, but he's only doing it out of fear. He doesn't want to see me lose control, and this topic has me hanging on by a thread. I want children with Abby, but I won't be demanding them from her.

I tighten my fingers around the lace in my pocket. "We should discuss Alpha Theon. I suspect he's—"

The chamber room doors burst open, cutting me off.

Jackie comes storming inside a moment later, with Kie and Abby in tow. Kie refuses to meet my eye, and Jackie looks suspiciously pleased with herself. It's enough to have alarm bells ringing in my head. What has he done?

Abby looks around, her eyes darting between the chairs. She doesn't know where to sit, and I use Jackie and Kie's distraction to wave her over.

"What's this?" Anox asks Kie.

Abby nears, and I pull her onto my lap. She smells like Kie and me, and I bury my face against the side of her neck with a contented sigh. I never thought I'd get to enjoy her like this—not after everything Kie and I did to her. I'm going to soak it in.

Jackie sits across from Lady Cassandra, welcoming herself into our space. Kie takes the seat on my left. He's still avoiding eye contact with me. If Abby weren't in my lap, I'd be strangling him. I'm unsure what he's done, but I don't like it.

"I have offered Jackie a position on the council," Kie says.

Jackie beams, clasping her hands on the table. Lord Bishop and Lady Cassandra look confused, their eyebrows pulled together and their lips scrunched. Anox is the only one who takes the information in stride.

I faintly remember Abby suggesting the idea to Kie this morning, but he vehemently disagreed. I assumed that was the end of the discussion. It seems my assumption was wrong.

I tighten my arms around Abby's middle. "Was this you?" I whisper into her ear.

She doesn't respond, but Kie gives a curt nod. He's pissed.

"Jacqueline?" Anox asks. "A council member? Why was this not discussed with me?"

Jackie clears her throat and straightens up. "Their Majesties chose to keep the decision quiet while I was investigating the attack on our queen."

She referred to Abby as her queen. It's a subtle gesture, but it's meaningful. I slide my hand down Abby's thigh, trying to read her emotions. She doesn't seem angered by Jackie's presence, so I won't be, either.

I understand why Kie is uncomfortable with the faerie, but I have no history with Jackie. I'm not pleased with the way she treated Abby in the bathhouse, but seeing Lillian drown her lessened much of my anger.

She was humiliated. It's enough for me.

Anox leans back in his chair. He doesn't look as upset as I'd expect him to be. Maybe he sees through our lies. This was a last-minute decision, one made by our mate. Or perhaps he's too pleased to be upset. He actively participated in the discussions regarding Kie and me taking Jackie as our wife.

Several moments pass before he speaks. "Council members must be voted in. I have not—"

"Nonsense, Anox," Jackie says, smoothly cutting him off. "This couldn't be discussed with you or the council, not when it was one of you who organized Abby's execution."

Lady Cassandra recoils. "One of us?" Her gaze flickers between Anox and Lord Bishop. "Who?"

I wonder the same thing. When Kie rattled off his list of suspects, none of the council members were on it. We would've never allowed Abby near them if they had been.

Jackie smirks. "Did you know Lord Bishop took out a loan against his estate late last year?" She levels her stare with Lord Bishop. "It's a shame how far your family name has fallen. You were once renowned for your propensity to manipulate magic, but you're nothing more than a beggar in expensive clothing. Rumor is you were denied a loan extension last month."

Abby runs her fingers up and down my forearm. I see where this is heading, and my body is on edge and ready for a fight. I want to rip Lord Bishop's heart out through his throat. I want to watch him choke on his blood. I want him to suffer.

Instead, I remain rooted to my seat. It takes all my self-control to do so.

"When word about Abby and Lillian spread, you were approached by a shifter. He offered you a hefty sum of money to kill Abby, didn't he? Gave you a stone filled with gods' magic and laid out what I must admit was a flawless plan. Nobody anticipated Kie being able to overpower the magic, though."

Kie overpowered gods' magic? How strong *is* he?

Abby shifts. She must be wondering something similar. I tighten my grip on her, using her to remain calm. Lord Bishop is much too close to my liking. One wrong movement and I will decapitate him. The sight will upset Abby, but it's a necessary evil.

Lord Bishop shakes his head, his mouth gaping. "That isn't true." His gaze snaps toward me. "You have to believe me! I have no idea what she's talking about. I would never—"

"It's interesting that you were approached *before* Lillian was discovered as a fraud," Jackie continues. "Why Abby?"

Kie rises. "Alpha Theon and Callie knew that Abby is our true mate." He stands behind Lord Bishop's chair, holding the man captive as he speaks with Jackie. "How do you know this?"

"I have several connections within the Redstall Forest," Jackie admits. She turns toward Abby. "The favors I called in were valuable, but I will consider the council position fair payment."

Jackie has shifter connections? I shouldn't be surprised. Most faeries would never consider it, but Jackie's never been afraid to get her hands dirty. It makes her dangerous, and it reinforces our need to have her on our side.

Jackie points a finger toward Lord Bishop. She's enjoying this.

"You are a sneaky, sneaky boy," she teases. "It was a good idea, truly. One that would've worked if Kie were weaker."

That's not entirely true. Had Kie not been able to save Abby, I would have murdered every faerie within the room. They can't hurt Abby when they're dead. I would've saved her. It just would've been slightly more violent.

Chapter Thirty-Four

ABBY

MASON IS PAINFULLY stiff below me, his muscles tense and unmoving. I curl my fingers around his wrist, holding him in place. I can tell he's a second away from lunging across this table, and I'd love for him not to do that—especially while I'm still sitting in his lap.

Lord Bishop is fumbling, his vibrant, violet eyes darting rapidly between Mason, me, and Kie. They show the most fear when they land on Mason. Everybody knows he's the wild card, and from what I've heard, he has a long and dark history of murdering faeries.

Jackie's smirking. She's pleased with herself, and I imagine she must feel like the faerie version of Sherlock Holmes.

"And what proof do you have?" Lady Cassandra asks. "An accusation of this scale surely should have some proof beyond the words of a *shifter*."

Woof. Mason shifts below me. I dig my nails into his wrist.

Jackie gestures toward Lord Bishop. He's trembling. "What more proof do I need than this?" She makes a good point.

Lady Cassandra rises, disappearing from the room a second later. Where is she going? Nobody follows her, but after a minute, she returns with four guards in tow. These aren't the regular guards who patrol the grounds. These ones are huge, and they're wearing silver armor.

They line the back of the room, waiting for orders as Lady Cassandra returns to her seat.

"Lord Bishop… Anthony." It's Anox who speaks. "Is this true?"

Lord Bishop shakes his head, the motion panicked and jerky. I'm having a hard time feeling bad for him. If what Jackie says *is* true, then he tried to kill me. And for what? Money?

"I had no choice," he mumbles. My eyes narrow as Lord Bishop locks gazes with Kie. "We begged your family for help, and you've offered us nothing but well-wishes and nominal support. We can't survive off that."

Kie recoils. "What the fuck do you expect us to do? We have an entire kingdom to run. Your inability to properly manage your household finances is not our problem."

He makes a good point.

"I didn't know she was your mate," Lord Bishop continues. "I swear! I never would've accepted had I known. I thought she was just some random human. Nobody would miss her, and—"

Mason speaks up. "Get him out of here." He's fully quivering below me, the telltale sign of a shift. "Bring him to the cells."

There's a moment where nobody moves.

"Now!"

The four guards Lady Cassandra brought in move forward in one fluid movement. They force Lord Bishop out of his chair, and a tingling warmth covers my body. I recognize it as magic, but it's stronger than it was the day I was attacked. It's seeping through me, hopefully as nothing more than a preventative measure as Lord Bishop is removed from the room.

I make eye contact with Kie. He's tensed in concentration, and his eyebrows furrow before his attention snaps toward Jackie. The newest council member is staring at me with unnerving focus, and my breath hitches as I realize she's also using magic to protect me. She offers only a wink, and when the door slams shut behind a shouting Lord Bishop and the guards, some of the tingling vanishes and she looks away.

Kie's magic remains, though, even as he slouches into Lord Bishop's empty chair and drags a hand through his hair.

"Was my father involved?" Mason asks Jackie. "Did your contact say which shifters were behind the attack?"

Jackie shakes her head. "No, and I doubt that's information I'll be able to get. Shifters protect their own, but Lord Bishop might be willing to share some additional details for a leaner sentence."

"There will be no leaner sentences." It's Anox who decides this. "We need to make an example out of him. Your rule is strong, and there *will* be punishment for acting against the crown." Anox points at Mason. "You will be staying far away from this. Prince Kieran and Jacqueline will facilitate the trial and subsequent punishment."

Mason scoffs. "You can't expect me to hide behind Kie. If the crown is strong, it will be strong *with* me."

Kie shifts in his seat but remains silent, letting Mason and Anox sort through this themselves.

Jackie's watching with poorly conceived excitement, and I'm already regretting offering her a council position. I didn't realize Anox would demand that she and Kie do things together, and I don't like the implication it sends.

It's too late to reverse the decision, especially since Jackie has already accepted it and Anox seems so taken with the idea.

Mason and Anox stare at one another, neither willing to concede.

Kie finally speaks, cutting through the tension. "I will not be seen with Jackie until Abby has been titled." Anox frowns, and Kie continues. "I will not be earning the affection of my people at the detriment of my mate. The faeries will know who Abby is, and they'll know nothing will ever come of Jackie's position on the council."

Jackie speaks. "You should let Mason participate in the trial. He'll grow angry, and it'll please the people to see Abby in action." She gestures to where I'm holding his wrist. "They'll find her ability to tame him encouraging."

Mason grunts, and the next thing I know, I'm being carried out of the room. The shifter is furious—I can tell by his heavy footfalls and the way he shoves open the chamber room doors. He can't just up and leave in the middle of a meeting.

"What's your problem?" I hiss.

"I am *not* defective," Mason says. "Nor am I a wild animal."

"Mason, you are very literally a wild animal." He's living in denial if he thinks otherwise. "You have virtually zero patience, and the faeries are terrified of you."

Mason doesn't respond, and I peer over his shoulder. Kie's still sitting at the table. He looks mildly annoyed, but it doesn't seem like he's planning on following us out of the room. I suppose that's good. He can catch me up later.

I want to know what the plan is concerning Lord Bishop.

Mason carries me home.

"Explain," I say the moment we're alone.

Mason finally sets me on my feet. "No. I don't wish to."

"Well, it's a good thing you're an adult who understands that sometimes you have to do things you don't want to do." Mason tries escaping into the kitchen, but I'm hot on his heels. "I don't think there's anything wrong with them acknowledging your violent tendencies. You've killed faeries, for fuck's sake."

Mason darts into the living room, trying to get away from me.

I sigh. "Mason, literally everybody knows you're out of control. The faeries are terrified of you, and I'm pretty sure they have been since the day you arrived in the capital."

He's still frowning, and I pull him into a hug.

"Isn't this nice?" I tease. I press my chin against his chest and peer up at him. "Don't you enjoy me calming you? If it makes you feel better, I'll let you tell people you boss me around when we're alone."

Mason shoots me a dirty look. "I already tell them that."

The corners of his lips twitch, the slight break all I need to see. Mason's embarrassed by Jackie's remarks, but he enjoys my teasing. I've never played with Mason like this, and I like it.

"I don't understand why you're so embarrassed," I say. "I don't think you're weak because you need some help leveling out. Besides, I kind of like the implication. You're unhinged, and you need me to function."

I slide my hands up the back of his shirt.

"Would you like to—"

The front door opens and Kie steps inside—with Jackie, Anox, and Lady Cassandra trailing behind.

"Sit," Kie orders us, pointing to the dining table. "We aren't finished."

I sit. Mason stands in the corner of the room, rebelling.

"We need to discuss Abigail's coronation," Anox says. He gives Kie a sharp look. "We should do it alongside a formal announcement of Jacqueline's new position."

He's looking for any way to soften the blow that a human is to be the queen consort. I don't take offense to it, but I'd be lying if I said it didn't hurt my feelings just the slightest bit. Being a human isn't this awful thing they're making it out to be.

Anox chews on his bottom lip. "I'd like to do it today. This confusion with Lillian and Abigail has gone on for too long, and we should coronate her, then announce Jacqueline's position on the council and Lord Bishop's betrayal in one fell swoop."

Today? Doesn't that seem a bit soon?

"Abby hasn't had time to prepare," Kie says.

"She saw His Majesty's ceremony, did she not?" Anox asks. "She knows what to expect, and the sooner we get this over with, the sooner we can focus our attention on the shifters."

Mason presses himself against the back of my chair, his hands landing on my shoulders. "What do you want?" he asks me. "We'll support whatever you decide."

What do I want? That's a good question, and I have no answer. I want this drama to disappear so I can be the pretty princess I've always dreamed of. I highly doubt that Ariel and Cinderella had to deal with this much politics.

"I want my family there," I decide.

Lady Cassandra taps her fingers against the table. "I can retrieve them."

Kie nods. "Yes. Go."

I press my lips into a flat line. It's nice to know that bringing them here has been this easy all along, yet somehow, I've been made to go all this time without them. I've been missing my family, which I haven't kept a secret.

Lady Cassandra leaves, and our front door slams shut a second later. I turn toward Kie. "How does she know who they are?"

Kie smiles. "We know everything about you."

That's not as comforting as I believe he intends it to be.

"Wonderful," Anox says, bringing his hands together. "We'll hold Abigail's ceremony this evening, and tomorrow, we will begin a plan of action against the shifters."

Mason sucks on his front teeth. "The shifters are primed for war."

Anox nods. "As are we."

"Are you sure about that?" Jackie asks. "We have no means to fight against delysum, and the border cities will bear the brunt of their attack. If the shifters strike, thousands will die."

This was briefly discussed yesterday, and I stare at the table as Anox explains everything the council spoke about during the last meeting. It's hard to believe it was just yesterday that we met with Alpha Theon.

Anox and Jackie argue, the two rehashing the same argument Kie and Mason had with him last night. They come to the same upsetting conclusion, too. There's no avoiding this. The shifters have spent years priming for war, and the time for passive action has passed. They don't care to negotiate with us, and if we let them set the terms for the fight, we stand no chance.

The faeries have to act.

Anox and Jackie leave. I remain seated, still staring at the table. I'm going to be a queen, the faerie who tried to kill me is probably going to be executed, Kie's ex-lover is now part of the council, and my mates are preparing to go to war.

Kie stands and paces the length of the room. Mason's the only one who appears calm and collected, which is a surprise. It's usually the opposite.

"My family doesn't know that faeries exist," I say, shifting their focus to something less unsettling. "I'm nervous to see them."

Kie leans against the wall, his arms crossed over his chest and his shoulder pressed against the plaster. "Why are you nervous?"

"They're going to be upset with me. I left without warning, and I should've reached out sooner."

Mason shrugs. "You can blame us."

"I intend to."

It is mostly their fault, after all. I decided to leave the human realm, but they decided to trap me here after discovering my relationship with Lill.

"I'm nervous, too," Mason blurts out. He joins Kie in his pacing. "What if your parents don't like me?"

"I won't tell them everything," I promise.

Mason drops his head, staring at the ground. He kicks his foot out, scuffing it along the floor before giving a jerky shrug. "You don't have to do that."

"I know."

I listened to Kie when he said he's afraid of his mistakes being held over him for the remainder of our lives. I want to move past this as much as he does, and I don't care to revisit it with my family. They won't understand, not that I blame them. They haven't seen how hard Mason and Kie have worked to fix things.

There's a knock on our front door. Is that them? Already?

My heart lurches, and I spring forward and rip open the door.

The second I see my mom's long, brown hair and damp eyes, I burst into tears. I don't mean to. I told myself I wouldn't cry, but I can't help it. For a while, I feared I'd never see her again. I thought I'd be sold to Zaha, forever removed from everybody and everything I've ever loved.

Mom pushes past my father and Lady Cassandra, and her comforting arms surround me within seconds.

I knew I missed my mom, but I didn't truly let myself feel it until now. I was in survival mode, and then I was distracted by Lill, Mason, and Kie. Being in her arms and smelling her muted vanilla perfume is a sharp reminder of how much I've missed her. It physically hurts, like a knife between the ribs.

"Baby girl," Mom chokes out. "My baby girl."

She's sobbing into my hair, her cries so heavy her chest is heaving against mine. A second pair of arms wraps around me, and I turn and bury my face against my dad's soft shoulder. I don't think I've ever felt so safe.

My brother clears his throat. He's moved closer, but he hasn't joined in the hug. He fiddles with the hem of his ratty high school football t-shirt, nervously tugging at the small hole in the corner. He looks worse for wear. His dark brown hair is unusually messy, and it's been a few days since he last shaved.

My dad doesn't appear much better. Dark bags sit below their matching brown eyes, and my dad in particular looks like he's lost a few pounds. Is this because of me?

Aaron licks his lips. "I suppose you and Lill weren't lying about faeries, after all."

I let out an unattractive snort. I spent years trying to convince him and Tommy Knocker that Lill was a faerie, but they never believed me. I'm going to make Mason transform into his animal form later and scare him.

"I told you so," I say.

Aaron's bottom lip wobbles, and he sucks his cheeks into his mouth and glares at the ceiling before joining the hug pile.

"You stupid fucking bitch," he says. "We thought you were dead. We had search parties and everything. I was researching bodyless funerals."

I let out another laugh, but it sounds more like a cry. "I'm so sorry."

Aaron and Dad back away, but Mom continues staring like she's afraid I'll vanish before her very eyes. Mason and Kie still stand off to the side, and Lady Cassandra is nowhere to be seen. The path outside the front door is empty, excluding the guards who usually mill about.

Mom glances at the two men hovering behind me.

"And who are they?"

Kie smoothly interrupts. "Let's take a seat, shall we? There's a lot to explain."

Chapter Thirty-Five

ABBY

KIE EFFORTLESSLY TRANSFORMS into the perfect host, an award-winning smile plastered across his lips as he guides my family into the living room.

My mom holds my hand, her grip borderline painful. I'm sure she has a million questions—I would if I were in her position. My dad is quiet, and he's wearing the expression of a man who's mildly convinced that nothing happening around him is real. His mouth is slightly open, and his gaze continually flickers around the room.

It's not every day a woman magically appears in your home and tells you she's taking you to a faerie realm where your missing daughter is about to be crowned queen.

"So…" Aaron says, sitting on the edge of the couch. He looks between Kie and Mason. "You're a faerie, and you're a… werewolf? That's what the woman who brought us here said."

"They call them shifters," I correct him. "But, yeah, it's pretty much a werewolf. Just without all the whole moon and garlic lore."

"Garlic is vampires," Dad absentmindedly says.

I nod. "Right."

Aaron drags a hand through his hair. Mason blinks, his eyes narrowing in on my brother. I wince.

In an effort to keep him calm after I was attacked, I told him all about my childhood. Amid my panic, I didn't think to explain that despite Aaron calling me a troll and bullying me relentlessly, I still love him.

Mason's holding a useless grudge in my honor. It's cute, and it makes me feel a bit bad for conveniently leaving out the parts where I was just as mean to Aaron.

"Mason's the shifter," I say, placing my hand on Mason's shoulder. I give him a warning look, one he either doesn't notice or chooses to ignore. I assume the latter. "I left the human realm to save Lill, and I met Kie and Mason shortly after arriving here. They were traveling together for some personal reasons, and they've kept me safe." That's a lie. I continue. "They're also my mates."

I'm met with three blank stares.

My back breaks into a cold sweat. "The people here have predestined soulmates. I'm theirs."

Mom gulps. "*Both* of them?"

I nod. I don't care to get into the nuances of my relationship, and I mentally prepare for the questions to come. My time here has been complicated, and my family doesn't need to know about it. If they stay here, which I hope they will, they'll eventually learn.

I hope they choose to stay.

My brother has a budding career, but my parents don't have much tying them to the human realm. They have jobs and friends, but they're both only siblings and my grandparents are dead. I want us to stay together, and me leaving isn't an option.

Dad clears his throat but doesn't speak. He looks at a loss for words. I don't blame him.

"And Lill?" Aaron asks.

Fuck. "She's…" I start. "Things are complicated with her right now. She was here for a while, but she left. It's a lot to explain."

Dad nods. "And where exactly is *here*?"

This might be harder to explain. I tighten my grip on Mason's shoulder, unsure where to begin. Probably from the beginning.

I start with Lill's sickness, something they're already aware of. Her health has been visibly declining for years, and I explain how delysum helped preserve her magic before diving into my grand plans to save her.

Even Kie and Mason are hanging on to my every word, and I realize I've never shared the full story with them.

I talk about Samuel, how he bought me dinner and gloves in exchange for a kiss. Mom and Aaron manage weak chuckles. Kie, Mason, and Dad don't find it nearly as funny. Mason's shoulders don't pop out of their sockets, though, which I consider a victory.

I talk about my walk from Callonton to Farbay, leaving out the part where I slept in a stranger's barn.

Mason trails a hand down my spine, his lips brushing against my ear a second later. "You'll never be hungry again."

I momentarily pause. I haven't said anything about being hungry, but he's reading between the lines. I was practically starving, but that's not a piece of information I care to admit to. I want everybody to think I was independent and resourceful as I navigated the faerie world by myself.

I was being heroic. At least, that's the picture of myself I'm going to paint.

Kie props his elbows on his knees as I begin discussing my time in the Redstall Forest. I give a watered-down version, conveniently leaving out how Kie and Mason threatened to murder me and then decided to gift me to Zaha.

My voice grows hoarse as I get to the part about Lill. I explain that Callie is alive and found a way to fake a bond between Lill, Kie, and Mason, and tears begin leaking down my cheeks as I share the queen's murder and Lill's disappearance. I leave out the details of Lill being responsible for the murder. I just can't bring myself to say it.

Kie takes over when it becomes clear I'm struggling to continue.

He lightly touches on the conflict between the faeries and shifters before finally dropping the bomb that I'm going to be crowned queen consort this evening.

"This evening?" Mom repeats.

I nod.

She falls silent again. It doesn't sound real. None of this sounds real, and I didn't realize how absurd everything has been until I said it out loud. It's no wonder my parents are staring at me as if I've grown two heads.

"I think I need to sit down," Mom eventually mumbles.

She's already sitting, and Dad wordlessly rubs her back. Even I'm struggling to wrap my head around everything, and I'm the one who lived through it.

Chapter Thirty-Six

ABBY

TIME WITH MY family passes too quickly. One minute I'm pretending to be interested in Aaron's love life update, and the next they're being politely ushered away by Kie so I can prepare for my coronation.

Mason has been tasked with keeping my family occupied and safe. The idea of my grunting mate trying to entertain my family would be mildly comical on any other day.

His eyes practically bulged out of his head when I gave him the order, but he's the top man for the job. Besides, we all know Kie's the best one to help me prepare. Unlike Mason, Kie cares about faerie traditions. He'll take this seriously.

Two women flitter around me, one braiding my hair into an intricate faerie hairstyle and another trying to teach me the words I'll need to repeat to Anox during the ceremony. She's growing increasingly frustrated. I'm trying my best, but the pronunciation is complicated.

The short-haired, violet-eyed diction coach repeats a word I've been struggling with, and I resist the urge to rip out my hair as I attempt to copy her. My tongue doesn't want to form around the vowels, and the more I try, the worse it gets.

Kie's standing by the front door, closely monitoring my every interaction with the two faerie women. I've gathered that he wasn't involved in the decision to have them help me prepare, and he argued with them at the door for several minutes before grudgingly letting them inside. This must be Anox's doing. Or maybe Jackie's.

I attempt the word again, my fists curling when everything comes out wrong. Why can't I get this? It shouldn't be this hard.

"Let's take a break," Kie suggests.

"Yes." The diction coach nods. "That's a great idea."

She storms from the room, letting the front door slam shut behind her. The young girl styling my hair takes a minute longer to complete what she's doing, and she offers a gentle pat on my shoulder as she finishes and excuses herself. She hasn't spoken a word, but she seems nice. She's been beaming since stepping into the room. She's young, too. I'd guess she's only about thirteen, but Kie didn't bat an eye at her age, so I haven't either.

I faintly remember Lill mentioning once that it's common for children of court to be given small jobs. Maybe this is one of them.

I'm taking it as a good sign that the faeries are trusting their children around me, not that I'm much of a threat. Even at thirteen, I'm sure that girl can whoop my ass.

I wait until Kie and I are alone before speaking. "Tell me more about this whole palm-cutting thing."

It's what I'm most nervous about. Mason cut open his hand during the ceremony, but I have a low tolerance for pain and I don't heal the way the shifter does.

"What are you looking to know?" Kie asks. "It's done to show commitment. To show that you're willing to bleed for your people. You don't have to cut your hand as deeply as Mason did, but you will need to draw blood. It's unavoidable."

I groan, and Kie laughs. "I promise we'll make it up to you."

He stalks toward me, his piercing gaze roaming down my frame. I've changed into a thick, blood-red dress, one picked out by Kie himself. It's low cut, and it's been laced so tightly that my airflow is restricted. I'm not a fan of the lack of oxygen, but Kie obviously enjoys the way it pushes my breasts up.

Kie eyes my chest. "This dress is going to drive Mason crazy."

I frown. "Is that all?"

Kie likes the dress, and I want him to tell me so. I don't enjoy him hiding his compliments behind Mason. He can say them for himself.

"I love it when you wear red," he finally admits. "And I love it when you wear the clothing I picked out. It makes me..."

He trails off, and I bite back a smile. "It makes you what, Kie?"

The way he's looking at me, all need and desire, makes me feel powerful. I enjoy knowing I affect the faerie prince.

His hands land on my hips, heavy and warm, and I can barely contain my excitement as he circles me. I don't spend much alone time with Kie, and I'm looking forward to getting to know him better.

Kie's chest presses against my back, and his hot breath brushes over my shoulder.

I shiver, desperate to know what he's planning. What's he like when the shifter isn't breathing down our necks?

"I'm going to dress you every day of our lives," he says.

I don't mind giving him that control. He obviously loves it, and I don't have a huge desire to pick out my own clothing. It would be nice, but it's by no means a necessity. I express myself in other ways.

Besides, I secretly love the idea of being treated like a precious treasure, dressed up and paraded about. I want to be spoiled and pampered and have every stressful decision taken away. It's not something I'm supposed to admit as an independent, grown adult woman, but it's how I feel.

"How are you?" I blurt out.

A beat of silence, then, "What do you mean?"

"I'm just… I hope you know I'm here to talk if you ever need it."

"Is this about my mother?" Kie asks.

I half shrug, half nod. "Amongst other things. I know it's against faerie tradition to mourn, and you're exceptionally good at ignoring your emotions, but I'm here if you ever want somebody to talk to. I do care."

Kie's warm breath brushes over my neck. "Thank you. I—" He clears his throat, then continues. "It hasn't been easy, but there's no point in dwelling over the things I can't change. I admit I miss my mother and sometimes I'm upset with Mason's recent turn of events, but it helps to focus on the positives. I have a mate, and I have an esteemed position on the council. I'm satisfied with that."

"Are you?" I push.

"I am. I promise you I am."

Kie slides his hands up my waist, bunching the fabric of my dress along the way. Then one of his hands slips down, quickly finding the hem of my dress and disappearing underneath. My breath hitches as his palm lands on my bare thigh.

"Are you excited to be our queen?" he asks, changing the subject.

His wandering hands are distracting, and it takes me a second to answer. "Yes," I admit. "I'm nervous, but I want people to know who I am to you."

Kie kisses my temple, his fingers trailing between my thighs.

"What are you doing?" I ask.

"I'm rarely afforded the opportunity to be alone with you.

Mason is incessant." Kie shrugs. "I'm taking advantage."

My skin is on fire. I blame the mate bond. It draws me to Kie and Mason, turning me into putty whenever they look in my direction.

I spread my legs, inviting Kie to continue.

"Do you like it when I take control?" he asks.

Yes. No. I don't know. Why does it matter?

It's hard to think when he's ghosting the tips of his fingers over my slit, teasing me with the promise of his touch. I spread my legs further, but he doesn't take the bait. It's frustrating. Mason would've been inside me the moment I spread my legs. He would've had me bent over within seconds.

"Do you like it?" he repeats.

I groan. "Why?"

Kie circles my clit, his lips curling where they press against my temple. "Abby…" He's taunting me. "Tell me or I'll stop and call the diction coach back inside."

I panic. "Yes! I like it."

Kie hums, pushing my underwear aside and slipping a finger inside me. He's gentle, moving slowly. I'm still sore from last night, and he seems to sense that as he presses his palm against my clit. I've never particularly enjoyed being fingered, but it's good with Kie. Mason, too. They know what pace to go and what pressure to use.

"Take out my cock," Kie orders.

My hands shake as I reach behind myself, scrambling to find his zipper and undo his pants. Mason's going to be pissed when he realizes what Kie and I did while he was babysitting my family. I'm excited.

Kie's already hard, and he hisses as I finally get a hand wrapped around him. Despite his calm exterior, he's aching for me. His length tells me everything he doesn't.

"Bend forward." I do as instructed, bending at the waist. Kie pulls his finger out. "Good. Put me inside you."

He bends his knees, lowering himself, and I guide him toward my entrance. It takes a bit of maneuvering, and I quickly realize this angle isn't going to work. I'm a little too short, and Kie's a little too tall.

"Shit." Kie huffs, pulling me toward the couch. "Don't tell Mason about that."

Kie sits, pulling me down with him. My back presses against his chest, and I lean against him before continuing. We both sigh when he finally slips inside. Kie's thick, and it takes a second to adjust to the stretch.

"Fuck," Kie groans. "I want to be inside you always."

He tightens his grip on my hips, silently urging me to rock. I'm more than happy to, desperate for the pleasure his touch brings. The pressure is building with every drag of his cock, and I know it won't take long to cum. I suspect it never will with Kie.

"You're mine," I say. "This is mine."

Kie twitches underneath me. "I'm all yours. Always yours." He gasps. "Always yours."

My thighs are shaking, and I grab Kie's arms as my pleasure peaks. My orgasm hits me like a train, and I let out a silent scream as I come undone. Kie takes over, and low, filthy moans pour from his throat as he thrusts deep into me and stills, finding his release.

Kie drops his forehead against my back. "Mason's going to be pissed."

I shrug. "He'll be fine."

Mason's grouchy and possessive, but I don't honestly think he'll mind. He's always known he'd share a mate with Kie, and he doesn't seem particularly jealous of the faerie. I think, especially as our relationship grows and sex begins to feel a bit less novel, he won't bat an eye when I enter a room smelling of

Kie.

"Put your hand out," Kie orders. "Palm up."

I obey, and Kie grabs my wrist. His grip is light, and I gulp as he traces his finger over the spot where I'm expected to cut myself. I'm trying not to think about it, and he's not helping.

"I'm going to use my magic to piece your skin together," he says. "And I'll hold it together, molecule by molecule, until it's healed. I promise."

He shouldn't. I know how much that drains him, and it's a waste of his energy. I'm not looking forward to cutting my palm, but it won't kill me. I've experienced worse—my knees, for example. They're covered in scars from my time in Redstall Forest.

One look at Kie's stern expression tells me he's unwilling to change his mind.

I flush, deciding not to argue. "Thank you."

Chapter Thirty-Seven

ABBY

WE RECONVENE WITH Mason and my family outside the doors of the meeting hall where the coronation will take place.

Mason is on his last bit of patience. He wears his agitation on his sleeve and is not very good at hiding it. He tries, though. He nods politely as Aaron speaks, and he doesn't react violently when Mom loops her arm through his, her fingertips accidentally touching his exposed wrist. She pulls away the moment she notices, and Mason maintains his forced smile.

It's a sweet attempt.

They like him, and Mason has no idea what to do with that.

He's not familiar with loving parents. I don't get the impression that Alpha Theon or Queen Gitta were the most nurturing, and Mason has never brought up his mother. I suspect he's never experienced a healthy family dynamic. He needs time to adjust.

He hasn't been given much affection in his life, but he's about to be showered in it. My family is welcoming, and they're going to suffocate him.

"Are you ready?" Mason asks, smoothly pulling away from my mom.

He closes the distance between us in three long strides and only stops once he's hovering over me. I used to find this position so menacing. I look up, meeting his intense gaze.

"Yes?"

Mason's nostrils flare, and he shoots Kie a sharp glare before pulling me in for a chaste kiss. I'm afraid Mason will say something crude in front of my parents, but he holds himself back.

"I did not enjoy being away from you," he says instead, his voice low so only I can hear.

Mom peeks around Mason's shoulder. "You look beautiful."

"Thank you." I flush. "Did you enjoy your tour? I'm sorry I couldn't join you."

I hope Mason put more effort into this one than he did with Lill and me. He took confusing routes, which I still suspect was intentional, and he rushed me through the most interesting parts. I've had to learn everything myself, and I'm sure there's still a lot I don't know. The property is enormous, and there's so much to explore.

I suppose I will have a lot of time to learn it, though. If everything goes according to plan, I'm going to spend the rest of my life here. I haven't had a lot of time to digest that.

Mom smiles, patting Mason's shoulder. "It was fantastic. Mason is a wonderful host."

She seems genuine. That's good.

"I'd love for you to stay here with me," I admit. I planned to wait a few days before bringing this up, but I lack patience. "If you don't want to live on the property, we can find something nearby. Anything you want. We can give you anything you want."

Dad purses his lips. He's never loved change. Mom's opinion is relatively easy to sway, and Aaron will be on board. He's lazy like me, and he won't turn away from a life of luxury.

Getting him to leave would be more challenging than getting

him to stay.

Dad scratches his chin. "I'm not sure if that's—"

"We would love to," Mom interrupts. "Wherever you go, sweet girl, we will follow."

Aaron gags at Mom's compliment but then bobs his head. "I'll stay, too."

Obviously. He has nothing else going on in his life. He's finishing up his PhD in Clinical Psychology, which I suppose he's passionate about, but there's no reason he can't continue that here. I've met several faeries—Lord Bishop comes to mind—who could use somebody to talk to.

I turn toward the meeting hall, my heart pounding. I was almost murdered the last time I was here. I avoided sharing that particular detail when telling my story. It would horrify my parents, and they'd be demanding Kie open a portal and send us all home.

They're going to find out sooner or later. I'm hoping for later.

Kie pulls open the front doors, and I do my best to avoid looking at the throne in the back of the room as Mason leads me inside. The throne taunts me, bringing up memories and feelings I'd rather not think about.

My family follows me inside, and Kie joins them in the back.

Mason guides us toward the small, private room to the left, but we don't immediately enter. The room is sacred, and only a select few are allowed inside. My family will have to wait out here.

I admire the intricate detailing of the double doors. The architecture here continues to amaze me, and judging by the shocked silence from my family, it amazes them, too.

I turn, sneaking a peek at their expressions.

Mom's cheeks are splotchy, and she wipes at them to remove the evidence of her tears. Then she huffs and swipes at the air, annoyed by the flecks of magic floating in front of her face. I've grown used to the magic, but I'll never forget how distracting it was when I first came here.

Aaron clears his throat. "It's beautiful."

"Isn't it?"

"Are you ready?" Mason asks. "It's not too late to change your mind."

It is, but I appreciate the sentiment. I'm sure word of my new title has already spread, and I want to do this. It will make things easier for everybody involved.

Kie places himself on the other side of me, and I silently reach down and grab both his and Mason's hands. They link their fingers with mine.

Mom and Dad clock the action, their eyes momentarily darting toward my hands. I can't imagine how watching their daughter date two men must feel. Even I think it's weird, and I'm the one in the relationship.

They'll get used to it. I hope so, at least.

Kie steps in front of me, commanding my attention. "We'll be by your side the entire time."

I hold my chin high as Mason takes my arm and guides me through the doors. He keeps me close to his side, offering silent support.

Mason and I walk in first, with Kie trailing immediately behind. Anox, Jackie, and Lady Cassandra are already inside, impatience written all over their faces. We aren't late, but I'm sure they grew bored listening to our conversation outside.

Faeries, especially the ones here, don't seem to place much value on familial relationships. If they feel love for their siblings and parents, they keep it behind closed doors. I'm still upset that Kie wasn't allowed to have a private moment alone with his mother during her observance.

"Everybody can smell Kie on you," Mason whispers, his voice low. There's a slight pause before he continues. "It should be me."

I can't help but laugh. I stifle it quickly, but not quickly enough. Anox narrows his eyes on me, then shifts his focus toward Mason.

"Your Majesty," Anox says as we near. The council members bow, showing respect.

Mason releases my arm. My heart rate skyrockets.

The shallow pool is just up ahead, the shiny black stone where I'll smear my blood floating perfectly in the center. I eye it for a second longer than necessary.

Anox begins. I still may not understand the specific words, but thanks to my diction coach, I know what he's saying. He's speaking to the gods, introducing me to them. I highly doubt the gods give a fuck, and I bite my tongue as Anox gestures for me to enter the pool.

I kick off my shoes, then step into the water. It's frigid, and I wince as it tickles my ankles. Mason lingers at the pool's edge, and I face him and Anox once I'm at the stone in the center.

The council members, Anox excluded, now stand beside Kie in the back of the room.

Anox continues.

I'm so glad I witnessed Mason's coronation, and I go through the motions and repeat all the proper phrases until we reach the time of the hand cutting. I'm not at all looking forward to this, but I refuse to show my fear as Anox hands over a knife.

Was it this sharp for Mason?

Every eye in the room is on me. The stares feel like tiny bullets piercing my skin. Kie said he would use magic to heal my hand, but this is still going to hurt. I bring the knife to my palm, holding my breath.

I dig in the tip and drag it across my palm, moving quickly. The cut burns almost immediately, and Mason reaches out and snatches the knife out of my hand the moment I'm finished.

He wipes it clean and hands it back to Anox, but I pay them little attention as I wait for the blood to coat my palm. I cut myself deeper than I intended, and the faeries better fucking appreciate this.

Once my palm is coated, I crouch and press it against the stone, proving to the gods and the faeries that I'm willing to bleed for them.

If this gets infected, I'll be pissed.

I leave a bloody handprint on the stone, and there's a noticeable warmth on my palm when I finally pull away. The pain diminishes, and my sliced skin pinches together so tightly that the blood stops flowing. Kie wasn't lying when he said he'd do it molecule by molecule.

It's almost impossible to see where the cut is, my skin pressed together so perfectly that it looks uninjured. I'm impressed.

I repeat the prayers the linguistics woman taught me. My tongue fumbles around the vowels, but I'm doing my best. I speak slowly, taking my time and thinking through each word.

The room is painfully silent once I finish, and it remains that way. Am I supposed to say something else? Did I mess up?

"Come on, then," Mason teases, extending his hand. "You're done."

I take the offering, letting him help me out of the shallow pool.

Dad stands directly outside the door, his ear pressed against it, and he jolts back as it's pulled open. Aaron snorts, and Dad's face turns a thousand shades of red. He was eavesdropping—or trying to, at least.

"Are you finished already?" he asks.

I nod. "Yeah. It's a quick ceremony."

Mason laces his fingers with mine. He's pressing against my cut palm, but it doesn't hurt. I hope it's not hard for Kie to hold the skin together.

"How was my pronunciation?" I ask Kie and Mason.

Mason squeezes my hand but otherwise doesn't answer. Kie grimaces, also not answering. It's confirmation of what I already know is true. I've never been good at linguistics, which is a fact my Spanish teacher loved to inform me of.

"There's a small celebration in the park, near the gardens," Jackie says, exiting the room behind us. "It was a last-minute decision, thanks to me. The time of you two"—she gestures to Kie and Mason—"celebrating monumental events privately is over. Your people enjoy a lively evening, and it tells them how to feel."

Kie furrows his brow. "Explain."

"This is a happy occasion, is it not?" Jackie asks, cocking out her hip. "How are people supposed to know that when you treat it as a dirty secret? They need to be told that this day is one to be celebrated."

Anox and Lady Cassandra exit the room, shutting the door behind them. They don't look particularly excited at the prospect of a celebration. Neither do I, if I'm honest. I haven't spent much time around the faeries of court, and I prefer it that way. Jackie makes a good point, though.

She's already proving her usefulness. I don't particularly love that.

Chapter Thirty-Eight

ABBY

THE NEXT TEN minutes pass in a blur.

Mason pulls me through the crowded outdoor corridors, leading me toward the gardens where this celebration is supposedly being held. He's pissed. So is Kie.

They want to hide me, keep me far away from the faeries who could make another attempt for my life at any given moment, but Jackie has ruined those plans. I assume the sheer number of faeries walking about the grounds is also her doing.

Maybe she's trying to murder me. We offered her a position on the council, but perhaps it wasn't enough. Maybe she's planning something bigger.

I chew at the inside of my cheek, my nerves getting the better of me. It's beautiful today, and a light breeze blows my hair into my face as we step out from underneath the trellis leading into the park.

"Wow."

Hundreds of thousands of small string lights have been strung from the trees. It's beautiful, and I can't imagine how stunning it will be when the sun fully sets in the next hour or so. They create a trail to a building deep inside the park, just beside a long row of hedges that I know lead to the gardens.

Hundreds of faeries surround the building, most standing on an expansive stone patio. They've dressed for the occasion and seem in good spirits as they chat and laugh amongst themselves.

Several servers are rushing around with trays of drinks and snacks.

This is nerve-wracking.

"Give Abby and me a minute," Mason says, turning toward Kie and my family. "We'll meet up with you shortly."

Kie doesn't look convinced. "Don't take too long. People are expecting us."

Mason leads me to the right, away from the hedges. The sun continues to set, hopefully allowing Mason and me to blend in with the shadows. I'm now a queen, and I need a minute of quiet to process that before facing the faeries.

Will they try to question me as they did to Mason? I know practically nothing about the faerie way of life, and there's no hiding that.

We reach a small building deep inside the park. It's surrounded by trees, giving a false sense of privacy. I promptly sit on the front cement steps, my legs splayed before me and my shoulders slumped.

Mason sits with me, his thigh pressing against mine. We don't speak. It's nice.

Mason's the first to break the silence. "You did well today."

I lean against his shoulder. "Do you really think so?"

"Yes."

We fall silent again. It's comfortable, and I let my eyes slip shut as I focus on the steady sound of his breathing. I'm beyond exhausted. It's been easy to ignore, but now that I have a moment to sit and relax, it's setting in. I need rest—and quiet.

"I don't want to go to the party," I admit.

Mason hums. "We can skip it."

"Jackie might lose her mind."

"She most definitely will," Mason admits. "But the faeries only care to see Kie, anyway. This celebration is just an excuse for Jackie to announce and brag about her new position on the council. Nobody will miss us."

"Kie will be pissed."

"That's never stopped you before," Mason teases. "Why let it stop you now?"

Mason rises. I hesitate, pretty sure this is a horrible idea, before taking his outstretched hand. Mason knows this world better than I do, and if he says I can skip the party, I'm going to believe him. He's an asshole, but he wouldn't suggest I do something that would genuinely upset the faeries. I trust he wouldn't.

"Where to?" I ask. "Home?"

Instead of answering, Mason drags me off the patio. His pace is fast, and I have to practically jog to keep up with his hurried steps. We eventually reach a row of carefully shaped hedges, and my heart pounds as Mason expertly weaves me through them. They're taller than I am, and while the sun hasn't completely set, it's dim.

It would be easy to get lost out here, but Mason maintains a tight grip on my hand.

We walk through rows and rows of hedges, eventually reaching the small courtyard where Queen Gitta's observance was held. I'm relieved to see her body has been removed, and I eye the stone slab where she lay before allowing Mason to pull me away.

Kie hasn't spoken much about Queen Gitta's death, and I wonder if he's affected by seeing me and my mom together. I can't imagine how hard it would be to watch somebody interact with their mother after I'd just lost mine.

Mason leads me around the party, careful to stay in the shadows.

I catch occasional glimpses of the celebration through the hedges, and what I see is terrifying. There might be more people there now than there were when I first saw it. How many faeries did Jackie invite?

We finally exit the hedges. Mason continues forward. The string lights don't stretch this far, and I rely on his sense of sight as we weave between trees. Where are we going? No trellises are overhead, so we must still be in the park.

Several minutes pass before we reach what appears to be some sort of abandoned brick tower. There's a stairwell winding up the side, and Mason urges me to begin climbing.

"What are you doing?" I hiss, stubbing my toe. "It's too dark."

Mason's responding chuckle feels almost threatening. "This building was closed up after a fire about a hundred or so years ago," he says. "Kie and I used to sneak up here and watch the garden parties back when we were too young to attend. You can see everything from the top."

I begin climbing, tripping every few seconds.

"Is this safe?"

"Of course."

I don't entirely trust that. This building must be at least three stories tall, and it's rickety as hell. The brick steps feel sturdy enough, but that doesn't mean they won't shatter beneath me. I have no interest in plummeting to my death.

At the top of the steps is a small rooftop. There's a narrow door in the center, but it's boarded up.

"That wasn't so bad, was it?" Mason taunts.

I shoot him a dirty look, then near the rooftop edge. Mason wasn't lying. We're well above the garden and hedges, and I can see the party.

It's hard to make out specifics, but I can see general faces and figures. I search until I find Kie and my parents. My mom and dad are with Kie, but Aaron has found food. He scans the long table, occasionally adding a few things to his plate, before being corralled to a small seating area with my parents. Kie seems to say something to them, his eyebrow furrowed, before hurrying away.

Kie attempts to weave through the crowd, but he's continually stopped by faeries looking to chat. I'd be annoyed, but he greets every person with a wide smile. He's well-trained for this, and I admire his patience. Someday, I'll join him for such things.

Today, though, I'm going to hide away with Mason.

"Do you enjoy sharing a mate with Kie?" I ask the shifter. I've always wondered. "I can't imagine what it would be like to share you. I could never do it."

Mason takes a second to respond. "I don't feel like I'm sharing you. I feel like..." He walks up behind me, placing his hands on my hips. "Kie is mine. I may not be sexually involved with him, but he belongs to me. I don't mind when my things play together."

That's not the answer I was expecting.

"I don't think Kie would be pleased to hear you say he belongs to you."

Mason shrugs. "I don't concern myself with how Kie feels." A beat of silence. "But don't tell him I said that."

I won't. I'm not interested in opening that particular can of worms. Besides, I'm pretty sure if I asked Kie the same question, he'd have an equally offensive answer toward Mason. Their relationship is entertaining. There's so much love between them, but they'd rather die than ever admit it.

"He found us," Mason says.

I already know who he's talking about, and I search through the crowd until spotting Kie. He's finally reached his destination, a standing table surrounded by Anox, Jackie, and Lady Cassandra.

He's speaking to Anox, but his eyes are on Mason and me. He doesn't seem pleased.

His hands are clenching and unclenching at his sides, and his jaw is routinely tensing.

"Mason...?" I look over. Mason grins at Kie, clearly pleased with whatever he's done. "What did you do?"

Mason licks his lips, his gaze heavy when he finally slides it toward me. "I assume Anox just informed Kie what I did with Lord Bishop."

What? When did he have time to do *anything* with Lord Bishop? He was with my family all day, wasn't he?

"What'd you do?"

Mason blinks, his lips curling into a cruel smile. It's one I haven't seen since the forest, and it sends shivers down my spine. I'm growing familiar with Mason's soft side, and I momentarily forgot that's not all there is to him. He isn't a good person. Not really.

"Tell me," I order. "Tell me right now."

"No." Mason shakes his head. "He's mine."

Mason watches my every move with unnerving intensity, like a predator waiting for the perfect moment to strike. My pulse is thundering through my ears, and I shake the fear out of my limbs.

"What did you do?"

Chapter Thirty-Nine

KIERAN

I'M GOING TO kill Mason. I'm going to rip out his liver and feed it to the pesky birds that live near the butcher's shop on the outskirts of Bellmere. Then I'm going to castrate him and offer his balls to Abby on a silver fucking platter.

"It seems he was abducted earlier this afternoon," Anox continues, his fury poorly concealed. "Only those with the highest clearance would've been allowed inside the cells, and the guards refuse to talk."

I frown. Mason has the clearance, and he also has the means to threaten the guards into silence. Leaving the shifter unsupervised was a mistake I should've known better than to make. I wrongfully assumed he'd feel responsible to protect Abby's family while I helped her prepare for the coronation.

"I'll take care of it," I promise Anox.

He nods. "I trust that you will."

My gaze momentarily flickers toward the abandoned building beyond the gardens. My mother had wanted to tear it down for several years, and I regret my role in convincing her to leave it standing. I have fond memories of hiding on the roof with Mason.

I'm going to tear it down with my bare hands.

There are only a few places on the property where Mason enjoys spending time, and the abandoned tower has always been one of his favorites. We used to love hiding up there when we were children, the two of us full of laughter and smiles as we talked poorly of the faeries celebrating below. I've become one of the faeries I used to mock. I'm sure that thought has already crossed Mason's mind.

He's standing on the rooftop, his arms around Abby and his chin resting on her head. He's avoiding me, running away like the coward he is.

"Where are they?" Anox asks. "This is Queen Abigail's celebration. Should she not be here?"

I frown, resisting the urge to glance toward the tower again. Mason hid himself and my mate well, cloaked in darkness and shadows, and I don't want to give their location away. Everybody of importance, from our top scholars to our military leaders, is in attendance tonight. Several of them have already stopped to speak with me.

"Abby's retired for the evening," I say. "Mason's gone with her."

Anox puckers his lips. He's annoyed, but he has no reason to be. My mother rarely attended celebrations honoring her. She felt her presence put the people on edge, and over time, that became the tradition.

The faeries knew that when they were invited to a celebration at the royal estate, they could attend without the looming fear of the queen's judgment. Even I'm drawing a few odd looks, and I hold no real power. Not anymore.

My gaze flickers toward Mason and Abby again. The sun is almost entirely set, making them nearly impossible to spot. I know where to look, though, and my frown deepens as I take in their new position.

Abby's straddling Mason, giving him love and affection he doesn't deserve—not after the stunt he pulled this afternoon.

Jackie places a hand on my shoulder. I brush her off. She's pushing her luck, and I'm too angry to remain diplomatic. I need to know what the fuck Mason did with Lord Bishop.

Lord Bishop confessed before the council. We aren't animals, and there is a process to these things. Mason can't take matters into his own hands, not when relations between the faeries and shifters are as tense as they are.

The faeries are looking for an excuse to be angry, and Mason is giving it to them. They won't care that Lord Bishop attacked our mate. He's a faerie, and Mason is a shifter. He needs to remain far away from the execution.

It was foolish to trust him alone with Abby's parents. I truly believed his desire to protect his mate's family would be stronger than his need for revenge. Abby calms Mason considerably, but he's still the firstborn son of Alpha Theon. His self-control is nonexistent, and I suspect he prefers it that way.

I sigh, dragging my fingers through my hair.

"I'm beginning to regret my endorsement," Anox says.

He's lying. Without Mason and me causing trouble, Anox wouldn't know what to do with himself. We keep his life interesting.

"I'll handle him," I repeat, displaying confidence I don't have. I'm not sure *anybody* can handle Mason—not even Abby.

Jackie grabs my shoulder again, her fingernails digging into the muscle even through the layers of my shirt. It's painful, and I know what it means. I hate that I have a secret language with her, that we've spent so much time together that I know what she wants without words.

It's a betrayal to my mate, and I suck in a slow breath before giving her my ear.

"Go," she says, her voice low. "I have this handled."

Anox brings his hands together with a loud clap, drawing attention—not that we don't already have it. Every pair of eyes in this garden is on me. The faeries are openly watching my every move.

"Yes," Anox says, his voice loud. "Help Queen Abigail tame His Majesty. Jacqueline has this handled."

I suck my cheeks into my mouth. "Do not disrespect our king." I push Jackie's hand off my shoulder. "He has been chosen by Zaha herself, and you will show him the respect he deserves."

I hold eye contact with Anox. I don't appreciate anybody speaking poorly of Mason, and he knows that. Only Abby and I are allowed to talk negatively about the shifter.

Anox lowers his gaze, submitting. It doesn't make me feel better.

"Go, Kie," Jackie repeats, her voice low. "I'll ensure Abby's family is brought to the royal guest suites, and I'll make sure the faeries leave tonight with nothing but positive things to say about your mate. I was raised to do this, after all."

I hate that I have no choice but to trust her. I need to secure Lord Bishop, dead or alive, before anybody realizes he's missing.

"If *anything* happens to Abby's family…" I start.

Jackie snorts. "You'll personally see to my death. I'm not concerned."

She spins on her heel and walks away, the gesture beyond disrespectful. She's letting her council position get to her head, and I mentally curse Abby for offering it in the first place. I don't think she truly understands the magnitude of Jackie's ego.

I make eye contact and offer friendly smiles as I make my way out of the gardens. Several people stop and talk with me, and I try my best to hide my annoyance as I answer meaningless question after meaningless question.

Almost everybody pries into my dynamic with Mason, eager for details I don't care to share. They want to know how we manage affairs and how we intend to move forward with Abby. I avoid most of them, but it's not easy.

It takes me almost thirty minutes to leave, and I storm through the hedges that will lead me to the abandoned tower. I practice breathing exercises along the way, hoping to calm myself before reaching Abby and Mason, but it doesn't work.

My blood is boiling as I climb the steps to the rooftop. I hear heavy breathing. Why do I hear heavy breathing?

"Mason!" I hiss.

There's no response, but I know he can hear me. He has the ears of a fucking bat. The brain of one, too.

I expect to encounter sex when I reach the top, but what I stumble on stops me in my tracks. What is happening? Abby is straddling Mason, but it doesn't appear sexual. They're both fully clothed, and Mason's arms are sprawled out to his sides.

Abby kisses Mason's neck and shoulders, quiet humming pouring from her throat as she runs her fingers through his hair. Mason throws his head back, his eyes squeezed shut. I don't understand.

"Mason," Abby coos. "Do I smell like you now?"

Mason shakes his head. "No. Keep going."

He's lying. She reeks of him. I can smell it from here.

Abby chuckles, probably seeing straight through his lie, before kissing along his jaw and scratching his head. Shifters love to rub against one another, but they usually do it in their animal forms. It's a way of forcing their scent onto things and asserting dominance. Sometimes they even pee on one another, and I'm beyond relieved to see that Abby and Mason haven't taken that step.

I walk around the pair, and Abby meets my gaze before

leaning forward and dragging her tongue up Mason's jaw. What the fuck?

I grimace, and Mason shivers. He's into this. I can't fathom why.

"What'd you do with Lord Bishop?" Abby asks, her voice low.

She knows? I'm surprised Mason told her. I thought I'd be the one to break the news.

He doesn't answer, and Abby scratches his head so hard, I wince. Is that not painful? It's followed up by a kiss, one I can tell Mason is greatly enjoying. I don't think I've ever seen him so relaxed, and I don't know what to make of it. She just might get answers out of him.

I press my lips together before sitting, letting Abby work her magic.

The sky is beautiful tonight, and I do my best to ignore the kissing sounds as I admire the stars. I love nighttime. It's peaceful, and there's nothing more calming than the quiet that comes with darkness.

The property is almost always sprawling with faeries, and I rarely get to enjoy being outside without being stopped by an overexcited person looking to speak with me about something unimportant. Mason doesn't have that problem, mainly because the faeries are terrified of him.

I'm the approachable one. It's both a blessing and a curse.

"Mason…" Abby whispers again. "Please tell me."

He grunts but otherwise remains silent.

Abby looks disappointed, and the corners of my lips twitch upward at the sight of her annoyance. Mason's stubborn, and she's learning that the hard way.

"I want the faeries to like me," Abby continues. She's pleading, almost even whining, which is new. I sit up, giving her my undivided attention. Mason does the same, his eyebrows pulled together. "They're going to blame me for this. You know they will. Please, Mace."

He opens his mouth, then clamps it shut. Then he does it again. And again.

Abby continues rubbing his scalp, keeping him docile and calm. I hold my breath, filled with hope. This just might work.

"But—" Mason starts.

Abby bites his shoulder, her teeth burying into the skin. He shivers, then slumps.

"He's inside." He jerks his head toward the boarded-up door beside me. "But he's mine."

Mason's head spins toward me, and he does a double take. His eyes widen, almost like he didn't realize I was here. I find that hard to believe. The shifter is always on guard. Always.

"He's not yours," Abby says. "Not yet."

I roll my eyes. Lord Bishop will *never* be Mason's.

I stand, ignoring the shifter's threatening stare as I approach the boarded-up door. It looks untouched, but upon closer inspection, I realize the wood planks are loose.

Fucking Mason.

Chapter Forty

ABBY

MASON IS RELAXED underneath me, and I hum quietly as I sift my fingers through his hair, playing with the thick, wavy dark strands.

Kie rips wooden boards off the rooftop door, low curses and occasional death threats pouring from his throat. I'm glad Kie came when he did. It took forever to get Mason to admit to where he hid Lord Bishop, and I highly doubt I'd be able to convince him to do anything about it.

He'd never let me inside the building, either, but he doesn't have the same reservations with Kie.

"Is it safe in there?" I ask Mason.

He grunts. "Wouldn't let Kie in there if it weren't."

My fingers slide out of Mason's hair, but he snatches my wrist and pulls my hand back to his head. I've spent the past thirty minutes treating Mason like a dog. I've pet him, licked him, done pretty much everything except sniff his asshole. He loves it, and he's practically jelly underneath me.

I can't help but smile. The big, bad shifter is weak and pliant for his mate. *Little bitch.*

My cheek is sore from rubbing against his rough stubble,

which doesn't feel great. Still, it's a small price to pay for information. Anox was adamant that Mason stay far away from Lord Bishop, which honestly should've been the first clue that Mason would do the opposite.

I've heard enough stories to know that Mason's never done well with being told what to do, and I suppose it was silly to believe his attitude would change now that he's crowned and mated. Mason is stubborn.

"What'd you do to him?" I ask, staring at the doorway where Kie disappeared.

I'd go in myself if I didn't already know that Mason would prevent me from doing so. I'm also slightly afraid that if I get up, he'll decide that he's changed his mind and stop Kie from collecting Lord Bishop. I have him agreeable and pliant, and I intend to keep him that way.

"Mason?" I urge.

He sighs, as if my questions are a bother. "Not much. He lost a hand in the transition."

My heart lurches. "You took his hand?" My voice is no louder than a whisper.

Mason shakes his head, the space between his eyebrows furrowing. "He chose to forfeit his hand engaging in a fight with me."

That's not how the faeries are going to see it. We've been trying so hard to appease them, and Mason's fucked it all up.

I honestly don't understand why Zaha put him in charge. The shifter doesn't seem to have much interest in being king, and Kie's admittedly the more levelheaded of the two. He makes better decisions. Zaha replaced a strong, caring leader with a volatile shifter who couldn't care less about the faeries.

Zaha's playing a cruel trick on us, and I've yet to understand her reasoning.

Mason turns, rubbing his cheek against my palm. "Have you had any thoughts about Anox's offer?"

"What offer?"

"To shadow him and eventually take over the kingdom's finances. I assumed Kie told you."

I jerk up. What? "I haven't heard anything about that. I'd love to."

I'm ready to work again, to have deadlines and projects and a manager to complain about. Anox is significantly more competent than my boss, Mark, but I already know he'll give me a lot to bitch about. And I'm exceptionally good with numbers.

"When do I start?"

Mason stares at me, his nose wrinkling. "Whenever you want, I suppose. I didn't think you'd accept."

"Why?"

"Because it's tedious work, and Anox is a nuisance."

I shrug. "I like finances, and he's not any more of a nuisance than you."

Mason huffs.

I admire the side of his head. He has nice ears. They're proportional to his head, and they're surprisingly soft. My lips curl as I recall tugging his ear when he was in his animal form. I hurt him, and he didn't retaliate in the slightest.

I don't know why that makes me feel so good. I've spent a long time being afraid of Mason, and I'm ready to move past it. We're going to be stuck together for the remainder of our lives. I should get comfortable with each of his forms.

"How many people have you killed?" I ask the question before deciding if I genuinely want the answer.

"Not nearly as many as everybody makes it out to be," Mason admits. "If you include the shifters we encountered while traveling to the portal of the gods and meeting with my father, nine."

Nine. My mate has killed nine people. I'm not sure if that's more or less than what I expected. It's not zero, that's for sure.

"I've never killed anybody," I admit.

Mason's lips twitch. "I've gathered as much." He wraps an arm around my waist, holding me in place as he sits up. "But Kie has killed five, so don't let him fool you into thinking he's innocent."

I glance at the doorway behind us, still waiting for Kie to reappear. What's taking him so long? Maybe Mason lied about hiding Lord Bishop in there. I wouldn't put it past him.

I drag my nails down Mason's head, scratching his scalp. He practically purrs, and he tightens his grip on my waist with a quiet moan. I shift my weight, trying to see if he's aroused, but there's nothing hard beneath me. This isn't turning Mason on, which honestly makes it weirder.

"We should check on Kie," I say.

I'm getting nervous.

Mason leans forward, connecting his lips to my cheek. Then he stands, bringing me with him. If he thinks I'm heavy, he doesn't show it.

"Kie doesn't need us checking up on him," Mason says. "He's a big boy."

As if on cue, Kie comes storming out of the doorway. I can tell by his hurried, stiff movements that he's pissed. Mason wordlessly sets me on my feet. I step between them, not in the mood for a fight.

"Not today," I beg. "Please."

Kie scowls, still glaring at Mason.

The shifter presses his chest against my back. "There's nothing you can say to me that I haven't already heard. You think I'm a fuck-up. You think Zaha made a mistake. It doesn't bother me, and I won't apologize for protecting my mate." Mason nudges me toward the stairwell. "Let's go."

"You deserved better," Kie blurts out. Mason stops walking. "You're a strong, intelligent man, and Alpha Theon made a mistake pushing you away."

Every muscle in Mason's body tenses, and there's a long stretch of silence before he clears his throat. "Why are you saying this?"

Kie steps toward us, but he halts when Mason bristles. The moonlight shines in his eyes, making the green color appear even more vibrant than usual.

"You're upset, and I understand why," Kie starts, "but we're a team. I'm not your enemy, Mace, and I don't want to be. You can't keep sneaking behind my back and taking matters into your own hands."

I step to the side, giving the two space. It's about time they talked things through.

Mason turns toward me. "Is this what you want?"

Why's he asking me? I nod. "Of course."

I mean it, too. Mason has strong instincts, and good things seem to happen when he works with Kie instead of against him.

"Relations with the shifters are worse than ever," Kie continues. "We need you to be on your best behavior. Abby and I need you on our side."

"I…" Mason pauses. "I will try."

Kie barks out a laugh. I'm not expecting it, and I jolt at its abruptness.

"You'll try," he says. "I guess that's all I can ask of the man who just chained up a faerie noble in an abandoned building."

Mason shrugs, and when I turn to look at him, I'm shocked to see he's smiling. "Did you see Lord Bishop's hand?"

"I saw that one was missing."

Mason's smile grows. He's proud of himself. I don't

understand men. "Is he still crying about it?"

Kie nods. "Like a fucking baby."

A warm hand lands on my shoulder. Mason gives me a gentle squeeze before nudging me again toward the stairs. "Let's get out of here," he says. "Kie will clean this up."

Kie snorts. "*Kie will clean this up*. Thanks."

I head down the stairwell and step into the park, and Mason quickly takes charge once he realizes I have no idea where I'm going. We manage to avoid running into any faeries—the guards excluded. Mason pauses once we reach the private path leading to our home.

"What?" I ask.

"Your family is staying there," he says, pointing to the house I briefly shared with Lill. I haven't been inside since she murdered Queen Gitta and vanished. "Would you like to see them?"

I nod, pushing my fears about Lill aside. "Yes."

We find everybody sitting around the coffee table, cards scattered about. Dad waves us over when he notices us lingering in the doorway.

Mason places a hand on my back. "Go," he says. "You should enjoy your time with them before everything goes to shit."

I suspect it won't be long before that happens. Alpha Theon will be pissed when he hears of my coronation and Mason's very public dismissal of the shifters. Things will grow even worse when they discover the faeries are moving troops into the towns bordering Redstall Forest. I'm not looking forward to it.

"I need to speak with the guards," Mason continues, drawing my attention. "Join your family. I'll be back in a minute."

Does he think I'm stupid?

"You will *not* be leaving this room," I hiss under my breath. "Now take a seat"—I point to the couch—"and don't fucking move."

My order is met with dead silence. I hold my breath, counting the seconds until Mason brushes past me and sits beside Aaron.

"I'm good at cards," Mason says. "Teach me this game."

Chapter Forty-One

ABBY

I WAKE TO a hard body pressing against my back. Kie's finally returned. It's about damned time.

He cuddles up against me, his warm body further pressing me against Mason's chest. I'm practically lying on the shifter, my left leg thrown over his waist and my arm sprawled across his chest. He's become my pillow.

A hand slips up my shirt, pressing against my ribs. I suspect it's Kie's, but I'm not entirely sure. Mason's just as handsy.

"Get it sorted?" Mason asks, his voice thick with sleep.

"Are you asking if I successfully cleaned up the mess you made?" Kie pauses before answering his snarky, rhetorical question. "Yes, I did."

Mason makes a quiet noise in the back of his throat, his lips pressing against my forehead. He kisses my warm skin before pulling away, and I do my best not to let the soft action get to me. I'm not used to these gestures, and I'm still learning to accept them.

Kie burrows his face against the back of my neck.

"I loved watching you today," he whispers. "It made me…" He pauses, struggling to find his words. "You're adjusting faster than I would if I were in your position, and it fills me with pride to see you succeed. I'm still drowning with guilt over how we treated you, but I'm so happy you're my mate."

My throat tightens, and I flip toward Kie. His violet eyes are duller than usual, probably from exhaustion. I have no idea what time it is, but I know it's late.

"Do you mean it?" I ask.

"Of course."

Mason rolls over, pressing himself against my back. "Don't roll away from me again."

I smile, and Kie ignores him as he continues. "We're going to have a happy life together. I just know it. I imagine our future is full of excitement, laughter, and maybe even a few children…"

He trails off, his voice growing cautious.

"I want children," I answer his unspoken question. "But not anytime soon."

Kie presses his lips together, trying and failing to hide a smile. He's pleased. I see how his dull eyes light up at the idea of future children. "We would never rush you, Abby. Children will happen on *your* timeline."

My cheeks flush. I clear my throat. "How large are shifter and faerie babies?"

I'm met with silence. That's all the answer I need, and I pray this realm has epidurals. If not, we'll be taking a trip to a human hospital. I want the sweet, sweet relief of drugs.

"I will allow your first child to be faerie," Mason says. "But it's my turn after Kie. I want a girl."

I snort. "You can't control that."

Mason shrugs, his chest rising and falling against my back. I like this topic of conversation. I enjoy the three of us discussing and coming to a mutual agreement on something important.

"Do humans have sex while pregnant?" Kie asks.

Mason sucks in a sharp breath, like it never occurred to him that humans might not. I pause before answering, selfishly enjoying making my mates sweat a little. Pregnancy comes with an onslaught of hormones and I might not want sex quite as frequently, but I'm sure I'll still want it.

"It's personal preference," I finally say. "I believe most women do. I will."

Mason relaxes, and Kie gives a jerky nod. "That's very good to hear."

I can't help but laugh. It's too loud in the otherwise quiet room, but neither of my mates seems to mind. Kie's staring at me like the sun is shining out of my ass, and Mason's wiggling against me like a cat in heat.

"You'll like me when I'm ovulating," I tease Mason. "I have a birth control implant in my arm that prevents me from menstruating, but when it's out, you'll have a guaranteed monthly lay."

Kie and Mason simultaneously freeze, and Mason's following question is so quiet I barely hear it. "Humans ovulate monthly?"

What? I pause, hesitating, before giving a slow nod.

"Shifters and faeries do so only once a year," Kie admits. He gulps, his throat bobbing. "There's a hormone spike in the days leading up to ovulation, and shifters are especially sensitive to it. I assume humans have a similar hormone spike?"

I nod again, and Mason buries his face against my shoulder with a low groan. My mouth grows dry, and I swallow past the lump in my throat as he rolls his hips forward, pressing himself against me.

"Why did you keep this from me?" Mason whines. He's hard, and the fabric of his underwear does little to hide it. "You're a cruel mate."

I open my mouth, but my words die on my tongue as I meet

Kie's gaze. He looks like he wants to devour me, and he holds eye contact as Mason's hand finds its way between my thighs.

"Take them off," Kie orders just as Mason's fingertips find their way underneath the front of my underwear.

Mason hates being told what to do, but for once, he obeys. He removes his hand, and he pulls his hips back just enough that he can slip my underwear down and off. There's a moment of shuffling before he returns, and I chew at my bottom lip as I realize he's also stripped himself.

My palm presses into the mattress, and I tap my fingers against the soft sheets before sliding my hand forward. I continue until I find Kie's bare chest, then begin downward. His abdomen is covered in lean muscle, and I feel every inch of them before slipping into the waistband of his underwear and finding the hard length that lives underneath.

Kie lets out a quiet groan as I curl my hand around him. I stroke him from base to tip, my lips twitching.

"Are faeries affected by the hormones, too?" I ask.

Mason answers. "Yes. Not as much as shifters."

Kie licks his lips, shifting his attention to Mason. "Turn her around."

Mason acts quickly. He flips me toward him, then grabs my leg and hooks it over his hip. My inner thigh stretches, but it's nothing to the stretch I know I'm about to feel in a minute.

"So soft," Mason whispers. One of his hands lands on my ass, and I flinch as he pulls the skin apart.

"*Mason!*"

He smirks. "You have *two* mates, Abby. Don't act coy."

Something hard and warm slips between my thighs, pressing against my ass. Kie's cock.

"Is this okay?" Kie's breath hits the back of my neck. "Can I have you?"

Mason trails his lips across mine. "Please, Abby."

Kie continues to play between my thighs, dragging the head of his shaft from back to front. I'm faintly aware I'm panting, my breath coming out of me in loud puffs.

"We want to share you," Kie admits. "Do you want that?"

I do. I honestly, genuinely do. Embarrassment prevents me from admitting that out loud, though, and I bury my face against Mason's chest as I bob my head.

Mason tuts. "Say it."

"No."

"Say it, Abby."

I lift my chin, looking Mason in the eye. "No."

He sucks his lips into his mouth, then shrugs. "Very well."

He tightens his grip on my thigh, pulling it further over his hip, before lining himself up with my entrance. His eyebrows furrow as he pushes into me, clear pleasure written across his features.

My toes curl as I stretch around him, my body still not used to his size. It'll take a while to adjust to these two men, but I'm patient. Mason doesn't rush things, either. He eases inside with soft, smooth thrusts, continuing until he's entirely seated.

"I know what you and Kie did earlier," he says. "You two are naughty."

Kie's hands run up and down my bare back, but he's no longer between my thighs. I wiggle back, subtly sending the hint that I want him, but he doesn't pick up on it. I try again, my frown deepening when he doesn't take the bait.

"Kie," I whine.

His fingers curl around my hips. "You don't wish to share us. I'll wait my turn."

"No." I huff. He knows I want them both. "I want you, too."

"Where?"

I wiggle back against him, inadvertently thrusting against Mason. "You know where."

"Say it."

I'm going to scream. "I want you in my ass, Kie."

Mason grunts, wrapping his arms around my head. "There she goes."

He finds his rhythm, pushing into me with even, smooth thrusts. It's so good, but I still want more. I want Kie, too. I've never done this, but I want to try. I want to feel them inside me at the same time.

Kie reaches over me, placing a hand on Mason's torso. "Slow down, Mace."

Mason slows, gritting his teeth in the process. I never imagined Mason would let another man tell him how to fuck his mate, and I like it far more than I should. I look up, locking gazes with the shifter. His bright-green eyes are half shut in pleasure, and he's biting his bottom lip as he rolls his cock into me, filling me with slower thrusts.

Kie reaches between my thighs from behind, and I practically choke on my spit as he wraps a hand around the base of Mason's shaft. The shifter stills, and Kie pulls him out of me so he can dip two fingers inside.

"I toyed with the idea of us sharing your cunt," Kie admits. "But we're too big for you. Your ass is better suited for me."

He curls his fingers, collecting my arousal, before shifting his attention to my ass. I instinctively flinch, and he pulls away as he's met with resistance. Blood rushes to my face.

"I've never done this," I admit. "I'm nervous."

Mason makes a happy little noise, continuing his slow, languid fucking.

"You've never done what?" Kie asks. He plays with my ass, waiting for me to adjust to the feeling. I gradually relax. "Taken two men or been fucked in the ass?"

"Neither. I've never done either."

Mason groans, and Kie slowly eases a finger inside. It's an odd feeling I don't necessarily love, but I trust Kie will have me enjoying it by the time he's finished.

"Neither have we," Kie says. My heart pounds, and Kie continues. "Mason and I agreed long ago never to take a woman together, and I've never had one in the ass. I'm nervous, too."

Mason chimes in. "I've never taken a woman that way, either."

"We're going to do this together," Kie promises. "I'll be gentle. It's just me and you."

He works his finger into me, moving slowly and giving me time to adjust before easing in another. The arousal he collected is drying, and he stops once friction begins. Mason twists away, and I'm greeted with the sight of the shifter's muscles flexing with each thrust as he reaches behind himself and rips open his bedside drawer.

"I thought you didn't bring women to your room," I say as he returns with a bottle of lubricant.

"I don't, but I masturbate." He shoots me a sharp look, as if sensing my impending teasing. "Shut up."

I snort. "What else is in that drawer?"

Mason hands Kie the bottle before reaching back into the drawer. I'm not sure what I'm expecting, but it isn't for him to pull out a fucking pocket pussy. The artificial vagina lands on the bed between us, and I take one look at it before grimacing and flicking it away.

"I also have a—"

I wrap my arm around Mason's neck and pull him close, shutting him up with a kiss. I don't care what he uses to masturbate, and right now, I'd rather him fuck me than explain.

He moans into my mouth, and he tosses the toy off the bed before cupping my cheeks and biting my bottom lip.

"I love you," he says as he pulls away. "I love you, Abby."

I gasp, and Kie works two slick fingers into my ass. It's hard to think with Mason in my pussy and Kie's fingers in my ass, but I don't need much brain power to respond to Mason.

"I love you, too," I say. "I love both of you."

Maybe it's the mate bond talking. Maybe it's not. I'm not sure, and I don't care. This is how I feel, and I'm tired of feeling guilty about it.

Kie's mouth meets the back of my neck. "Love isn't a strong enough word to describe my feelings for you, but I suppose it will suffice. I love you."

A third finger joins his other two, and once I relax, he pulls them out and lines up something thicker and warmer. Mason stills, halting so Kie can squeeze inside me. I breathe in through my nose and out through my mouth.

Kie takes his time, pushing inside with tiny thrusts. Mason peppers kisses along my jaw, distracting me from the slight hint of pain. I'm clutching his shoulders by the time Kie's hips are finally flush with my ass.

"There we go," Kie murmurs, smoothing a hand down my side.

I shift, painfully aware of how it moves them inside me. I've never felt so full. I'm bursting at the seams. I like it.

"I watched how you fucked yourself on Kie," Mason admits. "I'm going to make you cum the same way."

Kie and Mason pin me between them, then begin thrusting. They move slowly, one pulling out as the other pushes in. Both their hands are on me, sliding over every inch of my skin. It feels too good, and I can barely breathe.

"That's my girl," Mason whispers at the exact moment Kie

says, "You're doing so good."

I gasp, and they continue.

"So fucking beautiful."

"So fucking tight."

"I love the way you clench around my cock."

"You're going to make me cum."

"Do I feel good in your ass? I love you."

Mason grunts. "I love you more than Kie."

Kie pauses. "It's not a competition."

"Yes, it is."

My back arches, my thigh shaking where it's wrapped around Mason. I squeeze his shoulder, my nails probably piercing the skin as I desperately drag him closer. He's already as close as he can get, but the growing fire in my abdomen makes it impossible to think clearly.

"Please," I gasp. "Don't stop."

The drag of their cocks is overwhelming in the best way, like a shot of adrenaline straight to the heart. Mason wasn't lying when he said he watched how I rode Kie, and he figured out exactly how to move to make me cum from penetration alone. The angle is perfect, and the added pressure from Kie makes it even better.

Loud, nonsensical noises pour from my throat, and my mates continue their slow fucking until I fall apart around them. Mason grits his teeth as I cry out, clenching as I orgasm.

Kie moans. "That's it." He chuckles, then continues. "Look what you did to Mason."

I slide my attention to the shifter, a smile curving my lips as I take in his current state. He's gasping, short choppy breaths slipping from his throat as he fucks up into me.

"He's trying so hard not to cum," Kie teases. "Clench around him again."

Mason's eyes spring open. "Don't you fucking dare—"

His words are cut off by a throaty moan as I squeeze, clamping down around him. Kie hisses at the pressure, but Mason loses it. His face screws up, and he throws his head back as his hips jerk underneath me. He's cumming.

"Fuck," he grunts, stilling inside me. "You monstrous woman. I wasn't done."

I giggle, and Mason drops his forehead against mine as he pulls out. Kie quickens, taking advantage of being the only one inside me. I crane my neck to the side and look up at the faerie, pleased with what I see.

He's already looking at me, a soft expression I rarely see gracing his features. "Tell me you love me," he orders. "Not both of us. Me."

I place a hand on his thigh, stroking the skin. Mason wiggles away from me, letting my focus shift to Kie. Well, it does until my leg is pulled up and a mouth clamps around my clit. My entire body jolts as I look down, eyeing the head of messy brown hair between my thighs.

"I love you, Kie," I choke out, returning my attention to my faerie. "I know you're afraid it's only because of the bond, but it's not. You're smart and kind, and you're trying. That means so much to me. I'm excited to spend my life with you."

Mason moans, licking my clit in fast, firm strokes. If he has any issues with the fact that his cum is currently dripping out of me and his tongue occasionally dips too far back and presses against the underside of Kie's cock, he doesn't show it. I'm glad, because this feels exceptionally good.

I gasp. "I love you so much, Kie."

Kie grits his teeth. "I'm going to cum."

I clench around him, and Mason eases two fingers into me. His tongue is still on my clit, working me in rough repetitive motions. When he curls his fingers, I burst.

I claw anything I can reach as another toe-curling orgasm shoots through me, the feeling so strong, I can barely breathe. Kie finishes with me, thrusting in deep as he finds his release.

The three of us relax, falling limp against the mattress. Kie rests inside me for a while, growing soft, before making his retreat. I wince in discomfort, but I'm not in pain. I knew they wouldn't hurt me.

Chapter Forty-Two

ABBY

I'M LIMPING.

I don't enjoy it nearly as much as Kie and Mason are. I was under the impression Kie would use his magic to prevent me from feeling too sore, but he's doing a shit job of stopping the jolt of pressure that shoots up my ass with every step.

He and Mason are practically beaming with pride, their chests so puffed, I'm surprised they don't share blood with peacocks.

Mason huffs. "I apologize."

Anox pointedly ignores him.

I love this, and I smile to myself as I limp alongside them. Kie is forcing Mason to apologize for kidnapping and dismembering Lord Bishop, and Anox is not making it easy.

"You *will* forgive me," Mason continues, glaring at the back of Anox's head. "I was protecting my mate. You would've done the same."

Anox continues walking, pretending as if he doesn't hear the shifter.

"I think I might like him," I whisper to Kie.

Anox looks at me over his shoulder. "I like you, too, and I look forward to beginning our lessons this evening." His eyes then shift toward Mason, and he scrunches his nose before turning back forward.

I'm surprised steam isn't bursting out of Mason's ears, and I slide my hand within his before he does something stupid. I'm not expecting to encounter clammy hands, though.

Mason's nervous, but besides his sweaty hands, he's doing an excellent job hiding it.

"You've got this," I say, smiling up at him.

Mason glances down at me, licks his lips, and gives a curt nod. Then he turns back forward, his eyes narrowing at Anox's back. He's arguing with the faerie to distract himself.

I shove my hair behind my shoulder, my nerves spiking. We enter the park where the announcement is being held, and the pain in my ass magically vanishes the moment we come into view of the faeries already waiting for us. There are hundreds, and I keep my stride even with Mason's as Anox and Kie break apart.

Mason leads me up the tall podium brought in for the occasion.

My family is somewhere within the crowd. I don't see them, but I trust they're safe. Kie and Mason have assigned three guards per person, just in case. They claim there's always an increased risk when announcing to a crowd of this size.

Mason places a hand on the back of my neck, his fingers curling and pressing against my pulse point. I shiver but otherwise don't react as I stare into the crowd below.

A hush falls over the garden as the faeries wait to hear Mason's announcement. I can practically see their impatience. With all the change they've experienced these past few weeks, I can only imagine the fears rushing through their minds.

"Good morning," Mason starts, his voice booming. "I appreciate you coming out today, and unfortunately, I come to you with a startling announcement. It's been discovered that Alpha

Theon is housing a faerie fugitive, Callie Collins. In doing so, he's calling the Sylvan Harmony Treaty and his Alpha title into question."

Mason nervously runs his fingers along my neck, his palms sticky against my skin. This is a huge announcement, and it goes against everything he's ever believed in. Mason's drawing a hard line, choosing the faeries over the shifters.

"We have stationed troops along Redstall Forest," he continues, "and we're giving Alpha Theon one week to respond before considering the Sylvan Harmony Treaty null and void."

Chapter Forty-Three

ABBY

THE NEXT THREE days are a flurry of meetings, raised voices, and barked orders. I'm sure Anox has burst at least three blood vessels, and even Jackie arrived at a meeting with her hair undone.

"We've been housing him for—"

"I wouldn't exactly call it housing." Kie interrupts Mason's rant. "He's in the cells, without magic. He's pissing in a bucket."

Mason works his jaw side to side, his lips twitching and nose crinkling, before he shakes his head and continues as if Kie never spoke. "We've been *housing* Lord Bishop for several days, and it's time to move forward with punishment. I want him convicted and executed."

Anox sighs. "Yes, I agree it's time to move forward, but he's a longstanding council member. People are demanding he receive a proper trial."

"A proper trial?" Mason laughs. "I don't recall him giving my mate so much as a proper *conversation* before attempting to murder her."

I suck my cheeks into my mouth, not wanting to get involved. Anox seemed keen to punish Lord Bishop after the attack, but he's been dragging his feet. That, coupled with the fact we're still waiting to hear back from Alpha Theon, has Mason on edge.

I clasp my hands together, shooting Kie a glance. We should focus on Alpha Theon and the impending war, not this. The treaty was created around the same time Zaha destroyed the shifter lands, and as far as I'm aware, it's the only thing that's kept the faeries and the shifters from launching into an all-out war.

They both respected the treaty, skirting around the rules but never doing anything in outright opposition.

Without it, it's only a matter of time before shifters emerge from the forest trying to claim faerie lands. Faeries are strong, but they won't be able to defend themselves from full-grown shifter males equipped with delysum.

Mason told me how shifters live, how they begin learning how to fight from an ungodly young age. The shifters revere physical strength, and they'll cut through the small faerie towns like warm butter.

"It would be helpful if we set a date," Kie chimes in.

Anox frowns. "Lord Bishop's family has requested we allow them to conduct an investigation—"

"An investigation into what?" Kie interrupts again. Mason grunts out his approval. "He's already confessed."

Jackie, who's begun picking at her nails, glances up. "He confessed under duress." Her gaze pointedly shifts toward Mason. "Your reckless actions are the reason we're forced to delay. You should've stayed out of this, as we all agreed."

Mason bristles.

Jackie continues. "And as much as I *love* wasting our meetings discussing criminals already in our possession, I think our time would be better spent discussing the criminals who aren't. It's been three days, and we've yet to hear a response from Alpha Theon."

Mason leans back in his chair. "We gave him a week to

respond, and I doubt we'll hear from him with much time to spare. He wants us to sweat this out. He's hoping we'll change our minds."

Kie clears his throat. "Alpha Theon isn't going to extradite Callie. We already know that." He rests his head in his palm, lost in thought. "Have we heard anything from Kalix?"

Anox shoots Mason a sideways glance. "No."

Mason's younger brother is next in line after Alpha Theon, but Mason hasn't seen or spoken to Kalix since Mason was sent to live with the faeries at nine years old. Kalix would have only been seven.

"Kalix hasn't been seen in over ten years," Anox points out. "There are rumors he's dead."

Mason shakes his head, evidently refusing to acknowledge the possibility. Then he glances at the clock, checking it for the fourth time in the past fifteen minutes. "We need to leave," he says. "We'll continue this discussion another time."

Kie and Mason have been meeting the council several times a day, so I doubt this conversation will be postponed for too long.

I'm following the two out of the room a second later, much to my relief. This meeting lasted longer than expected, and I need a break. Anox had me up before the sunrise reading reports, and I'm exhausted.

I take this opportunity to squeeze between Kie and Mason.

The second we're in a private outdoor corridor, Kie wraps his arms around my waist and pulls me against his chest. It's hard to believe he doesn't have much experience kissing as he tilts his head to the side and drags his tongue against mine, and I curl my fingers around his shoulders as he guides me into a shaded alcove. It looks like a decorative pedestal once filled the area, but it's empty now.

My back hits a vine-covered trellis, and I gasp.

Kie smiles into our kiss, no doubt pleased to have earned a reaction from me, before dragging his hands down my waist. His mouth moves to my neck, sucking and kissing the sensitive skin at the base of my throat. I meet Mason's gaze over Kie's shoulder.

The shifter is leaning against the opposite trellis, his arms crossed over his chest as he glances left and right, ensuring no faeries wander into the area.

"I could take you right here," Kie admits. "I could hike up your dress and sink into your soft flesh right here, right now."

It's been days since we've been together. Kie and Mason have been busy, and all my free time has been spent with my family or with Anox. By the time we finally reconvene at the end of the day, we're exhausted. Well, I am, at least. I'm asleep the second my head hits the pillow.

Kie grabs my jaw, his fingers digging into my cheeks as he forces my gaze away from Mason.

"Don't look at him," he orders.

His other hand is pulling up my dress. The small alcove is private, but not *that* private. Kie doesn't seem to care, though, as the hem of my dress reaches my hips. He's undoing his pants a heartbeat later, freeing his cock. I can't believe we're doing this here.

Kie hikes up my leg, his eyes fluttering shut as he pushes into me. There's a slight ache as I stretch to accommodate his thickness, but it quickly vanishes.

Mason continues to watch from the opposite wall, his gaze heavy. He makes no moves to interfere, and his eyes continually dart around to ensure nobody has stumbled into the area.

"Fuck," Kie moans. "This is going to be fast."

I trail my lips to his ear, kissing the sensitive skin below it. I want Kie to smell like me, and I drag my fingers through his hair as he fucks up into me.

The faerie is mine.

Kie gasps. "I love you."

He shivers, then pushes deep inside. He's cumming already, and I tighten my leg around his waist. That was faster than I expected, which makes me feel better than it should. Kie must've been desperate for it. Desperate for me.

He pulls out with a low groan, and I bury my face against his chest as he yanks a small cloth out of his pocket and wipes between my thighs. Then he extends the dirty cloth toward Mason.

Mason snorts. "The fuck do you want me to do with that?"

"Throw it away," Kie says. "Preferably somewhere it won't be found."

"Why don't *you* do it?"

"I don't have time. Abby and I are going to be late."

Mason frowns, then snatches the used cloth. He looks disgusted, and he shoots both me and Kie a dirty glare as he shoves it into his front pocket.

"You two are vile," he says by way of insult. "Vile, vile degenerates."

Kie sets me on my feet and smooths down the front of my dress. "Did you hear that, Abby? Mason thinks we're vile, vile degenerates."

I can't help but laugh. I don't mean to, but it bursts out of me, anyway.

"Make sure Kie doesn't do anything irrational while I'm gone," Mason interrupts. Kie's not the one who does irrational things, but I keep that thought to myself. "I need to finish up with the council, but I shouldn't be too long. Twenty minutes at most."

Mason kisses my forehead, his lips lingering, before hurrying back toward the chamber room.

Kie is smirking, clearly proud of himself.

"Do you—" I start, gesturing toward his hips. "Should we stop by the house so you can shower?"

"There's no time." Kie shakes his head. "We're already late to meet your parents. We told them we'd be there ten minutes ago."

I bite back a smirk. "They're not going to mind, Kie."

Kie takes my hand, his bare fingers slipping between mine, and begins tugging me through the property. He does make a quick detour at our place, but only for me to use the restroom and for him to wash his hands.

"Let's go," he says, placing a hand on the small of my back. "I'm going to tell your mom it's your fault we're late."

Chapter Forty-Four

ABBY

KIE GUIDES ME forward, his pace so fast, I'm left with no choice but to jog to keep up. He's convinced my parents will be upset we're late, but they aren't like Queen Gitta. They won't care.

Mom opens the door with a smile. Her eyes dart between Kie and me as she steps aside and gestures for us to enter. My family has taken one trip back to the human realm to tie up loose ends and make sure nobody thinks they've gone missing, but they plan to make a permanent move soon. I'm ecstatic.

"Come on in!" Mom says. "You don't need to knock, Kie."

Kie grunts and steps past her, but not before I spot his smile. It's soft, maybe even a bit shy, and he does his best to hide it. He's unsuccessful.

Dad's on the couch in the living room, fully engrossed in a book on trolls. His guard brought him to the Bellmere library the other day, and he's taken full advantage. Beside the couch, stacked from the ground to his knee, is a pile of books he must have brought back with him.

"Morning," Dad says, not bothering to look up.

I sit in the oversized chair opposite him, and Kie lingers in the center of the room. He won't appreciate my guidance, so I remain silent as he looks around, trying to figure out his next move. Eventually, much to my relief, he decides to sit with me. He plucks me off the chair before taking the seat and placing me on his lap.

The front door opens again, and I perk up as Mason strolls inside. That didn't take long at all.

"Sorry I'm late," he says.

He awkwardly shuffles up to my mother, stiffly accepting the quick hug she offers. He claims to hate it, but the flush that spreads up his cheeks and neck says otherwise. He likes the affection.

A door in the hallway slams shut, and Aaron comes bounding into the living room a second later. His smile falls when he sees Mason.

"Where's Kie?"

"Kieran," Mason corrects him. He points toward Kie and me, alerting Aaron of our presence in the corner of the room. "His name is Kieran. You may call him *Your Highness*."

I shoot Mason a glare. "Be. Nice."

Aaron and I have always been mean to one another—it's how we choose to express our love—but Mason has difficulty understanding it. He met my brother with a grudge, one Aaron immediately clocked and decided to aggravate further.

He goes out of his way to make Mason angry, and he's not subtle about it. He's yet to realize how easy it would be for Mason to kill him.

"Yeah, *Mace*," Aaron says, walking into the kitchen. "Be nice to me. You don't want to get on Abby's bad side."

Mason stiffens, and I sigh. "Do *not* call me that."

Aaron turns, giving Mason his full attention. "Mace. Mace. Mace. Ma—"

I drag a hand down my face. Aaron's already screaming by the time I reopen my eyes. Mason has Aaron pinned to the ground, smashing his face into the rug with a loud, taunting laugh. It looks rough, but Mason's being gentle. He doesn't want to hurt my brother. He just wants Aaron to know he could.

Dad looks up, his eyebrows raised, before returning to his book.

"I should break your skull," Mason threatens. "I should crush it here on this fucking rug."

Dad flips to the next page. Aaron screams something about his arm breaking, which I can very clearly see is a gross exaggeration. Mason's barely touching him, and he even shifts to ensure he isn't hurting my brother—only humiliating him.

Mom sighs. "That's enough, you two. Help me set the table."

Mason releases my brother, who immediately scampers off the ground with an angry scowl. I can't lie and say I don't enjoy watching him receive the treatment he forced me to endure for most of our childhood.

"That was hardly fair," Aaron says, tugging down the ends of his shirt.

He strolls out of the room, but his gaze continually darts toward Mason as he carries plates to the dining table. He's on edge, waiting for my mate to attack. I'm happy to see it. It's what he deserves.

Mason follows Aaron into the dining room, looking around like he isn't quite sure how to help. I'm about to offer a suggestion when he leans down and whispers something into Aaron's ear. I can't fathom what it might be, especially when my brother barks out a loud laugh and hands over the plates.

"On the table," he instructs.

Mom frowns. "Don't pawn off your chores."

"He threatened to tear out my throat if I didn't hand him the plates," Aaron argues. "Seems I don't have much of a choice."

Mason doesn't bother denying Aaron's accusation, too busy setting the table. I'm glad he's found something to keep himself busy, even if it involved threatening to murder my brother.

Mom finishes preparing food, which really just means cutting up a bunch of fruit, cheese, and bread. Mason and Kie ensured all of my family's meals are taken care of, saving my parents the effort of cooking.

I suspect Mom likes the normalcy of cooking, though.

I sit at the table between Kie and Mason, biting back a smile as they each drop a hand to my lap.

"Have you heard back from your father?" Mom asks Mason, trying to start a conversation. "I overheard two women discussing him earlier today. They seemed quite passionate about the topic."

As it turns out, the faeries are passionate about many things. Most of them are relieved that the longstanding peace treaty has been dissolved. They're looking for any excuse to fight.

Mason grimaces. "It's not something I can discuss outside the council."

"I understand." Mom purses her lips. "What'd you two get up to this morning, then?"

"We can't discuss that, either," Kie says at the exact moment I say, "We met with the council."

He runs his thumb along my thigh, the gentle touch soothing me before I have the chance to regret saying the wrong thing. I'm still getting used to this.

"Did you two enjoy the theatre last night?" Kie asks, smoothly changing the subject. "I'm sorry we couldn't attend, but we try not to leave the grounds."

My mom opens her mouth, but her answer is cut short as Dad clears his throat, drawing attention. Mom makes a quiet, annoyed sound in the back of her throat, as if she already knows what's on Dad's mind and disapproves. He ignores it, too busy glancing at the ever-growing pile of books near the couch.

He has something to say, and he folds his hands together

before blowing out a long breath and speaking up. "The librarian wouldn't let me take out a book on plants. Why?"

Kie's chest bounces with laughter. Mom glares at Dad. She must have told him not to bring this up.

"We've recently learned some valuable information on an invasive plant, delysum, so I ordered our scholars to review our existing research for a few other plants," Kie explains. "They reserved several books, and while you're free to read them in the library, they must remain available for research."

Dad nods, seemingly finding that excuse acceptable. "Well, can you tell me when they're available to take home? The library chairs hurt my back."

I open my mouth, prepared to tell Dad that Kie has more important things to do than sit around monitoring some random books, but Kie's sudden grip on my thigh stops me.

"I will," he says. He's as much of a suck-up as Mason.

"What are your plans for this afternoon?" I direct my question toward Aaron.

"I'm heading into Bellmere," he says. "My guards say there's a popular, invite-only restaurant that's next to impossible to get into. We're going to use Kie's name to get in. Then we're going to visit a brothel near—"

"*Aaron!*" Mom hisses. "We're eating."

Aaron shrugs. "She asked. I answered."

"What brothel?" It's Mason who asks.

Kie's fingers, which have been tracing mindless patterns into the top of my thigh, still. I shove a piece of bread into my mouth, giving Mason my complete and undivided attention. I've heard all about his extensive history with brothels.

Is he going to suggest my brother visit a specific location or a particular woman? I like to think of myself as a relatively rational person, but I might lose my mind if Mason gives him a location and a name.

I know who I am, and I'll obsess. What made her so memorable that she's worth recommending to other men? Does Mason still think about her? Does he try to replicate those memorable things with me? Do I live up to the memory? I'll kill him.

Aaron glances between Mason and me, his eyebrows furrowed, before answering. "I've heard a few things about The Underground."

Mason's eyes dart toward me. "Don't go there. Faeries have superior immune systems, and we don't know how sexual illnesses manifest in humans. Something that takes a faerie a day or two to heal from might be enough to kill you. There are several establishments where the women are regularly tested and always wear protection. I'll give you a list later."

Kie's fingers resume stroking my thigh, but it's slower than before. Mom and Dad share a glance, and Aaron awkwardly bobs his head. I'm not sure how I feel. I suppose I'm glad Mason's looking out for my brother, but I don't enjoy the reminder that his entire sexual history is with sex workers.

Experienced sex workers.

"What about you, Mom?" I ask, eager to move away from the topic of brothels. "Any fun plans?"

"You seem to know a lot about brothels," Dad says, ignoring my attempt to change the subject. He sets down his fork, leveling his expression with Mason. "Have you spent a lot of time in them?"

Mason licks his lips, his back straightening. It's a far cry from the timid posture he usually uses around my parents, and I realize he's bothered by the question.

"Yes," Mason says. "I have." There's a brief moment of silence before he continues. "I am a thirty-year-old man surrounded by noblewomen faeries who either want to see me dead or wish to get pregnant and force a marriage. Brothels were my only option. Is that a problem for you?"

My dad's face grows red.

"Drop it." Mom's pointed words are aimed at my dad. I sink into my seat. She turns back to Mason. "My husband and his friends worked through my sorority like it was their life's mission, so he knows better than to judge."

Aaron smirks, crossing his arms over his chest. "Yeah, Dad. You were a real whore, weren't you? I faintly recall overhearing a story about you and Mom's second cousin."

Mason's fists are clenching and unclenching, and I place my hand over the one closest to me. I'm not upset, not really. Faeries and shifters are significantly more open to the topic of sex, and Mason was trying to help Aaron. He just went about it in the most uncomfortable way possible.

Mom hums. "First cousin, actually. Shall we talk about that, honey?" My dad's mouth opens. Mom continues. "I mean, if we want to question others about their sexual history at the dinner table, it's only fair we discuss yours, too."

Dad, whom I honestly think should be used to getting ganged up on at this point in his life, retreats. He carries his empty dish into the kitchen, and he glowers at us as he dumps it into the sink.

"I would like it to be known that I *never* had sex with your mother's cousin," he says. "And I don't appreciate the lies you three are keen to spread about me. I am a pure, innocent man."

Mason huffs. "So am I."

It's a well-timed joke, and I can practically feel the tension fade as a loud, deep laugh bellows out of Dad's chest. Even Mason relaxes, his shoulders softening and his harsh breathing evening out. This whole family thing is going to take a while to adjust to, but I think we're getting off to a good start.

Chapter Forty-Five

MASON

ABBY CURLS UP against me, her body warm and breathing even.

I love her most like this, when she's sleeping and comfortable and unable to tell me to stop staring at her. She gets angry when she catches me looking, which is bothersome. She's my mate, and I should be allowed to look at her whenever I please.

I'm just happy she allowed me to sleep with her last night. I thought she'd be too angry to let me join her and Kie in bed. She, Kie, and every council member were upset when I made my demands, but at the end of the day, I'm in charge.

Lord Bishop's execution was swift. Abby didn't want to attend, so she and Kie stayed behind while I watched his head disconnect from his shoulders.

It made me so fucking hard to watch the man who attempted to kill my mate meet his end, but I know better than to try to take that emotion out on Abby. I refuse to fuck her with anything but her on my mind.

I had other matters to attend to, anyway. Matters that kept me in my office until the sun began to rise. Matters that ensured sleep wasn't an option.

I've spent the past several hours watching Abby, admiring my mate and the tiny freckles that line her nose. They've grown more prominent these past few days, I think as a result of spending so much time in the sun.

I gulp, resisting the urge to touch her face.

Kie wakes slowly. His heart rate quickens as he comes to consciousness and realizes his vulnerable mate is beside him, and he lets out a quiet groan as he rolls to the side and spoons her from behind.

Abby shifts but otherwise remains asleep.

We should already be out of bed. I'm sure the council members are waiting for us in the chamber rooms. They're likely bickering about and adjusting the plans I typed up meticulously last night.

I should wake Abby up. We need to get moving, and she'll be pissed if we begin today without her.

Kie blows out a slow breath. He's fully awake and most likely running through the hundreds of scenarios we've spent the past week planning. He's also staring at me over the top of Abby's head, but I'm avoiding eye contact. I already know what he's thinking.

It's been a week. We've heard no response from Alpha Theon.

The Sylvan Harmony Treaty is broken.

We're going to war.

* * *

END OF BOOK TWO

A Sneak Peek:

Chapter One,
The Hidden Kingdom
(Book Three)

Chapter One

LILLIAN

EVERYTHING HAS BEEN a lie.

I hardly think through my actions as I rip open a portal and appear behind Queen Gitta. This is her fault. I don't know how, but I'm sure of it. She has everybody wrapped around her finger, and she poisoned my mates against me.

She cast doubt, and it grew thorns. I have thorns, too.

Her Majesty doesn't have time to register my presence before her head is in my hands and the knife I keep in my waistband is dragged across her throat. I press in deep, ensuring there's no chance of survival.

My arms shake with the effort, but adrenaline keeps me moving.

I'm certain opening another portal will kill me. I have no other choice. I rip one open, my vision blurring as I stumble through. Mom gave explicit instructions on where to find her.

Within a second of stepping through the portal, I realize I'm not where I'm meant to be. I'm in a forest, surrounded by trees so dense that the sun barely reaches the ground. It's dark and cold, far from the sun-soaked cabin I intended to travel to.

There's no magic floating through the air, either.

I'm in the Redstall Forest. Shifter lands.

"That was unexpected."

I spin, crouching low as my violet eyes meet crisp white ones. The man before me is lean, and he possesses no faerie or shifter traits. He's other.

He's a god.

I tighten my grip on my knife as his white eyes travel down my frame. Can he sense how weak I am? I've depleted the little bit of magic my body managed to store in the few days I've been in the faerie realm, leaving me virtually defenseless.

His gaze flickers to the right. "Kalix," he says, greeting somebody I can't yet see. "You're late."

Kalix. Mason's younger brother?

I shift my weight as another man appears. He's a shifter—there's no question about it—and he's the spitting image of his older brother. They share the same height, the same wavy dark hair, and the same vibrant green eyes.

Kalix buttons up his shirt as he weaves through the trees, his gaze darting between me and the god.

"I was busy," he says. He jerks his chin toward me. "Any issues?"

I remain quiet, listening and learning. Adapting. I can't open another portal. I'm too weak, and gods can manipulate them. I'd likely end up in the same spot, but significantly weaker. It's not worth the risk.

"Minor inconveniences," the god says. "She murdered the faerie queen, so enjoy dealing with that."

Kalix frowns. "When?"

"Right before I pulled her here. She was heading to some cabin down south, probably an agreed-upon meeting point with her mother."

What is Kalix doing with a god? Does my mother know? Does Alpha Theon know? Faeries and shifters have a long, complicated history with the gods. Everybody knows not to do business with them.

The shifters should understand that better than anybody else. They angered Zaha, and she destroyed the shifter kingdom. It's because of her that they were forced to retreat into the Redstall Forest.

The god pulls something out of his pocket. It's a thin, golden string, one I highly suspect is infused with magic. Within the blink of an eye, the god is in front of me. He ties the golden string around my neck with unnerving speed, and I hardly have time to react before he's gone.

He vanishes into thin air, probably returning to the gods' realm.

Kalix crosses his arms over his chest. "You're a tiny little thing, aren't you? Malnourished." I don't respond. He continues. "Figured Mason would've taken better care of you."

I fight back a wince. Mason's taking care of somebody, but it isn't me. He's denying the gift Zaha gave to us. He's defying nature.

I touch the golden string tied around my throat, then tug. There's a neat bow in the back, one that refuses to come undone. Despite how hard I rip, it doesn't budge.

Panic drives me to finally speak. "What is this?"

Kalix spins around, turning away. "Follow me," he orders. "My people are waiting."

* * *

STAY CONNECTED

SOCIAL MEDIA

Follow Invi Wright on social media to stay up to date on her newest releases, listen to her gab about romance & fantasy books, get regular book recs, and join a fun community of romance lovers!

TikTok & Instagram: @inviwright

EXCLUSIVE CONTENT & CHARACTER ART

Subscribe to **@inviwright** on Patreon for:

- Exclusive access to ongoing novellas
- Exclusive audio chapters
- SFW and NSFW character art
- Partake in polls (help decide what book she'll write next!)
- A free ebook copy of every book she publishes

COMPLETED WORKS

STANDALONES
The Nanny | A Nanny/Single Father Romance
Lord of Dread | An Arranged Marriage Historical Romance
Aine | A Dark Shifter Romance

THE FEMALE SERIES
The Female is a why choose demon romance with a dark dystopian setting, declining fertility rates, captured women, and three irresistible men.
The Female
Her Males
Their War
Chev's Mate
Queens

THE CURSED KINGDOM SERIES
The Cursed Kingdom is a slow burning, why choose romance with a mystical faerie realm, two infuriatingly attractive princes, and high conflict between the faerie and shifter kingdoms.
The Cursed Kingdom
The Shattered Kingdom

TRIGGER WARNINGS CAN BE FOUND ON:
inviwright.com

UPCOMING WORKS

STANDALONES
His Assignment | A Bodyguard Mafia Romance (Coming 2026)
The Dragon's Agreement | A Dragon Fantasy Romance
(Release Date TBD)

LAND OF WOLVES DUOLOGY
Land of Wolves is a high intensity shifter romance with fated
mates, government indoctrination that leads to painful betrayal,
and impending war between the shifters and humans.
Land of Wolves | Part One (Coming 2026)
Land of Wolves | Part Two (Release Date TBD)

ONGOING SERIES

Fates | Book Six of *The Female* Series (Release Date TBD)
The Hidden Kingdom | Book Three of *The Cursed Kingdom*
Series (Release date TBD)